Wages of War
Fred Croton

*Limited first hardcover edition.*
ISBN: 978-0-9745042-6-1

*Printed in the United States of America.*

www.patcheny.com

Wages of War

For Selma

# ONE

Before he left for Vietnam he did a curious thing. Deciding not to drive into Manhattan where any number of women would welcome his call and desire to spend the night, he drove instead to where traffic thinned; the highway dwindled to a two-lane road, and had the feeling he was going home.

Though he had not driven the road in years, each curve and rise came as no surprise as side-road businesses were passed, landmarks remained in their accustomed places, and finally the old town, diner, train station, movie house intact, with a nudge to the new: a disco bar, a bed-and-breakfast place. Then to the empty house, no curtains on the windows, no children there to comfort him. The marriage, sustained by annual relocations and quadrennial pregnancies, came crashing down one frenzied night with little warning. And he remembered, as he did every day of his life, that he'd left his children, left them, and there was no balm to soothe the pain that wracked his body, left him frozen, not against the chill, but against his vast capacity to bring misery into the world.

He might well have slept outside on the ground in the cold night, having traded the comforts of home for the immediacy of gratification. Instead, he wandered in darkness, needing neither light nor guide.

The kitchen floor had kept its red brick color and he remembered mornings cooking pancakes, tossing them to his kids, never missing their plates, their squeals of delight. Coffee and juice, glasses of milk, a glow on the faces of his sons and their mother from the heat of the wood-burning stove.

The white upright piano where he learned to play some simple tunes when his kids took lessons was gone. He ran his hand along the polished railing as he climbed the stairs, wallpaper peeling at the top of the landing, and looked into the small bedrooms where his children had slept. Books read, songs sung, good nights and good mornings, dotted the rooms and he quickly left them.

The bathroom, papered in a Victorian design, its claw-footed tub sure and squat, sat regally upon the floor. On a day he was in the bath after a morning of tennis, a weekend guest walked in, took the wash cloth and soaped his body, making him stand in order to be rinsed top to toe, top to toe. Toweled and dressed he joined his wife and bath attendant, now fixing eggs for her husband at jolly Sunday brunch.

But that was a long time ago. It was midnight and the moon lit the bedroom where he had slept with his wife. It had never been heated, depending for warmth on an electric blanket and little else. The night they moved in a small black bat was hanging upside-down on a curtain. He approached it with the curiosity of a city boy who'd seen the world, fetched a towel, felt its wings flutter under his hand, freeing it out a window, its eyes glistening as it wheeled then disappeared into the darkness of the trees.

In the attic of the old house he peered out a window at a darkened road he had walked in all weather and every season. Cows roamed amid the rubble of a great barn. Its vaulted ceiling, beams thrust into air, had been buttressed against wind and rain and weathering but not the gleam in the eye of an arsonist. On those walks he would drift into his dream-world ways recalling places and people far removed from this pastoral place. It would have come as no surprise to take the rise of the hill and, at the turning of the road, see that person from his past who had taken up his morning walk, be it dead father, old lover, an instrument of pride or cause for humiliation. Then the furies, the demons would strike, reaching deep inside, leaving him only the agony of regret. He's never delivered on early promises made. Never received instruction in the most elemental lesson--the piecing together of a life from its strings. Death, death, how was it he could call on it always, day in, day out, and it would not come to him?

From the top of the hill he would see, through the trees, smoke lifting from a chimney, silver maples dropping leaves to the ground, one of his sons chasing the other while their mother sat on the front steps reading a book. Autumn's glories turned to winter snow. Spring would come, its surprises concealed from summer heat and stillness. All seen, all loved. But the pain would not leave him; his face not reveal, give it away. But the children ever-watchful knew, as children always know, that something was amiss. Though Daddy smiled and played a while, he is distracted, he is so far away.

The wife's hook into him had been her fidelity, as each of the others had hooked him through devices of their own. And the children, the children. He had taught them the songs of his childhood, the legends of the gods, to scan a box score or a line of iambic pentameter. But they had also learned from his dejection, became infected by it; immobilized in turn, direct descendents of the house and line.

# TWO

So, why was he in Vietnam? Something to do, something to see, "My generation's war," he'd say. Another self-deception, having turned forty a few years before. Of course it would be secondhand. No guns, no noise of war, for sure. Another place to begin again, avoid the details of a past ever-present in the tyranny of here-and-now. A secondhand soul he was, and that was the alpha and omega of it.

Truth to tell he was broke, run out of favors friends would do for him. He'd heard they were hiring. Who was hiring? An American company, Dupar Construction, in business over there. What would he do? What difference did it make? Those who did the hiring hardly cared. They needed bodies to fill slots and got a nickel-plus for every dollar he earned on the job whether he worked or not. Cost-plus-fixed-fee they called these contracts, running into the hundreds of millions, with plenty extra set aside for administration, that's for sure. That nickel per dollar spent can add up, so he got his dollar, they got their nickel-plus, and we'll all be gay when Johnny comes marching home. God bless America!

His first days were spent wandering the streets of Saigon. Alone, confused by the world and they that dwell there. Lacking a wise teacher. Needing not a teacher but a savior.

It was early January, pathetic leftovers of Christmas a weird accompaniment to the fetid weather. Melancholy Americans walked the streets accosted by Santa Claus, holly wreaths, Christmas trees for chrissakes. And street beggars who knew the season was a time for special generosity from these giants in their midst.

He had memories of his own of Christmas past. One of nine in a family with no money, he'd shoplift gifts from the local five-and-ten. His sister's friends worked there, turning eyes away while the little thief went busily to his task. As a father he watched his own kids empty giant Christmas stockings then plough through piles of gifts spread under the tree. Jingle bells all the way. Not a sign of the Holy Cross. He'd abide a once-a-year visit to a High Falutin' Episcopal Church. For the music, he decided, putting up with incense and the rest of the nonsense.

Saigon in January was hot, drenched with humidity, streets crowded with bicycles, motor scooters, taxis, and military trucks joined by others loaded with firewood, fruit, vegetables, and flowers. Pedicabs moved languidly, their passengers indifferent to the labor of the drivers who seemed ancient of days, faces impassive as wizened monks as they went about their work in the chaos of sound offered up by the world around them. Beggars and kids on the hustle, along with prosperity around every corner. Streets filled with shoppers, their voices breaking musically into eighth notes on a scale and pitch he'd never heard before. Their laughter as they strolled together, ignoring the foreigners, deferring to none of them, displaying a special courtesy among themselves, a patience with one another, a sense of calm, of peace. Bright red decorations hung everywhere. Didn't they know red was the color of the other side?

He stood apart from the crowd, trying to guess where the war might be. It certainly wasn't here, on a corner of Tu Do Street where waiters served coffee at street-side tables to slight, smartly dressed men in lively conversation.

Their New Year celebrations at the end of the month, called Tet, sounded like New Year's, All Soul's Day, and Christmas. No one could explain it to him. He'd seen a thrown-away GI bulletin that said, "Avoid any display of emotion during Tet." What in the world did that mean? Rather than think about it, he watched the passing parade of good-looking women, ogled by hulking GIs in combat fatigues out of place against the bright colors surrounding them. He feasted on these women, believing his admiration different in kind, subtler in its appreciation. There was an enchanting quality, a spell spun by their movements and manner of dress. Most wore a long-sleeved white silk top, wide panels extending front and back to cover tight-fitting black pants. A hand elegantly lifting the rear panel inches from the pavement, a dancer's movement designed to arouse desire enhanced their unhurried, leisurely ways. It might be an illusion, but he'd been deluded before and looked forward to the spells bound to ensnare him.

Walking up Tu Do Street he came upon an immense cathedral square. The towers of the church bore down on those who entered and he followed the crowd through its front doors. It was noon, pews were filled, side chapels jammed, votives ablaze, flowers everywhere, a priest declaiming, the faithful responding. Soldiers, the old, the young, the well-dressed and those in rags joined together before altars, sacred images, The Holy Virgin. Imploring intercession, forgiveness, protection from the daily round of death and dying that confronted them. If it's the case that God tests only the strong, this would be the place to find out.

Why had he no memory of a simple faith? Was it because things were not so simple as a child? He walked deep into the thickness of sound, smell of candle wax, of incense. Chairs scraped, children cried. He was an intruder and left the cool darkness of the place for the bright sunshine that awaited him out-of-doors.

He came to the very corner on Tu Do where a monk had burnt himself to a crisp some months before. Across the street from that stain, in a tiny park, an empty bench beckoned. A woman in white, wearing rimless glasses, approached. What could this schoolmarmish type want, he wondered? She smiled and he smiled back. She put her hand in his, pulling him up toward a waiting taxi. In minutes they were down an alley and, with a bunch of boys watching, she led him into the dim interior of a small house. The living room had a shrine with simple flowers, a faded photo of a man, and lit candles, their flames fluttering from no breeze he could feel. A blind old woman sat by the shrine. Our lady in white pressed a bill into her hand, walked him to the bed and removed her clothes, gesturing for him to do the same. This can't be love he thought, not for the first time in his life. Indifferently, he partook of his first Saigon piece. Nothing special there, pretty much the same as always. A Euclidean Conceit, he realized. Over and done, he looked up and saw the boys watching through a window. He dressed, gave her five US dollars, and stepped outside. The taxi was no longer there and he began to walk down the long alley to the main street when the boys jumped him, trying to bring him down while reaching for his wallet, his watch, anything of value. He broke away, sprinting toward the street. There was still light in the sky as he hailed a taxi.

Carried away safe and sound, he had the crazy idea that Vietnam could be his deliverance. From what exactly? Melancholy, despair, sin, that's what. And repentance? Attracted as he was to so coarse an existence, repentance was no way out, no exit from reality. Vietnam might not transform, but devour him.

# THREE

It was time to stop by Dupar Engineering, Inc., to see how he might spend his days. They were paying him after all. In the midst of the chaos of a casually guarded compound, Vietnamese laborers stood about in dignified silence, Americans strode about with an air of purposeful disinterest. Filipinos, Koreans, Thais floated about as background. TCNs these were called, Third-Country Nationals. First Place given over to Americans. And, as a courtesy, in second place our comrades in arms, the Vietnamese. Third place, then, to the others, the TCNs, who were everywhere.

At the personnel office it was quickly noted he lacked an engineering background or accounting skills. "College?" he was asked. "Yes." "Graduate?" "Nope." "What did you study?" "English Literature." The fellow across the desk amiably called out, "Another useless bastard come to join the war against godless communism." No one in the office bothered to look his way. "Well, let's see how you can be useful around here." He checked a list before him. "Here we go, Director of Public Affairs, that should be a match for your literary career." He said this with a smile, adding, "The job is to keep everything private, not public. We wouldn't want the home front knowing any of our dirty little secrets would we? Take a walk around the place and introduce yourself. You might as well find out what's going on around here." And was handed a sheet of paper with names of Vietnamese, or so he thought. "You'll need to hire a translator who knows his way around. They've all been cleared by security, whatever that's worth. Talk to them at our downtown office, it's easier for everyone."

The single-story building's narrow hallways were painted light gray. The only amenities he noticed were attractive Vietnamese chicks walking past him with a quick evaluating glance. The TCNs stepped aside as he passed, an odd sort of deference to perceived power. A futile try at a military air pervaded the place, defeated by raucous laughter and conversation among American civilians who cared not at all for the protocols of Army life.

He walked into the Chief Accountant's office. Follow the money, right? And met Charlie Bonham, a double for the overweight personnel guy, with the same early morning booze habit. Charlie had a sign behind his desk. "WASTE NOT, WHY NOT?" And was happy to explain that every turn of a wheel, every meal cooked and served, every rat poisoned or not, every minute of every hour worked, was billed double to our dear old Pentagon. "Our guys in the field are too dumb or lazy to fill out the paperwork. We know they're doing the work, we got to make it up someway." He said this without guile, no attempt to hide. "The military always signs off on the billing. We know we're in this together and take care of each other, let me tell you. It's the way things go around here." He pointed to a neatly dressed, fiftyish man at a corner desk. "Last month he retired after thirty years checking on companies like ours for the Corps of Engineers. And here he is, knowing all the ropes, and working for us at triple his old salary. He's the envy of all his pals in the Army who can't wait to get out and come to work for us."

Wandering the hallways, he spotted the Procurement Office and entered, noticing that he'd immediately aroused the suspicions of a tall, lean cigarette-smoking American who slipped a sheet of paper into his jacket pocket. James Lee, Colonel, US Army (Retired) waited for the visitor to state his business. On explaining himself he was asked, or ordered, to take a seat. "Procurement," said the colonel, "is not about pimping." He waited for this joke to settle in on his listener. "Though sometimes, duty will call, and a man's gotta do what he gotta do." He did not think it necessary to expand further. Straight talk, man to man, that was the ticket, wasn't it? "Most of our buys are made stateside, the big stuff. But the little pricks running the country want their share and we spread it around like horseshit on a field of corn." The colonel looked him over, gauging how much to reveal since you never know when the Feds or the Army's Criminal Investigators might be poking around. "Vietnam is running with every kind of hustler and con artist. It's goddamn embarrassing the shit they'll offer me for a favor. We know there's a lot of stealing, bribery going on. The buildup is happening so fast we figure a twenty percent slippage is something we can deal with." That about summed it up for the Colonel, who rose. "Public Affairs, eh? The less I see and hear of you the better job you're doing." They shook on that. "Take a tour of the country, but stay off the roads, they're ain't many that are safe. There's a war on, you may have heard. The less you see of it the better for you, believe me."

He began to catch a whiff of something familiar, the stink of corruption, rancid as a side of beef left in the brutalizing sun. Deceit, betrayal had been the standard in his life. And here, in Vietnam, he was quickly learning it was the currency of business as usual. Out of harmony with himself as always, he wasn't sure what it might mean, but had a sense the game he'd played all his life had found a home.

# FOUR

Arrangements were made to interview for a translator. Three men and a woman awaited him in the reception area at Dupar's downtown office. The soul of good manners, he beckoned the very well-dressed woman to join him in an inner office. Within moments he realized she had to have bribed her way into the interview since her English was near to non-existent and had other talents to exploit. The next two seemed disappointed that he wasn't in procurement and saw no future working without the possibility of a little extra coming their way. This left the runt of the litter. Also the oldest, wearing a worn-down brownish suit ready to part from its lapels, perhaps five feet, thin to emaciation, eyes shining too brightly, a smile to match. Mr. Ninh had been a journalist, claimed to know everyone in the business, and more. He needed the job and to his joy and surprise was hired.

Was his new boss looking for a place to live? Surprise, surprise, a first dividend. Mr. Ninh happened to have a friend in real estate with an office right across the street.

An over-eager landlord, not wanting to miss a day of rent, took him to an apartment while it was still occupied. Marble floors and overhead fans in a large living room looked out on the remains of an old garden. He knew it would be right for him. The bedroom door was open and he walked in on a half-dressed American, the flesh piling up on him, going gray at the temples. His uniform showed off his rank, a full-bird colonel, packed bags made it known he was going home, that very day, to loving wife and family. But what really caught his eye was the beautiful child in bed. She seemed to be about twelve, but had to be older, he thought. The colonel saw his appraising glance and said, “She comes with the apartment. It’s up to you. An extra hundred a month should do it.”

“No thanks, I’ll make my own arrangements”

“Suit yourself,” he said, as he pulled on his Air Force blue jacket. “I’m going home.” Before he went, the colonel left behind this pearl: “You know what this war’s about? Asian pussy. And it’s worth fighting for. What did old George Patton used to say? ‘Save the fucking for the fighting men.’” He blew a kiss to his beloved, and was gone.

Puzzled by this rejection of an obvious good thing, Mr. Ninh shrugged, smiled, and negotiated a lease with the landlord on reasonable terms, no doubt collecting a piece of the action for himself. No problem there. We all gotta make a living, right?

The happy landlord left them. And off they went to celebrate at dinner. A taxi took them through town to a section of Saigon that suddenly lost its French Colonial look. They were in Cholon, the large Chinese quarter, stopping on Hung Vuong at The Fuji Restaurant and Cabaret. An odd choice, a Japanese place, they entered an immense room with a stage festooned with dancing lovelies. Ninh saw his approving smile before being grandly welcomed by a tall Chinese in a tuxedo who managed the place. Ninh introduced his new boss and they were led to a stage-side table. Ninh, pleased, said, “See, I know everybody important.” Their drinks served, Chinese cuisine his preference, Ninh ordered for the two of them after a toast to a good start to working together. His own attention was on the dancers, more interested in showing their lovely bodies than their talents in any other realm. The front tables were occupied by affluent-seeming Chinese and Vietnamese huddled together in serious talk. A waiter came over and whispered something to Ninh, who rose immediately and walked over to a table with four Chinese men, one so immense in weight he might have been a Sumo Grand Champion had he been Japanese.

He turned his attention to the dancers, attracted to one with an air of boredom about her every move. She wasn't there to worship Terpsichore or any other muse he could recall. He guessed she was available to an offer for her services, moving indifferently while waiting the call.

Two chairs had been added to the big guy's table and Ninh brought him over to meet his friends. Mr. Big, Eddie Fong, turned out to be the owner and spoke enough English to be understood with a little help from Ninh, who intruded, sometimes unnecessarily, to show he was part of the conversation. Two of the others were Eddie's sons, already showing signs of joining him in the sumo ring. The fourth, slim and tough, very tough, never took his eyes of the fresh kid on the block, this American new to them all. The bodyguard, he figured, and wasn't surprised when he could make out the shoulder holster beneath a finely tailored jacket. A jovial welcome to Saigon was offered and accepted with thanks. He quickly surmised that Ninh had somewhat overstated his new boss' importance to the company he worked for, but let it ride, amused and wondering what would be coming next. "Did he know a Mister Lee, Colonel Lee?" "Chief of Procurement?" Yes he did. Mr. Ninh sighed with pleasure. Of course his boss knew everyone, and would be able to help, for sure. What kind of help? A small problem with water and ice. "Water and ice?" he asked. Eddie Baby had a big contract to deliver both in purified form. Unfortunately, a delivery, somewhat contaminated, was made to an officer's club. The discomfort this caused many a member, there to enjoy a drink or two, need not be described. Colonel Lee had cancelled the contract. Reaching to touch the arm of his new friend, Eddie Fong said, with deep friendship and sincere feeling, "I know you can help."

He could have said, "Sorry," paid his check and left. But his baser self always at the ready, led him to an overwhelming question: "How big is the contract?" A question that led the boys around the table to know he was in the game. It was in six figures. A low six, but for water and ice? "I'll do what I can. But Lee will have to be taken care of." This last turn of phrase needed to be translated by Ninh for Big Eddie. A quick conversation he did not understand ensued. Eddie looked him over carefully as Ninh translated. "The colonel has already been taken care of."

"For how much?" He asked. Eddie nodded to Ninh. "Ten percent when the contract was signed." They all looked at the American who, guessing, said, authoritatively, "He'll want ten more." Eddie annoyed, said, "Five now, and five more if he renews the contract for another year." What the fuck was he doing, he wondered, having no idea how his buddy the colonel would react to all this. Big Eddie looked his new pal over carefully, trying to gauge how much of the extra he'd be keeping for himself. Another cost of doing business with these crooks, he figured. After a moment, Eddie said something and one of his sons jumped up and left. Then, looking carefully at Ninh, he said, "We'll have the cash before you leave." That look was clearly intended to deliver the message to Ninh that if things went wrong, he'd be the one paying. Ninh smiled that smile of his. Then Eddie, to seal the deal, decided on a bonus extra. A choice of dancing girls was available for his pleasure. When he made his choice known, Big Eddie slapped him on the back. "She's my special one!" He shouted with glee. "A lucky choice for the two of us. I make a special exception for you." Big Eddie staggered to his feet, fighting off his son's assistance, and he and Ninh were left to their dinner. Nothing more needed to be said, the deal was on and only awaited a conversation with Colonel Lee.

After dinner Ninh disappeared and a man in a bright golden-colored Chinese silk jacket took him backstage to a warren of small rooms, whorehouse in style. A door was held open and he found his little dancer, still in her costume, languid as before, awaiting come what may. The sheet on the bed was sodden to his touch so he kept his clothes on as she dropped her panties to the floor and sat alongside him. With a quick unzip she brought him to a hard-on, sitting on his stomach, clothes and all, while expertly placing him inside her. The best way for her to fuck Fat Eddie who otherwise would have crushed her while she hunted for his dick. But that was Eddie. Now she was riding him, trying to force his come, trying to get it over with. He wouldn't cooperate and she slid down alongside him onto her stomach. He rolled over on her, dick sliding past her ass. She reacted by rising up on her knees placing him at the opening to her asshole. Somehow she found a way to place her palm, filled with a soft warm cream, in a smothering movement across his cock, and he heard her grunt as he plunged in, feeling the smooth sides of her capturing him, her sphincter tightening and releasing 'til he came, went limp inside her as she kept moving, pretending to want all of it. He fell back as she rose to put on her panties. She had another show, another something to do. He reached into his pants and held out a 500-piastre note as a tip, which she snatched on the way out. Snatched. Lovely word, that.

He found his away back to his table where Ninh sat with an odd, somewhat stupefied look on his face. No smile, a faraway manner connected to a few hits on an opium pipe, beyond caring who knew. A box was before him on the table. Inside, what had to be thirty thousand dollars in neatly wrapped hundred-dollar bills. "Christ almighty," he said to anyone who cared to listen. If it didn't work out with the colonel he'd get it back to Big Eddie with his regrets. He was already ahead, what with a free meal and a free piece of ass. Way ahead.

It had been a long, devious day. Climbing into a taxi, he gave the name of his hotel, then, remembering, showed the driver his new address that Mr. Ninh had written down for him in a curious script so remote from American penmanship. Ninh had also arranged for his belongings at the hotel to be picked up and delivered to his new abode. A regular Major Domo he was turning out to be.

Climbing a flight of stairs, key in hand, aware as always of first things in his life, he entered the darkened apartment. Feeling for a light switch he flipped it and saw a woman jump to her feet. A scrawny thing, a face too old for her age, wearing a white smock, she began to gesture with hands and words that she would clean for him, wash his dishes, launder his clothes, as she had for the recent tenant. Showing fidelity to her station she took him into the bedroom to see how she'd unpacked his bags and put away his things. He nodded his thanks. She took this as agreement for their future together and offered an open palm to him. "Ten dollah," she said. Not caring if this was for a day or a week he gave her the ten, she took it and fled.

Wandering the minimally furnished apartment, a cat sniffing out its potential, he was satisfied. Not content, never content, but reasonably satisfied. A galley kitchen, a large open space with a couch, side chairs, lamps, and further along a dining-room table near to windows looking out on the courtyard garden. The bedrooms were decorated in French Boudoir, homage to the imagined predilections of the rentiers. He would take advantage of that offering, he well knew.

Everything in his suitcases had been properly stored, save for a small metal box on his bed. It was locked and he had its key. Opening it he fetched a beautiful object wrapped in an oiled cloth. A Colt Python 357 Magnum, Royal Blue in color. An "Aristocrat of Guns," "Rolls Royce of handguns," it was called. An acquisition bringing him to the edge of High Society. "Nothing but the best," he mockingly told himself. He flipped open the empty cylinder of the revolver, and loaded, one at a time, six .38-caliber bullets. Feeling the heft of a six shooter in his hand, admiring its design, the solid under lug running along the bottom of the four inch barrel, he brought the gun to full cock, a phrase that always amused him. Satisfied that its action would guarantee maximum efficiency, he wrapped it once again, returned it to its box, put it away. And so to bed.

# FIVE

He walked into Colonel Lee's office with not thirty thousand but fifteen in the box. The remainder was in two envelopes holding seven thousand five hundred each. He'd play the colonel, hoping to hang on to the one or both of the envelopes. Lee, suspicious as always, eyed the box, no doubt having seen one like it before, and took him into a back room.

After a minimum of pleasantries he told the colonel he'd met a friend of his, Eddie Fong, the night before. "You sure move fast, don't you?" the colonel said, without giving away a thing.

"He told me something about a contract…" But before he could finish Colonel Lee interrupted with a vehemence reserved for junior officers. "Yes, and I cancelled it on that fat prick. How dare him deliver contaminated water to a group of my fellow officers? I was at the club that night. Can you imagine how it felt being upbraided by colleagues of mine staggering around with shit in their pants? You're goddamn right I cancelled on him." And that seemed to be that for the colonel about to dismiss him, coming to a halt on hearing, "Mr. Fong would like to make amends." Colonel Lee, Retired, thirty years in uniform, having watched young punks pass him by on their way to a star, was wary as a jackal. Is this stranger sitting there out to entrap him?

"Amends?"

"Yes. He wants to give back to the government, through you,

of course, five percent of the contract. As a penalty, of sorts." He sat back, as though finished, but added, "On top of the original ten, of course."

"Anything else?" the wise colonel asked.

"Oh yeah, he'd like an extension of the contract in exchange for another five percent discount to the government."

"So, how did you make the acquaintance of Eddie Fong?" the colonel asked, pleasantly.

"My translator took me to The Fuji last night. Running into him was an accident."

"An accident?" The colonel said this as assurance that there are no such things as accidents. "What did you make of the floor show? Find anything interesting?" He had to admit that he did. "I bet the fat bastard told you you'd picked out his favorite."

"That he did."

The colonel let out a little laugh. "That's his line. Uses it all the time." Warming to the conversation he inquired, "The little sour-faced one, right?" Right as rain, he told the colonel. "And you fucked her in the ass?" He stated this as fact, not a query, clearly having been there, done that. "Sure you fucked her in the ass. It's the way all Chinese chicks take it. Their version of Planned Parenthood."

The colonel, having decided that no Fed would allow consorting with a whore, even in the line of duty, bought in on the deal. The box was handed over. "I assume you're being taken care of as well," the colonel said. "That I am," he replied. "I'm taking it out in trade." Knowing bullshit when he heard it, the colonel put his little box in a bottom drawer, bringing the meeting to a close.

He walked down the hallway, light of head, near to clutching at a wall. Fifteen thousand dollars in his pockets, no feeling he had sinned. Not at all. Joy in his heart, a great elation. What a land of opportunity Vietnam might turn out to be!

## SIX

He left it to Ninh to bring the good news to Fat Eddie. It would be worth a hit or two of the pipe for him. Fifteen thousand was a very good score, and he thought about a time when he was maybe fourteen, and fifteen dollars was really big money. Gambling in his neighborhood went on without stop. Numbers, the trotters, baseball in summer, football in fall. Most of the action was at the local pool hall where he hung out with his pals honing hustler's skills, watching and waiting for what might come along. The place was connected, of course, and the local Goombas came around each day for their piece. An odd sort of moral fervor saw to it that no one in high school could place a bet. Good little capitalist, he saw a niche market, printed up the football point spread, took bets from the Junior League in his neighborhood, and sent runners to all the local high schools. A quarter was the minimum bet, the good little losers were everywhere, and the money rolled in.

One day after a very good weekend he sat with his pals in a local deli, enjoying his pastrami when a guy in a shiny suit, white-on-white shirt, and really ugly tie walked in, looking for someone, and he was that someone. Sitting down in a booth he pointed and gestured him over. Making a point to first finish his sandwich he pushed past his pals, and hiding a pounding heart, sauntered over and sat down. It was early November and winter had not yet settled in. Outside a grey sky darkened the streets. Football season was in full flower. The biggest college games of the season were coming up. And Sunday was the pros. The finger pointer, noticing his meandering eye said quietly, carefully, "Look at me." His head jerked to attention at this command. In a mirror he saw his buddies staring across the room. No waiter had dared approach the table. "How old are you?"

"Fifteen last week."

"Well happy birthday to you." The birthday boy thanked him. "Look, enough of this bullshit. You know what this is about. No more booking bets, and that's it, got it?"

Kid that he was, he said, "Where else can they get down, you won't take their action."

"Look, you little kike, don't give me back talk, you shut it down today."

"Where do you get this kike stuff?"

"I know a Jewboy when I see one."

"My mother, not my father."

"Yeah sure. What the fuck we talkin' about here? This is what it is, no more bets, no more nothin', you got it?"

He got it all right. No more pastrami, back to hot dogs if he could afford them. Mr. Tough Guy looked at his defeated quarry. "Jewboy or no, you're a smart little bastard so we got for you."

"What's that?"

"You can run numbers for us."

"No thanks."

"Suit yourself. The party's over." He walked out. The counterman relaxing for the first time shoved a knish at him, saying, "You look like you could use some nourishment." He took the plate, went back to his boys in the booth, a lesson learned. That the powerful hold sway over their minions, that try as you may, there's no beating them. Small victories would have to be taken in small ways, a little cheating here and there, a minor theft or two, betrayals large and small. A nice way to get life started. Happy Birthday to you.

# SEVEN

The next day he boarded a C130 at Tan San Nhut Airport for a pre-dawn flight up the coast, maybe 200 miles, to Cam Rahn Bay. He'd been told it was worth a look. Grabbing an empty seat, if that's what a crisscross of webbing hung from the plane's bulkhead could be called, he found himself alongside a broad-faced, heavily built civilian. They nodded to each other, barely able to talk above the roar of the revving engines. The plane, fully loaded, began its slow movement down the tarmac and even more slowly, lifted off and made altitude. His seat mate reached into a bag, and to his surprise, fetched out a copy of Camus' *L'Étranger*. In French no less. Unable to resist, he shouted over the noise, "Êtes-vous Français, monsieur?"

Our Francophile closed his book and introduced himself with a smile. "Non, monsieur, je suis Américain."

He would never see his Franco-American friend get past page one of that book, but no matter. Johnny The Greek, who seemed to know everyone in Vietnam, would become his guide to the things of this world that seemed to matter most: good food and drink, access to the right clubs, the highlife as well as the low, a Greek Virgil, laughing his way through not-so-sacred woods. They exchanged those parts of their stories they chose to tell. The Greek, an engineer and Cal Berkeley football star, or so he said, offered his version of the life of a ne'er-do-well who'd washed up on this shore. No judgments, no sighs, nor what-the-hells. They were a pair. Half–educated, an eye for the chippies, a willingness to take chances, working for the same outfit. It was all they needed to know about each other. A jeep waited, after the short flight, to whisk them off to breakfast. In the morning light, the sun still moving upward into the waiting blue sky, he caught a glimpse of thousands of workers, their equipment, the construction of docking facilities and buildings of every kind.

Over coffee, John described what the place had looked like before the buildup. Heavy forest growth reaching near to the water's edge, vast stretches of sand and beach, a small detachment of the Vietnam Navy looking after an old French base. From the terrace of the Officer's Club he watched as concrete piers, huge in length, were nudged into place by small tugs. The advance of civilization seemed ordained, a necessary evil. "Look at that," John pointed. "Those piers were built on our East Coast, and here they are."

"Through the Panama Canal?"

John, still at his Eggs Benedict, waved him off with a fork. "Panama Canal? Never happen, much too big. Them suckers were floated past the canal, round the Tierra del Fuego, across the wide Pacific to Cam Rahn Bay." Breakfast consumed, they headed off to Dupar headquarters. Air condition-chilled to the bone despite the off-shore breeze, the office had an air of serious work being done, big money being made. John introduced him around before going out the door with a crew of engineers, leaving him in the company of a medium-built, short-sleeved American whose bulging dark eyes looked him over. He had gotten used to these suspicious looks, chalking it up to the paranoia of those fearing to be caught with a hand in the cookie jar. But Mario Perry had a small problem, which he revealed to his visitor when he learned he was about public affairs.

It seems Mario had been putting his desk to use of an afternoon as a place to fuck his little file clerk. Nothing wrong with that, is there? Except that her husband worked in the office, took great umbrage when he'd found out, rushing in on them in the midst of their brief encounter to cause quite a scene. "Of course the little bitch cried out that she'd been raped," Mario, indignant, asserted. "Raped? Ain't no such thing in this country." Turns out loving husband buys her story, has newspaper connections in Saigon through his family, is pressing charges, and it all will be in the Vietnamese papers any day now. Mario looked at him. No anguish, no remorse, nor shame, but terrified fear. "My job is on the line. Anything you can do?" He hadn't a clue, but said, "I'm back to Saigon this evening, let me see." He collected the names of the injured parties, walking out into the sunlight, a jeep waiting to take him on a tour of America at its best.

Growling earth movers, their huge front blades knocking back the forest near the beach, made way for progress. Metal mats for a jet landing strip two miles long were put in place by hordes of Vietnamese men and women overseen by tough-looking Korean taskmasters. Fuel tanks, their immense circumferences an assault on what remained of the natural world, sat squat and sure. The building of the pyramids must have looked like this. He didn't have the time to check it out, but had the feeling things were on the up and up out here, no place to make a dishonest dollar. That little fifteen thousand dollar bonus he'd earned told him he wanted more, on the lookout for come-what-may.

On returning to Dupar HQ he found his new pal Mario waiting to take him to the airport, handing him an empty attaché case while telling him he could catch an earlier chopper flight. He listened as Mario said, "Those pricks who make the passenger manifests figure you to be VIP or CIA. Wait and see, we don't got to say nothin' to them and you're on the next ride out." And, he was right. GIs on the way to R&R or home were ignored while special attention was paid to a civilian who'd spent the day in Cam Rahn Bay and needed to get back to Saigon on matters of importance. Important to Mario anyway.

The chopper's noise made talk impossible, and the uneventful ride to Saigon gave him a chance to look at the countryside, water buffalo at work in flooded rice fields, peaceful farm villages, cool green fields rushing up then falling back behind. Farmers had long since learned not to look up since trigger-happy gunners, mistaking a waving arm for a hostile act, had gunned so many down in mid-smile. Our gunners, young and hyper kids, watched every move below, swiveling guns on their mounts and letting go a burst once in a while, more for target practice and release of tension than anything else. An uneasy calm came to him. The old agitations, festering within, dropped away for a while.

The sun was setting and it was growing dark. The lights of Saigon were coming on as they flew over the darkened curve of the river toward the center of the city. "That field okay?" The pilot pointed to an open space below where young men and boys were playing soccer. "Yeah, fine." The chopper swiftly dropped toward the field, scattering the players as it landed long enough for him to jump out, stride to a waiting taxi and head for home.

# EIGHT

Mr. Ninh joyfully reported Big Eddie's gratitude at the contract's renewal. "You can visit him any time," he said with a wise smile. They were eating breakfast near his apartment on Cong Ly. The street, lined with magnificent tall trees, trunks massive, gnarled, leaning branches offering welcome shade against the brutal sun. He couldn't tell from Ninh's chatter how much Eddie might know of his keeping back five percent for himself. Not that it would matter to Eddie, he figured, since he was willing to give up the thirty thousand anyway.

But Big Eddie could wait. He told Ninh about Mario's problem and the story about to break in the local papers. Ninh shrugged, a near to Gallic imitation, and said, "My friend is the Minister of Information, would you like to meet him?" Of course he would. The restaurant had a phone, and an appointment was made for that very morning to meet with Minister Tho, allowing Ninh the satisfaction of showing his American boss that he might need him more than he knew. He inquired of Ninh what he might bring along as an offering, assuming any favor would need to be well compensated for one so high and mighty. Ninh, shaking a finger, grandly announced. "Nothing. Tho is my school classmate. A bottle of Johnny Walker Red, nothing more." Chastened, he put himself in Ninh's hands. This little dope addict might just be a real find.

The Ministry was a bit of a walk, but, protected by the shade trees, it gave him a chance to check out the neighborhood. Cong

Ly, a main route to the airport, had its usual flow of traffic. Motor bikes worked their way around stalled cars, riders on bicycles made their way at a more leisurely pace, street vendors setting up stalls for the lunch crowd chatted among themselves. Down a street he spotted a quiet patio within the chaos. Bahai Center, a sign read. The patio, filled with flowers and a flowing fountain, seemed to shut out the chaos of the street. As he marveled at this aberration, a man emerged in monk's robes, bowed, and welcomed them. To Ninh's great relief, the boss declined the invitation. They did stop at an NCO Club for the whiskey.

As they approached a three-story building in French-Provincial style, an immense yellow flag with three narrow red stripes hanging from an upper floor, Ninh became giddy with expectation. "My friend the minister will take care of everything, you will see." He had no idea what this could mean, but followed along, taking an ancient elevator to a third-floor reception area with marble floors, French tile decorating the walls, elegant sofas and chairs occupied by Vietnamese men smoking, talking quietly, paying no attention to the new arrivals. No attention, that is, until Ninh approached the reception area to state his business. And a moment later, a thin, very handsome man came bounding out, all but lifting Ninh of his feet in an embrace. The astonished looks on the faces of the lobby sitters led him to understand this had to be Minister Tho. Confirmed by Ninh's smile that said, "See, I told you so, he is my good friend." Tho's arm around Ninh's shoulder, the three of them entered an inner office.

The minister spoke English, near to fluently, having attended by his account Santa Monica Community College in California for two years. "Ah, the beaches, the girls, blue eyes and blond. I drove a Mustang convertible. Very popular. I love Americans." That being established, and a polite inquiry made as to the nature of the visit, Ninh signaled that the loved American should explain. The incident, the outrage, the possible negative publicity was reviewed for the minister, who asked for the names of the Vietnamese involved. When Ninh supplied them, Tho said, "Oh, that family. I know them." Lighting a cigarette, he added, "Of no importance." In some odd simulation of a Hollywood movie heavy, he let exhaled smoke circle around him. "What would you like me to do for you?" Ninh, with apologies to his boss, spoke to his pal in Vietnamese. It was a long conversation, allowing a look around the office. Framed photos of Tho with LBJ, McNamara, Westmoreland, a panoply of our leaders in this war, offering proof the minister was very important indeed.

Tho, assuming his minister's mantle, returned to English, saying, "The injured parties need an apology, and, he paused, "Compensation. Five hundred dollars should do it, but a thousand would be preferable. As to the press, that family has connections with only two newspapers that no doubt already have the story." Turning to Ninh, he signaled him to go on. Mr. Ninh, enjoying his moment, sagely, quietly, said, "The minister is proposing that we shut down those two papers for a week, citing newsprint shortages. The story would be old news by then and not be published."

"Holy shit," he thought. "They'll shut the bastards down, just like that." There had to be a reason for this war, and it here it was: suppression of the First Amendment. But that was an American conceit, civil liberties and all that. There was a war on, wasn't there? Uncivil liberties is what's called for. His meditation at an end, he thanked the Minister for his kind intervention in this embarrassing matter. Ninh broke out the whiskey, Tho insisting on a toast to friendship with filled tumblers at 10:30 in the morning. Doing his duty, he downed the glass, strong drink at this hour staggering him as he stood with his minister friend who asked a favor. American entertainers were coming to Vietnam in droves to amuse the troops. Could he make an introduction? Of course he could, hadn't Tho already mentioned his interest in the blue-eyed blondes of the world? They returned to the reception area, Tho walking arm-in-arm with the two of them, then imperiously pointing to a gawking pair sitting stiffly in their chairs, led them to his inner sanctum.

Walking away from the ministry, Ninh, puffed up with victory, happily accepted the thanks and praise. "Why, with your connections, aren't you working in a big job with the government?" he asked. Ninh put out his hands, and shrugged in a nothing-can-be-done gesture. "My family is from the north. Northerners are smarter, quicker than people from the south. Even though I came here many years ago they envy us, don't trust us." That was the answer, and he let it go at that. He thought to ask Ninh if the clever northerners would prevail in the war, but decided to let that one go. Ninh pointedly mentioned the American entertainers Tho was interested in. That would be the payback, but he had no idea how to pay the debt owed.

Back in his office, he called Mario, who was bothered more by the apology than the money, but agreed to go along. "I owe you," said Mario. "Anytime," he replied, remembering the scope of the work up there. "Count on me if you ever need anything up here," Mario told him. He decided to bank the offer against some future need.

# NINE

John the Greek invited him for drinks at his club, the Circle Sportif. Using his new friend's name an invisible barrier fell. Led to a table overlooking the tennis courts, he found John watching Nguyen Cao Ky, the notorious Number Two in the VN government, at play below them. Pleased to see his guest impressed, John flagged down a waiter and drinks were ordered up. A friend of John's came over to say hello. His name, Casanova, caused him to smile as he was caught up in the grip of a handshake guaranteed to break a bone or two. Jean Casanova was muscular and menacing, compact as a fire-plug, and did not take kindly to amusement at his name. "I'm Corsican," he said in a growl of a voice. "From the South." As if that explained anything. A few more words with John, and he was gone. No more was said about Mr. Casanova.

He heard French spoken at a nearby table by Vietnamese men drinking and enjoying themselves. No other Americans were in sight or sound. A ball being hit or missed, laughter over ice, the absolute tranquility of a late afternoon was simply what it was, nothing more or less.

They sipped their vodka-on-ice, John offering congratulations on his handling of Mario's little problem up there in Cam Rahn. "You'll get yourself a reputation as a fixer," he said. It surprised him that John seemed to be in the know on the details of the fix, but never mind. John asked what it took to make it happen. "Nothing more than a bottle of Johnny Walker Red," he was told. "And an introduction to any American song and dance girlies coming over to please the troops. Got any idea where I can find them?" John, whose own taste in these matters centered on local talent, chuckled at this Vietnamese passion for the round eyes. "To each his own," he mused. Then, all-knowing, told him the local USO club is where they congregate before traveling out to the bases. "I've seen them in the god-damnest hairy places, right within sound of the guns. And they sure aren't making any real money, so it must be for love." That tip digested, they went off, leaving the general to cheat on line calls as he played away at his game.

Walking down a side street, the Greek was obviously heading somewhere. Entering a store, shelves empty except for a few odd boxes and cans gathering dust, John was welcomed as an old customer by a doleful East Indian. Writing out a check to cash for a thousand dollars, receiving a pile of piastres he didn't bother to count, John casually asked the exchange rate. "One ninety." The legal rate was one twenty but this was the Indian's business: black market money changing. Completely out in the open. Nothing black about it. Checks, not cash for chrissakes.

John did what he could to explain it all to this innocent abroad. To put a stop to corruption, inflation, God knows what else, U.S. dollars were banned from use. The army issued something called Military Pay Certificates, MPCs, in denominations of one, five, and ten bucks. GIs, too lazy to exchange MPCs for piastres, paid bar tabs, whores and other needs with these MPCs, which were illegal for Vietnamese to possess. What was a decent hardworking whore or pimp to do? Why, trade these worthless MPCs for piastres on the black market, at a rate well below the legal exchange. And what was the hard working Indian to do? Why, trade these piastres and MPCs in exchange for checks in dollars written on good old American bank accounts.

When it was noted that these checks cleared through a Hong Kong bank, some surmised that some of these dollars might be going to Red China, the supplier to North Vietnam of beaucoup arms. Anything is possible in this most impossible of worlds. And so he joined in the game, cashing his check for piastres, earning a fifty-percent discount on his rent and other necessities of life. As for the MPCs? That was another black market deal that could wait another day.

Down the street, a small crowd had gathered. Curious GIs and amused Vietnamese watched as two Americans in their fifties tried to push past local cops blocking their way into a bar. The two grew loud and insistent. "Whadda ya mean I can't go in? I own the fuckin' place," one said, as one of the cops pressed a hand on his soft, fleshy stomach. When he threw the cop's hand aside a second cop drew his gun. The crowd stepped back as the two pairs stared each other down. Almost on cue, a grossly fat American stepped out of the bar. One of the Americans under the gun called out to him, "Boyle, go back in there and get Suzie." Boyle looked at him almost sadly. "Suzie ain't here."

"Whaddayamean, she ain't here? She's runnin' the place for me." Boyle stepped forward. With a slight movement he caused the cop to put away his gun. Then Boyle placed an arm around his American pal. "She sold the place last night."

"Sold it! She can't do that, I had all my money in the place."

"Well. That's what she did and you got nothin' to say." He shouldered his way through the crowd, spotted John and gave him the high sign. He tagged along, joining The Greek and Frankie Boyle who stalked down the street shaking his head at the foibles men are heir to.

The three went into a nearby bar. Boyle ordered three beers, not bothering to check anyone's preferences. John made the introductions as Boyle, using the bottle as a pointer, sized up the stranger before him. "That's a fuckin' good lesson for you, what happened out there just now," taking a swallow of the beer, draining the bottle, replaced before he set it down.

They knew Boyle intended to continue. After all, he seemed the expansive sort, not given to meditative silences. "That poor fucker, I told him not to get involved with that bar. 'It's a money machine,'" Boyle mimicked the sucker. "'A money machine.'" He shook his head. "A money machine, all right, but not for him. I told that dumb son of a bitch no American could own a business like that in Saigon. He sez to me, that's taken care of. All the papers are in Suzie's name." He spun his bottle in the direction of the bartender. "Suzie, for chrissakes. That ain't even her name. He still don't know her real name even though they lived together for five years." His third beer was before him. "So he puts up all the money, her name goes down as the owner. Six months later she sells the fuckin' place right out from under him. Go figure. I know I can't."

Boyle turned to The Greek. "So, who's your fuckin' buddy, Johnny?" With a smile, John began to explain. Boyle waved him off. "You play golf?" He shook his head. "Another useless fucker come to town. Don't nobody play golf anymore?"

"He chases pussy," John volunteered.

Boyle glowered over his beer. "Chasin' pussy is not a sport, it's an act of charity. Especially around here."

"You still screwing your caddy?" John inquired of the golfer in their midst.

"Sure," he replied with a smirk. "It's a different kind of 19th hole." As he spewed beer, laughing at his own bad joke, he turned to his new friend. "Don't get any funny ideas. Out here all the caddies are chicks." Boyle seemed to be looking him over for the first time. "You're from New York, aintcha?" He nodded. "I could tell. Jewboy?"

"My mother, not my father."

"Yeah, sure," said Boyle. "Comin' to my birthday party?" John nodded, yes. "Bring your pal along. Let's pay up and get outta here. I got a tee time in half an hour."

# TEN

"Jewboy?"

"My mother, not my father."

"Yeah sure."

Where had he heard that one before?

When he was a kid, Jewbastard was one word. It was something his father taught him. "Jewbastards, Jewbastards," he would cry. One word. The only way he knew to say it. Jew forever linked with bastard. Inextricable. It was the beginning of his religious education.

When his mother married a goy, "Worse a thing than garbage," her family held a wake. She would be ostracized for all time, confirming for her husband that the Jewbastards were all the same. Whether he worked for them, bought from them, was treated by them or cheated by them, they were all Jewbastards, entrapping him in the catch basin of his rage, his bitterness.

Though that rage was hard-earned by years of disappointments, he must have been so hopeful at first. An adventurer even as a boy, he slipped into the Great War of 1914 underage, barely fifteen. Thrown into the trenches, he stood and fought until felled by a burst of artillery fire that sent a piece of hot metal cutting across his body, leaving a long scar, but lucky to be alive. One of that peculiar breed, a boy-soldier who sneaks off to war and lives to tell the tale.

Boarding a ship to Canada, he crossed the border to America on a 48-hour visa. A visit lasting more than fifty years. An outsider from day of birth till day of death, he passed on this edginess to his son who knew, who heard, that his father's bag was packed, abandonment near at hand. But, despite humiliation, desperation, hunger, a life beyond poverty, the father had stayed with his family. Though he spoke of bag packed, passport in hand, ready to go, ready to hit the road, he would do anything to earn a dollar or two to keep them together. The son, looking out the window of their apartment one day, saw him sweeping the street, pushing a Department of Sanitation broom. On their own street! And there was the time the boy was in the park on a Sunday and saw his father with a shoe-shine box, bending the knee to those Jewbastards for a nickel a shine.

This miserably begotten son was kept standing outside the door while those inside decided his fate. They'd allow him within sometimes, but the fee for entrance was beyond his means to know or pay. Allowed to the perimeter, the rim, of the charmed. Letting him circle, looking for access. Letting his talents be either not enough or too much for any of them. Let him be turned away by word or deed. The son learned to get a step on the opposition, be it a lovely woman, a wife, a boss, the world. Wasn't that what he'd been taught, seeing his father driven to his knees?

When he was nine years old, the old lady who lived next door took him into her kitchen on Friday nights to light her stove in exchange for a few soft candies wrapped in cellophane. Outside, a man on the street promised to pay him ten cents to go with him to the rear of a large room filled with high-backed benches to flip on electric switches. He did so and asked for his dime. "Come back tomorrow night," the man told him. " I have no money now." Thus his religious education continued: Jews couldn't light matches, were afraid of electric switches, and were cheap, cheating sons of bitches.

Flickering light cast large dark shadows across the walls of his kitchen. A lit candle was sunk into a glass with strange writing on its label. He watched the wick and flame and the shadows it had formed, afraid to touch the glass, knowing dimly that it was something special and important to his mother. He never understood why, when the flame went out that the glass would be used and washed and rinsed and handed about like an ordinary thing. He never touched it, remembering the peculiar quiet that came over his mother who never said anything about the candle in the glass. It was a memorial to the dead. And his mother was Jewish. But his father was not.

Though taken from school at the end of sixth grade and put to work at twelve, his mother could recite every line of poetry she'd ever learned. Portia, Barbara Fritchie, Tennyson, Houseman. The lines would come tumbling forth, declaimed in a schoolgirl style "Lives of all great men remind us, WE TOO can make our lives sublime and departing leave behind us FOOTPRINTS in the sands of time." In a wistful mist of melancholy, her children her only audience, she would cock her head, look past the littered table, battered chairs, the couch and lamps that crowded the room. Look out into the gray world, smile, and oh so sweetly say, "The quality of mercy is not strained, it cometh like the gentle rain from heaven upon the earth beneath. It is twice blessed — It blesseth him that gives, and him that takes. Tis mightiest in the mightiest." And she rode through the glories of that speech till "therefore Jew, though dust be thy plea, consider this, that in the course of justice, none of us shall see salvation." The complications of the words were lost to him. But the cadence, the sounds, the language were there to fill the air, nothing moved, and there was stillness for a while.

The songs she sang had another message for the growing boy — songs of betrayal, duplicity, the cheating of a heart in love. He learned from his mother, "A woman's a twofaced, she gives you the big talk, but when the big talkin's done...." And, "Oh by Jingo had a lover, she was always under cover." He grew accustomed to the tone and tension and message in these songs his mother sang. Readied an entry into a world he knew would betray the innocent, exploit the unwary, break his heart. He needed to prepare. Isn't that what the songs his mother taught him were all about?

His parents rarely went out at night but one time they did, returning with a hoard of things to eat. The older, wiser kids grabbed for packages of sweet cakes called macaroons. There were jars of awful-looking white balls in liquid, and a flat-looking square something that was tasteless and crumbled in his hands. His sisters and brothers laughed at him as they sang, "Matzoh, matzoh two for five, that's what keeps the Jews alive." It was a holiday.

His parents had been to where free food was given to the poor. A great argument broke out between them over what to throw out and what to keep, until his father gathered up the laughable matzohs and other signs of his humiliation, and threw them out the window. This could not only have been about being poor and being humbled by our poverty. This was about something else.

The following day he went to visit his best friend, Jerry, and heard his mother say, "A goy in my house on Passover?" He didn't understand. He had been welcomed at Jerry's house, fed by Jerry's mother, helped with his spelling and arithmetic, and was not welcomed on this day called Passover. And his religious education continued.

The next morning, a Sunday, he slipped out of his apartment heading to the park. It was quiet and the early April morning was cold. He shivered on a hard bench, his sweater and shirt — relics handed down from his brothers — too thin to warm his bones. When no one showed up, he went over to the street where some of his friends lived. He spotted Danny Abramowitz and Leon Kaminsky, both dressed like they were going to church. They looked at him with equal curiosity since he was wearing his usual Sunday rags. He asked, "How come you're so dressed up?" They stared at him in disbelief. "We're goin' to services." "On Sunday?" he asked.

"It's Passover," they said.

"But it's Sunday," he continued to remind them.

"It don't matter what day it is," our Daniel pointed out, "Passover is Passover."

Then something was shouted at them from an upper window. They ducked inside the building, leaving him alone once more.

"Screw it," he said to himself. "I'll go find Curran and Esposito over on Third Avenue."

When he got to their building he found them dressed up in suits and jackets, standing around with some other guys. What was going on here?

He said to Michael Esposito, "How come you're dressed up, you're not Jewish."

"Jewish? Are you fuckin' crazy? I ain't Jewish."

"Then how come you're so dressed up?"

"Cause it's Easter," said Saint Michael, "And we gotta dress up for church."

Now, isn't that a laugh riot? That the Confluence of Waters represented by the two great faiths could, by a trick of calendar and fate, fall on the same Sunday, returning a boy to confusion and solitude? Praise God from whom all blessings flow.

When he was about 13 he was given and old team jacket as a gift. He didn't care, either way, about the huge white Star of David decorating its back. Walking home with three pals through an alien, Irish neighborhood, a voice called out "Hey, Jewboy." He turned and saw a boy his age hanging out the back of a parked truck. "I mean you, Jewboy," said the hanger on.

He turned to his friends and said "Let's get him," and moved toward the truck. A canvas curtain hung from the back obscuring voices and laughter from inside. Picking up speed he leaped up and in one motion pulled the creep from his perch into the street, jumped inside the blackness of the truck, throwing punches, knees to the balls, fingers to the eyes, hearing yowls of pain and fright and then total silence. He realized he was alone and peeked outside. Three guys were limping down the street and his friends were nowhere in sight. When he caught up with them they said, "Are you crazy, they could've killed you." He looked at them in amazement. Hadn't they heard what he'd been called? These three friends he had known for years and to whose Bar Mitzvahs he had not been invited. Why was that? Was it a question of a gift? These friends had run the other way as he moved forward defending a faith that was theirs, not his, and that he knew to be a source of agitation in his own home.

His mother's father, who Lear-like had grown old and a burden to his other daughters, made daily visits. Tea in a glass and the occasional handout would be exchanged for a hand on the boy's head, a muttering of strange sounds and words. Each time they moved, and it was often in those days dancing one step ahead of the landlord, his grandfather would move around the corner. Once, his mother asked him to visit grandpa in the synagogue. He went up to him in his place, saw his surprise, felt his embrace and the touch of a small, black cap quickly placed on his naked head. And felt the brushing of a bird's wings when the old man placed a white shawl across his narrow back and shoulders, handed him a book he could not read, pointed to a spot on the page and began to recite, moving back and forth, rocking and reading, rocking and reading.

In junior high school he began hanging out with the hoods, jokers who didn't need school. They sat together in assembly one day when Mr. Rabinowitz, the assistant principal, showed a movie that he said might be hard to watch but which they had to see. From the screen, images of the dead, stacked, tossed, and discarded came before him. Then a room filled with bones, then living creatures, with such eyes as no one could have seen before. Eyes popped from their skulls, listless, with Jewish stars sown to their striped uniforms. Some had their shirts off and their ribs seemed to have no flesh, protruding through the skin. It was horrible to look at. One of his bunch began to laugh and others joined in. Rabinowitz switched on the lights and raced down the aisle ordering the row of hooligans to his office.

"I never laughed Mr. Rabinowitz, believe me, I never did laugh."

On the day he had been drafted into the Army, a moment came when he needed to decide something. A simple enough matter for men filling in a form asking pertinent data on birth, parentage, schooling. The form asked: Religion? A blank line came after the question. A blank to be filled in. He passed it by and went on. When the form was completed he sat back and a sergeant came behind him, glanced down, and said, "You haven't filled in your religion."

"I don't have a religion, sergeant." The sergeant looked at him and said, "You got to put something down, anything." Easy, isn't it? Easy enough to put down Protestant and join the bland race. Or, why not Episcopalian, Presbyterian, Lutheran, Baptist, Congregationalist, Methodist, Adventist, Disciples of Christ, AME, Church of God and Prophecy, Iglesia Pentecostal, along with the Heavenly Host borne by the Holy Father offering safe haven, ticket to heaven?

In the seconds he had before the form would be replaced by another, he had to decide, and please a sergeant he would never see again.

He wrote, "Jewish." And that was that. Jewish he would be. Jewish on dog tags he was ordered to wear around his neck. Jewish on records trailing him everywhere. Jewish to his fellow soldiers, a North Jersey redneck bunch, who made him pay for the folly of his choice.

Jewish? Not him. But the metal tags around his neck stamped it loud and clear. They had a Jewboy in their midst and they'd let him know he'd chosen neither wisely nor well. His explanations to those who'd care to listen made no sense. His father was Protestant. He was half-Jewish. "Yeah, sure."

He arrived at an Army base in the south one Sunday night and found an empty bunk in a long barracks room containing twenty or so beds. While he unpacked his stuff, others came in. One approached him. "Where you from?"

"New York."

"Me? New Jersey. This place is the worst." Carlucci was his name and he had the look of too many schoolyard brawls, graduated to numbers running, minor burglaries, a broken head or two. The two of them were getting along, jabbering about places they knew in Manhattan, the common ground of a northern soldier in the alien south. Getting along just fine. Until Carlucci noticed something, stepped forward, lifted his new pal's dog tag and said, "Jewish, huh?"

"My mother, not my father," he replied. Carlucci turned, Brahmin in contact with an Untouchable, went to a group of his buddies, jerking a thumb over his shoulder. "A Jewboy."

And that was that. And what that was involved nights and days of minor annoyances, petty criminality, insults ordinary and extreme. He would laugh at them and tell them they were fucking crazy. Though one night, returning late, lights out, he approached his bunk and saw his bed and locker turned upside down. Suddenly, the lights were on, the room came alive as the others jumped out of their beds screaming, "Jew, Jew, Jew." Their faces were serious, contorted, drunk, their eyes on him as they approached, forming a circle around his upturned life. He turned to the one closest, who happened to be the biggest, throwing a punch, hoping to get an eye. But the bastard was too quick, the blow landing on a cheek. Big Boy came after him and, shit, he knew what he was doing. All he could do was try to keep from getting too badly hurt. Bored in on, sized up, shown the left jab, letting a right-hand feint be blocked, the big fucker came back with a grin and a left fist too quick to be stopped by anything other than Jewboy's nose. Blood came pouring forth, drenching his shirt, pants, shoes, spattering guilty dog tags.

They all went back to their bunks, one of them, a real Christian that one, throwing him a towel. The lights went out, they all went off to sleep. He was left to wash the blood from his face, wipe his blood-stained shoes, remove his bloody shorts and pants, and put order back into his world. And he wasn't even Jewish.

On the morning after he awoke to silence and a swollen nose. The mirror showed a black eye and he dressed for the day, left alone for once by God's avenging angels. During the morning he was told to report to the Chaplain's Office. What's this, he wondered? He found his way to the Army Chapel that looked like all the other buildings on the base, maybe a little neater. He'd never been inside and noticed that the chapel was set up to be all-purpose, all-purposeful, all-knowing. The three great faiths could commingle. Everything known to the civilized world accommodated. Up Torah on Friday night, down on Saturday, in time to set the table for Catholic Mass on early Sunday morning, which in turn gave up the ghost, cleared its jugs and wafers, making way for progress, Protestant style, a service at 11:00. A late enough start to clear the head, early enough to make the opening kick-off. God does move it right along, doesn't he?

A door opened and he saw a smile approaching, a shining silver bar on one lapel, the other with a Star of David. A nametag — Meyrowitz — on his left breast, a skullcap adorned a head of thinning curly black hair. First Lieutenant Meyrowitz. Jewish Chaplain. All out there to be taken at first glance, face value. "Good morning, good morning," said Meyrowitz, beginning to offer his hand but joining instead in the salute that the wise private proffered. It was the Lieutenant's turn to take in the GI-issued fatigues, the decidedly non-regulation busted up face that stood before him.

"Let's go into my study, why don't we?" And the officer led the soldier into a room with a bible open at his desk.

"I'm working on this week's sermon." It brought the rabbi no response. "Where are you from?"

"New York."

"Oh, I love visiting New York. I'm from Cincinnati."

"Uh, huh."

"Look, I know what happened to you last night, do you want to talk about it?"

"It was a fight."

"Where I come from nice Jewish boys don't get into fights." He chuckled.

"I'm not a nice Jewish boy."

"Of course, I didn't mean it that way. You are a man among men doing your duty, an important duty, for your country." The soldier sat before him in silence.

"I haven't seen you at services. Why not join us this Friday night? You'd enjoy the solidarity. It can get very lonely here, you can feel isolated when you are used to being among your own. Your buddies come from an entirely different world and it would be easy enough to fall into their ways, assimilate their values, don't you think?"

"There's not much chance of that," he replied.

"Your Jewishness is looked upon, probably for the first time in your life, as an object of real bigotry. You can shelter yourself from such attitudes in New York, but here you need to seek out those who share your values, your traditions. And we are here for you, ready to take you up."

"Can you get me a transfer to New York?"

"That's beyond my power. I'm here to offer a means to assist in the difficult adjustment you must be experiencing in leaving your heritage, your environment, for a place that must seem so alien, so far away. Oh, I empathize, I truly do. I'd love to be back home in Cincinnati this minute. But, I'm here. And like you, I need to live with that fact."

"Uh, huh."

"In ten days it will be Passover. The local community is inviting all Jewish personnel to a Seder on the Second Night. Join us. Wonderful people live in this area. Fine Jewish families. And some good-looking daughters, not incidentally."

"Thanks, but that's where I'll be in ten days, New York, on leave."

"So you'll be with your family on the holiday — wonderful!! What synagogue do you belong to?"

"I don't belong to a synagogue."

"None? I see. You're about twenty-two?

"Right."

"A college education?"

"Uh, huh."

"Haven't been to services in years, I suppose."

"Right."

The rabbi sat in silence for a moment. "Well, you might be interested to know that this is a dilemma for Jewish America today. You are part of a trend toward secularism and denial. A cause for great concern."

He made no response, not even a silent nod of the head. The rabbi looked at him, pointedly. "Have you read Philip Roth?"

"Yeah, sure."

"This is a writer whose books go beyond denial and cross over to Jewish self-hatred," said Rabbi Lieutenant Meyrowitz, who paused for emphasis. "These are books that," he raised a finger, "that, like a thief in the night, can creep inside all of us and turn self-mockery into self-destruction."

"I think some of it's pretty funny," said the private.

"What's funny?" asked the lieutenant.

"Oh, the unopened liquor bottles with drink recipes hanging from their necks, all that fruit in the refrigerator. That sort of thing."

The good lieutenant looked at him, keenly, man to man. "I'm here to help you. I'm here to provide for your spiritual needs. But you have to meet me halfway. Now report back to duty. But remember your other duty, Defender of the Faith, and when you do, I hope to see you at services Friday night." He rose, silver bar sizzling in the sunlight.

The good soldier rose with him, offered a snappy salute, turned, and walked away.

Jewboy? Yeah, sure.

# ELEVEN

The Saigon USO, exuding good cheer in the midst of the raucous hullabaloo of hookers, pimps, and touts, offered safe haven to those avoiding temptation. Coffee the strongest drink, along with cookies and cokes to wet the whistle, rang the bell for sobriety. Fresh-faced kids in uniform were exchanging dollars for piastres. At the legal rate no doubt. A chance for somebody to make a bundle on the side, his corrupt heart told him. But never mind, off in a corner he spotted what he needed. John's tip had been right as rain. Four American women and a man, suitcases piled around them, sat tired, a bit confused. The youngish women had a showgirl look. The much older man, a dreadful hairpiece slipping from his pate, was checking the condition of a portable keyboard.

The entertainment has arrived, he told himself. Watching from across the room, searching for Minister Tho's reward, a lion on the hunt, ready to cull the weakest gazelle from the herd, he set aside, with regret, the blonde. Too young for his mean purposes, he thought. Of the remaining three, the oldest, dark hair, dark eyes, had a suspicious air, a hardness about her that would do him no good. He moved toward the group having identified his quarry, slim, gamin-like with an open face that could be put to his advantage. He said hello. Relieved to meet a non-military American, they told him of their exhausting trip from New York by military aircraft. His sympathy aroused, he offered strong drink at a bar around the corner. To his delight, dark-eyed Dolores came along with her buddy, little Sue.

Settled into a booth at the bar, he established where they would be staying. Happy to be in the hands of one so knowing, they told him stories of Broadway road shows around the U.S., dancing in the chorus, waiting for the break they knew to be coming. Twenty weeks of work followed by twenty weeks of unemployment insurance was how their mean years went by. He offered to take them both to dinner the next night. "Why not?" He had his round eyes. Act Two could wait until tomorrow.

# TWELVE

His two dancing girls, dressed for an evening out, were whisked away by taxi on a dizzying ride to The Fuji, his new haunt in Cholon. Ninh would bring the minister after dinner for a just-by-chance rendezvous. When Big Eddie spotted him with his two beauties he would have leapt into the air with expectant glee, had he been able. Sweet faced Sue and dour Dolores, stunned by his great bulk, smiled, a bit nervously, at the attention. They did look good, the two of them. Bright contrast to Chinese men in dark suits, their bored women picking at dinner. The show had begun, the headwaiter marched them down to a table near the stage, flourishing menus. Big Eddie sat nearby, ready to pounce.

His companion of the other evening was not out there. Performing backstage, he figured, and listened to his new friends make mocking comments on the gyrations going on before them. They were pros, after all, entitled to their opinions. "I bet you could show them a thing or two," he said. An idea, a dark fantasy, began to seep into his thinking.

"You bet we could," said Sue. Dolores said nothing at all, sensing things about him still unrevealed. Dinner, selected by the headwaiter, had arrived. The table was laden with a feast for a dozen, crab's legs, noodle dishes, things no one recognized but delicious. Sue ate with glee in great quantities. Dolores, only tasting each dish, asked, "What else do those girls do here?" It was a statement within a question whose answer she knew. In his best avuncular style, he had to sadly admit that some of the girls made themselves available to paying customers. Dolores, more amused than impressed by his reticence and concern, moved her eyes back to the stage.

"The two of you could be headliners here," he said, not sure exactly what he was formulating.

"Oh, wouldn't that be nice," Sue, chopsticks poised over yet more food, exclaimed, silenced by a very severe Dolores who looked at him, beginning to divine where this was going.

"We're under contract, we've got work do to here," Dolores said.

"Oh," he said casually. "How long does the contract run?"

"Three months." As she said this, a chair was brought to their table, and Big Eddie, no longer able to keep away, joined them. He watched as this great whale of a man, with word and gesture, charmed the table. An after-dinner liquor was served, compliments offered on the quality of the cooking. Compliments, as well, from Eddie about the beauty of the lovely women before him. Sue's enthusiastic laughter was in contrast to Dolores' studied coquettishness. "Curious," he thought. "She doesn't have to play up to Eddie. Does she want something?" Since he was playing at his own game, he'd have to watch her at play, wait 'til later, if ever, to find out more.

A loud entrance behind him, the look of surprise on Big Eddie's face, and he knew that the minister had arrived. He turned to see Tho, impeccable in a dark linen suit, make his way toward them, gladhanding here and there. Ninh was nowhere to be found, no doubt impatient to score his little hit. Eddie, realizing the game was up, no sense in reaching for what no longer was there for him, shook hands with the women, testing their receptiveness, allowing his hand to linger a tad too long in each of theirs. Take what bit of flesh you can, when you can, was his M.O. He'd bide his time and wait for what might develop.

Tho, treating Eddie like a waiter, ordered champagne. Introductions made, the champagne popped and pored, Tho sat back pleased with himself as he assayed the possibilities before him, once again into his "I love America'" routine. Sue giggled over her bubbles, Dolores sipped quietly, languorous, indifferent, her eyes glancing toward the stage now and then.

Fat Eddie, ignoring Tho with a contempt bordering on murderous, asked his new American friend about the girls. "From New York, musical comedy stars, and movies too," he said with slight exaggeration.

"Sing and dance?" asked Eddie.

"Yes, here to sing and dance for American soldiers," he told him.

"Work for you?" Eddie wondered.

"Yes," he lied.

"Work for me?" Eddie was imagining his club with round-eye stars of stage and screen, American big spenders joining his regular crowd, tables going to the highest bidder. He'd be coining money. "What can I do?" he asked.

"Five thousand a week," he replied.

"Three thousand," Eddie said with finality.

Having no idea if he could bring this off, he hoped the girls would jump at a thousand a week. A three-way split, reminded his egalitarian heart. "Let me see what I can do," and returned to his table.

The minister, in high spirits, invited them to a private club for a nightcap and dancing. Sue loved the idea, and Tho had his reward. Dolores, bored, jet-lagged, watched the happy couple take off, leaving the two of them in silence. He looked at her, as she watched the action on the stage, not talking, not listening to his try at conversation. He didn't have much time, and couldn't divine a way to make his pitch. She was hard to read, offering little to hang onto, 'til he said, "Don't worry about Sue, she'll be OK with Tho."

"Sue can take care of herself. I'm not worried about her at all." She said this with a defiance bred by too many encounters with backstage lover boys, hangers-on around the road shows she'd been with over the years. He sensed an antagonism, not toward him, directly but to his kind. He decided to plunge in. "You and Sue could make a lot of money in this town." She eyed him, trying to gauge the implications of his suggestion.

"Doing what, exactly?" she asked.

"What you do best, singing and dancing. Right here, in the club. A thousand a week for each of you."

"How do you know that?" She asked, eying him as if for the first time.

"The owner of the place, the fat one, mentioned it to me."

"Mentioned? Is it an offer or isn't it?"

By their questions you will know them, and knew he had her on his line. "A definite offer," he said.

"What about housing?" she asked.

He thought a moment. Not quite sure how, he said, "That'll be taken care of." He assumed Eddie had plans for them beyond the talents on display and would have them fixed up in a nearby little love nest. Reading his thoughts, Dolores, a Gypsy with his palm in her hand, said, "And what else might be involved?"

"What do you mean?" our naïf manqué replied.

"I mean the extra-curricular crap the girls up there put up with."

"You wouldn't be involved with any of that," he said reassuringly.

"A thousand a week each," she repeated.

"Yep, that's the deal."

"Sue will jump at five hundred. Make mine fifteen hundred." Another blow for sisterly solidarity, he said to himself.

"And what about the USO?" he asked.

"We go off tomorrow," she said, "Back in two weeks." Patriotic to the core, she added, "If everything is as you say, we can cut out on them." He thought this a terrific way to do business and brought Fat Eddie over to say hello to his new headliner. Dolores, clearly repelled, turned on the star quality, leaving Eddie staggered by its potential. This was a very tough guy, allowing himself to be charmed for the moment, already counting the return on his investment.

He took Dolores back to her hotel. She'd see to it that Sue came to the party, and they exchanged a brief, tentative handshake. He decided to return to The Fuji and Fat Eddie to close on the deal. In the taxi, he mused that he'd be a pimp once removed if Eddie had his way. But never you mind, he reassured himself, working for the Yankee dollar was an option for any of them, why should these lovelies be excluded from chasing the dollars down? He fit right into the life. A war was going on out there somewhere, yet he was living the high life, comfortable among the corruptible.

Eddie, at his usual table seated between his sons, seemed to be expecting him. As he walked over he quickly noticed the bodyguard at a table immediately behind that immense back and head. The table was covered with emptied plates, leftovers from a greedily consumed, enormous meal. He sat down and was offered a glass of whiskey, politely passing on the chance to add ice. This was Fast Eddie, after all.

"The girls are in." On hearing this good news, Eddie took a toothpick from the table inserting it into the great maw of his mouth and waited to hear more. "They'll be wanting you to pay for an apartment or hotel. And a plane ticket home." Eddie nodded OK. It would give him that much more control over them. "And they'll need dressing rooms, backstage."

Eddie asked, "They know what happens there?"

"Yes, they know all about it."

"And they'll go along?" He had no idea how to answer this question, knowing this was the crux of the deal for Eddie, his vision of five-hundred-dollar whores returning his investment tenfold.

"If you sweeten the pot, yes."

Eddie plucking the toothpick, from his jaw, said, "And you'll be getting yours from the three thousand a week." He said this not as a question, but as one businessman to another, and saw his new partner nod in agreement. "And anything more for you?" Happy to pass on a pimps profiteering, he grandly waved off any suggestion of more.

"It's all yours, Eddie," he said with a smile. The bodyguard had yet to take his eyes off him. The menace of his presence assured him that Eddie had means of persuasion beyond his wish to know.

# THIRTEEN

He was on his way to Frankie Boyle's birthday party with a gift, his favorite whore. A light knock at his apartment door one Sunday evening found a waif in a long tan raincoat standing there. She looked at him with a mouth promising instant liquidity and said softly, "Suck your cock, mister?" It turned out to be the only English she had ever learned. It was that exact emphasis on "your" as she made her kind offer that caused him to pass her through to his bedroom where, after establishing her sex, "Never can be too delicate in these matters," he said to himself, settled down and watched as she worked at her trade, never removing her raincoat, never missing a beat, her eyes on him from time to time, a little wary perhaps, 'til he stopped watching and it was over, sweetly done and not a drop spilled to the floor. The best investment of five hundred piastres, in one of the great whistle jobs ever, he concluded.

Arriving at Boyle's, air conditioners blasting away against the heat, he saw that everyone there had the same idea. So much for an original gift. Paid for the day, the girls had turned up in party outfits, chattering among themselves like kids at school. It was their eyes that gave them away. Eyes that darted about on the lookout for the main chance. A guy he knew came up to say hello and pointed him in the direction of Boyle's bedroom. "Have a look," he said.

Boyle, old Asia hand and Vietnam hustler, was in bed asleep, not hiding a beer-belly gut. On either side of him, one young woman sleeping, another filing her nails. A grenade launcher and a box of shells sat by the bed. Closing the door, his whistle job at his side, he turned back to the room, taking in the crowd of construction stiffs, engineers, retired military types, already drinking, already drunk. After she pointed, he fetched her a coke and vodka-tonic for himself. His ladylove found a girl she knew, that took care of that, and he was on his own.

The large living room had no trace of anything beyond suburbia, no suggestion of a place outside America. The garrulous gang congregated around a long curved wooden bar served by a smiling bartender rapidly producing drinks on insistent command. These fellow workers of the world were his new companions and he stood among them, drink in hand, trying to get a feel for the place.

A clamor went up as Boyle entered the room. Wearing a pair of boxer shorts and nothing else, he padded toward the bar, pinching an ass or two along the way, shaking a few hands, being kissed by one, two, three girls. Turning to the crowd he said, "Thanks a lot, you guys are tryin' to fuckin' kill me. There's more to life than pussy, though I ain't figured out what it is yet, unless it's drinkin' or playin' golf with some colonel and takin' his money off him." He took a long swallow from the drink he'd poured.

"Well, I'm sixty years old today and still fuckin' like a monkey. I waved good-bye to the fuckin' Frogs in '54 and stayed around knowing that cocksuckers like yourselves would start coming in ten years later. And here you are, screwing things up, raising the price of pussy, putting up with outrageous shit from broads who wouldn't be good enough to clean out a Frenchman's asshole, and being fucked over by every gook landlord in the country." He was in high disdain now, indictment unfinished. "And spend your time thinking about going home, for chrissakes. I went home, four years ago. My daughter got married. 'This time for keeps Daddy,' she said for the third time. I was going to stay a month. After a week I got nothing to say to my old lady and I'm ready to pull my pud. 'Fuck this,' I said, and took a plane out of McGuire the next day. And twenty hours later I was home, right here in Saigon. Where I ain't some fuckin' old man like I am stateside."

Boyle, done with denunciations, headed back to his bedroom, gathering up two nearby women, the best in the room, saying, "Come with me honey, I'm takin' a shower and need a little assistance." Before he closed the door, he turned once more to the room and said, "Thanks for the gifts, you guys. Help yourselves to the leftovers."

Hash and grass kicked in around the room. Music came up and awkward dancing began between unmatched pairs. Over in a corner an older Eurasian woman caught his eye. Left behind as evidence of the French presence, she let it be known she'd been the last mistress of the last French General in Vietnam. And here she was, reduced to scouting possibilities among this crew.

The French before they were run out had done their hundred years and done it right, by God. True colonials, treating workers and women with abuse, disdain, meted out with liberté, égalité, fraternité. Gaining the respect and admiration of those they fucked over with that peculiar French ability to draw you into their orbit, yet keep you on the outside with contempt enough to make an Englishman blush. Oh, yes, the French love of hierarchy was a natural fit for the Vietnamese love of intrigue learned from the elegant Chinese over the centuries.

Then, Whoa Nellie!! Here came the Americans. That special breed called GI, or construction crew redneck, mixed with a sprinkling of professional types who had the one thing in common: They'd learned good manners from their mommas and poppas, and the Heavenly Father watched over them so long as they did honest work, respected women and children, and kept from excess of the flesh.

These cowboys, plowboys, dough boys, descended on a country used to abuse and were heard to say, "Thank you, ma'am," held doors open, practiced what'd been preached. Oh, they knew they were superior all right. "Look how small them fuckers is." Against our planes, our guns, our PX, our PAX Americana, they would be as nothing. But within that day-to-day condescension they held out a hand to shake special to the good old U.S. of A. And were met by the long-suffering Vietnamese with first wonder, then amazement at the antics, gullibility, generosity exported by these sweet innocents. "American like everything quick, like everything at once. American like no bullshit. Give GI way to get truck washed, cock sucked, bag of H, kilo of hash all in one place and make big success. American civilian here longer time, have more money. Good. Fuck him different."

He wandered over to mademoiselle and introduced himself.

"Parlez-vous Français, monsieur?" she asked.

"Would you like to dance?" he replied. She moved with him to the center of the group of dancing drunks who'd already begun to slip away to side rooms to hone newly discovered skills in the art of love. He could see in her eyes and face an interest in opium already out of control. No hard stuff at American parties, she settled for the hash. After a while they wandered out of the room together. "Let's watch what's going on," she said.

Two women were listlessly playing at being lesbians while an old retired general, now a construction superintendent, took Polaroids, placing each photo in an album, carefully posing them in a different position, never speaking, never smiling, a regular sort of guy in every way.

A fight broke out over some lovely. Two fall-down drunks were swinging at each other in a narrow hallway, their fists smashing plaster wallboard. The lady in question stood by, comforted by friends, while these knights contested for her hand. One of the drunks, exhausted, did fall down. The other, forgetting what the fight was all about in the first place, said, "Where's the shithouse?" and staggered away.

He spotted a bunch he knew and drifted toward them. Guys who'd spent their lives married to broads gone to fat serving up TV dinners, watching the game shows, an occasional toss thrown in when convenient. And now on their own, surrounded by the young, the slim, the available, becoming conversant with around-the-worlds, doing it in twos and threes. Convinced it was due to their charm, their American charm, that the slim, the young, the very beautiful, petted, caressed and courted them.

For the first and last time in their lives they lived in a place where anything that could be bought they could afford. It would never be the same for them, they had the sense to know it, ride it, and be damned.

At the after-party Boyle convened a group of drunks that assembled at his house on weekends. To a man they'd tried The Program, and to a man, stumbled off after a Step or two. None the worse for the experience, maintaining that peculiar straight-backed look that comes with being stiff with drink, they listened as Boyle explained the intricacies involved in turning a hundred dollars in MPCs into a thousand-dollar U.S. Treasury check in seven quick transactions. "There's army post offices all over the goddamn place," he said. "You go to one and buy a U.S. hundred-dollar money order with MPC. Make sure it ain't made out to nobody. You bring it to the Indian. He gives you 150 MPC for it. You go to another post office and buy a money order for the 150. And go back to the Indian and he gives you 225 for it. Have you got it?" Boyle grew both agitated and pleased as he went on: "Post Office to Indian, Post Office to Indian. Before you know it, you got a thousand MPC in your hands that cost you less than a hundred and you go get yourself a check for a thousand U.S. dollars and bank the son-of-a-bitch, just like that. Get it?"

The assembly shook its collective head, getting nothing more than refills. "The Jewboy gets it, right?" Some in the crowd turned to the heathen in their midst. It was a Sunday after all.

He decided to let this anointing pass. "Yeah, I get it. If it's so easy, how come Quinn was picked up last week for black market money dealing?"

"Quinn is a greedy asshole like all fuckin' Orangemen. I told him, goddammit. I told him over and over, no more than three or four times a month. That crazy fucker was at it six days a week. Jesus Christ almighty, what kind of fools does he take them to be? Of course they picked him up. Three or four times a week, tops. They'll never bother you if you take three or four thousand a week out of the country. It's practically legal." Boyle's Sunday sermon had come to an end. He grabbed his golf bag and headed out to the links.

The men in the room continued drinking away their Sunday afternoon. And began comparing tales of others they knew who'd come to grief here in Saigon. A Texan who knew his way around had a preacher's carry to his voice. Taking discreet nips from his whiskey-on-ice he sermonized to the flock that gathered round.

"Didja hear what happened to Dave Conrad? He's that smart-alec son-of-a-bitch civil engineer over at building maintenance. Well he's been shacked up all pretty and nice with this gal for maybe three years. Got hisself a house, filled it with stereo, TV, furnished top o' the line throughout. Even got a back-up generator to protect his freezers and shit when the power goes down. Well, Dave has got a daughter stateside who's giving his ex-wife trouble, so the kid, maybe 17 years old comes out to Saigon to visit. Likes it at first. Dating some GIs, you know what I mean. After a while she begins to get tired of the place and puts up a whine about nothing to do. You know what I mean. So Dave says he'll take her to Bangkok as soon as he can swing visas for the two of them. The kid gets all excited and begins to count the days to leaving, when there's a screw up the day before the trip. Now, the girlfriend has an uncle who's a big shot in the police. She needs him to sign something about his travel. Dave asks her what it should say. She doesn't know exactly. 'Look honey,' he says, 'I got to go to work, so I'll sign this blank sheet of paper here and you fill in whatever it is, okay?' And that night she's got the visas for her sweetheart and his daughter, drives them to the airport and a week later picks them up. He's got a great gift for her, a gold and pearl necklace. And the daughter seems happy as can be.

"Well, they get back to the house and her brother is there and her uncle, the police chief, so he pours them each a beer and they're talkin' when he notices a small TV is missing from the kitchen and asks about it. 'Oh,' says his ever-lovin', 'I gave it to my grandmother.' 'Gave it?' he says. 'Gosh, you can lend it to her but I don't think you ought to be giving it to anybody.' Well, that's when the brother and the uncle stop drinking their beer and she says, 'Dave you should know something.' And pulls out this here piece of paper which says, I, Dave Conrad, hereby turn over all the goods in the house on 14 Duy Tan Street, Saigon, to my faithful companion Thu Hop Lac. Everything in the house that could be moved is listed, and right there at the bottom was ol' Dave Conrad's signature, witnessed and notarized." A general head shaking and clucking sound filled the room. The wages of sin, oh yeah.

The lesson of this cautionary tale properly absorbed, a congregant freshened his drink, stood at the bar and proclaimed: "What I don't understand is, how, with all the cheap pussy there is to be had in this here country, a white, American soldier I heard about can get himself in the mess he's in. One Sunday morning, the boy I'm talking about had the duty over at the Motor Pool. He's trying to sleep off his Saturday night in the cab of a truck and this child, maybe 10-11 years old comes over and is hasslin' him to buy something from her and he keeps wakin' up and wavin' her away. She gets up real close, pushin' her boxes of chew'n gum at him and he swings at her just to get rid of her and goddamn, this little kid goes flying and bangs her head and is out cold. He goes over and, shit, she's not passed out, she's dead, blood coming out the back of her head. So the boy grabs her up, tosses her into the truck and takes off looking for a place to dump her. Down a side road he tosses her over into the brush. And then somethin' comes over him, I don't know what, but he yanks down his pants and throws one to her — God Almighty that's just what he does do. 'Course they catch the dumb son-of-a bitch and charge him with rape and murder. The Judge Advocate assigns him a lawyer who must'a been a smart Jewboy 'cause they drop the rape charge seein' as she was dead and there is nothing on the books about that. But the murder charge sticks and he's off for Leavenworth where he'll be splittin' rocks, not skulls, for a goodly time. Now what I want to ask is this. What is goin' on in this country that can bring an American boy to do a thing like that?"

No answer being offered, the meeting came to an end with agreement to meet again, same time, same place at Frankie Boyle's free lunch.

Free Lunch? Bullshit. Every one of these suckers had access to military equipment soon to be declared junk. And Boyle would be there for pick up and delivery to willing buyers. He didn't know that then. It wouldn't have meant much to him anyway. He'd had enough to eat and drink, made polite goodbyes, and headed out the door. He could count on his whistle job to show up later on this Sunday afternoon.

# FOURTEEN

The stories he'd heard back at Boyle's, tales of things that can so easily go wrong, reminded him he had a few of his own to tell. Memory was a gun placed to his head bringing the snap, crackle and pop of bullet to can't-miss target.

The taxi toward home passed a small park, bikes everywhere, tall trees giving shade to men chatting, children at play. Recollection overwhelmed the here and now, bringing back a story that began with the ordinary, obligatory lie: "I love you, I need you." A lie most women accept with a regretful, dismissive smile. But one woman built from these false premises a logic that carried him forward swiftly, unerringly, to her door one night, suitcase in hand, ushered in with a wondering smile.

The year before had tumbled and tossed, a prelude to the good life to come. He had believed in it, convinced by her argument that had begun with a convention, an expression of interest, mere words, "I love you, I need you, I cannot live without you."

He spent that year ferrying between lives, finding his only peace in travel between the stopping points, amazed at how little she comprehended the real situation. Oh, she understood about the kids and all that, had two of her own, but never could follow his desperation through its maze. He waited patient as a monk for passion to fade, interest to ooze, his inevitable disappearance to occur. Hadn't it always been that way? Why should this one be different? Wasn't it his obligation to be a step ahead, too quick for them, sure in the knowledge that the dealt hands are not the only cards in the game? It all came to a bad end anyway. Yet, he moved in to live happily ever after, haunted by his absent children, a shock to his friends, his dirty secret out.

When her teen-aged son asked for help in tying a necktie, he leapt to the task. The two of them faced a mirror as he patiently went through the intricacies of a Single Windsor. The boy watched carefully, getting it right the third time and was gone. He stood before the mirror, recalling his father's breathing, anxious and deep, when concentrating on any task. He saw his father in the mirror, felt his father's breath on his neck. All that remained was to look into his own eyes. He'd taught another woman's son a simple task. But not be there when his own sons would need his encircling arms.

# FIFTEEN

This woman in his new life, more by example than instruction, began to make him over a chip at a time. Oh, she was a pain in the ass from time to time. But his readiness to dismiss, put out the lights on a woman, had shifted in the present case to patience. He would sit back, not cut and run, if a moment or a night came when things seemed tame, dull, without fire. He'd sit back, knowing with certainty that good times would burst forth again. Loving it, as she cleared away the debris of accumulated leaves and weeds, shooing away the flies, and offered up a hundred ways to rescue him from despair.

He showed her as much of himself as a man could as she turned him away from melancholy a shadow at a time. He saw the possibilities of a life beyond the momentary, how he might live a decent life if he behaved decently. And it had started from Lesson One: "If you do not treat me kindly, I'm gone. There's a corollary, being good to yourself. But that's too complicated. So we'll start with something easy. I want respect, kindness, attention, love, fidelity. From you, all of the time, constantly. You got it?"

Yeah, he got it. And, felt sheltered by her demands. He'd been a sailor with a port in every girl, and now a safe harbor beckoned with a come-hither wink. Home-cookin' and sexy, an enticing combination for any wanderer, he ate what was put in front of him, licking the dish clean.

Fidelity could actually be fun, he realized, with the amazement of a Rip Van Winkle who's been sleeping around for twenty years and awakens one day to discover he is tired, very tired. That fidelity is at least as much fun as fucking around was a secret no one had ever shared with him. He didn't want to overdo it. Fidelity was not for everyone. His balls still stirred when a good-looking woman strolled by. This was not sin, but synapse. Neural, not neurotic. Our bodies, our selves, right?

He'd shifted his brain from its age-old patterning, reversed the flow of instruction. No longer would balls dictate to brain. Brain would issue orders. And balls, good soldiers, would bitch and groan, then shoulder heavy packs, follow orders, follow commands. A disciplined brigade, no longer a rabble that took no prisoners, leaving the field littered with wounded, ever-ready for the next encounter.

That the brain could rule the balls was a heretical notion to one who knew the corporeal held power over the vagaries, the spirituality of good intentions. How had this transfer of power occurred? What negotiations, deliberations between opponents had taken place? The mind, in an astonishing, breath-taken-away leap had made its escape. Balls not brains, his coat of arms had read. But that peculiar notion of courtly love had given way to devotion without fixation. He could sit and wait, with pleasure, the arrival of his one-and-only.

He knew enough to be cynical. Was wise, beyond his care to disclose, how much he did know. And he knew women. Knew them to combine fidelity and forgetting of vows; devotion and the breakout of passion; sensuality then embarrassed indifference. Knew them to agonize over temptation, then fall, giving in to splendid moments only to regret what could not be restored. A regret fleeting as the moment of engagement that caused the twinge. Then sigh, rising from fresh bed or greensward, a semblance of dignity restored as easy as an errant lock of hair is patted and pinned.

Though the evidence of his own life, and that of others who'd drifted away, gave the laugh and the lie to such possibilities, he was convinced, he was certain, that he and this woman were the truth within the fable of the matched pair. He'd beaten the house at odds of thousands to one. He'd joined with his honey in months and months of pleasure, delighting in the company of a difficult woman.

Difficult? I'll say. Her demands were impossible. She would tell him what she wanted, why she wanted it, and when. None of it could be bought over the counter. It was a prescription for change he was expected to fill.

Look at how decent she'd been about that phone call from an Old Flame. It was not in character for her to be so forgiving. A call from a long-forgotten name or face, a postcard from a lapsed old love, would cause a metamorphosis from kitten to killer. She'd tear finger from hand, hand from arm, and arm from torso. In a word, limb from limb. He reached for his mail in fear, the phone in trembling. The old denial-with-a-twist routine was no use. He was innocent. Could he command the oceans or the air to be still? He was being kept in touch. What could he do about that?

"Plenty," she thundered. "And you know it." Lightning would descend on his halo. He'd look at her in wonder. She meant it.

"I don't care about your history, goddamn it. But you won't live if you repeat it." That's what she'd said after a call one evening, when the zephyr of understanding gave way to gale-force tempests. Her voice, ever gentle and low, took on a bellowing cadence that would blast any heath, turn Lear himself to sanity. He'd gotten off the phone as quickly as decency would allow. But Tyrannosaur Regina demanded explanations, disallowed protestations, put a stop to all attempts at ordinary communication. Didn't he say she was impossible?

# SIXTEEN

The love of his life was leaving town for a week. Keeping a promise to go to Paris with an old friend. A woman friend, needless to say.

The night before she went away they made love with a sweetness he'd expected. But the tenderness, after so many nights and months together, was new to him. Their lovemaking, never the same, was pleasure, sensual pleasure. He often looked at her, puzzled at what had brought these unending waves of good feeling, and good, very good sex. And it came to him, the reason why, when they celebrated six months together. Six whole months that had withstood his smoldering desire to hit-and-run. Something had happened within him. Something had changed. He had learned the pleasures of fidelity, been granted a wish from his fairy godmother. A magic wand had been waved, turning him faithful to a woman for the first time in his life.

They were at the sidewalk of the departure terminal. Out of the car, she hugged him hard, kissed him swiftly, sweetly, and was gone. On the drive home, he took the long way round, toward the ocean, feeling that peculiar lightness that was so familiar; another one down, another lap to go. He parked the car at the beach to watch surfers and the surf, equally mindless, move toward shore, then back again to be met by another cresting wave carrying them along, buoyant and bubbling, until sand was all that remained, and they turned once again to the new wave, the next one.

A plane roared overhead, he saw Air France markings and guessing it was her plane, saluted, in the French style, and drove toward home, stopping at a liquor store to buy a bottle of champagne for a party to which he'd be going by his lonesome. No big deal, right? He could go to a party, dangerous territory in the past, without the protective armor a mate provided. He was sure he could handle it. A week from now he would proudly stand before his addiction counselor and say, to applause, "Hi, I'm a recovering sex junkie." Watch and see.

The living room of the apartment was decorated with Navajo blankets. Eye Dazzlers, they had come to be called, their diamond-shaped design appreciated by us moderns for psychedelic qualities. They no longer offered the other gift, smallpox, carried to unsuspecting Native Americans by the New Americans. Wrapping themselves against the cold, they died, the blankets left behind for traders, then galleries and auction houses in the Old West. From Hogan to Hollywood in one hundred years.

A mixed bag was seated around a fireplace, intrigued by their Human Potential. EST freaks were busily getting it and acknowledging each other. Scientologists, levels above clear, were whispering their secrets. A woman began to talk about Primal Therapy, and how it had all begun for her when Janov led her through screaming to an awareness.

He listened to this for a while and began to earnestly talk about a spin-off by followers of Janov, Primal Defecation. This caught the attention of the crowd. "Defecation is an act of courage," he told them. "The child holds on. The adult encourages the child to give it up, join society. The child's fright, confusion and pain is relived in these sessions, and inhibitions fall away, until, in the bliss of recollection the shit comes pouring forth and it's okay, no need for tears. A time, at last, for reconciliation of child and man." They all sat, staring at him. "Besides," he concluded, "It's a great cure for constipation."

The primal screamer got up and left. Others turned away from the Jeremiah in their midst. A woman's voice behind him said, "You think you're the smartest ass in the room, don't you?"

"No, he began to insist, "That really happens." "Now you're shitting me," she said. They both laughed and he saw that she was very beautiful, and maybe 25 years old.

She established some facts. " Single?" He didn't hesitate. "Yep." "Straight?" "Oh, yeah." They spent an hour passing along biographical tidbits, amusing each other, allowing no one else onto their little island. He actually believed it would end harmlessly enough. How could it not? He dressed out-of-fashion, had few apparent physical qualities, even a bit of a belly on display. What was that expression they all used? Built? Un-built he was. Maybe a diamond in the rough, but who could tell without bringing chisel to stone, and banging away?

She lived outside of Manhattan, naming a posh suburb. Would he like to see the place? Why not, thought our hero, nothing to lose but my chains. And so it was they departed, watched curiously by other revelers.

Driving along the Westside Highway, the Lordly Hudson apt companion to the flow of northbound traffic, she pulled her Fiat Spider into a dark spot facing the river and the lights of George Washington Bridge. They left the car, walking to a parapet. It was the edge of the world. They looked over and down and out at the view. Behind them in the darkness loomed the high walls of the Cloisters. Across the river, a stretch of blank dark stone formed the Palisades.

A car beam broke the spell of the darkness, then back to black again. They had not spoken when she said, "This is where the kids come to neck."

"I'm no kid," he replied.

"Well I am," she said, and grabbed his face in her hands, looked into his eyes for not a moment too long, and kissed him. He accepted this favor. No confusion, not yet. What's a kiss between friends? Hadn't he told her he was a single fellow?

She took him home. A cottage behind a large house on a wooded estate. When they stepped from the car a sweet odor filled the air. "Night-blooming jasmine," she said. "It's special to the season." Her place was filled with books, and a pair of men's sneakers, which he paid no mind. Poetry was everywhere, on tables, on shelves, on the refrigerator. Good stuff. He let his eyes run over titles of the living and great dead while a heavy tiredness overcame him. As they began to talk, she allowed as how she'd be a poet. It revived him and they scampered about the room pulling poems from the air or from the volumes at hand.

She made a pot of coffee and they sat quietly in the kitchen, where he noticed a birthday card. It was from her father, she told him. It quoted something she didn't recognize. He looked at the line: "I knew a women lovely in her bones," and recited the rest of the poem to her or as much as he knew of it. A pretty sexy poem for a father to send his daughter, he thought. He didn't tell her he'd known the writer before she was born.

"You are for real, aren't you?" she said.

He shrugged. "How old have you gotten to be," he replied.

"Twenty three."

Oh, what the hell, he decided. I'll give it to her with both barrels, and recited a poem by Dylan Thomas. Yes, goddamn it, Dylan Thomas. "Twenty-three years remind the tears of my eyes," he began. He was shameless, this gay seducer, no doubt about it.

When he was done she took both his hands, pulled him toward the bedroom, down onto the bed and began to remove his clothes. Ah, the uses and abuses of literature, he thought, not for the first time, and began to move toward her. She was out of her clothes and alongside him with her hand on the back of his neck. " Let me do you first," she said.

Where do these children learn this kind of talk? Don't their parents pay attention? But he stopped kidding around when she lowered herself to the foot of the bed and, starting with his toes, began to oil his feet, his legs, his thighs, rolled him over and oiled his back, his bottom, a teasing finger finding an opening and probing for a moment to test his receptivity, never touching his cock, not yet. Then up to his neck and down his back, every ridge in his spine getting its full share. Her hands moving to a measured, unhurried beat. Total silence, save for their breathing and his murmurs of delight.

She opened a large drawer at the side of her bed, rummaging around with one hand and keeping the other on his ass. She found a hand massager, which she applied to his back. Its gentle vibrations soothed him as he turned his head and saw in the drawer every tool and device designed for a grownup's playground. Vibrators in all sizes. Braided cords and silken leather, eyeless masks, feathers, fantasies, foolishness. And this on his first free night in town.

He was brought back to attention when she rolled him over on his back and a slightly medicinal smell came to his nostrils as she began to stroke his balls with an astringent, which made them taut, then quickly applied a warm thick oil, which made them full again. She finally allowed his hands on her, but was still not done with him. She reached into her concupiscent cupboard and fetched a small vibrator and began teasing his bottom, balls, and cock. Watching his eyes, running the devil's device up and down, then, in a flash of pussy and thigh, straddled him, cock enfolded by a picture-perfect vagina.

As she felt the beginning of the end, she quickly rose off him saying, "Just a taste for now, and squeezed the head of him with a quick knowing pinch, rolling over on her back to rest them both for a while.

They had their week. The sneakers turned out to belong to her ever-loving live-in companion who'd gone camping. Relieved, he was able to honestly describe his situation. His faraway sweetheart's kids with their father, he needed no further explanation. It seemed to suit her fine. What a wonderful generation this has turned out to be. What a convenience, this juxtaposing of spousal schedules.

They shared one another's beds with the fervor of limited expectations. He knew he could handle this. Knew when the week was over and his honey returned to his bosom, it would be back to business.

He and his child bride spent their last Saturday night together. Plenty of time Sunday morning for the clean up. Time for sex, even a little bit of love, and a poem about a dream of dying in a wreck. Curious choice, no? He recited the last three lines:

"That dream has not come true yet. Knowing what
Inexhaustible patience genuine darkness is

Capable of, I'd say, though, that it will."

"Is that yours?" she asked.

"No, no," he said, "It's by a guy named Sissman. It's called 'Death by Blackness.' It's about Bessie Smith bleeding to death in a car wreck. And he's dead, too."

"Sissman?"

"Yeah, he wrote the poem while he was dying."

He presented her with the volume as a last offering. And so it ended for them. They both had world enough and time to repair the universe.

# SEVENTEEN

A freshly made bed and fresh flowers about the house, he awaited his deliverance, acolyte before he knew not what altar, save that old Bromo Seltzer, amor vincit omnia. Her plane was late. She arrived exhausted, grateful for her bed and his company as she fell asleep. It was not too late for redemption, he prayed. He would begin again to practice this new discipline, fidelity. He would go forth and sin no more. The tenderness and faithfulness would multiply and became a part of him again.

He tried to cuddle up against her and a curious thing occurred. Climbing into his marriage bed he felt sullied, unclean. He tried again, hugging her close for a while, slipped out of bed, leaving her reaching for an empty space before settling back to sleep.

Outside, an edge of twilight lit the tops of trees. He moved around restlessly, flowers he'd bought for the occasion disappearing into the darkness. A dog barked, another answered. It was night, at last. The crescent moon low on the horizon, glowing in reflected light, carried its hidden burden. He walked back to the bedroom, a stranger in his bed, not for the first time. A stranger he'd awaited, expectant and excited, though not for the first time either.

Sliding in beside her sleeping form, he continued to feel dirtied, sure the scent, the stench of the week's adventure had left him fouled. He could not touch his longed-for ladylove. He came to the realization he was a moralist, there existed a set of principles by which he lived. If he wronged another the penalty was final: no appeal to a higher authority. He came to understand, too late for forgiveness, that complaints he levied against his wife grew from his libidinous ways. The wife had been just fine.

Three months later it was over and he doesn't bother to return her phone calls. The love of his life and the life he'd left behind were both over. The woman in question could not be blamed. She had taken what had been freely offered. The children were holy innocents. His wife might be charged with negligence, but no jury would convict. The guilty party was clearly identified in all the photos. He of the too-broad smile or somber glance was guilty, would serve his life sentence, and good riddance.

He'd made his escape. But what price this precious pearl? The final reckoning not yet in. Add this to the tally – seven years later his firstborn son was dead, killed by the accidents of fate and overdose. Put that on the bill, he's picking up the check. A son whose golden ways had lit his father's universe had been abandoned. Though he'd seen him as often as he could, it was abandonment. Though he took him shopping, cooked meals, loved him, dearly loved him, there was no taking back the facts in the case. Each time he saw him he had said good night, goodbye, and left. Each time together was a reenactment of the final parting, which had come too soon.

They had walked together one sunlit October day carrying a bat, ball, and gloves, returning home, to what no longer was his home, the silences growing between them. His son spotted mulberries out of reach above his head and he lifted this boy who'd soon outgrow him, holding him tightly round his legs, while the boy harvested berries.

"Dad, you're squeezing too tight, don't worry, I won't fall."

Dad was not squeezing, son, he was holding on, holding on. The boy wiggled free, ran to his house with a quick goodbye, then out of his life with no farewell, no, none at all.

His mother, no judgment here he prayed, no judgment, had let smoking dope replace the TV as baby-sitter. She, with her own problems, had let him drift — worried probably, concerned, no doubt, having no way to deal with a boy whose father had moved away and kept in touch by telephone. When it became too much for her, weeping, she let the boy live with his father. At fifteen, this boy with a fierce dope-smoking habit arrived sullen, stoned, professing ignorance of anything save his rock-and-roll guitar and music, music, music. He stayed four months to finish out the school year, announcing from the first day that he'd be leaving, that this man who set down rules about school and study and work and dope was not his father. But that first night, as he fell asleep in what had been his father's bed, his face took on the image of that golden boy and his father watched him, watched him for a long, long time.

Within days the boy had gotten into a drug-related scrape at school; at his father's insistence, joined a baseball team, which proved useless, his grace on the field destroyed by love for a grass no longer connected to any playing field save his own mind; tried but failed to get a part-time job, since he insisted that his hair could not be touched by scissors or comb. For him the Stones strode the world and Dylan? God bless us all, we were doubly blessed to occupy the same planet as the sainted Zimmerman.

Word came to the father that his son had been driving with some friends and taken a curve too soon, too late, and hit a wall, that death, oh blessing at the last, was instantaneous.

No man should have to bury his own child, or so they say. It had been his reward to do so with no way to mourn save solitary recollection, no consolation for his grief nor wish to speak for fear that glibness would reduce the pain.

He dared not look to the mother of his son.

"You killed him, you son-of-a-bitch," she said. "Killed him with your own hands." He had turned away from her, dumb, frozen, not answering her accusation, believing at that moment and for all time that she was right. A car crash had merely been the instrument. The uncontrollable substance in his son's blood and brain accompaniment to what had been transfused long before the alphabet soup of chemical compounds with strange sounding names took him to faraway places. The boy had been a victim of his father in ways his mother could never understand. It had been in his blood, all right. Blood tells by what it shows, isn't that so? But in all the telling, there is so much that goes untold. It was there long before a line of cars, a group of mourners, does what it must do. Move toward the public burial place. And along with the conveniences of coffin and plot and earth, covers over secrets at rest in the privacy of forgetting.

# EIGHTEEN

John the Greek drove him toward the Saigon River for dinner at the Club Nautique. Every war since Troy has a city where the best of everything is available to those of special status. Why should this war be different? The Greek had come to Saigon well before the build-up and joined these clubs, now closed to any American, a regrettable exception high-ranking generals and ambassadors. They had their apertifs, their petites salades Niçoise, their tournedos de bouef, la bouteille de Pommard (1964), raised their hands against the dessert cart but les cafés, les degistifs, d'accord.

"Any luck getting to those USO gals your pal the minister is after?" The question seemed innocent enough. He told John that his tip about where to find the girls had been just right. Tho had met two of them, made his choice, and that was that. Ninh had reported that the good Minister Tho was very happy although Sue had needed a bit of convincing. "Don't ask," he decided, not wanting to know more.

While waiting for coffee, he noticed three Vietnamese women sitting nearby, chatting in Vietnamese and French with an occasional English word bringing them to polite laughter. The youngest of the three caught him staring at her and slowly, too slowly, moved her gaze inward. She had that indefinably soothing manner so many Vietnamese women held dear. The long black hair, the wide eyes, the high forehead, the voluptuous cheeks and arching neck were not the thing, not at all. An unhurried, relaxed air, a sense of calm, a movement of hands, lean of head as she played her body like an instrument meant to captivate, sitting there with friends, amused along with them, allowing into her world this foreigner who would not stop staring. The Greek caught him at it and told him, without having to be asked, that he didn't know them, that they were very upper class, very rich. Measures, then, would need to be taken. He near to crossed himself when she rose and headed for the loo. He did the same, and taking no chances, idled outside the door until she emerged and, pushing his French to the limit, asked her name. "Thanh," she replied.

"Mademoiselle Thanh?" he inquired. And got a nod and smile for his labors. He tried to stagger through an invitation to lunch the next day at this same place.

"Why not?" she said, in perfect, careful English. "And, may I know your name?" She returned to her friends unescorted, he returned to his table with a great smile on his face. The Greek had caught it all.

"Very impressive," he said. "But, you'll never fuck her."

"Getting laid is the easy part in this town," he replied. "By the way, I'll be using your membership in the club for our little rendezvous."

"Avec plaisir. Monsieur, avec plaisir," the Golden Greek replied.

# NINETEEN

And so they had lunch. Thanh was forty minutes late. He'd gotten up to leave when he saw her walk through the door of the club offering a confident, appraising smile. No apology offered or required, they were seated at a corner table and he thanked her for coming. She said it was an opportunity to practice her English. Which was quite good, he pointed out. And so it began, with this mysterious girl/woman telling him about her studies at the Sorbonne, her English classes in Saigon. As she spoke, he listened carefully, and tried to divine the source of her power — it was the only word he could think of to describe her presence. It was not sexual, though her lips, her eyes, the rolling movements of her hands gave promise of the possibilities. Nor was it about wealth, or family position. The tranquility he'd seen the day before was part of it, but not the all of it. He'd have to wait, to learn what could be learned. He was good at this sort of thing, very good. But this was a different time, a different clime that needed to be puzzled out a heartbeat at a time.

"What about the war?" he asked.

"The war?"

"Yes, we sit here in this lovely place with a war going on all around us."

"My country has always been at war," she said. "With the French and for centuries before that the Chinese. We've fought our enemies and won each time."

"And who is your enemy this time?" he asked.

"Not who you think. We in the south share the same wish as the VC, but we go about it in different ways."

"And what is that?" he asked.

She looked at him carefully. "We both want to live our lives without foreigners. The VC wants to bleed you to death. Our generals want you to spend yourselves into exhaustion so that you finally quit and leave. Both things will happen."

"I understand about the VC, but what do you mean about the generals?"

"Look around you," she said. "The company you work for is building airfields, roads, and everything else. From this and many other things our generals are stealing millions. You can't tell me you don't know this."

None of it was said as an argument. None of it was more than a quiet description of her world. "Every week a group of generals and their aides flies off to Bangkok, suitcases filled with American money. They return with the suitcases so heavy they need help to carry them. And why are they so heavy? In Bangkok they trade your dollars for gold and return with their diplomatic passports and no questions asked. All this fighting and dying is to make them rich."

It was remarkable, he thought. She showed no rancor; spoke matter-of-factly, between sips of coffee. He had not come to Vietnam a naïve believer. No domino theories for him, no crusade against godless communism. With more than an inkling of what was going on, he was here for the ride and had nothing to say.

She took his silence for skepticism, and said, "Let me tell you a story." He leaned forward, his hands placed together as an odd sense of expectation came over him.

"My family has a pepper plantation in Pleiku. Do you know where that is?" He nodded. "Three years ago there were no Americans in my country, or nearly none. The war had come to a halt. Maybe it's all over, we thought.

"My brother was an officer in the army and told us the Americans were leaving Vietnam. The small American base where he worked was going to be closed. He invited me there to meet his American friends who would soon be gone. I was quite shy, but I had seen these Americans in town looking quite chic in their berets and so I agreed to go with him.

"The base was outside Pleiku and we drove to a gate and were passed in. My brother showed me the fences of barbed wire around the base. It was not very big but many Vietnamese were working there. We walked toward a second barbed wire fence. My brother told me that only soldiers were allowed inside this fence. They couldn't trust the workers, who might be VC." She interrupted herself. "Does this interest you?"

"Of course, of course. Go on." He sat up straight in his chair.

"We walked toward a third fence which surrounded buildings and big guns. My brother told me this was where the American soldiers lived and no Vietnamese, even he, were allowed to enter. He went to the American guard and asked for his friend, who was called on the radio and came out to greet my brother with an embrace. He was so tall, so handsome. I was introduced and he seemed so gracious and kind. My brother's English was very good and I was only beginning to learn. It may be because of my brother that I have tried to learn English. I suppose you wonder why I am telling you all this?" He gestured for her to go on.

"So you were getting ready to leave. To leave us in peace. Your Mr. McNamara was in Vietnam one last time before you were to go. Two nights after our visit, my brother left for his post. He was responsible for security inside the second ring of barbed wire. That night we heard loud explosions from the base and gunfire that lasted all night." She fell silent.

"What happened?" he asked.

"What happened?" Her voice took on a tone that seemed to come from the very deep. "What happened was that the first ring of barbed wire had been blown away and the second ring had been cut the night before. Some VC even got past the third ring of wire. The Americans' only means to defend themselves was to lower their big guns and fire them as though they were rifles. Many were killed, the attack failed."

"And your brother?"

"Dead, of course. Dead because he was betrayed. Not by the VC, but by those generals around McNamara who caused the wire to be blown and cut so that the war would go on. And your Mr. McNamara fell into their trap."

She came close to curling her lip in contempt. "They know more about you than you will ever know about them. And instead of peace, we have war and the millions to be made from war. She stirred the spoon in her cup and decided to change the subject. "Where do you live?" she asked. He told her.

"Can we go there? I'd like to see it."

They rode to his place, off Cong Ly, in silence. He tried to make some sense of what he'd heard at the restaurant. Back home he'd followed the arguments for and against the war and had guessed it made no sense for us to be there at all. But he was here, and learning why, from a girl who'd caught his eye and was coming back, he hoped, to his bed. What more could he hope for?

He and Thanh climbed the marble stairs to his apartment. She took in the flowers placed in tall blue jars around the living room, chatted with the maid who offered a cup of tea. When she wandered into the bedroom he followed. Too eager, perhaps. Before he had a chance to close the door, she smiled and slipped past him out of the room. "Thank you for lunch," she said as she approached the front door, pausing to brush her fingers over reddish-pink gladiolus in full bloom. He walked toward her, she offered him a cheek to be met with his own, and left him with a smile.

# TWENTY

Back at work at the Dupar offices, he wandered about the compound. Colonel Lee in serious conversation with a Vietnamese foreman, the mélange of other Asian workers separating themselves from day laborers by imitating the dress of their betters, those Holy Americans who strode the earth in PX chic. Vietnamese silently clambered aboard waiting trucks. A day's work for a day's pay, no more than that. As the compound emptied John the Greek arrived, was hailed down, and they entered his office to begin a workday of their own.

"I knew you wouldn't fuck her," said John amiably when he told him about lunch with Thanh. He shrugged that off, wanting to talk about Pleiku.

John had been at the base the day after the attack to put up new security lighting. "Everything had been blasted away. The fuckers cut through the wire all right. It had to have been the day laborers. And the VC got away without a single casualty. Our guys were blasting away at everything that moved and only killed South Vietnamese soldiers, the poor bastards.

"McNamara? It was McBundy who was there, but what's the difference? She's right about one thing. We were shutting down. I saw the orders. The contract that year was for three hundred fifty thousand. And now look. Two years later its five million and counting. Sure they wanted us to stay. I wouldn't have put anything past them to keep us here. They're coining money from it. But putting one over on McBundy? It's possible, but I don't know." John had no more to say about Pleiku.

"What's Frankie Boyle up to these days?"

John replied, "A little bit of everything. Salvage, money changing, you name it. Been here for years and years. Knows every police chief and province chief in the country. Drink his booze, eat his grub, listen to his bullshit, but stay away from him." He said this last evenly, near to a threat, more a warning. "He'll never do a favor for anyone unless there's a payoff in it. And, you don't want to ever need a favor from him." Then he added, to push the point home, "He'll take your pound of flesh, and more."

"What are you into?" He asked John.

"Work and love, baby. Work and love," he said with a grin.

Speaking of work, his showstoppers should be back that evening. He was tempted to tell John about the caper, deciding against it, still not sure his scheme would go down. "World enough and time," he said to himself.

## TWENTY-ONE

The girls were staying at the Ideal Hotel, one of dozens sprinkled around the city, gimcrack built to accommodate the unending flow of Americans rushing in to stake claims on Saigon goldfields. An unmanned reception desk announced the blank dreariness of an empty lobby. Bare fluorescents cast an unremitting glare on vinyl-covered chairs and sofas. A bit too early for the normal quota of denizens to be around after a night's serious carousing.

Dolores was sitting alone in darkened corner. He walked over. Accepting his presence, she looked him over, near to tears. There had been an accident. A four-jeep convoy had been racing to their next stop. She and Sue, second in line, watched the lead jeep carrying the other two women lurch on a curve, turning over as it hit a tree. The driver was dead, her two friends hurt badly, very badly. "How are they doing? He asked.

"I don't know. They were flown to a hospital on Okinawa. 'They'll never dance again."

"And Sue?"

"They had to give her something to stop her screaming. She's calmer now, and wants to go home. Who can blame her? Before the accident we were living in disgusting tents, mud up to our asses, mosquitoes everywhere. A goddamn horror show, I can tell you." His Fuji deal slipping away, he offered a commiserating cluck, dismissed by Dolores with, "And that's not all. Those clubs are goddamn whorehouses. Women brought over from the states, supposed to be entertainers, are turning tricks between the acts." Though it shouldn't have, this bulletin from the front surprised him. He'd have to check it out, he decided. Not the part-time hookers, but curiosity about the reach of Gomorrah into the war zone. That could wait. For the moment, he had other things on his mind.

"How is your music man doing?"

"Tommie? Funny thing. I told him about your proposition and he was interested. Now I don't know."

"Are you still game?

"Sure I am. But we'd need Tommie to handle the music. He knows all the show tunes and would shape up that joke of an orchestra back at the club. Five hundred a week, plus housing, should do it." She was all business, as he tried to decide if Tommie's five hundred should come out of the three thousand Fat Eddie had offered. That would leave five hundred for him. Is all this worth it? Sure it is, he quickly told himself. It was action. He was in the game. But, Tommie would need convincing to be brought back into the fold.

As he mulled this over, Tommie and Sue came out of the elevator. She looked wan, broken, a child in misery. Tommie had her by the arm, a bit over-solicitous, as they walked into the lobby. Dolores rose, taking charge of Sue who gamely smiled a real-trouper smile. Leaving Dolores to work on Sue, he took Tommie down the street for a drink, settling on a strategy to entice this sixty-year-old sagging wreck to stay around a while.

They entered a bar with too-loud music, a good mix of soldiers and civilians and, most important, beauties abounding to make an old man giggle. Set upon by two girls, maybe fifteen, he waved them off, wanting something older, better quality. Tommie looked out at a scene he might have imagined in a boyhood dream. Girls at the bar pawed at their loves of a moment, their hands inside zippers bringing shouts of laughter from happy recipients of such special attention. He left Tommie to his ogling to find the manager, telling him to bring over the best in the house to a nearby booth, handing him a big bill for his troubles. Two lovelies emerged from the scrum and took up residence with them as they sat down. Drinks were ordered. Saigon Tea for the ladies. Non-alcoholic, outrageous in cost, the opening price for admission to such hallowed ground. A toast made to good health and happy times, Tommie, sitting between his two beauties, allowed a cosseting, a shower of attention, to be bestowed on him.

A quick study, Tommie, becoming accustomed to such attention, learned his girl's name was Ruby. Another round of Saigon tea ordered up, Ruby's hand went from the back of his neck to the inside of a thigh, causing Tommie to jump for a moment, then settle down, accepting into his life this long-overdue gesture of affection. As Ruby murmured sweet nothings into Tommie's ear, his host whispered into the ear of the girl at his side. Lucy was her name, and she was game for come what may. Turning toward Tommie, she joined Ruby in romancing him, a bulge in his pants bringing smiles of delight as they lifted him away from the table to the convenience of an upstairs room. He watched the handsome threesome climb the stairs, Tommie looking back for a moment for an encouraging word.

He was not alone in the booth for a moment before being joined by a roving beauty. "You lonesome? Buy me Saigon tea?" Graciously demurring, he rose looking for the bar boss. He'd told Lucy not to ask Tommie for money and had to settle up. Tommie, no doubt, would be hit up for a tip for special services rendered. But that was between the three of them. Standing at the bar, a voyeur peeping at the spectacle of his own life, he downed a beer, watching boys and girls at play, sour beer spilled on the floor sticking to his shoes as the music goes round and round. No brass ring for him on this carousel he was riding.

As that thought settled in around his guts he was rescued from its implication by the sight of Tommie descending the stairs looking — how best to put it? — like a man who in a quarter of an hour had had his brains fucked out. The girls, already looking for fresh meat, left him in his daze. He'd be musical director. He was sure of it. Sold American!

Tommie, newly minted man of the world, walked back to the

hotel, grandly describing to his pal the goings-on in the upstairs room. "They really seemed to like me." He let that small deception fly on its own, as Tommie added, "They only wanted a bit of money. For mama san. I gave them a couple of bucks each. Think that was enough?" Assured his generosity was sufficient, they entered the lobby to find Minister Tho, Ninh alongside, in urgent conversation with Sue. On spotting Tommie chatting amiably with his new best friend, Dolores, dark eyes glowering as Tho held Sue's hands warmly in his, walked over. And sensed immediately that Tommie was in on the deal, not least because he exuded the musk of a man who'd been taken in hand by whatever had gone down in the past half hour.

Sue sat in a quiet corner with Tho. The accident was big news. Why, in a land where assaults against body and mind left thousands maimed, would this be so special? And was wise enough to supply the answer. Injured American women were the exception to the rule of the jungle that applied everywhere else in this broken country. Tho had learned of the accident and the injuries, and by the way, Ninh added, he also knows about the deal with Fat Eddie. "The water contract?" he asked.

"That too, but Tho doesn't care about that. He wants to see Dolores and Sue at Eddie's club. He thinks you are very clever." He said this with the admiring smile he displayed for all occasions, overcoming his boss's inclination to wonder how this news spread so fast. Ninh might be working for him, but no doubt served other masters as well. It was something he needed to remember. Not duplicity, exactly, he thought. Divided loyalties were as much the local currency as anything else.

Dolores, impatiently interrupting Sue's tete-a-tete, pulled her up to her feet, announcing, "She needs to rest."

"No, I'm OK," said Sue. Then, smiling at Tho, she added to Dolores, "I'm going to stay and do the night club shows with you." Minister Tho, statesman, sat back quietly, diplomatically. After all, his work was behind the arras, out of sight, managing these affairs of state. Dolores, seeing what was up, not troubled enough to leave behind fifteen hundred bucks a week, let Sue make her deal with that devil, saying, "You've still got to rest, let's go upstairs." Tommie, in need of a bit of rest himself, followed along. He stood there, this American, this foreigner, with Ninh, servant of two masters, alongside. Stood silently for a moment until a chuckle, a burst of laughter, hilarious slapping of backs carried them out of the hotel into the bright Saigon day. Tho's driver leapt to attention, holding open the car door. Tho, waving majestically, left them to bring the news to The Fuji and Fat Eddie.

# TWENTY-TWO

Their taxi to the Chinese Quarter came to a sudden stop at an intersection on Le Loi. American MPs held up white gloved hands as open-backed trucks swiftly passed, sunlight catching the darting eyes of American kids in battle gear, faces stoic against what would soon confront them. This was, at last, evidence of war. Where he was a fixer. Hadn't he accepted that title with a touch of pride? And a bribe taker. Hadn't he lasciviously counted his fifteen thousand over and over, stunned at his great score? The long convoy went on and on as he recounted his sins. How could everything he'd dreamt about, imagined, come to this? He had no answer to questions too frequently asked. Life offered not instruction but the tedium of repetition.

Bored with the waiting and the counting, he turned to Ninh. "I want you around to translate for me with Fat Eddie." Knowing of Ninh's need for a quick hit, he promised it wouldn't be too long before he could catch his ride to happy times. Ninh nodded, alertly, and said nothing. The taxi finally got going, the convoy no longer an intrusion, and they were at The Fuji and its warm embrace of a large lunchtime crowd, dancing girls on display. Eddie, at his regular table pleased at the good news offered up about the American girls who'd soon be working there, balking at the idea of paying anything extra for Tommie. The clever bastard had sensed the eagerness with which the deal had been brought to him. "Three thousand a week is all," he said. Turning to Ninh to translate, he offered free meals and entertainment as a sweetener. Not much of an offer. Pussy was cheap in this town and no real inducement. Good cooking was something else. But this was not about fucking and food. This was action, the game, and he went along. When he asked about the living arrangements, Eddie barked an order to one of his sons who jumped to attention and Eddie went back to his meal. Number one son took him, Ninh following along, to a hotel down the street. They were shown two suites decorated in tawdry Mandarin red, cheap lacquer furniture, sexy lighting. Each bedroom taken up with an immense bed. To accommodate an ever-hopeful Eddie, he supposed.

Back at the restaurant, he saw that Ninh growing fretful, distracted, would not be of use much longer. Quickly, he told Eddie the girls would be moving in the next day, that Tommie should be at another hotel. No sense letting him in on any dirty little secrets that might transpire. Besides, after that romantic adventure at the bar, Tommie might want his own bit of privacy, don't you think? He tried to negotiate a two-week advance. Eddie, balking, said, "I pay once a week, on Saturday night, after the show." No sense arguing the point, but he hated the idea of being the weekly paymaster. Eddie would beat him out his share, if he could, and let it go at that, releasing Ninh to slip away to his stairway to heaven.

# TWENTY-THREE

The way Dolores told it, on her first night in the new digs a soft knock on the door found Fat Eddie standing there, his great bulk filling the door frame. Apprehensively, she allowed him to enter and her expectations were met when without a word, he grabbed her as she pushed away. But Eddie had her pinned against a wall, thrusting at her, pumping away in a weird silence until she felt a shiver from him, and he was done, having come inside his pants.

Eddie had taken to a chair, his heavy breathing coming back to normal as she stood in place and heard him pronounce his terms of employment. That there were to be two shows a night, with an hour in between. In that hour, and for an hour after the show, she should be available for one-on-one entertainment. It was not a threat, more a business proposition. At two-fifty a go, how could she refuse? An extra five hundred a night, no rough stuff. And, by the way, Eddie expected her to bring Sue in on the game. "How will Minister Tho take to that?" she'd asked Eddie. And learned that Tho had major responsibilities at home, and more on the side than he could presently handle.

She described this to him coldly, scientifically, an anthropologist observing as she herself was being observed. They were sitting at a table in the restaurant, a rehearsal about to begin, chairs stacked, a cleaning crew at work, sunlight dimly seeping through dirt-encrusted windows. It was a place that belonged to the night, to darkness.

He sat there, listening to this woman describe her introduction to whoredom in a third-person way, as if talking about someone else. "By the way," she asked him. "Did you know about all this?" He was able to honestly say he knew nothing of it. Though a man could surmise, he supposed.

"What about Sue?"

"She was a little doubtful at first. But she's in. I reminded her she'd been giving it away free for years, to see it as just another one-night stand. She saw the logic in that." Then, with a sisterly sigh, she said, "Dear old gullible Sue."

"And what about you?"

She looked at him, not wanting to answer or confess anything to this stranger who'd gotten her into this. "I'm not sure. Little Susie should hold them for a while." Sue's second career floating in the air, she rose to greet the dancing girls who'd assembled nervously on stage. His little friend, everyman's favorite, offering Dolores a shy smile he'd never seen before.

Tommie was already at work, teaching his backup orchestra tempos and rhythms new to them. Their common language music, they quickly got the beat while Dolores showed the girls dance steps, allowing an occasional giggle over a lapse or two, demanding strict attention. Sue, vocalizing with the band, was delighted with Tommie's work. It was fun to watch it come together. No business like show business. Leaving these troupers to their work, he left for home to dress. Opening Night beckoned, its amusements in all their variety awaiting those that seek them. He imagined himself the impresario, another fiction to add to a growing list of self-deceptions.

## TWENTY-FOUR

A crowd outside the club jostled to gain entry and he elbowed past, spotting Eddie all smiles, sons in tow, bodyguard nowhere to be seen, counting money with his eyes as the suckers poured in. There was a thick mob of drinkers at the bar, every table filled, a jabbering buzz. He spotted Colonel Lee, Retired, at a table in the company of an older American woman. He went over to the pair and, to his surprise, met Mrs. Lee. The life of a wife of an Army officer is not a happy one, and her soft fleshy face and charmless southern accent, betrayed a discomfort here among the heathen. Before he got too caught up in the tedium of conversation, Ninh, who seemed to know Colonel Lee, came to the rescue and he was led to Tho's table and a grand welcome.

The preening Minister, Scotch in hand, chased off a minion to make way for his American pal. The table, all men, watched him closely as Tho, showing off his English, told him Sue was his special girl and they'd be celebrating after the show. He had a feeling the good minister knew nothing of the entre-acte business she'd be doing. But never mind. Love will conquer all, or so they say. The large room went dark for a moment, causing an anxious murmur from those who remembered there was a war on. But why worry about that? A single spotlight came up on the stage and Sue in spangled costume, showing cleavage, leg and thigh, belted out a song that few in the house could possibly understand. But no matter, she was soon joined by Dolores and her girls who had learned to can-can, driving the crowd into a frenzy as legs kicked high. Vive la France! And Dien Bien Phu, too.

Then a duet of Broadway tunes, Tommie at the keyboard, frantically keeping the beat for his boys. Tho was entranced, gripping his American pal by the arm to show his delight. It was all worth it, he seemed to be saying. The war has brought us together, Vietnamese and Americans, shoulder-to-shoulder in solidarity against the Reds. Brought together in this room filled with drinking and laughter, and prospects for a bright future. It was all worth it, don't you think?

Dolores, more dancer than singer, had stepped forward for a solo turn. A sexy, contralto voice added to the touch of mystery she offered, on or off stage. The whole thing was coming off amazingly well, he thought. After all, these were nobodies, hopeless losers on the road to nowhere. Yet they were professionals, highly trained to please. He hadn't forgotten that Dolores and the others had joined in with this corrupt crowd, dumping the USO and the entertainment of our brave troops at the first offer that came their way. And Dolores had beaten Sue on five hundred of the thousand she might have earned; then convinced her that hookerdom was just another way of playing make-believe.

The show came to a crescendo of dancing, singing, and wild applause. The lights came up and he watched as Eddie's sons ran between the tables picking up small slips of paper then bringing them to Daddy for review. Daddy looked at a slip, crumpled and tossed it to the floor, raising a giant paw with four then five fingers raised as more slips came his way. It seemed to be some sort of silent auction. After a time, two men, wallets in hand, were escorted by the boys to Fat Eddie, slapped a quantity of bills on the table, and raced exultantly to the hotel next door. A group of men headed backstage for between-the-acts divertissement available to the under-bidders. Meals were served to those willing to pay a double cover charge for the next show. No dollar would be left behind by Fat Eddie, who happily counted out three thousand dollars to his paymaster. Giddy with delight, they toasted their success not noticing one of the winning bidders approach, furious, speaking in rapid fire Mandarin. Fat Eddie, appalled, looked away from his red-faced friend. In English he said, "Mr. Chin tells me the dark, tall one, who cost him seven hundred dollars, talked for half an hour but wouldn't let him touch her." And then burst out laughing as he added, as an afterthought, "I don't think he understands English." The second high bidder came along brimming with happiness. Good old Sue had come through, thanks be to God. He left Eddie to deal with his little problem. The second show was about to begin and he thought the better part of valor was to skip out, letting the chippies fall where they may.

## TWENTY-FIVE

Money was be coming in from all sides. And it made him restless for more. Stopping by the Dupar office, where no one seemed to care where or what he'd been up to, he collected a list of NCO Clubs. The brief description Dolores had offered of the clubs and their shenanigans begged to be checked out by one with a curious turn of mind. Since Dupar's business was maintenance at locations large and small he needed no excuse to show up at any of them. He settled on Tay Ninh, fifty miles from Saigon and close by the Cambodian border. Offered a lift by car, he demurred, the better part of valor a chopper ride, not the chancy highway.

The NCO Club did not disappoint. Of good size, a reflection of the large number of our troops there in need of distraction it offered, in midday mind you, a raucous crowd around pinball machines and one-armed bandits busily sucking combat pay from player's pockets. Perched at the bar, four long-legged birds of a feather, two white, two black, genus americus, chirped happily, surrounded by young buckos eager to sample the merchandise. All of it a pathetic attempt to bring a touch of home to the troops. A jukebox, gobbling quarters, added to the din. Booze, the smell of dope, set in motion the manic atmosphere. Everything was for sale, a profit made at every corner or so it seemed. A spot cleared at the bar when one of the lovelies slipped away, a happy lad in tow. Taking up a stool, he found himself in a familiar conversation.

"New here?" he was asked with a winsome smile.

Recognizing the opening line of a barroom pick up, he answered, "Just visiting. How about you?"

"I'm Judy, an entertainer."

"USO?"

"Nope. Booked over here by an agent. Two shows a day. Good pay." She paused. "Plus whatever I can pick up on my own."

"Oh?" he smiled in reply.

She took this as an interest in her enterprise. "A hundred bucks." Placing a hand gently in his she promised, "I'll give you all you can handle."

"I'm sure you would."

This bright repartee was interrupted by a tall, rail-thin Master Sergeant with the air of a man who ran the place. Wary eyes too large for so narrow a face betrayed the jovial greeting he offered this civilian picking up on one of his girls. Learning he was neither a salesman nor slumming, Sergeant Fell, the glad-handing done, showed him around.

Away from the bar a large back room was set up as a restaurant. Tables were filled, but few were eating. At the tables, he saw a box of Craven A's passed around. "Pretty fancy cigarettes," he remarked to the sergeant, who grunted, "I don't get it. They love those boxes, but not for the cigarettes. That's O.J.'s they're smoking. And it ain't Tropicana. His guest looked puzzled. "Opium joints," he said casually. "When the Army cracked down on grass, our soldier boys turned to the hard stuff. No smell, no trace. Brilliant of our glorious leaders, eh?"

"How do they get it?" Sergeant Fell looked surprised he wouldn't know of such things.

"Kids in the ville sell them for a buck a pop. A morphine high? Five dollars a vial. And I hear heroin, ninety-six percent pure, will be coming in soon. Then, it'll really hit the fan." As he said this, a group of soldiers shuffled in indifferent to them, someplace else far from here, quietly, impressively, under the influence.

"Not good for business," the good sergeant said. "They come

in here shit-faced. And it ain't from my beer and whiskey, I can tell you. Try to stay high for their year here, then get the fuck out."

They stepped outside to look at diesel generators humming away assuring air conditioners, reefers filled with beer, Cokes, steaks, would remain war-zone chilled. Nothing too good for our boys. Three giggling young lieutenants walked past, the smell of grass all over them. Whispering out of respect for his superiors, "Officers, for chrissakes. Should be ashamed of themselves," he groused, watching his thirty years of lifer Army service, his Club Manager status, swatted away by the appalling sight of these gentlemen soiling the uniform of their country.

Back at the bar Sergeant Fell seemed pleased with his guest's manly choice of hard liquor over beer. The girls out of sight, he chanced asking about them. "A booker in Saigon supplies them. Flies them in on tourist visas. Must be hundreds of them, at every club in the country. Expensive, but they're good, singing and dancing their little asses off to entertain our boys hungry for a look at an American broad."

"I got a feeling it's not the only hunger they feed." Fell topped off his glass. "Strictly up to them. I see no evil." A fight broke out between pinball players. "Shit," he said, and went over to separate two kids in no shape to do real damage. Calming them down, he strode back to the bar. "Had lunch?" Hamburgers and French fries, pickles on the side were served up with a beer set before each of them by a GI bartender.

Part-time whores in a free-fire zone of dope and booze, slots and a penny arcade of other games, a Wurlitzer grinding out tunes. This was America at war. Waving a hand around the room, he asked, "Where does all this stuff come from?"

Dipping a French fry in mayonnaise, popping it into his mouth, Fell replied, "The equipment? Bought through a purchasing agent in Hong Kong. Easiest way to do it. You can't imagine the salesmen crawling the place like goddamn peddlers, might as well be Jews. Hong Kong is one-stop shopping." Fell, as an afterthought, said, "Used to be two sources there. But one got an exclusive somehow.

Every club in country has got to do business with him." Lowering his voice, Fell knowingly said, "They call the American who got the deal, The Money King of Vietnam. Big shots over here are on his payroll. Under the table, of course." Fell's admiration for this coup suggested the chicanery implicit in such dealings. "When there were two competing I'd go off to Hong Kong and play 'em off against each other. Them Hong Kong women is somethin' special. Been there?" No, he hadn't been. "Don't miss it, you won't regret it."

The ease of Fell's conversation smelled conman to his guest. Not that it takes one to know one. He didn't think himself a con artist, not having a talent for dissembling. He was merely a schemer in the company of a master sergeant who lived a life of small deals, taking whatever came his way. "Gonna be busy the next few days. A four-day truce for the Tet New Year." Then, with a mocking tone, "The ARVN don't fight worth a goddamn, and might as well stay home anyway. Just gives our kids a break, and they sure take advantage." This indictment of our allies in the war was interrupted. A boy soldier, smug smile on his face, came in from a back room, followed by Judy, who took her spot at the bar while handing Sergeant Fell two twenty-dollar bills. Pocketing them without a word, he turned to his guest, who'd seen enough and would be heading back to Saigon that afternoon.

# TWENTY-SIX

Returning from his foray into battle in Tay Ninh without an angle to exploit, he climbed the stairs to his apartment to find an envelope from Thanh under his door inviting him to a party at her house to celebrate the Vietnamese New Year. He delighted in the invitation. "Not bad," he thought to himself. "In town a month and making a major local scene."

The sound of weeping, despair, brought him to a window overlooking the garden to glimpse a woman dressed in white, the color of mourning. Each day at dawn's early light she seemed to be proclaiming a steadfast love. Later when twilight began its slow creep to darkness, her cries filled the room. None of his neighbors had any explanation other than that she was crazy. But this was not a lamentation that had its source in madness. It was sadness, profound misery. He would have to ask Thanh, who'd slipped out and away from him in the week since he'd last seen her. The sexual glue that connected to a woman had not yet begun its ooze between them. Until then she'd be no more than a vague wisp awaiting the corporeal strut to begin. He'd taken for granted that she'd be back in his life. All that could wait. Let her play me as she chooses, he thought. All in its own time. The party was the following day. The sky turned dark and the weeping woman turned silent, waiting for the dawn.

## TWENTY-SEVEN

A bottle of Johnny Walker Red carefully wrapped as a gift, he walked with jaunty air along streets jammed with shoppers buying flowers, food, and drink. This thing called Tet allowed a manic, festive mood to fill the air. Hundreds of stalls sold decorated paper lanterns, hanging strings of gold-colored plastic coins, rows of bright red calendars. Exploding fireworks could be heard everywhere. The staccato sound of a string of firecrackers thrown into the crowd caused no more reaction than amused laughter. A four-day truce added to the happiness. No guns of war, for now.

The crowds thinned as he turned onto Mac Dinh Chi Street, whose French Colonial villas radiated a we'll-be-here-forever dignity. So much for French hubris, he thought, admiring the wrought iron gates, the well-kept lawns and flowers, the fancy cars in the driveways of two-storied houses that might have been in Nice or Cannes.

As he walked to the end of the lovely block, a building like some monster from an alien planet rose into view. High walls surrounding a concrete and steel six-story structure in pristine white and out-of-place ugliness assaulted the street. At the corner of this fortress our flag and our American Embassy established its power over all it surveyed. Averting his eyes from gun turrets, high metal gates, sandbags and barbed wire, he saw Thanh's house directly across the street, walked in and entered another world.

In the thicket of officers in uniform and civilians in suits he spotted Thanh fussing over a group of elderly Vietnamese. She gave him a welcoming smile and with a gesture showed she was busy for the moment. Working his way through the crowd he stopped before an ornate wooden altar festooned with cut branches bearing small yellow flowers, plates of fruit, candies, cups of wine, and oddly, a pack of Marlboros. At the back of the altar, faded photographs of old men alongside a fresh photo of a handsome young man. Her brother, he bet, as he felt a touch and Thanh was beside him. His curiosity about the altar pleased her and she unwrapped one of a pile of green square packages heaped before them. He nibbled from her hand and tasted sticky rice flavored with meat and a green bean paste. "Chung cake," she told him. "A gift for our ancestors. We only make them during Tet." So that was what this was all about, honoring the multitude of dead relatives. Barely remembering his own grandfather he asked about a group of octagonal shaped boxes decorated with pictures of sage-like men. "Kitchen gods," she said, smiling, "We hope the good food and drink will make our ancestors want to join us for the holiday." That was just about all the superstition he could take, for now.

A man in a white suit and pink Hermès tie sat at a table before a quantity of red paper. A small group of Vietnamese had gathered. A murmur came from the group as he paused, then, with deliberation, dipped a brush in a small pot of black ink and swiftly drew elegant Chinese characters. A teenaged boy, probably his son, took the paper and pinned it to a wall behind him. He continued in this way, to the admiration of his friends, until the paper was exhausted and the wall covered with exquisite calligraphy. Thanh told him it was an old, forgotten way to make such things and the man who still practiced this tradition was her father. When he rose from his chair she introduced them. They shook hands, Poppa turning away with his daughter who had other duties.

At the bar, he tried conversation with two Foreign Service types careful to spout nothing but the party line on any subject until he could take no more of it. A group of field grade officers allowed him into their orbit. He was here, wasn't he? And therefore must belong. These officers and gentlemen were doing their year, getting their tickets punched is the way one put it. Knowing that duty in a war zone was a convenient prelude to promotion so long as they kept noses clean and Efficiency Reports golden.

How to explain the feeling of being among the false and pretentious under false pretenses of his own? He did not belong in this crowd, had gotten in on a pass. Yet no one seemed to care. You dressed right, going out for the evening, you ate and drank with decorum. Didn't everyone? If the talk shrank to the microscopic, what difference did it make? Why get agitated? Why get carried away?

These Generals-in-Waiting, working on second and third rounds of double martinis, groused about drug use among their minions. These candidates for the Twelve-Step Cure where shocked, chagrined that dope was slowing the war effort. The most senior of this bunch, gin sloshing from glass to fingers, said, "Goddamn marijuana. It's everywhere. Our infantry go on patrol, into combat, stinking of the stuff." Heads nodded, sagely, in agreement. "I hate to say it, but the Marines have it right, court-martialing anyone caught, no matter with what. And our way is to turn our backs on everything except the dealers and hard drug users." A younger officer said, "And the hard stuff costs nothing. There's more shooting up than shooting at the enemy." Then quickly added, "Or so I've heard."

He listened to this high-and-mighty prattle, this critique of GI's surviving the tedium and terror of the war on grass, and anything else that came their way. Deciding to offer illumination on one point he offered, "Our guys are smoking opium, not shooting up." And it mattered to them not at all as they turned away toward the bar, pleased to be within the confines of their kind.

At the end of the evening Thanh approached. He expected no more than a polite goodbye, but was surprised and delighted when she asked if he could take her to Dalat the following weekend. He wasn't sure where or what Dalat was, but promised himself he'd soon find out. "Leave The Fuji and its follies behind for a while," he said to himself, knowing it would catch up to him sooner than later.

# TWENTY-EIGHT

Dalat, a mountain town in the Central Highlands, had brought cool summer weather to the upper classes for years. South Vietnamese generals, their families, and politically important friends carried on a tradition from the Roaring Twenties when an Emperor built a palace here, followed by an upper crust eager to do the same. These days the mountains were running with Vietcong, but a deal had been struck, a rapprochement between parties bringing the pleasures of Dalat to higher-ups on both sides. The VC danger was directed toward Americans, and few were willing to risk it.

The airport, located in a valley between two mountain ranges, was shrouded in thick fog. Only after their Air Vietnam plane touched down could he see the terminal through the fog. "Oh, what we'll do for love," he said, half-aloud, as his knuckles turned back to pretty pink.

Thanh had arranged for a car: a vintage Citroën with high, rounded fenders, running boards, polished chrome. The driver, handling bags, opening doors and closing them, slipped into the driver's seat and took off for the Dalat Palace Hotel. Thanh took his hand. It was the first time she had ever done so, and spoke to him in French, pointing at the driver. Look at that, French back in, Americans out. Go figure. She sank down into the car's soft seat and closed her eyes, her hand still at rest in his.

They arrived at a grand hotel, high hedges trimmed with care, tires on the gravel driveway offering a soft yielding sound, an entrance with expansive terraces on all sides. Small balconies outside upstairs windows looked out on a garden saturated with hydrangeas in lovely pastels. The bags deposited, he made a move to pay the driver. Thanh shook her head. The car would be theirs for the duration of their stay. He was pleased. Pleased by the hotel, pleased by the car and driver, though he'd have loved to get behind the wheel. Very pleased to think of the evening that awaited him.

When they entered their rooms, a suite overlooking the main garden, he hardly minded the worn carpet, window trim in need of paint, or the dilapidated luxury of vulgar extravagance. There was a war on, wasn't there? The rooms, in blues and yellows, were furnished with tightly upholstered chairs and that empire-look, French in every way, which was all the rage in the twenties. The conquerors, conquered, still retained their sway in matters of taste. For the upper classes, anyway.

They'd had an early start that morning, and Thanh seemed fatigued. He asked if she'd like to rest. It was an innocent request. "No," she said. "I'd like to go out," and went to her suitcase for two wrapped gifts.

He dutifully followed to the door and down the stairs to the waiting car. At Thanh's instructions, the driver headed out on a two-lane road crowded on both sides by tall trees whose foliage darkened the way though it was the middle of the day. He wondered where they were going. "To visit a friend of mine. I hope you don't mind." He took her hand to show agreement. She allowed this simple gesture and he marveled at his pleasure in the rhythms of a slow but sure courtship.

As they climbed steadily, the occasional opening in the woods revealed a grand chateau. Then, hillsides thick with what he was sure were marijuana plantings being carefully tended by a family of farmers. The deep pine forest flashing by might have been in the American Northwest, but he knew it was not. Knew that not so far away, deep heat and sweat and pain filled the air. Knew this sanctuary was temporary for all who came here.

Thanh said a word to the driver who slowed and turned off the road to a clearing in the woods. A young woman, a child in her arms, stood in the doorway of a small neat house from a fairy tale. Thanh left the car and ran to the door. He watched as the child shyly turned away and the two women exchanged greetings. Not joining them, he watched the scene play out before him, trying to discern what was going on. The driver handed him the packages from the front seat and he entered the house with the others.

"This is my friend Tu, and her son, Nguyen." Thanh offered the gifts, a blouse for the mother and a toy truck for the boy, pleased at his eagerness to accept it. Tu left the room and returned with a large tray of food. They sat down to a lunch of soup, spring rolls, and thinly sliced beef and condiments he learned to wrap in a large lettuce leaf and hold in his hand. They giggled as juice ran down his arm and delighted to see his eagerness to try nuc mam, a fish sauce with a vile odor but sublime taste. Tu left the table to bring lunch to the driver and he watched as Thanh played with the boy. A domestic moment. He had seen it before. But this was here, an enchanted cottage in the woods. Thanh looked up and smiled. His reward for making this possible?

When Tu returned, the two women began to talk and he stepped outside to see the driver nodding off behind the wheel of the car. An opening in the woods behind the house led to a trail and a brook whose waters were ice cold. He felt the chill reach up his arm, enjoying the sensation, crossed the brook and continued down a path toward he knew not where, nor cared. A strange path, an unknown destination, was not new to him. He moved ahead, sensing no danger, expecting little more than the pleasure of footfall, the songs of birds, whispering of the trees. He was nowhere and everywhere. It seemed to be his way. Not intentional. No plan, neither of certainty nor escape from chaos, confusion

He had sons of his own. And fondly remembered they'd been two years old once upon a time and he'd done what he could to treat them decently. No one could ever say they suffered violence, as long as violence is defined as blows struck with hand or fist. He had loved his children. Held them close, giving them everything he could. Then left them. Left them so abruptly.

He'd spent a lifetime looking back, but they'd turned away, were gone from sight. He tried to be their father, but the awful deed was done. His children looked upon him as a sham. There can be no father without a mother. They knew this fact of life. Did he think they were stupid? He had been their father. And now he was gone. Was he there when they woke up? Was he there when they came home? Was he there when they needed him or when they didn't need him at all?

One day he'd mumbled some words about loving them but not loving their mother anymore. And was gone. A few days later, he came back to collect some things. His youngest son, not yet eleven, came in to the bedroom as he tried to detach a tie rack from the closet wall. He asked him to fetch a screwdriver. Can anyone imagine? He'd asked his son to be accessory to the crime, and didn't notice the silence with which he'd followed his orders. A dutiful son had helped his Dad dismantle their life. The boy had probably forgotten that. It falls to the father to remember, it falls to the son to forget.

He would visit his children to be comforted. Familiar rugs and furniture, pictures and lamps, all in appropriate places. Nothing had changed after all. He could feel the knobbiness of a worn couch as he passed on to one or the other of the boy's rooms. "Hi," he'd say. And they'd barely look up, more attentive to the television and its antics than his tricks. That was normal for two growing boys, wasn't it? They had their priorities in the order that preserved the sanity and sanctity of home. Ignore the father in their midst. Choose the TV Dad who goofs and gurgles on the screen while loving wife forgives and doting children put up with his inanities. The flesh and blood father, aware of the niceties, waited for a commercial to intrude.

"How are you?" he asked.

"Fine," they both answered, too quickly, too much in chorus. And the father fell silent before this onslaught. Frozen by the awfulness of the trap he'd set for himself to do more than acknowledge what was before him. He was an embarrassment, a nuisance, really. They wished he would go away. Or come back. One or the other, but now and forever. The father/visitor had no business here. This was their house now. Their mother made a point of not being around. Why did they have to pretend? It was left to the sons to comfort the father and they weren't interested.

The TV show came to its happy end. TV Father smiled at knowing mother and children. He too, would be back next week. Familiar, forgiven, all's right with his world. Lucky him.

"Are you hungry?" he'd ask. They'd nod.

"I'll fix us some supper then. Anyone want to help?"

"I've got homework," said one.

"I've got to make a phone call," said the other.

He fled their indifference for the calm of the kitchen. He could still provide for them, goddamn it. Cheeseburgers he'd prepare the way they liked 'em without having to ask. Fresh cut French fries cooked to a sizzling, golden turn. Steamed broccoli with a mayonnaise and curry sauce they way their mother made it. Then vanilla ice cream with hot fudge and cream that he whipped up himself, and slathered over the top of his final offering to these young lords whose favor he begged.

They ate in a silence controlled by a vow to show no more gratitude than necessary to this supplicant. He collected a "thank you," and thought he heard a begrudged, "This is good," when his back was turned. Sixty minutes to prepare. Six minutes to consume. They cleared their places. The older of the two said, "Leave the dishes, I'll do them later."

He knew what later meant. Later was when he would be gone. His son had said to leave the dishes. But wanted to say at the top of his voice, "Leave MY DISHES." Had chosen to let the pathetic father/servant off for the evening. Off and running. And the father did leave, counting the words exchanged as precious. Ever hopeful, next time he'd get there earlier. To bake a cake!

He knew there was no quality to the time spent with his children. Except emptiness. The emptiness of silent, sullen acknowledgment of his existence. He accepted these blows as he leapt with alacrity to the cross he'd constructed. But they'd outsmarted him, would not participate in his self-martyrdom, self-mortification. Thumbs up, they'd said. Let the bastard live. Let him burn here on earth, not in hell. The possessions of a lifetime were no longer his. He'd been disinherited by his own will. Signed off on by not two, but three witnesses. Nothing remained for him but to close the door as quietly as he could.

"Goodnight," he said.

"Goodnight," they had replied. But it was early. Too early for bedtime. Too early for goodnights. Too early to be tucking anyone in. He should have said goodbye. And, goodbye, his children should reply.

He looked at his watch. He'd been walking for an hour, and turned back. Saigon and its madcap days and nights had been swallowed by these woods. The sound of rushing water from the nearby stream, the well-trod path touched by fallen leaves, the sighting of blood-red wildflowers brought him to recall that old *New Yorker* writer who had said, "The suicide doesn't go alone, he takes everybody with him." And the old Frenchman who'd written, somewhat in contradiction, "We want to die because we cannot cause others to die." Odd, that such thoughts offered a sense of calm.

Leaving the cover of the trees, he walked back to the little cottage. Thanh was relieved to see him, concerned about his disappearance. She'd had a chance to talk with her friend, and as they readied themselves to leave, was overjoyed when the little boy let her hug him as they said goodbye. The tiredness he had noticed earlier in the day overwhelmed her. Exhausted, she lay her head on his shoulder and fell asleep as they drove off.

Awakened by the sound of tires on gravel, she stirred sleepily. At twilight the lights at the hotel entrance glowed with an expectation that matched his anticipation of the evening to come. Bed covers had been turned down by attentive staff. Thanh went into the bathroom. Hearing water running into the tub he slipped out to have a drink at the bar.

The dining room was empty except for an older Vietnamese couple eating an early dinner. An elderly waiter stood at hand, eager to please, disappointed that he turned down a table in favor of the adjoining bar. He ordered his drink, remembering Thanh's reminder to speak French, and examined the polished wood of the bar. Red banquettes ringed the back wall. Not a soul in the place. He sipped vodka. Russian vodka, he noticed with a smile, and wondered where the war had gone. He'd seen nothing of it but army convoys bawling their way down streets and highways, young soldiers looking out at the passing scene heading toward they knew not where with a crazy mix of bravado and trepidation. Taking a last pull from his drink he thought about another, then remembered he had a matter of importance to attend to up those stairs.

The room was in darkness. Through the open bedroom door he saw Thanh, eyes closed, in the large bed. She seemed a child tucked in for the night. He showered, his body responding to the warm water in a prelude to arousal. He slipped between the sheets, feeling the silk on his skin and rested there, enjoying the sensation before turning to Thanh, on her back, breathing evenly.

She was naked, he was pleased to see, and he put his hand to her face caressing her cheek. She stirred, but her eyes remained closed. He took this as a response and kissed her mouth. Her lips were waxen. It was the only word to describe them. Gently turning down the coverlet and the sheet to look at her caused her to reach for the covers. He pulled them back over her. But he'd seen the sweetness of her body and decided it was time to begin the slow move toward what he'd spent the day awaiting. He kissed her again, with no answering interest. He ran his hands down her neck to her shoulders and breasts. She seemed to be unaware of what he was doing, what was happening to her. He was good at this, very good, and grew puzzled as none of his loving attentions drew anything from her. He wondered if he should go on. It was not his game to force an unwilling object of his desire. But he continued. Mouth to breasts, reaching down to thighs, the probing finger, the tongue within after parting her legs. She made no sign as he felt her go wet, found his way inside her and waited for her to move, to react. She did not. She lay there, accepting whatever he would do. Giving up, he decided to finish it off, put an end to unhappiness. And so it was that he was done. She turned over on her side and went to sleep.

He leaned back on his pillow and wondered what it was all about. He'd been through the awkwardness of many a first time. The getting to know you kind of thing. But it always had a frantic excitement, early notice of things to come. This odd encounter made no sense. Clearly she didn't want any of it. This wacky romantic hideaway in the middle of nowhere would have made sense if she wanted to get away from Saigon for a hot weekend. But she was cadaver-like and he might be weird, but necrophilia ain't his game.

His agitation brought him up and into the outer room. Thanh never moved. Blissful sleep, he snorted to himself. Opening the door to the balcony, he stepped outside and felt the chill of the mountains come over him. He grabbed a heavy robe thoughtfully provided by management, and went out again, protected against the night, further comforted by the perfumed air carrying the scent of unseen flowers. The moon, bless it, had risen above the trees and cascaded its light onto the hedges and pathways. Shadows crossed the gravel. Topiaries, carefully carved into the shapes of birds and animals, stood out in relief. It was a sight for the gods. No sound, no light save what came from the heavens to cast its shadow where it would. He drew it into himself, hoping to remember it forever.

# TWENTY-NINE

The next morning, after a night of troubled sleep he reached for already gone, half-remembered dreams. Thanh stood over him, smiling and dressed for the day. Another morning with another woman after the night before. As he indulged in the melancholy of reminiscence, she tossed him the robe he'd dropped to the floor, the gentle odors of breakfast delivered to a table in the outer room bringing him back to the moment.

She allowed him his leisure, but seemed anxious to get going, so he quickly dressed and they went once again down the grand staircase to their waiting car. A group of men in full hunting kit, shotguns at their sides, looked them over, not approving of the happy couple. One made a sneering remark. Thanh allowed her face a flicker of reaction then a cool, dismissive glance and they were on their way to the Central Market. Along the way houses obscured by cascading bougainvillea in shades of red, hibiscus blossoming, roses everywhere, in February no less.

Wealthy Vietnamese women trailed by servants selected from every sort of game for the week's meals. Pheasant, rabbit, sides of venison, and smoked trout were sold at stalls by women dressed in glorious reds and blues, matching ribbons descending from their bodices. Mountain people, husbands famous for ferocity and courage available to the highest bidder in the faraway war.

Small mountains of rice, in different sizes and shades of white, were on display. Thanh, taking small handfuls, brought them to his nose to show him that each had its distinct essence. "What's this?" "What's that?" he asked, with a child's curiosity. "Stems from the lotus." "Flowers from the banana tree." "Celery in Chinese style," she answered. He picked up an artichoke no bigger than a silver dollar, alongside asparagus in a shade of green as fresh as the morning's harvest. "French bamboo," she called it. He let it go at that, amused by this disparagement of so fine a vegetable.

They stopped at a fruit stand where he picked up something small, brown-skinned, and covered with spines. Thanh asked the woman for a knife, split it down the middle, peeled it, placed it in his mouth, delighted at his shock tasting the sweetness and softness of a fruit so diabolically hidden. After choosing a large bunch of flowers among hundreds of varieties of orchids in every color and size, she was finished with her marketing. On the walk to the car he stopped, in wonder, at a stall selling the freshest fish and clams. My god, he thought, they had to have been flown in that very morning. They would be returning to see her friend and hoped he didn't mind. Not at all, he shrugged. And off they went, the happy couple, for a repeat of the day before.

On this second trip he asked to stop before an immense, silent chateau that loomed on a hillside, its magnificent grounds, grand allée formed by tall trees, more inhibiting than welcoming. Thanh told him, no surprise, it was owned by the richest general in Vietnam. Later he saw modest, well-kept buildings with dozens of kids running around watched over by nuns in old-fashioned habits. "A place for children whose parents are dead," she said quietly. Then a decrepit, run-down home with more kids. "The same thing," she told him.

"They look so different," he said.

"The first is run by the Catholic Church. They have all the money."

"And the second?"

"Buddhists. They have nothing."

Later, he pointed to the farmers at work on an immense growth of marijuana plantings. Thanh refused his wish to stop the car. "It is dangerous. The general who owns all this property is very unpleasant." No doubt an understatement, he decided, and let it go. Obviously it was the cash crop of choice, grown in this friendly mountain climate for users at the NCO clubs he'd visited. He had seen the two ends of the supply chain and his fervid mind began to think how he might mess with Mister In-Between as they turned off, once again toward the enchanted cottage.

The driver brought in the great quantity of purchases from the market. Thanh carried in the flowers happy that the little boy, less shy, played and read with her. Tu made soft spring rolls from thin sheets of rice, then prepared a lunch of fish ball soup while steaming the largest artichokes he'd ever seen. When Thanh softly, urgently called her name, Tu went to her. He followed behind and saw the child asleep in Thanh's arms. Her face was alive with pleasure, and something impossible to divine passed between the two women.

On the ride back, Thanh once again fell asleep against his shoulder until they reached the hotel. Taking coffee in the downstairs lounge, she thanked him for making the trip with her. He had wondered why she'd needed him along at all, but decided not to press his luck and let her gratitude convert itself into something a bit more satisfying. Hope does spring, does it not?

He asked about the group of hunters they'd seen that morning. "Nouveau riche," she said, adding, "two of them worked for my father."

"And now?"

"They own trucks that deliver supplies to the bases." That dismissive tone piqued his egalitarian soul, but rather than take it up with her, having other fish frying, let it pass.

She hoped he wouldn't mind if they had an early dinner. Another good sign, he thought. He ordered escargots, le truite almondine, une petite salade, and she ordered escargot as well! Garlic for garlic, excellent! He marveled at her appetite as she ordered les tournedos meunière, frittes, une salade. Which was washed down with a fine

Montrachet. Plus, for him, a glass of pouilly fuisse.

They talked casually about the meal, the wine, the hotel. Enjoying the pleasure of one another's company. He tried to get her to talk about the war, remembering the fierceness of her opinions at their first meal together. But she preferred to talk of other things. All was going well until he made a mistake. He asked a simple question about the little boy. Where was his father? Thanh's face and mood changed in an instant. But she did not answer. Instead she began mildly asking him questions about himself. Like a good cop, she said, "Of course you are married, with children." Not a question, a statement of fact.

"Divorced," he said.

"How is it all Americans in my country are divorced?" He let her wise query bring the meal to a close. No coffee? No dessert? No digestif? Nope. They went to bed.

They lay beside each other not speaking or touching. Their early -morning flight to Saigon would be bringing their time together to an end. "He's your son, isn't he?" Her reply was to turn away from him, closing down this idyll and falling fast asleep. So much for bad intentions, he said to himself.

The next morning she was friendly, polite, and eager to return home. On the way to the airport, he asked why she hadn't made the trip without him. She seemed surprised by his question. "I wanted you to see another part of my country," she said. "You liked it, didn't you?" He left it at that.

# THIRTY

As a demonstration of devotion to duty, he sat in his office early on a Monday morning drinking lousy coffee, musing on the splendid start to the New Year. This first month, filled with the joy of money earned licitly and otherwise, the newspaper caper, The Fuji adventure, Thanh and Dalat, and whores selectively chosen within the multitude of possibilities, brought him to an expansive view of the universe. These happy thoughts were interrupted by Mr. Ninh bringing news of a narrower world. That Dolores had spent the last two nights in jail. She'd been taken from the club for failing to have a work permit. Fat Eddie was behind it, of course. He didn't like her reneging on the deal they'd made. He looked at Ninh, who was in on everything, and asked, "Should I do something?"

"No, it all will be taken care of today. Jail is a very unpleasant place." Ninh said this with the understatement of a man who knew of such things. "Dolores will get a work permit and go to work." More understatement, he realized, with mild amusement. He thought it a good idea to avoid The Fuji at least until payday. He'd get the story from Eddie, no doubt. And hear plenty from Dolores.

Ninh casually, slyly, asked about his trip to Dalat. His first thought was to demand of Ninh how he knew this. But wait, this was Vietnam after all. Conceding the point, assuming Ninh would likewise know about the girl, he asked about Thanh's family. Ninh, pleased to see the Boss aware of the niceties, offered up what he knew. "Her father is an important man. Not a minister, though he could have a ministry if he wanted one. He is number one at the Export-Import Bank. Very important. He approves everything coming into Vietnam. Everything. Liquor, beer, things for the house. And everything that goes out from here."

"What goes from here?"

"Many things," Ninh replied. "There is much to be made from the leftovers of war." He let that last resonate for a while, as Ninh added, "Minister Tho is very impressed by your new friend."

"And her father," he answered.

"Oh, yes. For sure."

No point in asking Ninh how or why Tho was following his movements. No harm in that. It might even provide him with a little protection. Everyone around here could use a bit of cover. He asked, "Do you know an American they call 'The Money King of Vietnam?'" Ninh looked past the question, tried to figure what it might be about. "Ronald Steele, a very big man. Very important. Very rich. Even Minister Tho stays away from him."

"How come?"

"I saw him at your embassy once. A big party. He is old, has trouble seeing, trouble walking. When he came into the room, it got very quiet. Then an American general rushed over, followed by our Prime Minister. I watched as he sat in a chair while people took their turn to greet him." Ninh paused, "I didn't want to go near, it felt dangerous, but I couldn't resist and heard him talking perfect Chinese to the head man of the Chiu Chao."

"What's that?"

"A gang. But more than a gang. They are like the government in Cholon, controlling everything, black market, girls, opium. Mr. Steele is their partner, I think. But I prefer not to know." Ninh's discretion left him wanting to know more. John the Greek would be bound to know this Mr. Steele.

Having delivered his news and information, Ninh was released, happily waltzing away, glad to have been of use. He was left alone, to think about Thanh, and her powerful father who must be in on every dirty deal this side of living life in the chaos of war. She'd already brought him into a world of privilege, and he wanted more, willing to trade bad sex for access. Besides, as he lovingly, smugly, would often say, "Sex is the easy part in this place." He could hope that such discernment would bring its own rewards. Not wishing to confuse matters, he filed away any possibilities Poppa presented. He'd been here only a month, after all, and much more was to be learned, might come his way.

He left his office for a stroll down the hallways of Dupar Construction. It had been a while. Avoiding Colonel Lee, he heard laughter and entered a room with coffee pot, assorted stateside cookies and candies, the whiff of whiskey in the morning air. Americans only, some of the same bunch he'd seen at Frankie Boyle's birthday party. The personnel chief he'd met in his first days shouted out, "Here comes Mr. Fixer!" The crowd grew silent, having heard that story of his rescue of their buddy up in Cam Ranh. The silence, out of respect for his title, showed an understanding that A Fixer could be a troublemaker, too. Each of them, in his own way, was up to no good, and didn't need anyone around to remind them. He sniffed at this hostility, wondering if Boyle, who he barely knew, might be behind it. The personnel guy sensed this as well, rescuing him by making a joke about his failure to hire anyone for his operation. "To do what?" he asked.

"To build your empire," one of them offered.

"Get 'em on the payroll, added another, "It don't matter what they do. Bring 'em on. It's company policy."

The Personnel Chief, demurring slightly from this crass assessment, agreed that adding to payroll was a good thing. "We have six slots for writers," he offered.

"Write what?

"Jesus Christ," an old-timer bellowed. It don't matter what they write, or what they do. They can write up the fuckin' menus in the mess hall. That's what they can do. Just bring 'em in. The more the merrier."

Each and everyone in the room looked at Mr. Fixer. It was two-bit crap, but all they had to play with. The lesson over and done, attentive to their duties, they returned to their respective stations.

Power corrupts, you say? Absolutely.

# THIRTY-ONE

Time to face the music; he walked into The Fuji in mid-morning, taking a chair at a rear table to watch Dolores in rehearsal. She seemed cool as always, unperturbed by what had fallen to her in the past few days. Tommie was pounding out a tune from Carousel as she showed her girls new steps. The little Chinese girl, no longer sour of face, quick to learn, had become the lead dancer.

Eddie came over to tell him business was booming, all was well, no problems, everything just fine. He asked Eddie about the jailhouse, causing Eddie to pound him on the back while bursting into loud laughter. It was his only reply and he left, the great bulk of him lingering as a presence in the air. Dolores, distracted by the joviality, called a break. The girls scampered off the stage, followed too eagerly by Tommie who had learned to know a good thing when it came to hand.

He walked down toward the stage meeting Dolores halfway. She paid no attention to this little courtesy and he joined her at a table. She looked across at him, through him, her eyes not focused on a spot but a point in time, whether in her past or future he couldn't tell.

"I heard about the jail," he said.

"Heard?" Her voice was a growl of fury. "And what else have you heard?" Mocking him as she repeated the word, staring into his eyes, daring him to speak again.

"I was put in a small cell that morning and left there." Her voice, her manner, was neither angry nor resigned, a report to gods appointed to record the workings of the world. "That night two men in uniform entered. I'd had nothing to eat or drink. Another, an officer, came into the cell. 'You work?' He asked. I said no, with a shake of my head and he threw me to the floor, unzipping his pants, stopped by one of the others who quickly spoke to him. Whatever was said caused him to zip his pants and leave, spitting in my direction."

She began a slow rocking motion as she spoke. A sort of keening, an anticipation of what more was to be described. She was talking to herself, for herself. That he was there to hear it made no difference to her. "The next morning, one of Eddie's sons was there with the officer from the night before, repeating the same question, 'You work?' It was Eddie's question, being asked for him by these apes. I said, 'No,' and Eddie's boy said something and I was taken down dark stairs to a dungeon and pushed inside.

"The filth, the smell from a hole in the floor, flies everywhere, a rat nibbling in garbage, struck me first. In the dim light I saw men and women moving about and tried to find a corner to avoid their staring but it was no use. Women came over, hands begging for cigarettes, anything of value. I had nothing for them and they moved on. Men who were zonked out came to look me over. Warily at first, they grew bold, pawing at me as I pushed them away. In a far corner a few men looked on, unsmiling. They seemed to have some authority over the cell. Over the hours I sat in my corner and watched as the women went over to these men accepting a cigarette, or a plate of food, in exchange for sex right there on the floor." At this, she stopped talking. Not that she was done, not yet. All this was prelude, he felt, for what was to come. "Late that night, I dozed off, shaken awake by hands holding me down. Other hands were ripping at my clothes, stretching my legs apart. A man was atop me, I felt his disgusting cock at my belly. I bit his face, and he pulled off and away as I screamed, screamed so loud and long it must have frightened them in some way and I was left alone 'til morning."

He thought he saw her tremble as she compulsively told her tale. Eddie's son had shown up again that morning asking the same incoherent question. "You work?" She'd had time think about it, and this time nodded, "Yes." She'd trade five hundred extra a night, for this pesthole. Eddie's boy gave her an encouraging pat, ignoring her repulsion at this touch, and they left the prison for what awaited her outside.

Tommie had come on stage, noodling at the piano. The girls were drifting back, practicing their steps. Dolores looked on at this safe haven before turning to him again. She seemed to be relating this tale as a punishment and finished off with a flourish. "I got back to my hotel that morning wanting only a shower. I paid no attention to a man sitting outside my door. When I left the shower, Fat Eddie was on my bed, on his back, naked. His grossness overwhelming me, his eyes on my body, he beckoned me over."

Sitting at the table across from Dolores, he shook his head, knowing what would be coming next. Her voice took on a mild questioning tone, asking," Do you know what it's like to fuck a man whose little dick is hidden within the folds of his disgusting body?" This was rhetorical, no doubt. "You have to climb aboard this great pile of flesh, looking for a way to put him inside you and get it over as quickly as you can. And then, as you slide off this pig, you find out that the guy sitting outside is part of the twenty-four hour guard that's gonna keep you from disappearing." She rose from her chair, no interest in his reaction to what she'd related.

As he watched her return to the stage, her body moving to the music, he granted that her only way to escape the jail made sense. But she could easily slip her guardians. Eddie probably had her passport, but she could throw herself on the mercy of the American Embassy and chance they'd be sympathetic, never a sure thing. So, why is she staying? Could it be that extra five hundred bucks a night? Her calm in the face of this sex slavery was disconcerting. Was she saving for a rainy day? Corruptibility has its own rhythm. A slow but steady beat, reaching to its crescendo. Once caught by its rhythms it becomes what we are. Dolores would do her two shows a night, plus another two for her extra five hundred. No more no less.

The rehearsal was over. The restaurant needed to prepare for the lunch crowd. He wandered back stage on a whim. The cubicles were empty, the chorus girls gone until evening. Hearing a familiar sound from a rear cubicle he tiptoed over. Dolores was stretched out on a narrow cot, eyes closed, face in sweet repose. The source of her ecstasy everyone's little Chinese favorite, head bobbing up and down between Dolores' thighs. He allowed himself a Peeping Tom's little pleasures for a while. Eyes open, a sound escaped Dolores' lips leaving them to an exchange of smiles across the tiny room.

## THIRTY-TWO

John The Greek, back from a stateside trip, joined him for Saturday night at The Fuji talking with admiration about the anti-war stuff going on back home. But grumbled mightily at the contempt shown for GIs, back from their year in Vietnam, vilified by kids their own age for simply following orders. "I couldn't believe it when I heard about it. Had to go see it for myself. And I did. Our guys, many of them back from all kinds of hell, climbing off planes after a twenty-hour flight were jeered at, reviled by chicks and freaks of all kinds. The puzzled, stunned looks on those GI's faces were enough to make me weep. I told some in the mob they ought to be at the Pentagon, not hassling this poor bunch of guys lucky to be alive. They examined me with the disdain they'd learn to show for the short of hair and long in tooth and returned to their sport." He spoke with the tired tone of one who'd seen too much, knew too much. When they entered the hullabaloo of The Fuji, he watched as John and Eddie clutched at each other. Old friends he guessed, not at all surprised, as Eddie finally turned to him with a vigorous welcoming handshake.

Walking down front to their table, he saw a sprinkling of his American colleagues in the crowded room, loudest of them Frankie Boyle, who was quick to notice the special table arranged for the two of them. They waved their hellos to Frankie and sat down as waiters brought plates for a banquet that magically appeared. Accepting this largesse, they ordered up drinks and he thanked John for his advice on where to find the USO girls. John, curious about the deal, asked for details. He filled him in on the accident, Tho's intervention with Sue, the trio's willingness to dump the USO for the big money Eddie was offering. John's admiration for his wheeling and dealing turned to a low whistle of surprise when he added that the girls were turning tricks, two a night, for the highest bidders. "Eddie claims to be splitting fifty-fifty with them."

"For now, at least," John replied with a smile. "You've made him an even bigger man on campus. He already has his string of cute Chinese hookers. Now he's got round-eye pussy for sale." John, too discreet to ask what his host might be gaining for himself, listened with head shaking-wonder at the story of Dolores' jailhouse blues. "She's lucky she got out alive," he said. "What Fat Eddie wants, Fat Eddie gets."

Seeing an opportunity, he asked the Greek, "Do you know this guy Steele?"

"Ronald Steele? What do you know about him?" John asked quietly.

"He's called The Money King, how come?"

"Cause that's what he is. He's drawing down big millions every year. Some of it even legitimate." Bringing an end to the subject he added, "And it's all you should want to know." John returned to the tender morsels within his stone crabs.

"How is it he speaks Chinese so well?"

"Jesus, you're a persistent bastard." Placing his chopsticks at the edge of his plate, John said, "He grew up in China with missionary parents. No doubt it was from them he learned the value of The God Almighty dollar." Rather than continue with an anti-clerical rant, John went on. "When Mao took over in '45 and threw out all the foreigners living in China, Ronnie baby managed to stay behind working for the People's Daily as a translator. He got pretty close to Mao's inner circle, so I heard."

"Was he a party member?"

"I don't think so," replied John. "He made himself useful bringing in luxury goods for Mao's special friends."

From Maoist to Money King, he thought. Communist to capitalist, a well-trod path.

Ninh approached, seeking permission to join them, quickly offered a seat at the table. He sensed John knew Ninh, but let it go as the show began. It was slick as always, bringing cheers led by Americans after each number. The big event was at intermission when little papers flowed like a river in Eddie's direction. Pasha-like, he looked them over, glancing at his watch. His showgirls had dutifully returned to their rooms. Thirty minutes of their time, no more than that, was up for sale. After five minutes of frenzy, Eddie sent his sons to collect the winners, and his winnings, which he stuffed into his pants without counting. The crowd, engaged with the happy extravagance of it all, went on to satisfy gustatory appetites at table or backstage for the all-you-can-eat-pussy special. Oh, the joy that comes to a man watching an entertainment featuring come-hither gyrations, sexy torch songs, and able to partake of pleasures widely promised but not always delivered.

Frankie Boyle came over and sat at the table, picking at a left-over plate of crabmeat with his fingers. "Some idiot assholes paid a thousand fuckin' bucks each for that American nookie. Amazin' isn't it? Ain't a piece of ass in the world worth that kind of money. If the pussy had been that good back home I'd a stayed in New Jersey." He pronounced this verdict as a man would who knew the value of things. He would have continued, but fell silent watching one of Eddie's boys approach the table and hand the Jewboy a thick envelope. Boyle was not yet over his quizzical staring when envelope in hand, he went backstage to do a little business. Chinese men, making delicate adjustments to their clothes, left the cubicles and their less-expensive sweethearts of a half hour. No rest for weary girls, unless you consider it restful lying flat on your back taking on come what may.

Ninh brought him three envelopes and he counted out fifteen hundred for Dolores, and five each for Sue and Tommie. Ninh, watching with hungry eyes, said nothing. Five hundred-dollar bills bounced in his hand until he added two more to the five hundred due Sue and Tommie. "Dolores gets the bigger money. Tell the other two Eddie's giving them a raise." Taking the envelopes, ready to do what was asked, Ninh paused as his boss quietly rubbed the last bill between in fingers finally saying, "I want you to take over the payouts. I'll clear it with Eddie." Ninh nodded as a hundred dollars came into his hand. "For you. Every week. Say nothing to Eddie or he'll fuck you out of it, understand"? Ninh understood, all right. He stared at the bill in his hand. His salary was a hundred a month and this crazy American was giving money away. Can they all be as rich as is said? Sue and Dolores returned from their break and Ninh dashed off to make his deliveries, carefully folding away the fresh hundred-dollar bill that was his very own.

He'd washed his hands of the foul mess, leaving behind a pimp's commissions. Not from some moral fervor. It was a spur of the moment kind of thing. Not worth thinking about. And Fat Eddie was one scary son-of-a-bitch to be avoided. He returned to the table, Boyle gone, thanks be. John told him he'd be leaving. A predawn flight to Danang awaited him. Happy to get out of there, he asked, "What's up in Danang?"

"A few things I gotta take care of. Are you game to come along?"

He was game, for sure, willing to suffer a pick-up at four in the morning. "No sacrifice too great," he solemnly intoned. And away they went, leaving The Fuji behind for a while.

# THIRTY-THREE

The nasty trill of a bedside alarm clock grumbled him awake at 4 AM. John would be picking him up in fifteen minutes. Enough time to pop on clothes, wash up, grab an overnight bag and shuffle down the stairs to the deserted street. Cong Ly, silently watched over by magnificent tall trees, awaited the dawn and the choking traffic to follow. He absorbed the quiet into his sleepy soul, kept from agitation by this moment of calm. Before he had to think about it a single pair of headlights came up and John was there. Mumbling their good mornings, he was grateful to see that John's ebullient nature was subdued by the early hour. They drove in a comfortable silence than can fall between pals traveling together with no more between them then the next destination. At the airport, a courier plane offered coffee and local pastries to its VIP passengers. Another extra that comes from knowing John the Greek, he happily reminded himself.

After coffee he asked, "So what's doing in Danang?"

"We're opening up the Cau Do Bridge again."

"Again?"

"Yep, for the third time. We fix it, the VC blows it, we go in there and fix it again. It's on the road between Chu Lai and Danang and we got to keep it open." He began to grin that funny grin when marveling at the follies of this world. "You know, we get paid extra every time we repair the fucker. Maybe the local VC commander is on our payroll." He gave this some further thought. "Nah, I've spent too much time living in Berkeley. Then he added, as an afterthought, "It might be hot up there." It turned out he wasn't referring to the weather.

A company jeep was waiting at planeside to take them to the bridge. Along with flak jackets and steel pots. John, shaking his head in amusement, showed him how to adjust the steel pot's helmet-liner for a better fit. The weight of the helmet dropped his chin to his chest, but he could soon see the river and the bridge. Its blown sections had been repaired and were afloat waiting to be welded into place. John explained that a fifth, smaller section had to be added to the original four-section bridge because the VC charges that blew it had shortened it by a few feet.

Workers moving welding equipment into place were hunched over, moving back and forth crabwise. Tanks of the First Marine Division, heavy tanks, mind you, were all around the perimeter of the bridge ready for action. The flak jacket and helmet made sudden sense to him. These workers of the world, American and Vietnamese, were under fire. He came to this solidarity-creating conclusion as he jumped at the whistling sound of overhead artillery followed by the roar of exploding shells landing on the opposite shore.

Well, there's a first time for everything. As he mused on this point, work began in earnest. The final section had been floated into place when everyone scattered at the pinging sound of bullet on metal, a sniper attack. Two of the tanks nearest to him swiveled their turrets, cannons deafening him as they let loose in the general direction of the snipers. It fell quiet, but none of the workers moved. When the last section began to float away, John the Greek dashed onto the bridge, grabbed a rope, jumped aboard the barge, and began pulling it into position. The tanks continued firing. A reluctant American and two Vietnamese answered John's wave for help. With the section tied in place, John donned a welder's mask while the others warily joined him to finish the job.

Later, as they walked away, he said to John, "I didn't know you were a welder." John smiled that smile of his. "Never underestimate the Cal Berkeley Baccalaureate degree." They let it go at that. "Let's go back to the base for a beer. I want to show you something else that's going on."

He kept his helmet in place on the drive. A badge of honor not a badge of courage. But, fuck, he'd been under fire, hadn't he? Wowza!! It was high overhead, the flying bullets fifty yards away. But he'd seen and heard and been there. The rush was gone but the memory lingered on.

They drove onto the base. Force Logistics Command, it was called. Paved roads with sidewalks in place, a PX, a movie theatre, immense warehouses filled with supplies of all kinds. Fenced yards with every type of truck, bulldozer, backhoe, neatly lined up according to some military reg or another. Every military base looked the same. Neutralizing any landscape, bathing it in barbed wire, dull browns, all natural curves of the land converted to right angles. Neatness counts, he guessed. Order, precision, insistence on the rules of the game seemed to be anodyne to the chaos, confusion, terror of war. These rear echelon types would never know the smell, the screaming noise of combat. They had jobs to do, would earn their ribbon, able to say to their grandchildren of a night, "Yes, I was there." But in their heart of hearts these motor pool jockeys, supply sergeants, captains of logistics knew that they knew nothing of the horror, the horror.

In front of a building under construction, a sign read Hoa Khan Children's Hospital. "I've never seen a hospital in Vietnam for children." he said. The Greek turned to him. "Because this is the first one ever built. It's the third expansion and you don't have to ask why."

The explanation was at hand. Kids with stumps for arms or legs, some of them three and four years old. Others, older, their eyes filled with worry, trying to get the hang of canes and prosthetic devices. John knew one of the boys without a leg who smiled at him. They spoke in Vietnamese, John poking the boy in the belly as he said goodbye. Another ward, even worse, for burns. These kids were out of danger, but bandaged, immobile, waiting for healing to begin. Each one cared for by a navy medic, nurse, or doctor.

He asked John about the kid without a leg. "He got hit scavenging for brass shell casings. All the kids do it. They run into fire zones, jumping over dead bodies before the smoke clears. The kid back there probably stepped on an unexploded round. It happens all the time."

That seemed to finish it for John until he was asked why the kids were risking so much for used shell casing. John, sounding near to angry, said, "There's a world-wide shortage of brass. It's being eaten up by this war. Tens of thousands, maybe millions, of rounds are being fired, and they all use that nice shiny brass to keep their powder dry. The kids chance everything for a few pennies. Metalworkers turn them into souvenirs." He paused, the world's follies unfolding before him. "And who buys these lovely reminders of war? Americans of course. Who else would collect such things?"

His bitter peroration ended when he saw a nurse he knew. She greeted him with a loving hug, and walked him to the new operating theatre. Navy Seabees had built the place but special equipment that couldn't be obtained through channels had appeared on the loading dock. "Miracles do happen," John said, as they entered the surgery area. A tiny, tender child was being wheeled to the recovery room. He counted her limbs. All intact. Small favors, he thought. John slipped into the surgery, spoke to a doctor, and began checking out valves on newly installed oxygen equipment. Satisfied, he tested the backup generators. He was an electrical engineer — with all the practicalities that implied. But calling on that Greek heritage, he was also a philosopher of the old-fashioned kind, flux more than a term from physics or metallurgy. No certainties for him. That's for sure. His work done, they finally went for that beer.

The setting sun lit the South China Sea. What more could he hope for? They tasted their beers. The nurse he'd seen earlier walked in with a group of doctors, spotted John and joined them. Exhausted, she slipped into a chair, leaning back against its molded plastic to rest her weary frame. Her nametag read Brenda Bender. Dark hair, dark eyes, and a quiet about her that could not be mistaken for calm. Rather, it was a blasted look that told of long hours, patched wounds, surgeries, the dying, and the dead. John went to fetch her a beer and she sat in silence. He offered no small talk to this lovely woman whose weary face and eyes held dark shadows. Eyes that glimmered in thanks when John returned with her cold beer. She licked the foam from the bottle top with a flick of her tongue then tilted it back and took a long swallow, smacking her lips like no sorority girl. "You were supposed to be out of here three months ago," John said. "How come you re-upped? She brought the cold bottle to her cheek, her forehead. "Tom extended, that fool, and I figured it would be the only way to see him."

"He still on the Kitty Hawk?"

"Yep. Flying night missions and constantly bitching about the targets they're assigned. We get together every couple of days." Returning to the comfort offered by her beer, she allowed herself to look out to the glorious, reddening, dappled sky. "Our guys know we're caught up in an impossible, un-winnable war. Taking out chickenshit wooden bridges, replaced in hours, when Haiphong harbor is filled with ships loaded with war supplies begging to be blown away."

He watched as John shook his head in wonderment. Tom must be the boyfriend. But where did John fit in? He knew the Kitty Hawk was a carrier and landings and takeoffs at night were hairy-dangerous, or so he'd read. But he kept silent as the two old friends, or whatever they were, went on talking.

A doctor came over and thanked John for the surgery room equipment. John waved off the gratitude with a nonchalant toss of his hand. Brenda began talking about the children. "We're all doing twelve to sixteen hours on our regular jobs. Our guys come in with every kind of wound and mutilation. And we go about our business, keeping them alive. If we can. Some of them, when they wake up, curse us for bringing them back in the shape they'll be in for the rest of their lives." She paused, letting the memory of those moments pass through and beyond her. "Working with the kids has kept us sane." John didn't respond, but waited for her to go on. "Did you see that navy medic in surgery?" They both nodded. "He's out every day with his platoon. Every day. Facing every kind of danger and medical emergency. Any off-duty hour he spends assisting in the children's surgery. It keeps him human. Puts him back in touch with decency, no matter how horrific the wounds these children suffer."

John recalled when the hospital for kids had only eleven beds. "And now there's 130," she said. "And they're all filled. But what I want to know is how many more kids are out there? Did you notice how there are no family members with the children? Not all the kids are orphans. Their families love them, but what keeps them away is fear. The local VC warns them to stay away from Americans, but what's worse is the local medicine men. They tell them their children will come back with spells that will be very expensive to exorcise. Can you imagine?" She rose. "I've got to get some sleep, I've got the duty tonight." He watched as they exchanged hugs and cheek-to-cheek kisses. Before leaving she looked over at him and said, "Keep an eye on John, will you? Try to keep him out of trouble." She smiled. "Thanks for the beer."

A last dab of light remained in the sky. They'd be spending the night and went off to arrange a place to stay on the base. It was out of the question for John to eat in an officer's mess. He knew a great seafood place in Danang. Off they went, two good-time boys on the prowl for a decent meal.

Driving through the base he noticed Air Force and Army housing was clean and comfortable in comparison to the Marines, who seemed honor-bound to live in broken-down misery. It was good training, they liked to say, to live in Quonset huts that were a throwback to World War II, on dust-filled roads with no suggestion of privilege or favor. But sharp in dress. Shined boots and buckles de rigueur for these Marines.

Outside the base, a street running with bars called Texas, New York, Suzie Wong had touts hailing down strolling soldiers out for an evening's entertainment. It was payday and things were jumping. They passed this glitter in favor of a restaurant with a tank in its window filled with fish awaiting evisceration and preparation. Vietnamese and a few American civilians sat at tables laden with immense platters of shellfish, crabs' legs, and things from the sea he'd never seen before. They sat down and two bottles of Muscadet appeared without warning. How in the wide world did this joint come up with Muscadet? Life's mysteries continue mystifying, he thought, as he dove in. The freshness of the mussels did not surprise him. Hadn't he seen the sun set on the China Sea? Between gulps of white wine, he asked, "How do you know Brenda?"

John looked at him. "A good meal spoiled. But I suppose you had to ask." He dipped a lobster chunk in the butter sauce but gave no reply.

"Is that pilot her husband?"

"Yep, he sure is." John waved down the waiter and ordered a fish dish. The Greek, normally wildly expansive about the women in his life, was not giving anything away. It brought an end to that line of questioning. A large red-skinned fish arrived on a platter, its succulent white flesh prepared to a god's requirement. They ate on. And drank on. The long day drawing to a close at last.

"I hear hard drugs are giving grass heavy competition these days," he said to John.

"Not yet, but it's getting there." As an afterthought, John asked, "You a user?"

"Nah. A little grass now and then. Not for a while."

"Corsicans run opium, but heroin is getting big for them. The more GIs come into the country, the more they bring in. Demand and supply my boy. Economics 101."

"What about opium," he asked.

"Opium is the local's way out of this craziness. Too much trouble for GIs with the set-ups, the hookahs and all that."

John seemed to know the score on just about anything going down. Chalking it up to John's long years here, he let any suspicious thought slip away.

That night, stretched out on a BOQ bed, he began thinking about those kids collecting brass for pennies on a battlefield. The risk to life and limb, the pity of it, should have overcome him. Instead, he began to think about the worldwide shortage in brass caused by the war. If Supply and Demand had done its inexorable work the market had prevailed and prices had soared. Any good capitalist, worthy to call himself an American, could see opportunity calling. Kids all over Vietnam could be put to work collecting spent shells. Always magnanimous, he'd pay not a penny, but a nickel, per. Collection points at strategic spots would use Vietnamese Army trucks to deliver the brass to a central point near Saigon. His buddy Minister Tho could make that happen with a phone call. There'd be enough profit for a payoff to everyone. Freighters, normally returning deadhead to stateside ports, would welcome extra income. Thanh's father would gladly sign off on an export license for a piece of the deal. Commodity traders the world over would jump at the chance to play. He wondered how Big Eddie might be of use in the deal. Leave him to his whores and his chop suey, he decided. Turning his eyes from the occasional risk to the kids, he would generously allocate a percentage of his profits to a Children's Welfare Fund. Who could ask for more? Everybody wins in this best of all possible worlds. He's a can-do guy, isn't he? What were the Robber Barons of yore if not can-do kinds of guys?

As these thoughts raced through his teeming brain, his hands gripped the sides of the bed. Anger surged through him and he jumped up to a window lit up by moonlight swinging his fist hard into the wall, his knuckles bloody against the blow. Anger had turned to anguish at the comfort, the ease, with which he exploited anything that came his way. Was he simply in a place that allowed him to be his worst self? Or, was this his true self? He had no ready answer, self-knowledge never his strong suit. Slinking back to his bed, not wanting to soil Government Issue sheets, he licked the blood from his hand falling into a not-so-innocent sleep.

## THIRTY-FOUR

Back from the perils of Danang, he was up early on a Saturday morning sipping hot coffee in spite of hundred-degree temperature that sucked air from his lungs. Under a ceiling fan, his bare feet begging for what little chill remained in the marble floor, he groused, "It's too hot for words." But the old Billy Holiday tune offered no way to be cool. A soft knock on the door brought no response from him, sure it was one of the up-early hookers looking for a little business. A second, louder knock and the calling of his name brought him to the door.

Thanh stood there, lovely as ever, looking impossibly untouched by the weather. He was delighted, hadn't seen her in weeks. It hardly mattered that she was with her younger brother. The soul of good manners, he welcomed them, offering café au lait, which they happily accepted. He fussed in the kitchen, grinding coffee, heating milk, setting out cups, hearing the two of them talking somewhat urgently. Carrying a tray, he walked into a little domestic scene when the boy got up to leave, swiftly, curtly ordered back by Thanh who took pastries from her bag. Moon cakes, she called them, the sweet paste inside their hard exterior perfect with the coffee they shared. She seemed to have something on her mind; began inquiring about the company he worked for. Her oblique way of bringing it up led him to wonder if she wanted to ask for something. She turned to her sullen brother who spoke no English, and asked him a question.

Then said, "My brother is in his last year of high school and has his highest grades in math and drafting."

He congratulated the boy. "Will you go on to university?"

Thanh said, "No, he will be drafted into the army first."

"It won't matter, your father will land him a safe job in Saigon." He didn't know what to make of the silence descending on the room. The boy made to leave again and his sister uttered a sharp command, causing him to sit down. Something was up. This wasn't American-style family business and bickering. He waited. Finally Thanh said, quietly, with an effort to speak so directly, "If he has a job as an engineer with your company he won't be drafted." The boy had to have some English because he began talking rapidly in Vietnamese. He couldn't tell if his speech showed anger or any emotion at all. Thanh gently said a word or two that silenced the boy.

"You want me to get your brother a job?" She nodded. "But he doesn't speak English." She simply looked at him making no reply. "OK, I'll try. Why can't your father do this for him?"

"Because it would be unpatriotic. It would hurt his position in the government. My brother wants to go into the army and volunteer for the most dangerous work. Paratrooper. Ranger. To avenge his brother's death." She paused. "He is the last son left in the family." She said this quietly, an indictment of herself and her sister for not having been born boys. He remembered celebrating Tet at her house when male ancestors where honored and special mention made of future sons and grandsons not yet born. "Daughters are the children of others," an old man had told him. It struck him then as an oddity, a convention. But maintaining a male line meant life and death for a family. What a fucking country, he said to himself, not for the first time.

"Okay. I'll do what I can. But you have to tell me what sort of papers you need." Despite that odd experience that night in Dalat, her grateful look was one he hoped he could cash in on one way or another. She lost her evasiveness, was all business, producing a blank form in English and Vietnamese that needed to be filled out, signed, sealed, and delivered. He took it and she rose, extending her hand. A business deal, for sure. Remembering what he'd learned about her father he silently asked, But where my profit?

Getting the kid a job was no big deal. Half the local workforce was beating the draft in the same way. All that was needed was a signed statement describing this seventeen-year-old as being critical to the war effort in his capacity as a junior engineer.

Just like back home. The colleges and universities stateside were filled with scholar/draft dodgers. Or the Guard. Or, in a pinch, Canada, Sweden. The upper class turned underclassmen. And the true underclass? Why here, there, and everywhere in dear old Vietnam, doing their duty, as their betters grew wise into their junior and senior years. With grad school beckoning as final testament to the wisdom of avoidance behavior.

## THIRTY-FIVE

Ensconced in his office, awaiting come what may, he listened as Ninh, in his jump-start way, brought him news of good times at Camp Fuji. The girls were behaving, the money was flowing, Eddie was dancing in the aisles. Ninh, no doubt taking advantage of his hundred extra a week, was wearing a new suit, fresh shirt and elegant designer tie. That cash infusion to Ninh would buy whatever loyalty the little guy possessed. Or so he hoped as he continued to marvel at how Ninh seemed to know what was going on even as it happened. Wired, he was, in more ways than one. Ninh was about to say something about Tho and Sue, the little lovebirds, when Colonel Lee walked in. Out of discretion or fear, Ninh quickly left the room.

Sitting down, Lee said, "Nice deal you've got going in Chinatown." Was that a touch of respect within his mocking tone? Lee had never come into his office, so he must have needed something from him. And though in need, was incapable of charm. A thirty-year army career as either master or servant can do that to a man.

"I've got no deal at The Fuji," he told Lee. "Just made the arrangements."

Lee smiled. "Arrangements, huh?

"Yep." That's all there is to it.

"OK, never mind the bullshit. We got a problem, a big problem." He was wary of Lee, knowing he'd drop the dime on him, turn informer anytime, to save his ass. And waited to hear what might befall him.

Instead, Lee leaned forward. "Renewal of the contract for the whole goddamn job is in trouble. Over some fucking air conditioners. We're in a ninety-day window negotiating as a sole source, but a couple of senators from Texas are pushing for their own pals back there." He paused, puffed up with self-importance as he established the importance of it all. "There are two hundred air conditioners, purchased outside of channels, sitting dockside on a freighter in the goddamn Saigon River and we can't get them delivered"

"What's that got to do with anything?"

"The Corps of Engineers has gotten themselves nice new offices, thanks to us, with fancy BOQ's attached. Every swinging dick over there has something to say about our contract. Especially the two-star who'd sign off on the extension. And they're bitching and whining 'cause they're sweating their balls of without the air conditioners we promised them." He paused. "We're talking about big millions on the line here. If we don't find a way to cool their asses they'll hit us on non-compliance and we can all start packing to go home." Then, can't-help-himself mockery returning, said, with a pathetic try at a Jewish peddler's accent, "Vell Mistah Fixeh, any suggestions?"

On hearing this, he would have told Lee to go fuck himself. But business is business. "The boat is dockside?" Lee nodded. "Got a copy of the manifest?"

"I can get one," Lee said.

"Well, maybe I can help." After a moment he added, "It'll cost something."

"Ten thousand should do it," said Lee, expansively.

Lee's eyes popped when he heard him say, "Those air conditioners are stuck there because someone knows how important they are to us, it'll take ten times that."

"That's a hundred thousand," Lee cried out.

Not hushing him, acknowledging his sublime grasp of multiplication tables, he said to Lee, "It's peanuts. The cost of doing business. You said we're talking about big millions and, by the way, your own little tuchus." He let that little Yiddishism sink in, adding, "Think of it as a good career move for everyone." Before Lee had a chance to reply, he rose, dismissively, "Get me the manifest and the goodies and I'll see what I can do."

## THIRTY-SIX

Late the next afternoon a long line of trucks delivered up two hundred air conditioners. Installed that very night, they offered up the succor of cool air to our heroic Army Engineers. Lee was in ecstasy, hoping for an explanation, his only satisfaction the result not the details. And details aplenty could have been told.

Manifest in hand, he'd gone to Thanh's house that night to speak with Poppa. He'd worn a jacket, deciding to insinuate the hundred thou' in its inside pockets rather than show off the cash in a briefcase. Poppa welcomed him, grateful for his help in rescuing his son from military duty and pleased to hear he could offer a favor in return. He displayed the manifest, naming ship and cargo. Not a problem. Anything else? He had Thanh explain how much the company appreciated his consideration. Was there anything they could do to show thanks? He watched as Poppa raised his hands in a gesture to show no thanks were necessary; sure he could be called upon for any future help the family might need. And that was that. Poppa had other things to do. Thanh, invited to dinner, was regrettably busy.

He walked outside to confront a decision that comes to the life of every man. Patting with affection thick bulges showing on both sides of his jacket, the decision needed no more than the briefest deliberation. The hundred thousand would be his to have and to hold.

## THIRTY-SEVEN

In celebration of his four-month anniversary, he was off to the races. Saigon's Phu Tho Racetrack loomed over an out-of-the-way neighborhood, its grandstand forming a semicircle dwarfing nearby houses. Longchamps, it ain't. Any trace of La Belle France was obscured by a mob of Vietnamese men indulging their habit — the gambling away of wages, ill- or well-gotten gains. The track's common bond with its Belmont and Hollywood Park sisters was the touts, the hustlers, down-on-luck vagabonds congregating inside and out. He engaged one to place his bets and repaired to the reserved section of the grandstand. Lame, dispirited nags listlessly entered the track. Jockeys, equally emaciated, barely held on to the reins of their mounts. He soon learned that betting was a joke. The fix was in on every race, with a limited number of bets allowed on any one horse. He watched the mad scramble as local punters scuffled, in good humor, trying to get down on the horse of the moment. His agent returned after each race, the sad smile of a loser on his face, and received another fistful of piastres from Lord Bountiful. The shade of the grandstand barely made a difference to the rising heat and stifling, inescapable dampness. He raised his vodka tonic in a toast to spring. It was mid-April, and all the world was in bloom. For the first time he felt a longing for that vacancy called home. An early springtime snowfall would have given way to jonquils bursting their bulbs, the smell of lilac in the air, a dousing rain, a new baseball season.

How could he have known that bats and balls and gloves, reminders of what he'd left behind, were instruments to club and bruise and wound? His children, abandoned, had not allowed him into their hearts, begrudged admittance to the places where they played. Their rules were clear. He shall not speak to them before or during games. Nor offer any advice on hitting or pitching. This father, who had taught them everything he knew, and watched with joy as his sons exceeded him, was ordered to stand mute.

Searching out the schedule of the games, since his son had a lapse of memory whenever asked, he'd show up, slip discreetly into the small bleachers and watch as his boy, pitching that day, warmed up. He had known early on that the boy had the heart, the arm of a pitcher, and only needed instruction in pivoting the body, dropping the arm behind and way back, shifting weight while striding toward the plate, releasing the ball just so — strike three, you're out!!

All this he'd begun to teach and his son had learned his lessons well. But something had intervened between the seasons to prevent the father from working with the son. Those little details, which a wise father could teach a son while walking together throwing rocks or snow balls or skipping stones on water. Those everyday things were now lost to them. The son's vengeance was to ban his father from any moment of joy or instruction.

A small flaw crept into his boy's delivery. He was over-striding and simply needed to be told. He would adjust, if he knew, but none on the field knew his son as he did. It was a spring day in May, his son was not twelve years old, and he could no longer call his name, gesture with advice, whisper assurances and instruction between innings. A splendid day in May under a bright blue sky. At the end of an inning in which he'd struggled, the father could control himself no more, stood and called and caught his eye and made a movement with his leg and arm which would tell him everything at once. That he should shorten his stride, that he should release the ball sooner, that he was loved, dear God, loved beyond measure or gesture or telling, and it was sorrowful, so goddamn sorrowful, that it had come to this.

Alone at the bar, his back to the track, he ordered another, wondering about the ice in the glass, but let it pass, staring at himself in the wide mirror. What stared back was an overweight, out-of-sorts, forty-plus, going nowhere kind of guy. Ambition's early force had dissipated down the stretch. Or does he exaggerate, a too-equine comparison here at the races? The setting of records for speed, at a distance, needs breeding, nurturing, gamboling about, as a horse finds its legs. Careful training to saddle and starter's gate, a life of colors and crowds, music and mystery, hid the flaw that showed after he'd burst from the pack, breezing round the turn. The rest of the breed lagged back till the top of the stretch when horses behind, an ever-closer rumble, caught him, passed him, racing on to the wire. Under the whip, he'd finish up the track, out of the money, giving his backers a thrill for a minute. But a race at a distance goes two minutes, plus. Early foot, they call it, those keepers of records, and it's the call at the finish that counts.

Or, is he too tough on himself? Perhaps it's a question of equipment. Perhaps what causes him to shy, be spooked, is nothing more than a chance stirring of leaves along the rail causing a turn of the head, a break in stride to keep him from moving straight to the wire. A change in equipment, that's the ticket. Blinkers is what's called for. That'll keep him from distraction. That'll help his concentration. And if that won't do it, we'll geld the son-of-a-bitch. That'll get his attention, calm him down.

A loud braying interrupted his reverie. In the mirror he saw Boyle, with a band of merry men heading toward the bar. Frankie was spreading his winnings on the bar and ordering drinks for all. No sucker, he had the system down, and the winning tickets on the day's long shot. No escaping him, he went over to be greeted by his pal and introduced around. Boyle dismissed the idea of betting on any of the other races and settled down to bitching about the weather. "Wait 'til next month, you'll sweat your balls into a puddle. The rain and fuckin' humidity will soak your brains, the air so thick you can't breathe the shit." His chorus, nodding in agreement, fortified themselves against their fate with another round. Frankie, he noticed, had put his winnings in his wallet. No second rounds from this baby. One of the gang around Boyle seemed more amused by his antics than respectful. Marty Long was his name and when he said, "Around here it ain't the heat, it's the cupidity," Boyle missing the mot, demanded, "Marty, let's go back to your place, the air conditioning is going, right?"

Marty lived a few blocks from the track in a two-story villa surrounded by a high wall with a wide artfully decorated metal gate. A side door let them enter a flowering garden laid out around a fountain set within a rock formation. The two-block walk having delivered them to perspiring hell, the group stormed into the air-conditioned house. An attractive woman appeared. Marty quietly said something to her in Vietnamese. She left and a second woman, a maid, appeared with a mountain of cold towels that were offered around. The first woman never showed again, but the maid brought ice and snacks, cleared glasses, wiped spills, and scurried about assuring that all was right with the world.

He'd had enough booze for the day and wandered the house looking at the scrolls, sculpture, and ivory carvings that filled the living room, dining room, and hallways. He examined a scroll with a mountain painted in shades of brown and black and tiny figures walking in the distance. Alongside was another that seemed identical. When Marty came over he asked him why they were alongside each other and was told that one was Chinese and quite old, the other Vietnamese. "A copy?" he asked.

"Not really," Marty replied. Then asked him, "Which is which?" Fifty-fifty odds isn't bad, so he guessed and got it right. Marty had been collecting them for years and offered to take him to shops where they could be bought for next to nothing.

At a group of photographs, Marty, whose accent identified him as a Bostonian, grunted, "The family. Back Bay, all the way." Marty screwed up his face in front of a photograph. "That'll be me mum and me dad and me twelve brothers and sisters, praise up to God." His pass at a low-class Irish accent duly noted, they turned to a picture of Marty as a teenager in what looked like a seminarian's cassock. "Yep, that's me. My folks thought it a wondrous thing that one of their own would choose to be Christ's vicar on earth. They weren't pleased when I told them I'd learned I had a vocation all right, but it was for sex. And I'd learned that fact at the seminary. That got their attention, I can tell you. My dad came close to belting me when I told him that the Brothers had an odd view of celibacy. That sins of the flesh extended only to the opposite sex. Anything else was fair use. When I told them that their beloved Father Damian had laid hands on me and I'd poked him one in the eye, my mother, if you can imagine, smacked me one across the face."

He paused a moment glancing down at the pictures of his brethren. "I went off to Boston College and was thrown out after trying to major in dissipation. And here I am, in the safe harbor Vietnam offers to those of us in need of their ease." They walked back toward the living room. A roar of laughter greeted them. Doyle was in full entertainment mode. "Talk about a professional Irishman," Marty said. He shook his head in agreement. "But he's a clever son-of-a-bitch, and dangerous."

"How so?"

"Never you mind, my boy. And don't ever need to feel the need to find out why. Been here for years. Knows every police chief and province chief in the country. A good guy, but watch out for him. He's into a little bit of everything. Money changing, army surplus. He's a good guy to know, but don't ask too many questions."

He asked Marty about the woman he had seen earlier. "Think of her as my wife. Her name is Tu."

"Any chance we can look for those scrolls anytime soon?"

"Sure," Marty replied. "The best place is closed on Sundays. How about we meet for a drink at the Continental on Tuesday. Let's make it 12:30. I'll be dropping Tu off at the cathedral for noon mass." Marty saw the smile cross his face. "Somebody has to keep the faith around here." They shook hands on that one. A friend's been made. Let's drink to it.

# THIRTY-EIGHT

The terrace of the Hotel Continental awaited his pleasure. He'd be joining Marty Long for a drink, a bit of conversation, a shopping tour. A way to spend a Saigon afternoon seeking un peu de divertissement. The strolling hookers were pleased to show their wares. But beer was the indulgence of choice at this time of day. Hardly noticing the dense traffic on Tu Do he spotted Marty at a table close to the street and off they went, boulevardiers ambling down Le Loi toward the Central Market to visit the shop of Mr. Dat, an 80-year-old gentleman.

Marty told him a story, bound to be true, about Robert McNamara returning from a trip out here with three small antique ivory sculptures. At a dinner party back in D.C., dear Bob showed off his finds to an expert in the field, who regretfully told him the pieces were fakes. And to prove it removed a small cap from the top of one piece to show it wasn't ivory, but bone. "Nicely carved, however," the scholar was supposed to have said. "Well," Marty gleefully went on, "Mr. Dat was visited by a goddamn VN general who was coolly told: 'You look like you're doing pretty well by this war. Don't we all have the right to make a living?" And that was that. The old Whiz Kid himself being fucked by a people a lot smarter than he knew. And not for the first or last time, I'm afraid." A great story, he thought, as they entered the small store on Troung Dinh.

Mr. Dat rose with a courtesy that seemed outsized, and offered tea. As they sat in this spare room sipping from small ceramic cups, Dat and Marty chatted in Vietnamese. On the wall behind the desk an exquisitely carved wooden plaque imitated an unfolding scroll. A suggestion of flowers floated across its top. All this in soft gold, save for the deep black calligraphy emblazoned across the scroll's surface. Dat had been watching him. Marty said, "Mr. Dat thinks you have good taste to be admiring that plaque."

"What does it say?"

Dat said something that Marty couldn't translate. "I don't get the words but it's about the Mother Goddess."

"Mother Goddess?"

"She's a guarantee of prosperity. Don't you know women run this country? If you don't, look again."

Dat rose and ushered them through a doorway into a vast room. Objects, colors and shapes flooded over him. He tried taking it in all at once, staggered by its quantity and variety. Bright red lacquer boxes to carry gifts for a bride's family; small carved figures in green, red and black, holding musical instruments — water puppets, he was told; a wood block print of a young woman on an elephant — she'd led a rebellion against the Chinese conquerors a mere seventeen centuries ago; an odd group of large, wooden monkeys, long thin legs emerging from roughly carved tree stumps, found in Highland cemeteries; calligraphy, clay toys, colorfully glazed ceramics, all evidence of a splendid civilization unknown to him. Or had he been blind to it? Had the batik, the embroidered vests and collars, the ceremonial altars that engulfed him, been here all the time? He picked up a simple black cap adorned with silver coins and saw that the coins were French, left over from another war, another victory against a foreign invader. And began to feel an intruder, but this was business after all.

He took a liking to a tall document box. Ornamental tracery in ivory covered its front and sides. At least he hoped it was ivory. Its base and frame were of a dark wood and nothing more. The price Dat quoted brought a smile from Marty who began bargaining. Settling on a price less than half what had been asked, they left, with smiles all around. The best fifty bucks he'd spent in a long, long time. "Lunch is on me," he said happily.

# THIRTY-NINE

He had hoped to show his purchase to Thanh, who'd made another of her frequent disappearing acts. A day-to-day tedium overtook him. At loose ends, bored with the whoring, he stopped at the Blue Fox, a bar on Pasteur, an American joint serving up booze and grub to indifferent regulars. Décor was of no importance, booths, tables and chairs not for comfort or darkened for romance. Welcomed over to a table, he sat down, noting that the six women sitting there were American round-eyes. Probably office workers. DACS, Department of the Army Civilians in this hellhole of a place. The two youngest were in the hands of officers in fatigues. The other four had high hopes, surrounded by a bunch of fellow Americans drinking Bam y Bab, the local beer.

Of the four women on the loose, the oldest, so old she clearly could give a shit, was on her way to a royal sousing. She'd worked overseas contracts for years, seen everything, and fucked anything along the way she got her hands on, so she said. Ellie was her name and it was clear that the way this old gal got along was to be one of the boys. She was telling a story about getting clap from a colonel in Spain when we were building airbases there in the fifties that seemed to involve trying to buy penicillin on the local market. The oldest of the old boys was totally amused by her, grateful for the entertainment and the company of any women that reminded these poor, homesick suckers of stateside life. A waitress, slim, cute, cleared the empties and he ordered a round. One of the women, noticing this largesse, chatted him up. Within minutes he had her life story. Married, grown kids, divorced, out-of-work, a tax-free job, a chance to see the world beyond Ames, Iowa. Sensing his boredom, she turned to another worthy hoping to keep his attention. Ellie went on drinking and said to one of the uniforms, "I know why I'm here, to make a buck. What are you doing here?" The young captain began describing his rear-echelon job responsibilities when she waved him off. "I don't care what you do, I wanna know what this is all about, what are we doing here?" It was a stand-up question from a stand-up kind of gal. "I've been here over three years. When I first got here we could drive out to Bien Hoa without any trouble. It's 30 goddamn clicks up the road from here, what's that? Twenty miles? Now, three years later you can't even drive the goddamn road. You gotta take a chopper out to a Saigon suburb, for chrissakes. What's that all about?" She had the wrong guy to ask such questions. He'd made a career in supply and had no answer to a simple question, "What are we doing here, for chrissakes?" The captain, lacking intelligence or interest in infiltration, interdiction, had no answer for this drunken souse of a dame.

Walking away from the bar, he passed an American army compound, MACV, central headquarters for America's mighty war effort. Sandbags piled high against come what may, a leery pair of MPs, M-16s at the ready, peered out onto the darkened street. He quickly passed on to an intersection that always brought a smile to his face, the corner of Pasteur and Alexander of Rhodes. The only streets he knew of in Saigon with Western names. Pasteur he could understand, but that other Colossus? He strolled down Pasteur past the cathedral, past evening worshipers and ever-hopeful street vendors, and a sight that always made him look twice. Young Vietnamese men, some in uniform, walked by holding hands as casually as that. There was nothing queer about it, he'd been told, but had his doubts as a twosome passed by idly chatting away. He crossed Le Loi's wide expanse of boulevard where car and bicycle traffic waited eagerly for a cop, in a starched white uniform elevated above them, to whistle and wave his arms to send them rushing home.

Wandering in the direction of the river, he could tell he was drawing near when hailed by hookers in taxis looking for merchant seamen trade. At Nguyen van Thinh he saw a bar called the Single One. Thinking it would suit him he entered to find either sour faced men or hopeful hookers turning his way. "Not for me," he told himself, and saw a sign, HAPPY BAR, in tune with his mood. Perfect, he thought, the river can wait, and found himself in raucous, roaring, sailor heaven, Merchant Marine variety, not our boys in red, white and blue. With money to burn, hazard pay, bonuses — we were in a war zone, were we not, they were burning it, for sure, two-deep at the bar, glass in hand, enveloped by lovelies eager to fulfill any desire, inspire the lust in a man. Most were large, muscular. Some had beards, some tattoos, and large rings, silver belt buckles, gleaming cowboy boots. He was not dressed like this.

The crowd eyed him long enough to know he wasn't one of them and turned back to their own. He shouldered past, caught the eye of the bartender and escaped to the rear where booths were saturated with revelers, their women of the moment, and a noise level matching the bar decibel for decibel. He looked around not needing company; saw in a rear booth a group of kids, cameras around their necks. They wore Army fatigues, but weren't soldiers. Drinking, laughing, six of them squeezed together, watching the mad scene, freelance photographers he'd been hearing about. All but teenagers, they were getting pictures of the war suicidal to take, working in the thick of it all, getting killed now and then, but making names for themselves if they lived long enough. Ruddy faced, steady of hand and nerves, looking through a small lens to bring to the larger world out there a world they'd never know. He moved in their direction and saw a girl among them. They seemed to be trying to convince her to join along to the next bar on their hop. She shook her head pleasantly, and they left.

He watched her sip her beer, comfortable in solitude. "Not a chance," he thought, as she looked not at him, but past him. "No way," he decided. Taking a glance as an opportunity he approached and she became aware of this old guy, maybe forty, balding and with nary a tattoo, coming into her field of view. He smiled. She did not. He raised his glass to her. She reluctantly returned the gesture. "You're not a sailor, are you?" he asked. "No, and neither are you." He slid into the booth. She looked him over. "Cruising for sailors?" He burst out laughing. It was her first clue that this was a man interested in women and she unconsciously moved a hand to her hair. He told her he lived here, worked here.

"You're a DAC?" She spit out the word. He told her he worked for a contractor, vague about what he did. "So, you're CIA."

"No, no," he said quickly and heard her growl begin to lift in a contemptuous attack on everything he was.

"You're here making the big bucks, tax free no less, living like a goddamn king in the middle of a place where people are being blasted to pieces every day while you do another day at the office. Christ. How can you do it?" He had no answer, but did not evade the hardness of her eyes, which, he noticed, were dark and quite beautiful. "You'll never know, none of your kind will ever know, what's going on out here. You're too goddamned busy sucking on your beers and anything else your little hearts desire."

He had a feeling she wasn't quite through and she did not disappoint. "Have you even heard a shot fired? Or seen a dead and battered body? Of course not. As far as you know, there's no war, no one is dying, there's none of the chaos, the noise, the fucking smell, for chrissakes of dozens of firefights taking place right now thirty minutes from here." She quit her diatribe, prepared to dismiss him. He decided to stay and take his chances, quietly saying, "In strife bewildering we spilt blood enough to swim in. We orphaned many children, we widowed many women.'" He watched her take in the lines.

"What's that?"

"A poem, War Song."

She took a small notebook from her breast pocket. "What's that you said, 'Strife bewildering?' " He nodded as she wrote the two words down. "Who wrote it?"

"Thomas Love Peacock."

She looked at him and his optimistic heart sensed a softening. "Ain't that something. You come in here looking like a pansy and recite me a poem by someone named Love Peacock." She looked down at her notebook moved by the words she'd written. He decided to press his luck: "Sometimes a word is worth a thousand pictures." She looked up, "What's that supposed to mean?" "You're a photographer." "Yes," she said, very quietly, "That I am." He sensed the mood swing in his favor. "I came down here to walk along the river. Care to join me?" And the two of them walked past the milling crowd that made way with respect due to a lady and her gentleman escort.

# FORTY

The Seine she is not, the Saigon River. Though it would do for his purposes. They walked down Nguyen Hue, the mist engulfing them, pretty much in silence. The bright lights on the boulevard turned fuzzy and dim as they came to the point where an estuary, the Ben Nghe, merged with the wide river. Lined with pitiful shacks and sampans tied up on shore, the Ben Nghe was home to thousands of workers eking a living from traffic on the river. At a tree-lined quay a troopship unloaded its cargo of boys off to war. She paused, framing it in her mind, wishing she'd brought her camera. He concentrated on a slightly built boy burdened by the weight of weapon, backpack and duffel bag, apprehensive, eyes darting this way and that, called to order by a three-striper, reassured that someone was in charge, someone would be giving orders, someone would be looking after him.

Freighters in mid-channel, running lights dimmed, waited their turn at the piers. Small boats ran among them carrying passengers to the shore. It was sailor's night out after the Pacific voyage and the long wait offshore in the bay. Pointing to one thing or another, still hardly speaking, they came to a wide bridge filled with heavy traffic and strolling Vietnamese couples, crossed to its center to gain a mid-river view. Incessant truck traffic went past with a roar, the deep darkness of the river settling into them as they watched the current churn to a white froth for a brief instant before being swallowed up by blackness. He felt a touch signaling that she was done, wanted to move on. They continued across the bridge into Gia Dinh province, which he knew had seen the ferocity of the war at its further edges. She led him toward a stall on wheels with four stools in front. A restaurant. She was hungry and ordered a bowl of Pho, lacing it with a fish sauce so spectacularly odoriferous his gag reflex kicked in to her amusement. He called for a bowl of the same ignoring the best medical advice to avoid street food. The evening was going well, he thought. Following along with her mood and rhythm suited him just fine. It had worked for him in the past. She looked at her watch and told him she had to get to the AP office to check some photos. It seemed she was offering to take him along for the ride. Finishing her bowl with gusto, she lightly bounced from her stool.

At the AP office she was all business, bitching to herself about composition and contrast as she leafed through black and white prints. The lab guy, clearly respectful, stood by as she examined a contact sheet and quickly marked it up with a grease pencil to indicate the cropping she desired. He nodded and left for the darkroom. She was ready to go but watched him leafing through some of her prints. Spectacular, heartbreaking photographs of soldiers in action, or wearily at rest, or weeping at the sight of dead and wounded comrades. They'd become the common currency of war. Every magazine and newspaper had to have this fresh meat to be devoured by head-shaking readers.

He closely studied a photo of a single soldier, weapon raised at the moment of returning fire. The soldier's face showed fear and fury he'd never seen in any photograph. But there was something else, something that caused him to stare at the picture. She had come to his side, curious about his concentration on that one image. Then it came to him. A premonition. The soldier was point man for his squad, the first down the path, the first to catch the ambush or the booby trap awaiting them. That cold fury and fear she'd caught on film had turned to hot death for the boy an instant later. "He was walking point, wasn't he?" She nodded. "And he didn't make it," he said quietly. Again she nodded; surprised at his ability to read the photo so well. Where had she been to get this face-front view? Ahead of him, even closer to the danger, back turned to the gunfire that had broken out and killed him? Yes, that had been the case, she told him. It was the POV she wanted. And, he thought, that point of view had been worth her life.

He gently pressed her for more details. The firing had begun the instant she'd gotten the picture she wanted. She'd thrown herself face down, her head hitting against something hard. The rest of the squad, advancing, firing desperately, passed over her. A two-man ambush and they'd gotten them both. She'd raised her head to the silence, her head against the side of the dead soldier whose picture she'd snapped moments before. A medic helped her up, asking if she was OK. There was nothing to do for his buddy except carry him away. She watched that happen, following along, taking no pictures.

She halted her story, not used to talking about herself in this way. Interested more in the intensity of the scrutiny he'd brought to the photo he still held in his hands. He put the photo down, not wanting to give it up. It was a bond between them. He turned to this waif-woman, overwhelmed by an emotion akin to the love a parent felt for a brilliant, lunatic child.

They walked out into the warm Saigon evening. Together. It was what he felt and she, without word or deed, seemed to go along. Her talent filled him with admiration and remorse at his useless life. He'd never learned anything of substance, never took any talent and honed it to a point of perfection. A useless life.

It was late; the occasional taxi came by, slowed, moved away. They seemed to be drifting, the quiet letting one moment play into the next. No touch, overt or accidental, passed between them. He was content to walk down darkened streets indifferent to the possibilities of danger, feeling safe in her company, willing to get by on her luck, hoping for her sake it would hold up for a good long while. They came up on the Presidential Palace, its French Colonial grandeur encircled by a high, ornate fretwork fence and closed gates decorated with elaborate grillwork. Nervous Vietnamese cops and soldiers in starched uniforms looked out from sandbagged sentry boxes at all who passed. He asked if she'd like to go for a drink. The bar at the Caravelle was open until two. No, she would be up at five to rejoin her outfit, the 173rd, which saw constant action. She lived nearby. He walked her home.

Her name was Mara. "An Old Testament name, it means bitterness," she said, with an odd smile and left him at her front door, but not before he extracted a promise that she'd meet him on her return. "About five days, I think. Check at the AP office. I'll leave a message." He watched as she slipped through the gate of the villa, a resolute stride so much a part of her, never looking back, disappearing into the darkness beyond the doorway.

# FORTY-ONE

Happy to return to the normal chaos of life, a good excuse gave him the chance to spend his own five days up country in Nha Trang. He spent those days enjoying the seaside, taking advantage of the local talent, hanging out with fellow Americans who kept generators flowing, heavy equipment going, and making sure all's right with their world. The honest among them were paid for twelve-hour shifts. The greedy logged eighteen hours, though they all spent at least half that work time drinking at the club, or the local bars, or at the beach waterskiing, skin diving, or anything their hearts and minds desired. It was good duty. Safe, clean, air fresh as a sea breeze, plenty to do, pussy galore.

The beach stretched in a sensuous curve for miles toward a distant promontory atop which a tall tower, struck by the rays of the descending sun, glistened blood red against the darkening sky. His comrades-in-arms knew nothing about it, were indifferent to this speck on their horizon, save for one scholar among them who said, "They owned the place for a thousand years. They're not here anymore." He added, "Their queen had a hundred husbands. Sounds like my first wife." None remarked on this cuckold's confession. Who around here had not betrayed, and been victim of betrayal in their turn? Thus it was. Thus it would ever be. None of it was as important to him as this tidbit of information about that faraway, cliff-side tower.

It was time to get back to Saigon. Alone, he wandered onto the beach. Little light remained. The faraway tower was disappearing into the darkness. Yet it still loomed, a thousand-year presence in the land. Whitecaps began their roiling dance; a chilling breeze came off the water. He went inside to pay his bill. The waiter, pointing to the tower, told him in imperfect English that his uncle had a car and could take him there tomorrow morning.

So it happened that he changed his plans and found himself in an antique Renault driven by an even more ancient guide and driver chugging up, up, up a one-lane cliffside road, finally reaching the top to race along an edge offering such a stunning view of morning sea and sky that it would have meant nothing to him to be launched from that cliff into the welcoming heavens. Instead, they came to a stop beside a crumbling wall. An old man stood at what once might have been a gated entrance. A small bill was offered and silently accepted.

They passed through a dusty compound toward a hundred-foot-high tower. Two sets of low steps rose to an entrance supported by thick, rounded columns. Above the massive entrance two more levels rose skyward in perfect symmetry. The gentle waters of the bay, white clouds, the mountains beyond, were background to the silence, the tranquility of the place.

"Marco Polo? You know Marco Polo?" his guide asked him. He nodded, "Here. He came here. Seven hundred years ago, he came here." The old man shook his head in wonder at the idea. "To see the King of Champa. To see his three hundred children." A queen with a hundred husbands, a king with three hundred heirs. "A thousand years the kingdom, a thousand years." The old man seemed to be contemplating this immensity of time. "What happened to them?" asked the innocent abroad. "Vietnamese killed them. A thousand years." Was that defiance, or a cautionary warning he saw in the squaring of those ancient shoulders?

He followed his guide inside. The shock, the dismay of an immense room filled with figures on pedestals confronted him. Not animals he realized, but humans with the heads of elephants. "Ganesh," his guide whispered. As he strained his memory to recall what that meant, his guide said, "Elephant God." Gods they are indeed, in the place where they belong. He'd seen them in museums or for sale in galleries where sculpture was what they were. But here? Here they were Gods, surveying the world and all who dwell therein. Delicate carving brought out the refinement of the stone. A trunk bent toward an open hand that held a lotus flower. Massive heads atop broad shoulders seemed a natural evocation of animal and man.

As he looked at the strangeness of these beautiful things, their power overtaking him, he felt the return of an old regret. His base ignorance, his failure to follow through on study of any subject, his abject stupidity lashed, lacerated him. He knew a little bit of this, a little less of that, slothful to a turn. Steered to another room, a massive God in human form peered at him. Ten arms, a third eye, a Mona Lisa smile. "Shiva," he said. The old man agreed. One of the Hindu Big Three, he remembered. Shiva, Vishnu, and the big guy, Brahma. "See, I ain't so stupid a fucker after all?" he asked no one in particular. But this is a Buddhist country. Why all this Hindu stuff? He didn't know and doubted he'd ever know. He looked closely at Shiva, the Destroyer. Vietnam his perfect dwelling place. But Shiva restored as much as he destroyed, and women wanting children offered him their prayers. "We go now," the old man said. "Bigger place better place." They left this ruin of a sacred place, still sacred if he wished to guess.

The drive took them inland, into a valley, then another, and another. Brilliant green rice paddies, their single shoots emerging from muddy water, filled fields on both sides of a dirt road that unraveled before them. Farmers stooped to their tasks, backs bent, hands deep in water and mud. Immense water buffalo, their great curved horns pointing skyward, pulled wooden plows, urged on by the occasional gentle tap of a switch fashioned from a tree branch. A flock of snowy egrets, spooked by the car, took flight, white wings carrying them to a safer place. He nodded off, awakened when the car jerked to a stop. Overwhelmed by heat and the damp of his own sweat, he watched the old man in conversation with a woman outside what seemed to be a small store. Satisfied, he got back in the car. "Safe. No mines." With no time for this assurance to sink in, the car more antelope than automobile bounced through potholes, scrambling up the mountainside. About the time he could take no more, they came to a stop. Carefully lifting himself from the car, he followed along a narrow path closed in on both sides by high bushes, remembering the old man had said "No mines." But was still careful to walk a step behind. They crossed a sagging footbridge, then another. The path narrowed until both shoulders brushed dense foliage. Humming sounds of insects, a bird's sharp cry, the soaking heat on a path to he knew not where, exhausted him. The path opened and he saw a running brook course between heaps of rubble before disappearing around a bend toward tall trees. Piles of broken stone, sculptured pieces of arms and heads were scattered about, remains of the Gods he'd seen that morning. On the other side of the road, an immense crater filled with water was the burial place of a grotesquely leaning section of a huge red stone temple. He walked along the running brook but was brought to a halt by the old man saying, "VC here."

"Viet Cong! Here?" Panic in his voice, the adrenalin coursing through him, the fear gripping his insides, was shamed to calm when he was told, "Not now. Big bombs, very big bombs. All dead from bombs." Then added, "Hear planes, not see planes." As he listened to these fragments of language, he saw, on the other side of a tall stand of trees, the tops of towers twice the height of the temple he'd seen that morning. The Viet Cong must have used the place as a hideaway, a headquarters as safe from their enemies as it had been for their ancestors. Until the technology of war caught up with them, aerial surveillance brought the rain, the tempest, of B-52s flying high, dropping their loads as good boys always do on people and places and things deserving of their ardor. Thousand-year-old buildings turned to dust. A campsite blown to rags. Bodies pulverized. What might be left of the dead removed. Pro patria for sure. Which of our bombardiers could know anything about the Kingdom of the Champa? For that matter, what could those boys on the other side know of the splendid buildings they used for hideouts, for toilets, for sleep, for war? Did our enemies wander around in wonder at carved stone animals, topless towers, Gods whose names they'd never known? Shiva, God of Destruction was there, and had exacted his price at a rate of exchange leading to death. The miracle was that anything survived. But take bets on it, these sacred precincts, where the Gods have their sport with us, will be here when we are long gone and dimly remembered.

They walked past the destruction toward a ruin caused by insidious time. The havoc of weather, the drip of water, patient seedlings bursting through brick to reach for the sun, thick vines and trees a mournful accompaniment. Within the temple he saw, in the shadow of a wall, two voluptuous figures. Darling boobs, cleavage and narrow waist, hips a sinuous reminder of pleasure. Sex objects. It was time to get back to things he knew and could understand.

In the car, his wise driver, pointing to his stomach, asked, "Eat?" On reaching level ground, the car shot down a side road to a hovel beside a stream. An old woman, more gums than teeth, welcomed them with a smile. Outside the pathetic dwelling was a table and chairs. As he approached, the odor of cooking crept up to greet him. The old woman went into the house and brought out four trout so fresh they might have jumped from brook to plate. She grinned as he waved a hand in approval. His driver fetched large plates of spring rolls, their soft white wrapping filled with bits of shrimp and cut up greens to be dipped in a mysterious sauce enhancing their flavors tenfold. The trout split open, center bone removed, head intact, slathered in a green sauce smelling of garlic, all for him, of course. But our gallant insisted, absolutely insisted, on sharing two of the trout, anyway, with his providers. His largesse gratefully accepted, there they sat down beside the running waters, sampling the trout's soft white flesh. Who could ask for more?

But there was more. The old fellow went into the hut to get a large carton whose first use had been to hold cans of GI tomato sauce. He waited as the new contents of the box were revealed. The dishes cleared, twelve golden shapes, ten or so inches high, stood before him, exquisite versions of the women in stone he'd seen on the mountain. He became absorbed in the beauty of a piece, its sensuality, sinuosity. It exuded a languor, an indifference to those who might behold its breasts, nipples carved to a splendid roundness, a left hip thrust to one side. "Beautiful," he said.

"Old, very old. Of gold," he was told. "Champa. Maybe seven hundred year." One was handed to him. As it came into his hand he gently traced the carving with a finger, could see the refinement the piece possessed as it began to possess him in turn. He placed it carefully down on the table. "You like?" Of course he did. "Buy them?"

"How much?"

Any tradesman from Phoenicia to a present day souk would have been proud to see this old man quickly produce pen and paper, hesitate a moment as he calculated the measure of his mark, and with a flourish wrote one million. "For all," he said, gesturing to the lot. He assumed it was in Vietnamese currency, but even at black market rates it was beyond anything he could afford. All Americans were millionaires to these guys. Taking pen in hand he isolated one piece and wrote a price equivalent to two hundred and fifty dollars. The old man gravely shook his head, took back the pencil and brought the price for one to five hundred dollars. Caught up in the game, no way to know if they were truly gold, desire overwhelming caution, he offered six thousand piastres figuring, at black market rates, to cost him about four hundred dollars. A done deal.

The sculpture came into his hand. He felt it warm him, offer comfort to what might pass for his soul. The box repacked, they made their goodbyes. Let the seller pay for lunch. It was worth a detour, as the French like to say. Racing back to Nha Trang, he cashed a check at the local black-marketeer to pay off his merchant-driver, smugly congratulating himself, "Wait 'til Danny Long sees this."

On the way back to Saigon that evening, his idyll over, the big chopper descended suddenly to pick up a man who'd had a heart attack in a remote, up-country location. A Navy corpsman with him for the ride to a hospital, doctors, the best America could offer a

U.S. citizen. The man did not look good, his color gone, his eyes staring with fear and pain at this group of strangers accompanying him he knew not where. The kid medic in contact by radio with the hospital thirty-five minutes away had learned to handle the sucking chest wound, the blasted arm or leg, bodies half blown away but salvageable — wounds that came to the young. Trauma was his business, not the intricacies of a beating heart. The old guy began to slip, breathing erratic, eyes back in his head as the kid ran through his repertoire of skills that could not help this man who moved frightened eyes toward the cast of characters assembled for his last act. The helicopter steadily beat the air as the stranger floated on that sound, trying to emulate its regularity, slipping instead into a set of spasms, then the final gasp of breath. "Goddamn it," said the medic. Goddamn it, the living had to agree. His blanket a makeshift-shroud, the dead man went along with them on their journey back to Saigon.

He was not superstitious; did not think a man dying in his presence was an omen of anything. The bad luck belonged to the poor bastard who'd come out here to make a buck and instead had bought the farm far from home.

## FORTY-TWO

The job for her brother in hand he was determined to exact a pound or two of flesh by inveigling Thanh to pick up the work papers at his apartment. He called it fascination, more obsession, toward this woman so sensual-seeming, yet failing him in every way he might call sexual. Mara would be kept in reserve, a common way he had of doing business.

Early the next morning, quite early, Thanh appeared. The smile, the style, the welcoming cheek-to-cheek embrace had become familiar, not yet dulled by repetition, as she offered these delights to a stranger in so strange a land. A small overnight bag she carried gave him no pause since he'd learned to expect little from her in the realm of such things. "Why don't we go to Cap St. Jacques for the weekend?" she said, naming a remarkable stretch of beach by its old French colonial name. A few hours south of Saigon, it was now called, by the new order, Vung Tau. "When? Next weekend?"

"No. Today. Are you busy?"

"No, not at all."

"Can you get a car?" He had been using a Honda 250 to get around town, but could borrow the Greek's VW Bug. "How are you managing this?" he asked. "My cousin's family is in France for a while so no one is using their villa."

"I mean your parents, how can you…" She interrupted. "They're at our pepper plantation in Pleiku." The ever-dutiful, ever-obedient daughter was doing what all daughters do when opportunity lurks. That is to say, fuck around. The happy recipient of such favors could only reply, "Why not?"

Most roads beyond Saigon were hairy dangerous. A chopper, for safety's sake, was the transport of choice. But away they went, the happy pair on a fifty-mile jaunt to who knew where? Saturday traffic jammed the road to Long Thanh. From there, they dropped south past ruined rubber plantations whose thick foliage made wonderful cover for infiltrating VC. Near a bend in a river, as they watched the mix of river traffic, gunfire erupted from a side road in the direction of the rubber trees. Filipino soldiers manifesting great courage were firing from inside their armored vehicles. Leaves and trees were blasted away while traffic went its merry way in both directions. All's right with the world.

The hour's drive to Ba Ria, the next turnoff, took them deep into rural Vietnam. He had no doubt there was lots of army around, from both sides, but a pastoral air, a pace attached to growing things, an eventual harvest, the pleasures of the hearthside, seemed the controlling element. As he shifted gears her hand rested on his; when he glanced her way he found her eyes on him. Shut up and drive, hold on to the moment, he said to himself. And went on driving, feeling the touch of her hand.

When they reached Ba Ria, she asked him to stop. The tiny market square was mobbed. Not all of them shoppers. Whole families stared out at an uncaring world. A child, urged by an older sister, approached him with a hand outstretched. Thanh emerged from a store with two cans of Coke. Ah, America the beautiful, he thought, while placing a few coins in the outstretched little hand. As they drove on, he asked Thanh about the families gathered there. "Farmers forced from their land by the fighting. The VC goes into the villages and farms for food, and to hide. Your army forced them from their homes to keep them from helping the VC. Now they are in the towns and cities without work, or money or food to eat." Her matter-of-fact reply implied sadness, acceptance, a bit of anger. It was the way things were. They were drawn to a sudden view of blue water as the road came close to the shore then veered inland on the last stretch to Vung Tau. Car windows open to catch the welcome breeze, he drove toward the waters of the South China Sea, pleased with himself and his companion. She had him turn onto an unmarked side road leading to a wall and a gate that opened, as if in a dream, letting them inside the grounds of a chateau that might have been moved stone by stone from Brittany.

With barely a chance to take in the perfection of the place they were descended upon by servants who opened doors, grabbed bags, and disappeared into the house. An elderly couple, clearly in charge, awaited their arrival at the top of the stairs. Greeting Thanh with in-their-places warmth, they held open beautifully carved doors leading to the cool interior. Escorted up the stairs, feeling underdressed for the occasion, he took in the opulence of the place. One of the native-bearers held his bag before an open door. He watched Thanh head to a room down the hall. She turned with a smile, no doubt having anticipated his chagrin, and told him lunch was waiting whenever he was ready. My needs are many, he said to himself. And one of them is a proper lunch. He took in the sight of his monk-in-a-cell narrow bed. Only its size would suggest the ascetic life since the bedding and coverlet were piled high for comfort. A majolica ceramic bowl and pitcher rested on a dresser of polished pine. Either piece would have set an antique dealer's heart aflutter. The beauty of the little room carried his eyes toward a view of beach and sea. He sat on the edge of the bed, allowing a moment to come to his senses. This was not his life — it was only the life he was living. He would descend the stairs, walk out onto a terrace, table set for two, his darling awaiting him, old retainers standing by to seat and serve.

Monsieur would wish to approve the wine, non? A white burgundy, a Chassagne-Montrachet was set before him. "Christ in his mercy infinite, where did this come from?" he asked himself. Displaying delight prickled with amazement, his eyes rose to his eager sommelier. Sniffed, sipped, and approved with a knowing nod, he watched as two glasses were carefully filled. They toasted to health and happiness.

A white tureen was placed on the table. A wispy vapor came to his nostrils. "Bisque de homard" was quietly murmured as if lobster bisque needed any introduction. He barely remembered to offer "bon appétit" before savoring his first spoonful. Thanh smiled as he gave thanks for such an offering to the Gods. Small, discreet cubes of tender lobster floated in the combination of cream, brandy, fish stock, and lobster shells that had, no doubt, been crushed and added to the soup then carefully sieved away. And then the sherry, added at the last moment to make a bisque to be savored here if not in heaven. Thanh urged him to a second helping. He allowed a mere half-bowl, plus a refilled glass of the Montrachet.

As plates were cleared his eyes turned to the view from the terrace. The beach spread before them, glistening sand winking a welcome to one and all. Turning away from nature and nature's god he listened carefully as quenelles de poisson was announced. Carefully shaped white balls of fish poached to a turn were bathed in a white sauce tasting of pepper and nutmeg and cream. And was that a touch of parmesan melted within the sauce? The platter was garnished with shrimp, plump oysters, and mussels. Heaven can wait, he said to himself, and so can the shellfish, as he helped himself to the quenelles and sauce mornay. A second bottle was placed before him for his consideration. A Meursault from the Clos de Mon Plaisir. Indeed. "Will you join me in a glass?" our gallant asked his lovely.

"Of course," came the reply.

Politely waving of the need to taste before serving, he watched the pale yellow liquid poured into his glass catch light flowing over the shaded terrace, seeing the moment as an eternity. Eternal not in the sense of forever, but here, now. Before him a woman, a table laden with wine, and gifts from the sea. Sun, soft air, hovering help at the ready to assist. Wasn't it always thus? He had no gift for self-examination. The past? The future? Wrapped neatly into the present. An odd gift to himself yielding an empty return. Lunch was over. He begged off from dessert agreeing only to a plate of petit fours to accompany strong black coffee.

Thanh suggested a walk on the beach. Hot sun, four glasses of wine? A stagger, not a stroll, but he was game. A fulsome merci beaucoup was passed to the sublime cook who shyly accepted their thanks. Excusing himself for a wash-up he moved slowly up the stairs for one so young and strong. But the day beckoned, as did a walk on the beach. Isn't that what he hoped life to be?

The road to the beach was lined with families sitting alongside tethered animals and bags of possessions. They had that stoic look he'd begun to take for granted. But their listlessness was overwhelming. "More refugees?" he asked. Thanh nodded.

"It seems worse here," he said.

"They are rice farmers whose dikes have been destroyed in the fighting. There's no work for them."

At the beach, GIs played games with sports equipment made available by a grateful nation. Thanh wore a two-piece bathing suit covered by a gauzy white overgarment. The young buckos checked out his companion, staring a bit longer than good manners required. "Get your kicks were you can," he said to himself.

Aren't beach towns the same the world over? Sun-drenched, an anticipation, an expectation, of waves and surf and sand. The sort of existence that counts on first things: air, light, hard-packed sand wetted by the tides, softer granular sand out of reach of the water warming toes or a body in repose. Turning toward white sand and the South China Sea, he was drawn to the water's edge. A wavelet lapped at his feet. Oblivious to swooping gulls and swimmers splashing through their strokes, he marked the long curve of the bay as it rounded a far point.

So many walks on so many beaches. Wellfleet, Truro, Provincetown, and the edges of New York in God Bless America. Now, Vung Tau, Nha Trang, Cam Ranh in Vietnam. They each had taken his heavy tread, his trudging heart and given back no answers to questions lit by blue sky or moonlit night. The unremitting surf cursing or caressing the shore offered a place for footprints, rest, escape where he could lose the present, conjure past lives, past loves, and draw what sense he could from the repetitions of engagement and departure, optimism and disappointment crisscrossing his life. A mournful shuffling pace to match his mood of dejection, paralysis. A funeral pace with muffled drum, muted bugle, no trace of tears, weeping long since spent on other woes.

Thanh gently brushed his hand. He returned the touch with a slight caress. She seemed to want to make him happy. He grasped at her good intentions as they moved across the sand.

The warmth of the water coursing over their toes, they quickly escaped the crowd to find themselves in the company of scurrying sandpipers, pelicans wheeling through the air, hovering, swiftly dropping beak-first toward the water with a splash and a swallow. Dozens more arrived, given some secret signal telling of a school of fish passing through the water. No sound but the crash of large birds on water as they went about their business. Not frenzy, but calm, deliberate flight, search, dive, and capture.

They turned their backs to the sun as it began its descent across the bay, coming again upon GIs at play. A short distance away a group of lithe young Vietnamese laughed and lay about as any youth of the world would in this place. But there was something distinctive about these boys. "VC," Thanh whispered.

He stared back at her. "Here? On the beach?"

"Yes, they share the beach with us. Everyone knows about it." American soldiers, tossing around a football, could not have known about their neighbors. Or did they? In this war to bend all wars who knew anything to be straight and true? He let the mad scene play out. Watched his fellow countrymen horsing about in the sun while fifty feet away the enemy lurked, chatting amongst themselves, paying no heed to anything more than sun and sky and sand.

It had been the same in Dalat. A live-and-let-live deal with the devil. But who's from heaven and who from hell? He would have pondered this further but a gathering of people listening to an old man got his attention. They were following his words, some chanting along with him. It was poetry. Though not able to understand a word, he could hear a rhythm that had to be a poem. His audience, in the black dress of country people who'd fled the war, seemed comforted by the sounds of the song-like performance holding them together. A child listened intently, joining what must have been a refrain of some kind. He asked Thanh if she understood the words. "Of course," she said quietly, and turned back to the old man's voice.

"What is he saying?"

"It's a long poem."

"Tell me."

"It's too difficult."

"Try."

"I don't think I can." She was whispering, and he let it go, went back to watching this forlorn, desperate bunch transported to another time and place by the words and sounds around them. The old man paused for just a moment then began again.

Thanh turned to him. "This poem is for a baby sleeping."

"A lullaby?"

"I don't know that word." He leaned toward her. As he heard the music of the words in Vietnamese, she softly said:

" 'Little one, go too sleep. Sleep soundly. Mother's gone to market; father ploughs the field. Our parents toil for our meals, rice and clothing, making the land yield a good home. Grow up, study hard, little one, tend to our native place, mountains and river. Become worthy of the Lac-Hong race. Hopes met, our parents' faces will widen in smiles.' "

He grasped her hand in thanks as she hushed him into silence. A poem began anew and she recited,

" 'A lantern sways from the Banner Pole, the East wind rattles its panes. My love for you is deep-aching, endless. In the tipped dish, I grind ink for a poem: a poem...three or four, saying Wait for. Hope for. Remember. Love.' "

She turned away, not willing to look at him. He was stricken by what he'd heard. A lullaby. A love poem. The decencies of listening and chanting and respect for one another. The humanity of it all. He could take no more. They walked back to their car, but not before he gave a little bow, which went unnoticed, to the old man and his audience.

At dinner, a splendid dinner, he drank near to a bottle of fine Bordeaux. Ordinarily such a meal and such a wine would have been impressed on his memory, but it had flown by unrecorded. The chill in the air brought them to coffee and after-dinner drinks served before a fire in the grand living room. His thoughts continued to turn to those out in the cold night air as he poured a cognac. Those out-of-doors would have set fires for warmth, wouldn't they?

As he rolled his tongue around his cognac, Thanh turned double before his drunken eyes. Enough, he said, pouring another. Thanh talked quietly about the pleasures of the day. Thanked him for taking the trouble to drive down. He nodded, grinned, afraid to look more foolishly drunk. And he was tired. So awfully tired. He stood, and she was suddenly at his side, offering a discreet arm to steady him as they walked to the stairs. Holding on to the polished banister he pulled his dead-weight body up a stair at a time. She was amused by his toil and insistence that he would be all right, was fine, in fact. Until he pushed on his bedroom door, that gave way a bit too suddenly, and was saved from falling on his face by catching hold of her. She slipped this drunken embrace, with so innocent an intention, a seductive arm around his waist.

The narrow bed awaited, coverlet turned down. He sat, a penitent in his little cell, turning to put head to pillow, body to bed. And then another confusion was added to a confusing day. Thanh removed his shoes and socks. Lovely, that, he said to himself. Then she opened his belt, unzipped him and helped him out of his trousers, pulled the shirt over his head. Laid out before her, naked, shivering a bit, he wondered what could be next. She reached into a closet for a pair of silk pajamas and dressed him, turned out the light, touched his cheek with a loving hand, and disappeared.

He leaned back on the pillow. No part of the day to hang onto. No sense, no coherence. A spinning circle. Sworn enemies playing games on the beach within pistol range of each other. Lullabies, and poems of love, forever etched into the lives of eager listeners. How could this be? Grateful for the solitary confinement, he turned his face to the wall, missing out on the starry sky.

# FORTY-THREE

The morning came to his lidded eyes borne on a breeze, no comfort to the pounding temples of a man-sized hangover. A soft blue robe placed on a chair, the fragrance of coffee and fresh baking, encouraged him to slide out of bed, throw on the robe and investigate.

His quivering nostrils found their way to the breakfast room. A servant stood by, awaiting his lordship. Seated, he watched coffee and hot milk poured for café au lait. He nodded his thanks, welcoming its warmth, fearing its effect on his delicate stomach. He didn't dare attend a large woven basket, covered by a linen napkin, from which peeked warm croissants, a brioche or two, and, no doubt, for the truly indulgent, pain au chocolat. Small pots of butter, jam, and juice in a clear pitcher stood at the ready. Headache lifting, he took in the lovely French Provincial kitchen, the view of green hills beyond the bougainvillea, named after a Frenchmen, he recollected, beginning to think that a bite of that croissant might not be a bad idea.

He turned at the sound of Thanh entering the room. He rose to receive the lovely cheek to cheek kisses of her good morning greeting. She spoke, in French, quickly and pleasantly to the old couple. They asked if she slept well and her plans for the day. The chaste nature of their sleeping arrangement seemed to have pleased them. Protectors of womanhood, no doubt.

She sat across from him offering a smile, and a compliment on how well he looked in the blue robe. He noticed she was dressed not for the beach but for travel. So our little idyll is over, he mused, thinking as he always did that he'd never return. Concentrating on a feature of the room to retain, he caressed the polished pine of the tabletop, willing a metamorphosis to transform him into this permanent, impermeable thing.

The fingers of one hand idly moving over a small corner of the table, he watched Thanh bring cup to lips, take a small bite of the brioche, dawdle over a glass of juice, and felt the old exhilaration in the company of a beautiful woman. She watched him watching her, enjoying in her way his silent attention. He had hoped for another walk on the beach, a return to the house for a shot at sharing her bed, not looking forward to returning to noxious, noisy Saigon. But it was not to be. She told him there was no hurry but wanted to get back by early afternoon.

He rose. Thanh walked him to the stairs, quietly asking him to leave a small sum of money, nothing extravagant, on his dresser as a gift for the servants. He nodded in agreement. Almost as an afterthought, she took his hand and told him she'd meet him on the terrace, where she wanted to talk to him about something. He climbed the stairs, restored by breakfast, looking forward to his shower and wondering what this conversation might bring.

Walking onto the terrace the morning sunlight struck his eyes. Thanh was in silhouette looking out to the sea. Turning at his entrance, she came into full focus, beckoning him to share the view. He joined her, slipping an arm around her waist that she accepted, then drew him to a rattan love seat and sat beside him. Something was up. His intuition was rewarded when she told him her father needed help to make a business deal. "He needs two hundred thousand U.S. dollars."

He looked at her worried that she had surmised his score on the air conditioner deal. "I don't have anything like that kind of money," he quickly lied.

"No, no," she said. "He only needs to exchange piastres for dollars." Then added the kicker: "But he can only afford the legal rate, not buy dollars on the black market."

"But, that's a fifty-percent difference. He's got to use the black market like everyone else."

"A man in his position can't be seen to be doing such things." He'd heard that one before. She looked at him, all business. "Can you help us?"

He thought immediately of Frankie Boyle and all the warnings he'd had about him. How guys who worked with him got busted or tossed from the country. He couldn't possibly be a cop, but, no doubt, protected himself by giving up a friend now and then. "Maybe I can talk to someone," he said. She rose satisfied, her business done. The ride back to Saigon was oddly quiet.

# FORTY-FOUR

"Are you outta your fuckin' mind? Two hundred thousand U.S. even up for piastres? That's a fifty-percent premium your gook father-in-law is asking for. Tell him to go fuck himself." Frankie Boyle was in full rant and wasn't ready to quit. "What am I supposed to do with twelve million fuckin' piastres? Wallpaper my bathroom? A hundred thousand U.S. is worth eighteen million not twelve. That's a fifty-percent difference, don't you know that?"

"You already told me that, Jimmy."

"Well I'm gonna tell you again. Anyway she's a lousy piece of ass. They all are. So tell her to go fuck herself and find somebody else to steal it for her."

"OK Frankie, I just thought I'd ask," he said, and got up to leave. Doyle, raising his glass to stop him, took a swallow. "You speak French, doncha?"

"A little, not much. Why?"

"You know I've got a little war surplus business on the side, doncha?"

"Yeah, Frankie, I've heard."

"Sure you have. Well, maybe we can help each other out." Frankie waved him back to his chair. "I've got a load of junk in a trailer I made a deal on and have to make delivery. The guy buying don't speak any English, only Vietnamese and French. He's paying two hundred thousand U.S. for the load."

"What kind of junk is worth two hundred thousand dollars?"

Frankie looked annoyed. "If I name a price, and a guy meets it, what do I care? Look, here's the favor I can do for you. Bring me the 12 million, and you deliver the goods." He paused. Do you know how to unhook a tractor from its trailer?" He shook his head, no. "Well you better learn fast, cause the deal goes down tomorrow night. He pays cash on delivery and the payoff is all yours." Frankie sat back, pleased with himself, he had the Jewboy by the balls, and waited for him to say, "Deal, Frankie. I'll see you tomorrow."

He took a taxi to Thanh's house afraid of what he was getting himself into. Everything he'd ever heard about Doyle screamed, watch your ass, but he was going forward with the scheme. It was showing off to the girl, high-wiring it without benefit of net, it was stupid, so stupid it didn't bear thinking about. He left the taxi, rang the bell at the gate, and was soon in the presence of Lady Fair. He told her he needed to meet with her father. He'd have to have the twelve million tomorrow. Thanh sweetly told him she'd have it for him in the morning. "Nice," he thought. "The old man doesn't want to meet the American or get involved with the dirty work." Thanh, reading his thoughts, said, "My father thanks you. And I thank you, too." Then she delivered up one of those smiles. He guessed it was all worth it.

# FORTY-FIVE

Doyle, driving fast, crossed the river at Phan Than Gian Street onto the highway going north. Within a few minutes he pulled up behind a trailer parked on the side of the road. They both got out and, as the sky darkened, Boyle methodically checked out his newly-acquired skill, unhitching trailer from truck. He was told to drive exactly 14 clicks and turn off at the first side road on the left. They'd be waiting for him with the money in a clearing down that road. "Why not come along, Frankie? You're this far already." Not even an answering grunt. Boyle squeezed himself back behind the wheel and took off.

He watched him drive away, climbed into the cab, and turned the key. The engine growled alive. He'd never driven a ten-wheeler, but what the hell? Part of the fun, right? Pressing the clutch he felt for first gear. The truck lurched forward and stalled. On the third try he got the beast rolling in a gear that seemed acceptable and began to calculate 14 kilometers in U.S. miles, driving straight and true, whistling a happy tune, doing a little business, that's all.

He found the side road and entered the clearing, cut the motor, and waited in the silence and darkness. Four men in black pajamas, Uzis pointed at him, broke from the cover followed by an older man who said something, and the four lowered their weapons. The older man approached carrying a small attache case. He wouldn't have believed it, but Boyle, the prick, was capable of dealing with anyone, including the VC. He got out of the cab and, what the hell, extended his hand. Surprised, the other returned the gesture, exchanged greetings in French and walked behind the trailer. One of the armed men opened the door, and he saw boxes sealed and stacked, marked RADIO 2 WAY.

Opening two or three boxes and assuring themselves of the contents, two in the group saved him the trouble and unhitched the trailer as a second cab drove into the clearing. He pointed to the attache case and it was handed to him. He opened it and was amazed to see fresh U.S. hundred-dollar bills bundled in bank wrappers. A quick count came to no more than a hundred thousand dollars. Approaching the leader he said, "Monsieur! Non, non, non!" A hundred thousand dollars short and goddamned if he'd let them get away with it. And dumb enough to try to keep them from leaving until those Uzis pointed his way brought a change of mind. All that was left was to watch them hitch their own cab to the trailer and drive away.

He sat in the cab of the truck, out a hundred thousand. Ramming the engine into gear, he roared toward Boyle's, hurtling into the small compound where his house stood. He slammed to a stop before a stone barrier and leapt out, attache case in hand. At the door he heard music and laughter. Another goddamn Boyle party. He burst in and Boyle rose quickly and took him down a hallway, as he shouted, "It was only a hundred, you prick." Boyle grabbing his arm in a vise grip pulled him into a side room and closed the door. Shaking the attache case, he said, "I'm short a hundred grand, Boyle. Fuck you and your deals." He tossed the case at him and demanded the piastres entrusted to him by Thanh. Doyle tried to cool him down. "Forget about the piastres, and I'll settle with those gook thieves in my own way. I'll make it good. I got a deal a week going down. Relax yourself, for chrissakes. Come and have a drink."

You had to hand it to Boyle, he thought. Playing it cool and bluffing, he was sure. "Bullshit, Frankie, and stuff the drink up your ass. I need this money before the fifth."

"What the fuck is the hurry? What a minute, you're not falling for that fifth day of the fifth month crap, are you? Talk about bullshit. These fuckers will do a deal any day or night or month or fuckin' year. They'd do a deal dancin' on their fuckin' mother's grave. Look, I got somethin' comin' down next week. No gooks, no gun. Just a delivery. And it'll bring you your hundred thousand." "Delivery? Of what?" "You don't need to know, you don't need to find out. Are you in?" Maybe Frankie wasn't bluffing. "I'm in."

Frankie put a sweaty arm around him. "Let's go get that drink."

He pulled away slightly. "When is this coming off?"

"Next Thursday. The seventh. Look at that, Lucky seven." Boyle gave him a smile and stalked back to his party. He passed on any good ol' boy conversation and headed to Thanh's house.

A servant opened the door. Thanh and her family were at dinner. Her father looked up, then looked toward Thanh, who rose and walked toward him, confident, lovely. She took him into the parlor. Before they could sit down he told her he only had a hundred thousand and the rest would come next week. Showing only the slightest disappointment, she excused herself and brought her father into the room. He rose at the arrival of this rotund gentleman in white suit and another Hermès tie, welcomed graciously in French. It was soon clear that French was lost on him and Thanh began speaking in Vietnamese to her father who listened quietly, learning that his date with the fates was being delayed. Her father, looking him over carefully, said something to Thanh. "My father says he is sorry to make so much trouble for you and invites you to join us for dinner." Such an offer! Such magnanimity!

The great good manners, the generosity of these upper classes, his betters, never failed to intrigue him. Poppa might be out his extra thousand, but never blinked, showing a stoicism that had to connect to Buddhism. But the family was Catholic, he knew. Papist or not, Poppa placed his bets across the board.

He took his seat, nodding to his hostess, sipping wine from a crystal goblet. He partook, belonged. He'd arrived.

# FORTY-SIX

"So, OK, Boyle, what's the deal?" Boyle, golf bag of elephant hide at his side, was running late for tee time. But business is business and he collapsed into a chair. "And I want the whole story, Frankie, none of this bullshit about surplus junk that turns out to be new radios still in their boxes." Boyle eyed him and quickly dismissed the idea he might be a cop. Okay, Jewboy, he said to himself. The more you know, the deeper you're in.

"Didja hear about the drug bust at the airport last week?" He hadn't. "Ten KG of heroin, that's over twenty tons. A regular delivery coming in from Laos. It's the third time this month."

"So?"

"So that's what this is about. Somethin' is goin' on and I'm doin' a favor for a friend to help him out with a pickup."

"Of heroin?"

"No, you fucker, diapers for his baby. What do you think I'm talkin' about? Jesus!"

"I don't know Boyle, that's nasty shit." He wasn't sure if this was a moral judgment. Boyle, a good salesman dealing with an objection, looked at him.

"These people smoke and chew this stuff like aspirin. Head colds, arthritis, rheumatism, anything that fucks 'em up. They're desperate; the price on the street has gone nuts. We're doing a service, it's an act of charity."

"That's a new one on me, Frankie. What about the big users, the addicts?"

"You're talkin' stateside crap. The niggers and spics back there stealing from their mothers and peddling their sisters are fuckin' junkies." Boyle became indignant. "There's not anything like that goin' on here." He waited for some response. "Look, I got a golf date, are you in?"

"How's this supposed to work?"

"They figured another plane load would be picked up so they sent a load by truck. It's in town right now. You get the truck, deliver it, and the hundred thousand you need is yours. He paused. And an extra ten percent for you."

"When do I get it?"

"When you're done just come on back to Daddy Boyle's and it will be waiting for you."

"Where's the truck?" Doyle stood and grabbed his golf bag. "Parked on Ky Dong. It's only a few blocks long. Look for an old Mercedes truck with the number 913 on its side. Drop it off in front of the Bat Dat Hotel in Cholon on Dong-Khanh street. You know the place?"

He nodded. "How come you can't get some local guy to drive the truck?"

" 'Cause Americans are trustworthy, courteous, and obedient, like all good Boy Scouts. Hey, you'll be the first whiteboy in the drug business." Heaving the golf bag to his shoulder he moved toward the door. "I got a bunch of guys waitin' at the club who think they're goin' to hustle me. We'll see who does the hustlin'." He stopped at the door, remembering something. "Oh, yeah." He reached into his pocket. "I almost forgot." He tossed a key ring, adroitly snatched out of the air, and said. "See you later."

A taxi took him to Ky Dong out by the airport. As they neared the street, a noxious odor filled the air. The stench filled his lungs; he felt it on his skin. Ky Dong Street was an immense garbage dump. He'd finally gotten used to the heat of Saigon, but this was something else. Hot sun searing through piles of garbage cooked it to a fetid stew. He tried to imagine Thanh's father walking here. Did he even know of such a place? There seemed to be a hierarchy of scavengers. At the bottom, Vietnamese women wearing cone-shaped straw hats were picking up tin cans, removing their tops and bottoms, slitting them down their sides, flattening, then tossing them into large baskets. He seen them used as siding and roofs for the shacks that had grown around the city. Men broke up wooden pallets for bundles of firewood. Small children played at throwing rocks at rats, while older brothers and sisters searched through the wet piles looking for anything salable.

The taxi driver wanted out of there, pronto. He paid the fare and saw the truck, parked at the edge of a sea of rotted leavings. One front fender gone, it seemed part of the landscape. He walked past, nonchalant, on his way to an appointment. But there sat the truck, representing a hundred thousand plus and god knows what else. "Fuck it," he said aloud to no one in particular, jumped into the cab and rode away, not noticing a figure emerge from a shack and speak into a two-way radio.

The truck, a wreck on the outside, ran racing-car-right. He cruised his merry way, carrying his cargo of H to Saigon's Chinese quarter. He knew checks cashed at his black market money-changer always passed through a Hong Kong Chinese bank; the Chinese of Cholon were into anything that could turn a dollar or a dong. He had learned that dong is what the Vietnamese called piastres and begun chuckling at its absurdity when, suddenly, he was cut off by an Army truck. He jammed the brakes hard, bouncing head and face off the window. Dazed from the impact he was forced to the other side of the cab by a soldier who took over the wheel. Surrounded by Vietnamese police, he swore that no matter what happened, he'd bring that asshole Boyle down with him. As his head cleared a bit, he saw they were continuing into Cholon. He assumed he was off to jail. But why hadn't he been cuffed?

Instead of a police station, the truck pulled up in front of two-story building. He was pulled out, shoved inside, hustled into a back room. A mirror showed the swelling over his eye. The door opened and two men in raincoats, dressed like French detectives from the movies, entered. They searched him, looked through his wallet while trying to ask him questions in very bad English. "Who you? "What you do for truck?" "Why you durb?"

"No understand," he said.

Angrily, the senior of the pair said, loudly, "Durb!! Goddamn, why you durb?"

He began to be frightened, when it came to him. "Drive?" he asked. "Why I drive?"

"Yes, why you durb?" How to explain that he was doing a favor for a friend of a friend? It was the truth. Glowering, they left. And he was left with his thoughts. They might be cops, but this was no police station. They probably had stolen the load, but what did they want with him? They could have shot him on the spot. Instead, they were curious about him. A headache seized his temples, and he closed his eyes.

Loud voices outside awakened him. He'd been asleep for a while, undisturbed. It made no sense. As he came awake, he heard laughter and a distinctly American voice he recognized. Going to the unlocked door, he opened it a crack and saw a giant of a man, towering over the slightly built men in the room, slapping one on the back, putting an arm around another and, finally, advancing in his direction. It was Johnny the Greek. He opened the door to John, who drew him out with a flourish. Clucking solicitously over his battered face, "Mon ami," John said grandly, embraced him, and walked him toward the smiling group who so recently had held him prisoner. John shook hands with the older man who clearly was in charge, had him do the same, and sailed him out. He passed on John's offer of lunch at The Fuji, starved instead for an explanation. "What the fuck is going on?" Where are we going?"

I'm dropping you at Boyle's. Isn't that where you want to go?"

"Come on John, cut the crap. What was going on back there? How did you know I was there?" John smiled. "Didn't I tell you to watch yourself with that fat pig Irishman?"

"Yeah, yeah, everybody tells me that. So, what's going on? "

"Take care of business first."

When they arrived at Boyle's, John tossed his thumb at the house. "He's waiting for you." He slowly left the car, his head aching. John invited him to lunch the next day at Arc en Ciel. He mumbled yes, stumbling down the path. The door was opened before he reached the top step. "Holy shit, what happened to you?" said Boyle. He brushed past the solicitude, walked into the living room and wearily sat down. Boyle called out a girl's name and a pretty little thing came running with ice. He winced as she tried to apply a cold compress. But her hands did feel good on his neck. "She's one of the caddies I'm fuckin'. Cute 'eh? Remember I told you? The caddies are all little chicks like her. I bring one back after every round I play." He smiled at his wounded friend. "You ought to take it up. It's a terrific game."

Small talk, the prick is giving me small talk, he thought. But he wasn't interested. He waved the girl away. "What the fuck happened back there?" Boyle, pouring himself a drink, offered him one and was refused. "Listen, I gotta apologize. It was a fuckup. A problem in communication." He sounded pleased with his explanation.

"Commun-a-fucking-cation? I've got a busted face, and your talking like some fucking social worker." Boyle answered him by reaching behind the bar and handing him a cardboard box. "Here you go, one thousand crisp and shiny hundred-dollar bills. That should make your head feel better." It did, it surely did. "What about the extra ten percent?" Boyle airily gestured with an open hand. "Oh, Johnny had to spread that around to spring you. Didn't he tell you?"

"No, he didn't. Anyway, how did he know I was there?"

"A little favor he did for me. And for you too, in case you didn't notice." He looked at the box with Thanh's hundred thou, satisfied with the outcome, but wanted to know more. "Were those morons back there cops?" "Sure, they're cops. How do you think they make a living? Anyway, the fuckup was they thought you were stealing the load. Somebody had forgotten to tell them a round-eye was in on it."

“So I get a busted head ‘cause someone forgot to make a phone call?”

“Somethin’ like that. Listen, it’s all over, the deal is done, you did good. For chrissakes, you took out two hundred thousand in a week.” Boyle was returning to form.

He staggered to his feet, loot-in-a-box in hand. He wanted no more of Boyle’s rant. “You goin’? You’re gonna drop that off? Let me drive you, I’m goin’ into town anyway.” Doyle offered a hand to pull him to his feet. “What’s the address?”

“On Mac Dinh Street.”

“That’s where our embassy is.”

“They live across the street.” If he’d been less fogged in by his cracked head he’d have seen that Doyle, dropping him off, would now know where his girlfriend, and more to the point, her very important father, lived.

He approached the front door and the kid brother, still sullen as any teenager, stared at his busted face. He asked for Thanh and learned she was up in Pleiku with her father. He’d planned a grand entrance with the cash, hoping for some small show of gratitude. So, what to do with the cash he was carrying? It would be nuts to walk around with that kind of money or stash it in his apartment, and just as crazy to turn it over to this kid. He was saved from making a decision when the mother walked in. She saw his face, led him to the living room, and called a maid who appeared in a moment.

A tea service was brought in on a silver tray. Delicate cloisonne cups were filled. Sugar was offered and accepted. Her features were broader than Than’s, her height about the same. Dressed in lovely ao dai of white silk, a large diamond on her finger, she finally spoke, in French, something about his face he figured. He waved it away as nothing, a small thing. He’d hoped to tell Thanh the whole story. Instead he sipped his tea, letting it reach inside him, calming him after a day of garbage dumps, a car crash, and who knows what else might have happened. And for what? The action, sure, and the reaction from Thanh, which wasn’t going be. Her American has delivered the goods, period. No doubt, they would pass onto other things, other favors she needed.

He handed the box to his hostess. She opened it, eyes widening. Clearly she'd been in on everything. He wanted to take out the bundles of hundreds, count them before her. But he watched as she quickly closed the box, laid it off to the side, and turned to her tea. This is how the upper classes treat their help, he mused. Enough, he thought, I'm outta here. He rose, took her hand to gently press near to his lips, never touching, showing what a class act he was, departing for home and an aspirin for his aching head.

# FORTY-SEVEN

The Arc en Ciel, where he would be joining John for lunch, was in the heart of Cholon. In stores on the avenue dead ducks hung from hooks, near suckling pigs basted and roasted. A return to the scene of the crime. The Greek was beside himself, uninterested in anything more than busting his balls for getting involved with Boyle. "Those bozos were going to drop the dime on you, give you up as cover to get the green light for anything they were into. You were perfect. A goddamn round-eye caught with a truckload of the goods. You would have been the arrest of the year. They'd have been in the clear forever." His voice was rising in the restaurant, crowded with upscale types.

"So that's what my ten thousand went for, to buy them off?" He paused, pissed off. "I'd have dragged Boyle into it the first words from my mouth."

"Sure you would have."

"So my extra ten percent went out to protect him, too?"

"You got it, baby. You could have brought LBJ himself into it and you still would have seen years in the slammer."

"Why'd you get involved? Are you in on it too?"

"I owed him."

"Owed him for what?"

"Remember that generator I installed at that kids' hospital in Danang? Well, it was courtesy of the Frankie Boyle Marching and

Philanthropic Society." He paused long enough to catch his breath, or so it seemed. "And that deal out there in the goddamn woods could have got your head blown off."

"So you know about that?"

"Sure I do. Those fuckers could just as easily have taken the trailer and the tractor and left you with a dozen bullets instead of paying you off."

"Why didn't they?"

"They were first-time customers of Boyle's. That's why he sent you. He didn't know if he could trust them. He's ripped off all the time. He figures it's the cost of doing business. They get one chance to prove they're honest, if I may use such a word in this conversation. And you were, or could have been, the sacrificial lamb." John let this sink in to the innocent before him.

"Where does Boyle come off selling two-way radios to the VC?"

"First of all it isn't all to the VC. And if you ask him he'll tell you that they'll get it from somebody else, so why not him? The fact is the VC and anybody else is buying anything they goddamn want right off the ships as they come into the harbor. They place their orders from the ship's manifests, and it's cash on delivery. Isn't this a lovely war?" He receded back into his chair, seemingly done with his ball-breaking. "All this for that chick you met that day at lunch, right?"

"Right." He told John about the two-hundred-thousand-dollar exchange her father wanted at the legal rate. "She seemed in such a goddamn hurry. She had to have it before next week."

John told him, "Her father is like all the rest, his life controlled by the lunisolar calendar. The sun, the earth, the moon are lining up just so. He's got to make his deal, whatever it is, on the fifth day of the fifth month. May the fifth. Very auspicious."

"Auspicious? It sounds more like superstitious," he said.

The Greek waved at him with his fork. "This is a country of spirits and ghosts more alive than we'll ever understand. We'll never get it. We're here on a pass, if you know what I mean. And when we're out of here, the old ways will resurface. They've only been out of sight to the likes of us."

As this settled in around them, John added, "As long as I'm ragging your ass let me tell you something more. These people are all about their families. It's a wonder to behold, as long as you're part of it. But to get inside is near to impossible. You're not gonna marry her, are you?" No, he wasn't going to marry her. "And none of 'em fuck worth a damn, so it can't be about pussy." He had to acknowledge it wasn't about pussy, either.

"Sort it out for yourself. Enough of this bullshit. I'm gonna order lunch. On you."

# FORTY-EIGHT

Stretched out on the couch in his apartment, the overhead fan offering comfort from the heat of the afternoon, the concussion about healed, a residue of bitterness clung to him. If John was right, he could be dead. And for what? What madness sent him out on that lunatic chase simply to please a woman? He'd been forced to ask that question more than once in his life. The answers always partial, contingent on circumstance. Women were always there. It was a given in his life. Give this one up, boy, before it gets away from you. Other adventures await you. Things equal to the same thing are equal to each other, are they not? Euclid has his uses beyond plane geometry, does he not? He'd find out what John was up to these days and tag along. It was work, wasn't it? Work and Love. He'd hitch those twin ponies to his chariot and away he'd go.

He was determined to have no more to do with Thanh. Except on his terms. She'd have to seek him out. No doubt she would, said the egoist within, continuing to work on his behalf. The door to his apartment opened, and there stood his nemesis. He'd given her a key as a demonstration of his fervor and fidelity. She approached with a womanly manner he'd not seen before, her purpose to thank him for services rendered. He drew her toward his bedroom, surprised by her ardor, feeling the power of both the pleasure and the indifference that came over him.

Events of that afternoon did not deter him from a decision made. He had enough discipline to consider her visit a trifle, a bagatelle, not more than that. When they were done he'd simply sent her home, or wherever she might be heading.

Mara would be back from her constant to and fro from the war. He'd taken for granted she'd want to see him. And, right you are if you think you are. At the AP office a message from Mara wondered if he could stop by her place that evening. Indeed he could.

She was pleased to see him. The place was a frat-house mess, but never mind. Offered a cup of tea, he accepted with grace though preferring something stronger. She darted about, despite the exhaustion he saw in her face, and he asked about her week away. She dismissed the question with a gesture, cradling a teacup in her hands, its warmth a comfort to her weary bones. He watched as she curled herself into the sofa's cushions, sipping her tea, not offering conversation. He noticed things about her that were hidden from him when they had met that dark night. How the sunlight shining through the window brought a shimmer to her reddish blond hair. How she looked at him so directly, her eyes a shade of blue-green he'd only seen in paintings by old masters. She welcomed quiet, did not mind it at all. She seemed to be taking him in, taking his measure, making up her mind about something. "Strife bewildering," she said. "How is it you know those lines?" She awaited his reply to her simple question, still curled in her place, all but demure, sipping her tea. He told her he'd found it in a book he'd read many years ago. That he was attracted to the book because it had the word "Ambiguity" in its title. He stopped, fearing he'd reveal his lost soul, his easily apprehended weaknesses, and it would be the end of them. He was saved by a noise at the door and recognized one of her companions in the bar. Mara leapt to her feet and hurried to him as he dropped his bag and joined her in an embrace. No, he was relieved to see, not an embrace, but a long hug of welcome home, how wonderful to see you alive. The boy was desperate, he said, for a beer and a shower. The spell was broken, or so he thought. He told her he'd be leaving, hoped to see her again. "Why not dinner tonight, if you're free?" she said. They set a time and place. She offered a cheek, met by his, and away we go.

# FORTY-NINE

The My-Canh Floating Restaurant was Mara's idea. A place in town famous for Cantonese delicacies and a list of fine wines for the well-heeled to enjoy in the company of delicate ladies. Expensive. And he didn't mind at all. A crowded quay gave safe harbor to couples and families moving indolently in the heat of early evening. A small tobacco stand, a bicycle leaning alongside, stood at waterside. The lights along the way took on a golden glow as the bright sky, fading into twilight, brought that peace that passes all understanding.

An elegant gangplank, its railings painted a pretty pastel green, a blue canopy with a white scalloped fringe, protection from sun and rain, offered entrance. Traversing the twenty feet or so from shore to ship, he saw large glass windows looking out on the harbor, elegant customers enjoying one another's company. Four American buckos, in short-sleeved shirts and jeans, distinctive among them a handsome black face, had before them cans of Coke and a fine Bordeaux. Good buddies all. He cringed at seeing Coke added to a glass of the wine, but let it go when he spotted Mara at the bar. It held promise of a lovely evening.

Rather than linger at the crowded and noisy bar, they were led to a table. Following behind he saw how small, how vulnerable she seemed. Dressed in pants, of course, but a tailor's hand had shaped that cloth to match the curve of buttocks in a most delightful way. He couldn't imagine her standing still for a fitting, but then again, what did he know about women? And woman she was. Black jacket a perfect fit over a deep-green silk, open-collared blouse, a finely worked strand of silver setting of a lovely neck.

Waiters in tuxedos, busboys in starched white, scurried about delivering courses, swiftly replacing soiled plates. A mixed bag of American civilians, a sprinkling of French couples, Chinese and Vietnamese men with their lovelies accepting their due. A happy sense of entitlement scented the air. He was transported from the everyday. Able to forget his unlovely life. Able to concentrate his powers on the here and know. It was all there was. He had no recollection of what had been ordered or what had been eaten. A glass of wine, a single beer. An abstemious evening. His head clear, getting the measure, the beat, of each of her words as she quietly described, for herself as well as anyone, a war he'd never see.

"They call their buddies who've been killed, the lucky dead. Can you imagine? The unlucky living forced to be alive another day in this place." She paused. "I'm a fire-fight junkie, I guess."

"You're in as much danger as any soldier," he said.

"Are you asking me if I'm afraid? Afraid to die?" He had no chance to answer as she grinned and said, " 'My dying will be a grave matter.' "

"Oh, ho," he said. "Look who's using Shakespeare on me!"

Pleased with herself, she told him her roommates were having a party back at the house. Could they go back to his place? She giggled as her Romeo too-quickly grabbed the sleeve of a passing waiter, demanding the check.

And then the bombs went off.

"Like a movie," awful cliché, came to him. A silent film, a visual thing, an absence of sound before the screams of terror, of pain, came to him. A busboy thrown against a wall, his large tray of dirty dishes tumbling to the floor, stared in dismay at the sight of a hand separated from his arm. A waiter, leaning forward with a sycophantic gesture was covered in the blood of the patron before him. A Chinese woman he'd noticed earlier, blood now cascading from her mouth onto large pearls descending from a lovely neck stared at her companion sitting there, head torn from his neck. The glass windows had exploded, points of glass savaging flesh with brutal cuts. Bodies, the helpless injured, were everywhere. Those who could rushed the gangplank, trampling those who ran before. Pulling Mara along, he fled for the front door. Her ferocious grip pulled him down to the floor as she shouted, "No, no!" Then a second bomb went off, this time from shore. Perfectly timed Claymores, mines spraying deadly balls of steel slicing through what remained of the place, shredding to pieces those who'd dashed to escape. In the chaos he pondered if there was a Mr. Claymore? To join Mr. Gatling, Mr. Thomson, Mr. Kalishnikov, and other notables who'd given their names to those handy tools of destruction? Encircled by death, he left this crazy meditation to watch that handsome black soldier stagger, then fall dead, blood flowing from a grievous head wound.

And beyond crazy he watched Mara calmly, coolly taking pictures with a small camera she'd carried in her bag. Stunned, he looked on as she paid him no mind moving about, no doubt composing her pictures as she stepped over the dead and wounded. He approached, wanting to grab the camera from her. "What are you doing?"

"Let's go," she replied. "I've got pictures to scoop the world."

She was near to exultant as they threaded through the carnage to the shore where more horror awaited them. More bodies, more injured, the passersby of a few hours before, incidental victims of the attack. He slipped on pavement running with the blood of innocents. A mother, her dead infant at her side, cried out. He saw another family, the mother dying, father's body sheltering a crying baby. Nothing to be done, no one there to help. Mara had her pictures to develop, print, and sell to the highest bidder as desperate cries on and off the shore stirred the air.

She'd known a second bomb awaited the crowd, and saved his life. For that alone he didn't dare question her. Business is business, right? She sensed his dismay, and simply offered, "I'm a photographer, with a job to do. And the job right now is to cover the war." He said nothing, knowing his best-laid plans for the evening were over. Love and Death, that unlovely pair, had had their waltz, a bow at parting, with promises to meet again for another dance in three-quarter time.

# FIFTY

Time was out of joint, and he sat there in his apartment musing over the night before. A near-death experience it might be called. It was in papers all over the world, Mara's photos featured everywhere. Quite the coup for his little companion. Try as he might he couldn't rub from his mind the handsome black soldier who seemed to be walking toward him 'til he fell forward on his face, the back of his head no longer there. He didn't think Mara had gotten that picture. She'd slipped away again, following her passion, those war zones welcoming her with a warm embrace.

A knock, and Ninh was at the door. He knew about the bombing of course, and uncannily knew the Boss had been there. "How did you know that?"

"The girl who took the pictures is your friend." That was true, but how did he know that?

"Minister Tho is not happy about the pictures. The VC is claiming a great victory." That was the answer. Mara had been seen taking photos, and he'd been along for the ride.

"A VC victory? As many Vietnamese were killed on the shore as in the restaurant."

"They want to show no place is safe in Saigon."

Was that a touch of pride in his statement? Ninh was a puzzlement. He seemed to be in on everything. It was the value he added to his work, but mildly disconcerting. Could his hiring have been a set up designed to keep an eye on him? When Ninh said, "There are many good restaurants in town, maybe you will let me tell you about them." Holy shit, he thought, did Ninh know about the bombing in advance? Was protection money paid to keep the VC at bay? Or was something more ominous in play? He decided then and there he'd bring Ninh in on most of his dealings. Not the amounts of money involved. Too dangerous. He'd already been getting his from The Fuji deal. A hundred extra a week was plenty, and seemed to satisfy his needs. Ninh seemed not to have succumbed to the greed that had overtaken his countrymen. A suffering air engulfed him, gaining relief from the quietude of opium. "Are you married Ninh?" he asked, bringing forth a doleful reply. "My wife is trapped in the North, unable to be with me." A longing touched Ninh's voice, clouding his response. "A few weeks after we married, I came south to study before our country became divided. Millions escaped from the North, but my wife's parents were ill, could not travel." He had no more to say and turned away, looking north to conjure the face of his beloved.

# FIFTY-ONE

He had taken to sitting at the bar of Saigon's best hotel to watch the parade pass by. The Caravelle catered to quality riffraff exclusively: Reporters from big dailies, celebrities on display, businessmen on the lookout for any deal. And men in uniform, officer class, bringing a certain sense of urgency to Happy Hour. Blue and white décor, an obsequious staff, an odd absence of the hooker class, welcomed those who seldom strayed beyond the landlocked mooring of its rooms and bars. No dangerous Caravelle of Columbus, this safe haven.

He'd become a regular, more or less, joined by Ray Moore, an American reporter he'd drink with now and then. A raucous voice spewing forth with the urgency of a drill sergeant gave pause to their drinking. They turned to see the famous face of an aging actress.

"What the fuck am I out here for? Where's the fucking coverage? I'm busting my ass for this? So some shit ass colonel can get in my pants and tell his fucking buddies about it the next day at breakfast?" Carefully tailored combat fatigues, famous name tagged to her chest, mouth un-gagged, she worked them over. "What are you guys doing while I'm busting my hump? Not a word in the papers, no TV. Don't show me clips from those GI rags. Who gives a fuck? Where's the New York and L.A. coverage? What am I doing here?"

There was no story here for Ray, who paid no attention to this faded Broadway star in Vietnam to entertain the troops, bitching to her minions who had no answers, or cared that the room heard every word. "Who does she think she is," said Ray, "Bob Hope?"

She raved on, her uniform obscene contrast to three young officers who'd come into the bar, fatigues dust-covered, boots mud-caked, fresh from the field and the day's firefight. A thirty-minute chopper ride allowed an evening's peace after days and nights of death. Half an hour away fires they'd ordered set were still burning, boys they'd ordered forward were no longer screaming, morphine or their wounds quieting them for now or forever. Other ranks in the room, rear echelon types, clothes clean and pressed, ignored the intruders, managed to keep from looking their way. These three reminders of their soft life would not disturb their Happy Hour. But, wouldn't an appropriate dress code be in order?

Ray, clever newsman with the street wisdom of a New York Irishman, looked the three over as they sat at a table across from them. Being adept at these things, he gleaned their units by the patches at their shoulders knowing they'd been hit hard, again and again. Ray left him at the bar and wandered over asking, "Mind if I join you?" pulled over a chair and sat down, noting the trembling hands of one of the drinkers. The three of them looked up, but none spoke. "I got a feeling it was a tough day," he said at last. A grunt of assent was all he heard. "Then again, all the days are tough till you get out of here." He ordered a round, and asked where they'd been that day. One of them said, "Cu Chi." He'd hit the jackpot, knowing that if he kept things going he'd have his story.

And that's how it went for Ray Moore, intrepid reporter. Never in the field, head down over his booze, finding his war stories at the Jerome and Juliette Bar on the eighth floor of the Caravelle Hotel. He'd read Ray's stuff back home. It had the flavor of battle, fatigue, heroics, death. Including names and on-the-spot details told with a storyteller's art. A Homer he was, in every sense.

A few nights before, Ray, seriously drunk, had told a story on himself. His fame had spread, he bragged, and a newsmagazine wanted his picture. He readily agreed to pose at the daunting hour of nine. No sacrifice too great, he figured, and was met in front of the Continental Hotel, its terrace filled with breakfast boozers watching the action on Tu Do Street. The photographer had a Jeep and driver waiting when our faithless reporter, squinting at the sun, climbed aboard. As they drove off, he asked, "Where we going?" The answer caused him to say, "You got to be fucking kidding."

"No, that's what the magazine wants, you and some GIs at a defensive perimeter."

Handed a flak jacket that would barely fit past his gut, he looked at the offending article. "Turn this Jeep around." It was not until they got back to their starting point that he spoke again. "C'mon with me," and headed for the Continental's inner courtyard with its immense growth of decorative plantings. Struggling into the flak jacket, he found a thick stand of bushes. "Here's your fucking defensive perimeter." While life in the hotel swirled by, he set a pose. The photographer shrugged. And that's what ran in the magazine — stalwart reporter in the bush, eyeing hookers done for the night, walking past and looking for a little A.M. action.

As he remembered hearing Ray shamelessly tell that story, he watched him leave these three young soldiers and head to the elevator. To his room and typewriter, no doubt. It was his war goddamn it, and he'd cover it the best way he knew how.

Frankie Boyle, who had the same window table every night, came over and greeted him like an old friend, "How come you're sitting by yourself? People will think you're a homo or somethin'. C'mon over and meet some people." Frankie, polite as ever, made the introductions, "This is my Jewboy pal." Two strangers, an Air Force colonel and a smallish, thin-faced civilian, examined this rare specimen before them.

"Frankie, my Limey father would cut your Irish throat if he heard you call me that. He's seen the inside of more churches than your fat ass will ever see."

"But your mother's Jewish, right?"

"Right, Frankie."

"Then my money says you're a Jew 'cause that's how it's figured and you know it. Can any of us get into Iz-real? Any of us? Go ahead, answer me that. Only one can get in there is you."

"And the Arabs, of course," said the colonel, smiling.

Frankie Boyle could not contain himself. "A-rabs don't go nowhere unless the kikes tell them, isn't that right?" He paused. "Who would have thought them Jewboys could fight like that." And turned to the expert amongst them — "Where did the Jews learns to fight so good?"

"They've been at it for a long time," replied the boy with the Jewish mother.

"Well, they got a lot to teach us about handlin' the shit heels. Turn loose a battalion of them mother fuckers on the VC and this place would go quiet fast. Trouble is, they take over the black market and tailor shops and the PX and order matzohs served in all the restaurants." He turned to the full-bird, and said, "How come them Jewboys can kick ass like that and we can't get shit done over here?" The colonel cleared his throat and Frankie Boyle, shifting targets, said, "'Cause they don't have no niggers in the Jewish Army, that's why. You don't got to answer that one, colonel, it happens to be the fact. Let's go get a steak."

Descending to the cool, blue lobby opening onto the damp Saigon night, the colonel's sedan drove them at a crawl down Nguyen Trung Truc Street to the Embassy Hotel. Its penthouse terrace had a wide view of the city, the river, and flares slowly descending by parachute to illuminate paths of infiltration, glory, and death. Oh what a lovely sight, with sounds of nearby artillery heightening the entertainment. Son et lumière, Saigon style, courtesy of your friendly neighborhood war effort.

A combo began to play, a Vietnamese woman, old enough to have labored over Piaf's tunes, sang phonetically, "You don't have to say you love me, just be close at hand. You don't have to stay forever, I will understand, believe me, believe me."

He'd come here with Thanh and heard that song. An anthem for American boys and the girls soon to be parted by time and distance or those chance encounters that lead to bliss eternal. Thanh had asked if she could give the singer some money.

"Sure," he said, and asked for a Vietnamese song. She wrote a note and a waiter delivered it to the bandstand. The singer looked over in their direction, one in the band picked up a guitar, found his key and a lament filled the room, causing waiters and busboys, bartenders and bimbos to pause as she sang a song only they knew. A song of war, and the end of war, when a soldier returns to his wife and children and there is peace at last. Simple song. Simple story. It all sounds so simple, doesn't it?

Frankie interrupted this reverie. Curious about how he'd sprung loose those air conditioners, he wanted to know how he'd brought it off. Annoyed with the evasive answer, Frankie turned to the colonel for a quiet, whispered conversation. His other dinner companion, Joe Zeigler, was head of sales for the distributor of all the American beer sold in Vietnam. Frankie looked up for a moment. "Salesman? He's made more in commissions than the fuckers who own the distributorship. That's a fact."

Joe told him it was true, but his commission deal would soon be cancelled. "We got half a million thirsty souls out here wanting their beer. A million cans a day of dear old Bud and Miller Hi-Life." Drawing a breath he pronounced, "That's one hundred and sixty six thousand six packs, four thousand one hundred twenty five cases of twenty-four. Each and every day." He intoned those numbers as though reading from a pulpit, awestruck by their majesty.

The beer had been shipped in on military cargo planes. "Space available basis," with no delay to the war effort, he assured his listener, none at all. Mournfully, he added, "Some goddamn bluenose senator got wind of it and put a stop to the air shipments." He cursed the senator, who'd proclaimed his intention to save our brave boys from the immorality of two beers a day. "He'll just turn them to dope," Joe said. "Its our biggest competition. These kids are beginning to smoke here, there, and everywhere. It's a goddamn epidemic. And watch what happens when ODs start joining the casualty lists." He added, "We have to bring shipments in by sea. On slow boats to Indochina, and nothing to be done about it." As the steaks arrived he casually said, "I'll be needing an expediter." Frankie and the colonel had left their private conversation, and Joe had clearly meant that last remark for the guy who'd pulled off release of the imprisoned air conditioners. Caution, a rare interference to his way of living, led him to ask himself how everything he touched seemed to breed the nasty stench of possibility. Did everyone have a piece of the action? Or, was he being set up, a lamb sacrificed on a spit?

As the other three dug into their beef, he began another calculation: How much could be taken in on the million cans a day coming into Poppa's port? He had trouble chewing on a bit of steak as he surmised that a bounty of a mere penny a can would yield ten thousand dollars a day. That penny a can would mean nothing to Joe Zeigler. To protect his share, he'd have to become Poppa's bagman. A dangerous thing in a dangerous place. But he was jumping too far ahead. Joe would have to be talked to first of all. Frankie, bulging cheeks in full-mastication watched this Jewboy coolly pick up knife and fork and tried to figure how he'd had made those Saigon connections so quickly.

A glow of self-satisfaction warming his heart he turned to Frankie. "How's the golf game going?"

# FIFTY-TWO

Walking down Tran Hung Dao Street toward the Hotel Victoria, he found himself moving easily in the dank humidity on the way to breakfast with Ninh. "I've grown accustomed to the place," he hummed, as he eyed the ten-story hotel, constructed quickly and on the cheap to accommodate the never-ending flow of Americans who'd come to the party. Joe Zeigler would be waiting for him at The Continental, and he would have preferred to start his morning there, but Ninh was unhappy on that terrace, his unease caused by rumors that grenades would be tossed by motorcycle riders into the crowd of Americans congregating there.

The Victoria, to his amusement, advertised "Running Hot Water." A grandiose amenity, that. The elevator had conked out, and he'd be goddamned if he'd walk up the nine floors to the restaurant. Ninh, already on hand, was drinking coffee in the lobby. Coffee and croissant would be there in the moment it took a waiter to hustle up to the ninth floor, sprinting down the stairs to assure the warmth of breakfast. Accepting this breathless service as his due, he heard Ninh say, "A sad story to tell." Biting into his croissant he waited for Ninh to continue. "A very sad story," he repeated.

"Has Eddie stopped paying?"

"No, no. Something else."

Ninh's dramatics, always charming, he waited, letting him play it out. Finally he said, "My friend Minister Tho is very angry."

"About what?"

"Sue was with another man. It made him very angry."

"What happened?"

Ninh looked around carefully, then whispered, "He found her in bed with another man."

"I can't believe it."

"Yes. It's true. But worse."

"Worse?"

"Yes, much worse. Tho knew the man and when he shouted at him, his friend said, 'Wait your turn, I've paid five hundred dollars to fuck the American.' Tho pulled him out of the bed and began beating Sue. Beating her very hard." When his friend tried to stop him, Tho called out, his body guard came into the room and began beating the friend 'til blood was all over his face."

Mirth bubbling to his face he asked, "Then what happened?"

"Tho was choking Sue, trying to kill her, I think. Dolores rushed into the room, lifted Tho away from Sue and threw him across the room."

"Hooray for Dolores," he wanted to say. But let Ninh continue.

"Mr. Tho rose up with great dignity and left the room." He said this with the respect due a Minister of State.

But holy shit, what happens now? Ninh had found out all this from Eddie, who told him Tho had threatened to close his place down. The girls would have to go. Maybe he could do something. But why bother? He had no interest in the whole crazy scheme. He'd done what a man could do. Sue's blackened eye would heal; Dolores would have to say bye-bye to her little Chinese cupcake. Poor Tommie, he thought with regret. Leaving just as he was getting used to the good life. In farewell to Ninh, he promised to make up the hundred he'd be out and headed off to his meeting with the burgomeister.

# FIFTY-THREE

Ignoring Ninh's warning he courageously strode onto the crowded terrace of The Continental. An immense sculpture of two Vietnamese fighting men carved in heroic Soviet style graced the plaza outside. The terrace was an American hangout, attracting shoeshine boys and other assorted supplicants seeking the favor of the high and mighty. Tu Do Street traffic streamed by, motorcyclists, no harm, weaved through traffic. A sprinkling of the Dupar crowd was there. Having heard the air conditioner success story, they nodded to him with respectful glances as he scanned the room 'til he spotted Joe Zeigler at a rear table talking with two men in suits and ties. Sitting down, he thought about a second breakfast, ordered coffee and met the other two, overdressed in the morning heat. Andres Casanova, courtly, better dressed of the two, owned the hotel. He wondered if he was related to the Casanova he'd met with John but decided against asking, more interested that a Corsican owned one of the better hotels in Saigon. The other was an American, younger and awkward in dress and manner. Freddie Fazool looked like one of the Italian punks from his old neighborhood. The two of them had other business and left, with Freddie Fazool making a pass at a hard look in his direction.

"So, you a friend of Frankie Boyle?"

"No, I hardly know him. Been to a party at his house, that's all." Then he added, "I stay away from him, he dragged me over to your table."

"Same as me. He's got no friends, far as I can tell. He's an all-around hater," Joe said, chewing on a piece of toast. "With special attention paid to Jews, you may have noticed." That he had, and handled it by trading insult for insult with the Mick prick. "He's trying to hustle me into letting him handle beer deliveries to the local bars," Joe added.

"Will you play along?"

"Maybe. It never hurts to do a favor." He said this pointedly, hoping to engage his tablemate in the efficacy of such advice. Getting no response, Joe pushed his plate to the side. "Everyone's talking about how you are saving your company's ass." He nodded, accepting the compliment, waiting for what else might be coming his way. "I just might have a similar problem with my deliveries. There's enough inventory to cover 'til the first boatload arrives but then, I don't know."

He looked at Joe and quietly said, "A penny a six pack."

"That's fifty thousand a month."

"Is that what it comes to?" he replied.

"My commissions are nothing like that," Joe said, in wonderment at the cool demand presented to him.

"Didn't you tell me you're off commission, on a straight salary?" He decided to hold in abeyance a sweetener for Joe, if he resisted the deal, saying, "You don't owe your bosses a thing, sweating your nuts off out here, writing up orders for a million beers a day." He was beginning to sound like one of those Reds protecting the exploited classes. But wasn't this a Cold War battleground, The Armageddon the war hawks were always talking about?

Joe sat in silence, then said, "Twenty five."

"That won't cut it, these people who run the ports know the value of every nail and screw coming in here." Then presenting the dealmaker to Joe, he said, "I'll get them to kick back to you five, maybe ten percent. That'll make up for your lost commissions."

Joe smiled at this. "Five or ten?"

"Let's call it ten. A deal?"

"I'll have to check with my office, but they'll go for it. How are you gonna arrange the payouts for everyone?"

Making it up as it went along, he replied, "My guy has a Swiss bank account, you can be sure. Then again, he might want a monthly suitcase of cash to convert to gold. They love the sheen on those lovely bars. When you get the OK, I'll find out how it will go down."

And with that, a handshake between them, he would have left The Continental for a giddy stroll up Tu Do Street, but watched a bunch of very nasty, olive-skinned guys in suits emerge from chauffeured cars. Freddie Fazool led the group up the short stairs to the terrace to be greeted by Casanova with cheek-to-cheek kisses. Corsicans all, he guessed. Casanova wore a large gold medallion hanging from a thick gold chain he'd added for the occasion. His countrymen were accessorized the same. Some sort of club, he figured. With intentions well beyond the social. Something was up, he was sure, as his curiosity shifted to a splendid woman emerging from a car with another medallion-bedecked Corsican at her side who waved a greeting to his pals, then ordered the woman back into the car. His only purpose in that strange interlude to show off his beauty to the admiring gang he joined on the terrace.

A glimpse of the woman was enough for him to hail a taxi and gesture instructions, "Follow that car!" Just like the movies. The crawl in traffic allowed him to stare through her car's rear window at the pale skin at the back of her neck, the European cut to her hair pulled back in a chignon. All he needed, for now. After a stop, he watched her slip out of the car and walk into the best jewelry shop in town. He could have, should have, ended it right there, order the taxi on its way. But this impulsive act, bound to lead to compulsion, obsession, was something familiar to him. Not to get ahead of himself, ignoring any wisdom achieved from past experience, he left the taxi to watch her for a moment then entered the store. An attractive clerk greeted the rich American, who noted the special attention paid to his quarry by the shop's owner, who greeted the object of his affection, "Bonjour Mademoiselle Brame." So, she was a regular at the store, known to the owner who paid her the attention such a client deserved. An exquisite jade necklace was placed before her on a black velvet pad while the clerk showed him other jade pieces in vulgar gold settings, just the thing for a taste-deficient American.

Mademoiselle was wearing a rough silk white mini dress reaching to mid-thigh, of a cut and quality shrieking haute couture. Her dark blonde hair was equally à la mode, her skin cosseted by delicate creams and gentle hands. Savoring her body for last, he allowed his eyes to admire her bronzed thighs, tanned youthful face, her eyes of a shape he could only call exotic. Watching as she placed the necklace around her neck, watching as it fell to her exposed throat and delicately exposed cleavage, he was enthralled, in thrall, a better way to put it, as this exquisite woman turned to him merely to see what effect she might be having on her public. His appreciation for her favor duly noted, she turned to inquire the price of her bauble. The price, in his money, was ten thousand dollars and he watched her hesitate, only for a moment. It was enough to give him what he wished for. "Allow me to buy it for you," he said, quietly, casually. She looked at him as one used to such offers. Any question that she might not understand him, was answered by her gracious, smiling reply: "Thank you. I can buy it for myself."

"Of course you can, but I'd be happy to buy it for you, and, if you wish, never see you again." Amused by his little lie, she asked over tinkling laughter, "Why would I do that?" It was his turn to smile as he archly replied, "Why would you let me buy it for you, or why would you never see me again?" Charmed by his turning her question to his advantage, she said, "Why don't we find out?" The store owner, puzzled, not understanding a word, watched sadly as she removed the necklace. Our gallant, keeping to his word, picked it up from the counter. "Where shall I have it delivered?" And heard the answer to his second question of her when she named a nearby coffee shop, telling him to meet her there in two hours. "Would that be convenient?" she oh-so-politely asked. Oh, yes, it surely would. Her Loveliness turned away toward the door, leaving him with a wisp of perfume and an astonished shopkeeper told to hold the bauble for Mr. Rich American to return cash in hand.

The pursuit of women had been a commonplace, but he had to admit the price of admission to this mad chase was different. In the past the only cost the risk of being found out by his loved ones. This had the smell of another kind of danger, but what the hell, in for a penny in for ten thousand. Risk-to-benefit ratios were for the logical, the schemers. He preferred to concentrate on a green jade necklace descending from a white throat, reaching down into the happy valley. It was vision enough to send him scampering home to pull the cash from his hidden stash while whistling a happy tune.

But wait. He suddenly realized this little errand had distracted him from important business. Closing the deal with Thanh's father had priority, did it not? He never seemed to weary when women got in the way of life's demands. It exacted a price, he knew. But, oh the joy!

## FIFTY-FOUR

Thanh's father would be home for lunch promptly at noon, a habit of a lifetime. He'd need a translator and hoped Thanh would be there. She'd have no qualms about the wheeling and dealing. The offer needed to be presented carefully. The subtleties of bribery were new to him, but he was a quick study, eager to learn its nuances. Besides, twenty-five thousand a month should get Poppa's attention.

As he approached the house, its banks of roses all in bloom, his surmise was confirmed when a chauffeur opened a car door and Poppa emerged. He watched and waited a few minutes, then boldly walked to the front door and into another happy valley, real money.

Thanh, walking down the stairs, showed no surprise at seeing him. He told her he had a proposition for her father involving a large fee, could she help talk to him? She left him for a moment, returning with Poppa who eyed him with curiosity, as he was led into a side parlor. Quickly sketching out the deal he watched the father's face as Thanh translated into French. Why French, he wondered? Her father, responding in kind to Thanh, never looked his way before abruptly leaving the room.

He cursed himself for his ignorance of the language. And anyway, why weren't they using Vietnamese? He figured he'd blown the deal; Poppa was not susceptible to such shenanigans. Fifty thousand a month split two ways, less the ten percent for Zeigler, was down the fucking drain. As he got up to leave, Thanh quietly asked, "How will payments be made?"

"Holy shit, the deal's on," he said to himself. "When the shipment is dockside, ready for pickup, he'll have the money wherever he wants it."

"I'll be the one," she replied demurely. This should not have surprised this refugee from the mean streets, but shocked he was. Poppa's fingerprints would be found nowhere. It was Daddy's little girl who'd take the fall. The dough would be his, count on it. But he'd not see, hear, nor have his hands soiled by the evils of filthy lucre. She rose to join father and mother for lunch, no invitation forthcoming to the bribe maker. It's all in the family, no doubt about it.

Walking across the street in the shade of the high Embassy wall, it suddenly hit him why they weren't using Vietnamese. The clever bastards were keeping their business from the sharpened ears of servants ignorant of French. Clever was hardly the word. Poppa's caution was the watchword over all they surveyed. But, why should he care? Zeigler would deliver, he was certain about that. Twenty thousand a month would be his to have and to hold. And, really important, our boys would be getting their beer ration on demand. A fine, patriotic endeavor anyone would agree. Of course, Poppa had gone for the beer deal. With cash on the barrelhead, you betcha. A fifty-fifty split was honest enough he decided with a newly acquired munificence. Generosity was an easily acquired skill for a boy raised in deprivation.

Setting such fine fervor aside he was off, hippity-hop to the jeweler's shop, feeling a slight tremble across his fingers at handing over ten thousand dollars to the eager shopkeeper who, ever hopeful, pushed on him a tray of earrings. Politely demurring, he turned toward the coffee shop and his rendezvous with destiny.

The ten thou' was barely a bite from his new riches, an easy-come, easy-go attitude he maintained whether holding or no. What with big-dollar payouts in his future, a hundred thousand in a can back home, kickbacks here and there, and more to come, he murmured to himself, "You've come a long way, baby."

It brought back a memory from those early times, a sister's great act of kindness buying him two shirts, a pair of pants. Such ordinary things, but the pants were fresh and new, and fit him, black corduroy, Cour du Roi, Cloth of the King!! And so were the shirts of checked cotton, one green, one red, smooth and smelling sweet. All his life, until then, he'd dressed in hand-me-downs and the pathetic offerings of the charitable.

Later, at family gatherings, he invariably reminded his sister of her generosity, that happy time. He could still hear the corduroy squeak, still remember the bright colors of the shirts. He told her it made him see the possibilities that life might offer. She would smile, and they would go on to something else.

After their father died, she interrupted the story. "Don't you remember what happened after I bought you those things?"

"No, I don't."

"It was the beginning of school," she said. " I was a senior and about to quit my summer job in a department store. Momma told me I should quit school instead, that we needed the money. I was only sixteen, Momma had to sign me out of school. The guidance counselor begged her to let me stay and graduate. I was on the honor roll and had higher grades than any of those Jews in my class. Momma said I could finish at night, but I never did. Even though the war was on and everyone was doing good again, Poppa wasn't. So I went back to work at the store. I put in a lot of overtime one week and came out with a good paycheck. I bought a real nice coat for myself. Full length, dark green, for fall. You were about to start second grade and I said to myself, my little brother is going to look as good as anybody on the first day of school, and took you shopping.

"When I came home from work on your first day of school, Poppa was in his chair. I hardly noticed him sitting there smoking, and brooding. I took off my new coat and put it on the couch and you came running in from the kitchen wearing your new clothes looking so sweet and handsome. I asked you about your first day of school and you were so proud. 'The teacher told me I looked nice,' you said. 'I told her, my sister bought them for me.' Poppa jumped out of his chair, grabbing at your shirt, hitting at you. I got you behind me as his fist came down and screamed, don't touch his head! I pushed you into the kitchen, or out the front door, I don't remember anymore, and when I turned saw he'd got hold of my coat and was ripping it to shreds."

No, he hadn't remembered that. Hadn't remembered the terror he must have felt. Hadn't remembered anything like that at all.

A blaring horn caused him to jump back from a rushing car. When the light changed he crossed the street toward the coffee shop and a smile from the object of his affections. He looked at her, saying nothing, then placed a silk pouch on the table. The goddess accepted this offering, eyes showing no reaction as it sat alongside her café au lait and a half-bitten piece of pastry. He let this silence envelop them, allowing her the chance to escape, perhaps free him from what might be. As her hand caressed the bag in a single movement, it was clear more was to come. "You were quite amusing in the shop," she said. He guessed desire for amusement was at a premium for her. He'd heard other French women toss off the word with a charming lift of the head, mouth slightly open as "amused" left their lips. "How was it you were at the jewelers?" She asked.

He decided to keep her amused by answering, "I followed you in a taxi from the Continental Terrace." She nodded at this admission, accepting his daring as her due. "After you left your husband," he added.

She shook her head, indifferently, "Not my husband. He already has a wife." Displaying a way-of-the-world shrug as she waved a hand in the air, she said, "And anything else he might want." She had the freshness of the beautiful young, not yet touched by years. He was seeing her at the best she would ever be, that the glory and the freshness would soon give way to the onslaught of experience.

"A wife is far easier to manage as any man knows," he said, not surprised at all by her laughter at his mocking tone.

"You know something of such things," she said. Not an inquiry, a statement of men-as-beasts fact.

"Yes I do. But I also know that to manage a ménage is hard, very hard."

Her broad smile gave over to an admonishing warning: "Making a woman laugh can be dangerous. It brings her to wonder if there is more and she's often disappointed." Before he could frame a reply, she softly said, "Let me tell you another dangerous thing, my boyfriend is Carlos Fusina." Getting no reaction, she had to add, "He is The Opium King."

"Oh," he allowed himself to say.

"Corsicans are very jealous."

"It was his turn to offer a Gallic shrug. "Jealousy is not exclusive to Corsica." He watched her taking in this two-bit wisdom as she placed the silk sack inside a larger purse. "Ten thousand dollars," he said to himself watching it about to fly away. Hoping to keep her near for just a little longer, he asked about the men in suits he'd seen on the terrace that morning.

"Corsicans, all of them. Cousins of Carlos. They arrived from the island yesterday. He will be with them all day and all night." He was about to ask an indiscreet question about their business here, but this impertinence was avoided when she removed a gold pen and embossed leather notebook from her purse, wrote an address, inviting him for a glass of wine at six o'clock. "If you can," she said, turning an invitation into a challenge, amused once again as she saw desire overwhelm hesitation as he replied, "With pleasure," and watched as she rose from the table and with a leggy stride move toward a car that appeared as if a wand had been waved, and was gone.

"Oh boy," he said to anyone who wished to hear. A Corsican drug king. A jealous, Corsican drug king. The Emperor Napoleon had his Josephine, and he held in his hand a gold trimmed piece of notepaper asking him to cross to his own little Elba. Of course he would. Turn down a lady? Not a chance.

# FIFTY-FIVE

The address he held out to the taxi driver led him to a side street in Thanh's neighborhood. Close, but not uncomfortably close. They couldn't possibly know each other, but so what if they did? Stepping from the taxi, he stood before a grand mansion, another leftover of the latter-day French Empire. Down a short path, high columns supported a circular entryway. Carved wood double doors looked out on a tiled walkway guarded by squat, brightly colored porcelain elephants. Grandeur, it announced to all that came before it. It had to be home to The Drug King. Could she be sharing it with Carlos and his wife? A partial answer came when a door opened and his new friend stood there, a glass of white wine in hand, long hair reaching down to bare shoulders, so different from the tight bun he'd seen earlier, wearing a silk dress in light purple reaching demurely to her knees. Allowing him a cheek-to-cheek welcome, he was sure she'd changed perfumes to a heavier musk and imagined how she'd drawn a bath to cleanse herself from the heat of day to prepare for her gentleman caller.

The entry hall was decorated with scrolls, save the strange sight on a far wall of a large abstract painting in a myriad of colors. He stopped to look at it and saw that the blues and reds, deep orange and vermillion moved together in a carefully composed way, giving a feeling of solidity within the chaos of color. Neither of them had yet said a word. "It's a wonderful painting," he said. She'd been watching closely, and said, "Why is it wonderful?" '

"It's the colors, how they work together, and how it all hangs together," awkwardly repeating himself, but it seemed to satisfy her. "Is it from Paris?"

"No, from here," she said, leading him to a quick guess, "It's your painting, isn't it?"

Amazed to see a blush across her face, he heard her softly say, "Yes it is." And took the glass from her hand to offer up a toast to good work. Accepting this token, she led him glass-in-hand to the living room. A coffee table held small plates with pâté and soft, smooth brie. Champagne cooling in a bucket awaited his attention. He took a taste of wine from her glass, establishing a touch of intimacy. She knew the meaning of this gesture, accepting it in silence as he placed the glass down. He pointed to the champagne, she nodded, and he slowly pried up the cork allowing no more than a gasp from the bottle, then poured the pale liquid into delicate flutes. All this in a silence, near to pantomime, as they exchanged glances over glasses tipped up to wet lips and parched throats. The furniture in the room had no touch of Asia, its couches, chairs, lamps of contemporary design. One wall, in contrast, had charcoal drawings, and one large pastel, all beautiful Asian women young and old. Their frames were ornate, turn of the century. Champagne in hand, he went over to the pictures. She watched from the couch as he turned to her. "They're the same woman, at different ages of her life."

At that, she rose toward him. "My grandmother. Her husband, my grandfather loves her very much." She said this so simply, so much a fact in her life. "He was Counsel General, it caused him great trouble in his family and with his career to marry a Vietnamese woman. But he has adored her forever, drawn her portrait all of their life together."

"Do they still live here?"

"No, they live in Paris, with my mother." These tidbits of family history became important to him as he watched her unfold her story.

"My mother met my father, their only child, when he went off to Paris to the École Militaire. She looked at her visitor helping himself to the pâté. "He was first in his class and was posted back to Vietnam to fight the Viet Minh."

Knowing this story could not have a happy ending he put a cracker laden with brie back down on his plate. "He was at Dien Bien Phu and was killed there during the siege." Then, added quietly, "I was ten years old."

He knew the French had been defeated and run out of the country in 1954. It meant she was no more than twenty-two and seen more than her share. He wanted to hear more, learn why she'd returned to Saigon, and said, blandly, "So here you are, back in Vietnam." Her eyes jumped to his. Making sure this was an inquiry, not a judgement, she decided to satisfy his curiosity. "Carlos came to visit my family last year. Things had not gone well for them, or my mother. A diplomat's pension, a soldier's pension, is not much. My beautiful mother took a job in an elegant dress shop putting up with every sort of humiliation from their bourgeoisie clientele." As she said this, her eyes wandered to the luxury of her present existence, seeking forgiveness from some faraway person for the choices she'd made. "I had just finished art school, and Carlos, who'd been a high-school friend of my father's, took us out every night to the best restaurants, charming us as only he can. I assumed he was interested in my mother, and who wouldn't be? On his last night, he quietly slipped a thick envelope holding a great quantity of francs to my grandfather. Then, more discreetly, an envelope for me with a firs-class, round-trip ticket to Saigon." And then, in mocking parody of her guest's remark said, "So here I am, back in Vietnam."

Then, apropos the present situation, said, "I've given my driver and his wife the evening off." Sensing his hesitation, his apprehension, she said, "Carlos usually stops by before going home at night. But not tonight, since he'll be giving his cousins a good time." There was not a smidgen of anger, despair in her voice. An observation was all it was, a toting up of her deal with the devil. Then, to make a fine a point to it, added, "He's become trapped by the product he controls. It will soon be controlling him. He shows up here, useless to me as a man, barely able to talk, an addict on his way to destroying himself."

This flow of information began to overtake him. Here she was idly ensconced in her love nest, fucked-up loverboy out for the evening, servants away, suggesting a neediness he could try to satisfy. She interrupted his wandering in this labyrinth with an amused query, "Are you afraid to come to bed with me?" As she said this, she took up her Champagne, shifting her position on the couch, amused to see his smile at her challenge to him.

"If I'm afraid, it's to be afraid for you."

"Oh," she said, "you think you are too much for me?"

"No, no," he said, then realizing she was teasing, said, "When Carlos finds out, it will go very badly for you."

"It will be worse for you," she said.

He could almost hear a bell tolling its lugubrious warning. "So he'll find out." Not a question, a simple statement of what was to come.

"Yes, he will find out." It was his moment to flee, but he sat there looking into her face, detecting a vulnerability she'd never shown before. It took a fleeting second for her to rise from the couch. Before turning away, she put a finger to her closed lips, sending a kiss. "Meet me upstairs in a few minutes. I'm sure you can find my bedroom."

He watched her climb the stairs in full appreciation of the body moving away from him that would soon be his to have and to hold. "Run you crazy bastard, run," he said. "This thing will get you fucking killed." But no one was there to listen, least of all himself. He stood up, never looking for the exit. The stairway beckoned, he answered the come-hither call. His fate could wait. There was this business of pleasure at the top of those stairs.

"So, Americans can be good in bed, after all." It was a remark she'd made to fill an interlude between the acts. No chauvinist, he accepted this singular compliment with an inquiring, "Oh?" A dangerous game, that little word pushing its way into a lover's past. Her response led her to tell of Americans in Paris, "Eager as puppies clambering to get at me. It must be what a mother dog with a large litter feels like."

Her hunger for sex, intimacy maybe, was there from her first lovely gesture, greeting him at her open bedroom door wearing the jade necklace, sheer panties, sandals, and that's all. "I never seem to dress right for any occasion," he said, as she drew him in, not bothering to close the door, her nakedness giving him a chance to note what she had to offer. She indulged this survey, following his eyes as they examined her part by part, piece by piece. Head, and neck, and shoulders he knew. The green necklace reaching toward young breasts took up his time until distracted by a curve of waist descending to slim hips and thighs leaving firm legs for last. And then, she turned, twisting her head to look at him as he took in the sumptuous ass. She approached him, still standing there, and kissed him with an open, eager, wet mouth. He returned the kiss in kind as she backed him toward the bed, seated him, kneeling down to remove his shoes and socks. He looked down at her, "You don't have to do that."

"But I want to," she said, lowering her head to her task. Her hair, blonde with traces of a darker shade, billowed across her shoulders as she rose, breasts brushing his face, to remove his shirt. Undressing her man seemed important to her. A whorish payback, he imagined with chagrin, for the necklace he'd bought her on a crazy whim. His chest bare, she stood him up to open his belt, drop his pants to the floor, then lowered herself to remove them from around his ankles. He was thinking how clinical, how practiced an air she brought to the proceedings, when she tugged at his shorts, pulling them away, pressing a cheek to his still soft cock with so loving a gesture he decided all this was for him, only for him. Taking to the bed, he watched as she removed sandals, necklace, then jumped in beside him with a joyful anticipation he hoped to satisfy.

She was practiced in her craft, highly practiced, and she allowed him his way with her, biding her time, awarding points for technique, level of difficulty he chose to attempt. That was his thought, at least, as he worked away at her, gratified to hear murmurs of approval, feel her body shift with pleasure under his hands moving slowly across, around, within. It was all worth it, Opium King be damned.

He said this as he caressed her ever more slowly, something she'd signaled was better than best. Her eyes, her grandmother's Asian eyes, looked at him. "I knew you would be this way with me."

"A lucky guess," he said as finger and thumb quietly continued a rolling motion on the sweetness of certain parts between her legs. They kissed, and, keeping his fingers in place, caressed her cheek with his other hand, this gentle move causing her to grip the back of his neck and come in a deep heaving motion that seemed to go on and on.

Half-opened eyes declared, "Merci monsieur."

"De rien, mademoiselle, de rien."

He would have allowed her the rest she deserved, but alert to new possibilities, or remembering her responsibilities in the matter, she drew him atop her, knees raised in supplication, inviting him, pouring him, into her. It might have been what she wanted, but he had other plans, quickly withdrawing, to her wide-eyed surprise, to gather himself in his own time. He would not be hurried, damn it, his reward not yet up to risks taken. Carlos again, he knew. But let the ball roll, no matter where it may go.

His calculations completed, his darling on her back, he slipped aboard his pleasure craft, her knees once more unfurled, to offer a portion of the delights they'd share. It pleased him to note she did not need the distraction of acrobatics, not yet, anyway. She was content to remain in place, returning each of his slow-motion moves inside of her with rhythms, subtle variations on themes of her own. Forget pretty musical terms. This was carnal, flesh-on-flesh, the grinding of bones, until she cried out "Please," begging him to finally come inside her. On such red meat doth Caesar feed.

It was at this point of rest she'd made her remark about sex with Americans in Paris. Unable to resist temptation he asked, "And Carlos?"

"A typical Corsican. Did you see the gold medallions they wear around their necks? One side has a portrait of Napoleon, the other side his Imperial Eagle. They adore Le Petit General. And for good reason. Like Napoleon, they all have penises the size of your little finger. And treat their women like shit to make up for it." He wondered if this information about The Little General had come directly from The Empress Josephine, and while at it, whether her intimate knowledge of Corsican cock sizes was based on more than one little bit of evidence. But leave well enough alone he thought, and asked why those country cousins were in Saigon, and saw she looked at him carefully for a moment before answering.

"Their business is heroin. And they need a new supply." His puzzled look led her to add, "You Americans have won one war these days, anyway. Turkey was their source for poppy, but your government bribed the Turks to burn the fields and stop production."

"And that's why they're here?"

Ignoring the naiveté of the question, she shifted her body closer to him, "Prices have doubled in your America and in Europe. Not bad for Carlos and his friends, but they are desperate to find a new set-up. And Carlos has convinced them that Burma, Laos, and Vientiane can be Turkey all over again." As he listened, he realized this was the second time a woman had tried to give his innocent soul the lowdown on the things of this world. Thanh had elaborated on the corruption that continued the war, and here was another bedmate introducing another good reason to keep the fires burning. As he thought about this she said, with a petulant tone, "Haven't we talked enough?" And reaching for him, to check his readiness, she rolled atop him, smothering him with happy kisses, delighted her research had brought so happy a result.

Readiness was all, as she moved across him, using every bit and bite of him. He lazily placed his arms and hands behind his head as she happily worked him to her own ends. She took this as permission to straddle him, slide in and out of him, taking him any way she chose. He was a living, breathing, throbbing cock to her, nothing more, until she sensed it could go on no longer for him and seizing the time, ended it for both of them.

As she gently caressed him, he asked her name. "Roxanne," he heard her softly say.

"Roxanne," he repeated, as if making a liturgical response in the quiet that encapsulated them. Not the silence of strangers with nothing left to say. More the quiet of expectation against a future without possibilities.

She rose from the bed, heading for her dressing room, a very good thing over and done. But not quite yet. She turned to him and said, "Carlos is sending me to Bangkok next weekend to make a delivery for him. Why don't you join me? Think about it. I'll be right back."

"Delivery? Of what exactly?" he wanted to ask. Instead he awaited her return, in a pajama top reaching nearly to a point six inches above her knees. Reaching for his clothes, he said, "I'll meet you in Bangkok."

"The Oriental Hotel," she said, buttoning his shirt, letting him put shorts and pants on by his lonesome. Don't she love me anymore? he wondered. They walked down the stairs, arm in arm. She loves me she loves me not, he thought, as he said, "The Oriental Hotel."

"Friday night," she replied, offering a chaste cheek for his adoration.

Stepping out into the street, he checked left and right. Relieved to see no one watching the house he walked toward the nearby boulevard and a taxi home. Friday was a week away, time enough to attend to business of his own. Carlos, Corsicans, even Roxanne would be set aside as he waited for his ship to come in.

# FIFTY-SIX

The Reuben James, a freighter flying the Liberian flag, had left port on the West Coast seven days before, steaming for Saigon with a thirty day supply of the suds and Lord knows what else to satisfy the maw of war. It was due in that very day, according to Joe Zeigler. Cash would be king, he'd learned from Thanh, passing on to Zeigler the suggestion he buy larger and larger suitcases. Daughter and Company would get half the cash. Joe would get his ten percent, left to wonder about the payoff to his facilitator. Thanh and he would be in touch. An extra bonus beyond the twenty thousand buckaroos he'd be taking down each month. He'd already accumulated more than a hundred thousand dollars and needed to consider a safe haven for all this bounty coming his way. Something would come up he was sure, and let the days pass by, his freighter full speed ahead, steady as she goes across the silent sea.

## FIFTY-SEVEN

With nary a hesitation he'd booked a Friday flight and reservation for the weekend at the Oriental Hotel in Bangkok. Sure, he should have shut it down, let the one-night-stand be no more than that. But this one had that little extra beyond good pussy. A world he'd never known. He had a notion The Greek would know about such things and found him in his office in cozy conversation with a lovely Thai woman there to please.

"My new assistant," John offered as explanation for this adornment. She's got a civil engineering degree." Introductions made, the lovely left for her cubicle and he asked John about Freddie Fazool.

"Sure I know him." John said, waiting for more.

"I met him the other morning at the Continental, and later I saw him with a bunch of guys in suits and ties, Corsicans."

"Why did you think they were Corsicans?" There was a curious tone, almost a cop's voice asking his question.

"They looked just like that guy Casanova I met with you a while back."

"And?" This was not the voluble John he knew, offering opinions, information, without a qualm. He was holding back waiting to hear more.

Looking at John, he said, "A man and a gorgeous young French chick showed up." John remained silent. "He joined the crowd on the terrace and she went back to the car that brought them."

"That would be my pal Carlos and one of his women."

The temptation was mighty indeed to tell him he'd fucked the girl that day he saw her. It was a common thread to their talk. Deciding to leave that for another day, he asked, "And Freddie Fazool?"

"Ever hear of Sam Trafficante?" How could he not? Major Mafioso. Girlfriend sleeping with JFK. Havana, Bautista, Fidel.

"Sure I've heard of him."

"Freddie Fazool is his punk nephew." John watched this bit of information raise a whistle of surprise.

"I didn't notice him wearing a uniform, what brings him to dear old Saigon?" John took in this mocking remark with a smile, "He lives here."

"And your pal Carlos?"

"The heroin operation in Saigon? That's his."

"I knew that."

"So, why did you ask?"

"You know that woman he was with that morning?" John nodded. "I fucked her that night."

It was John's turn to whistle. Instead he cocked an eye. "Bullshit you did."

"Bullshit if I didn't."

John sat back in his chair, waiting for more. "I followed her in a taxi. When she left her car I chatted her up, she invited me for a drink at her place." Deleting the ten Gs for the necklace from the tale, he watched John take in this news with continuing disbelief.

"And so you fucked her."

"That I did," he said with prideful self-possession. "She told me your boy Carlos would be out all night with his Corsican paisanos. I guess she was lonely in her little love nest."

"So that's how you found out about Carlos?"

"Yep. And that he's taken to using, big time."

"My, oh my, listen to Mr. In-The-Know." John said this with a touch of respect, ready to hear more, amazed to hear what came next.

"She's going to Bangkok on Friday. Making a delivery for Carlos. She invited me along for the weekend."

"And you, you crazy bastard, are going?"

"Maybe"

"Maybe, your ass, you've already booked your ticket."

That has to be a good guess, he said to himself. "That I did, but the plane could leave without me."

"You are not only a crazy bastard, you are a suicidal crazy bastard. That will turn out to be a very expensive piece of ass." He offered that as a caution, hoping it would have some effect. "Carlos will find out. He may already know about your little peccadillo. The jealous son-of-a bitch has the houses of his girlfriends on 24-hour watch." John's remarks seemed to have no effect. "Where do you want your body sent? It'll be cut up into little parts. Probably while you're still alive." He wasn't kidding, or was he?

"So Trafficante's nephew is in on all this?"

"That he is."

"And the Corsicans are here to cut a deal on supplying the shit?"

His question led John to gather he knew more than he admitted. "You get that from the girl?" He had to admit he did. "I guess you did more than fuck her. A regular little talker she must be."

"She's pissed off at Carlos for all kinds of reasons."

"Why does she stay?"

"I don't know. He may be helping her family in Paris, they're pretty hard up."

John seemed to be avidly collecting this information. "The supply is here all right. Poppy is grown and turned into paste in Laos, Burma, Vientiane. They must be here to figure how to get the shit to Europe and the good ol' U.S.A."

He sensed that, for John, this wasn't chitchat. It was beyond simple curiosity. He seemed to know a lot and wanted to know more. "So, you're off for Bangkok. Been there?" No he hadn't. "It can be a fun place. Come back and tell me about it."

He left John to his Thailand import, loving the prospect of having more to tell, ignoring dire warnings. Friday would be upon him soon enough. Meanwhile he had other work to do. It might be said he'd become self-employed. Beyond the jobsite, that is. He hadn't been around for weeks. Not that anyone noticed. Still drawing down on the credit earned from pulling off the air conditioner delivery, he wondered how long his AWOL status would go unnoticed. The answer came when he came across Colonel Lee in the company of a two-star general. "Long time no see," said the colonel, introducing him to General Augustus Sinclair. In lieu of a salute, vigorous handshakes all around. Sinclair, tall and lean, the very model of a modern major general, was revealed to be chief procurement officer for the Corps of Engineers. A VIP being courted by Lee with a cloying sycophancy near to touching in its persistence. The general, leaving Lee behind, walked his new friend a distance away. "Lee's taken all the credit for those air conditioners we needed. But I happen to know it was your doing." The general said this with a welcoming smile for a job well done. And then said, "Come by my office sometime this week, I'd like to talk to you about a few things."

"Sure," he replied. "Tomorrow morning OK?"

"Good man," said Sinclair, pleased by his quick response. Lee stared from afar watching this repartee as the two of them parted company.

He left the compound, leaving Lee to his ass-kissing duties wondering, "What now?" That answer would have to wait. The beer baron would be in his office with that suitcase.

## FIFTY-EIGHT

Ziegler's office was up the stairs in a two-story building off Tu Do Street. Walls lined with beer ads pictured happy guys and gals enjoying the good life. What the war was about — wasn't it? Sitting at his desk, small suitcase to the side, he said, "I got trucks ready to roll dockside. This better not be someone's idea of a con."

Picking up the loot, waving it in nervous Nellie's direction, he replied. "Got yours?" Joe's grunt in reply said, "Sure I got mine." And that was that. Next stop the drop off, first taking his share. Twenty thousand dollars. All in a day's work.

Thanh, at home, accepted the suitcase, nothing so crude as to open and count it. He asked about her brother, a reminder of a favor from the recent past. Thanh, untouched as always by the heat of the day, was equally unfazed at accepting the payoff. So long as the cash was invisible, it didn't exist. The upper classes have lessons to teach about such things. Dalat and that odd encounter in bed seemed far away. The monthly bribe would be a continuing link between them. Another line to add to the equation beyond sex. If that was the deal between them, let it be. Money and sex, usually so compatible, held out no promise. His thoughts turned to Roxanne. Did Thanh know her? he wondered. But decided not to ask. And left with a politesse he'd been taught by her good manners.

Crossing Mac Dinh Street, a line of taxis waited outside the American embassy. Twenty thousand dollars stuffed in his pockets, he took off for home. Then, mirabile dictu, he saw a sight a wonder to behold. Offices of the Bank of America and Chase Manhattan Bank had opened for business for the first time, that very day. A long line, Americans all, waited outside each bank. He brought his taxi to a squealing halt and joined the crowd of laughing cavaliers with plenty to giggle at. Each of them held paper bags or boxes, or large envelopes stuffed with cash to deposit. Any amount was welcome so long as it didn't bring the IRS down on your head. It seems the folks in charge back home, poor fools, were trying to get control of out-of-control inflation by allowing these two great avatars of capitalism to open branches to aid and abet getting rather than spending. Profits from black-market dealings and from anything else that came their way were accepted, no questions asked. He joined the line outside Chase Manhattan like a regular fellow, listening to a fellow parishioner carrying a shopping bag holding at least fifty thousand dollars explain that they'd accept up to one year's salary plus anything you might claim as gambling winnings. A deposit made, relieved of this burden, his pockets empty, he whistled while he worked. Oh, what a lovely war.

# FIFTY-NINE

His weekly power breakfast with Ninh took him back to the café were he'd sat with Roxanne. Ninh was late, allowing him to look at the world around him. Concentration on that lovely woman had so distracted him; he hadn't noticed the movie theatre across the street with its rounded cement marquee, large posters of oddly round-eyed Vietnamese women in war-like poses. A row of tiny 50 cc Hondas stood sentry outside the café where an old woman in pajamas and sandals sat on the street selling small bouquets. A tree shaded the scene, motorbikes and pedicabs rolled by under the not-so-watchful eye of an off-duty cop paid to keep an eye on things. He'd already stopped looking, stopped noticing young men and their girls casually enjoying a morning together. No longer looking for the subtleties of Vietnam that had so entranced him in his first days here. As always, there was a war out there somewhere, but these everyday scenes dulled him to its meaning. He was grateful to see Ninh arrive, taking a seat on a padded folding chair, wreathed in smiles and apologies.

Breakfast ordered, he waited for Ninh's news, sure he'd have something for him. And he did not disappoint, telling of Dolores and Tommy's escape on a U.S. Air Force plane bound for the states. "Using USO identification and a little bit of charm," Ninh said. He wondered how Ninh might know that. On the other hand, he'd given up on figuring out how Ninh knew about his own doings.

"And Sue?" he asked causing a frown as Ninh replied, "Still at The Fuji, she spends a lot of time in one of the back rooms."

"Opium?" He watched Ninh shake his head and explain, "She shared a pipe with my friend Minister Tho and learned to like it too much."

"How is she living here? Is Tho helping her?"

"No, she's on her own." Ninh said this so quietly it could only mean she was turning tricks.

That was enough for him and he changed the subject by asking Ninh, "Do you know a big shot in Saigon called Carlos?"

Ninh too quickly looked up from his croissant. "Carlos Fusina? I don't know him but everyone knows about him." He nodded at Ninh, wanting more. "A crazy man. Very dangerous. People working for him kill on his orders." Remembering John the Greek's warnings, he did not smile, but waited for more. Ninh took a moment to say, "They call him The Opium King, do you know that? But something else is going on." Looking around him, he leaned forward. "Heroin is the new drug. Very pure. Worth big money. It might cause a war."

"A war?" he said, too loudly. "There already is a war going on." And found himself being hushed by Ninh.

"This is different. You heard about the big battle between Burmese and Lao generals?"

"No, I haven't."

Ninh, expansively, explained, "A fight over control of poppy fields. A very big fight, many killed."

Out of curiosity, he asked, "And who won?"

"A truce. Nobody won." And then he added the killer detail. "Someone in your government made the truce."

Trying not to look incredulous, but thoroughly flopping at it, he repeated, "Government? My government?" Then, putting a fine point to naiveté, asked, "Why?"

"Laos is your ally against the VC. Their generals need to be kept happy. The Burmese are only in it for the money."

Ninh had said, "Your ally," rather than "Our ally." This was enough, for now. Remembering his appointment with the general he decided to tell the clever bastard something he might already know or would soon find out: "I'm going to Bangkok for the weekend. A little R&R. Can I bring anything back for you?"

"A little gold bar is always welcome," he said with a big smile."

He had to be kidding, of course. But who knows? Ninh, a constant source of information and surprise, walked with him out onto the street, a jolly strut to his stride.

# SIXTY

MACV, MILITARY ASSISTANCE COMMAND a large, loud sign proclaimed to one and all. "Assistance, my ass," he said, as he walked toward two American guards laden with bulletproof vests, steel pots on heads, M16s at the ready. Half a million of our troops, Christ knows how many planes, ships, millions spent was more than assistance to a Vietnamese army that would run to fight another day. Back home "assistance" was a welfare check. Out here, the check was blank, filled in for any amount the payee chose. Sauntering unchallenged past the armed guards, his white man's face gave him natural access to the place. In the flag-draped reception area pristine floors offered a military sheen; soldiers in starched, knife-sharp pressed fatigues strode by suggesting urgency, high seriousness. It was all so clean, so faraway from the mess of battle. But, who is he to judge? He asked at a desk for General Sinclair. Within seconds he was greeted by an aide-de-camp to the general in tailored fatigues that gave a shape to her thighs that the Lord intended, a lift to her boobs for the delectation of all, hair nicely bobbed to military regulation. Allowing herself a brief smile of greeting, Captain Crawford was all business as she marched him down a well-lit hall to her general's offices.

The general was there to meet him; the captain disappeared under their watchful eyes. "West Point," he said. "Near the top of her class. Terrific soldier." Whatever his point, the two of them entered his office, windows draped against the heat, central air at full blast.

"Coffee?" Coffee was a fine idea against the chill. An intercom button pushed, a male voice answering, "Yes sir," was ordered to bring coffee for two. Within a breath's time a bright young three-striper rolled in a coffee service. The general genially waved off the sergeant's offer to pour. "Anything else, sir?" "No thank you." Did the sergeant leave walking crabwise backwards, or did it only look that way? The general pouring for the two of them said, "There's someone here in Saigon I'd like you to meet." That was getting to it, he thought. No further ado for the general.

"Who?"

"A very important business man. Very important to us." Sinclair said this with a man-to-man straightforwardness assuring the seriousness of the matter, whatever it was.

"An American?"

"Of course. He'd like to see you this morning." The general made that sound close to giving an order. Looking down at his unpressed slacks he was inclined to reply, just for kicks, "Not today." But left his rebel's heart long enough to agree, only asking the name of the gentleman so eager to meet him.

"Ronald Steele."

"The Money King?"

"A ridiculous title," said Sinclair, drawing himself up in the chair. "He's a legitimate business man."

That being said, and no argument offered in reply, he was ushered from the office, past the guards offering a snappy salute, returned with fervor, to a corner where a private car awaited. A little odd for a general officer to not use a staff car, he thought. But never mind, the driver took off without instruction and in the silence between them he tried to think why The Money King of Vietnam would want to see him. No time for such cogitation when the car pulled into the driveway of a modest house in a nondescript neighborhood. A peculiar location for one with so rich a reputation. Led to the front door by Sinclair, he entered an interior without decoration. Shades were drawn in the unlit room and he was taken aback to see an old man in a wheelchair, wearing dark glasses, who offered a hand in greeting across a wide and empty desk.

Sinclair took a seat to the side as Steele took in the new face seated before him. "My eyesight is going to hell. The wheelchair is something new. I got caught in a rockslide forty years ago. Crushed my back and it's finally caught up with me." His voice was direct, not soft exactly, but with a tone of both authority and weariness that suggested someone who'd seen many things and was tired, very tired. An elderly Chinese man was in the shadows and stepped forward when Steele spoke to him, then left the room.

"You speak Mandarin," he said to his host.

"Yes I do. But that was Cantonese. He's from the south."

"You were born in China."

"In 1914. My father was a missionary."

It meant he was in his early fifties and looked fifteen, twenty years older. Steele could see him making that calculation and said, "You're Jewish, aren't you?" He'd asked politely enough, not with the belligerent tone he'd grown used to.

"My mother, not my father," his tired reply.

Steele smiled, "My father, not my mother."

"You said he was a missionary."

"A convert, then a zealous preacher of the Gospel." His mocking tone gave him to understand this was not the son's path.

He noticed Sinclair squirm uncomfortably, not used to hearing such conversation. And grow more uncomfortable when he heard Steele say, "At eighteen I joined the Young Communist League. My own kind of conversion."

Talk about odd bits of news. When the general asked him over he was expecting to see chippies of all kinds, bodyguards in every corner, luxury to fit the needs of a Money King. Instead he found himself with a member of the CP who's proud of it. But there was more news.

"You've heard of The Long March?"

"Yes, I've read about it. Thirty-two hundred miles. Two Years. Made Mao leader of the country."

"Yes. It did. But it was half that distance. Doubling it made for good propaganda." Then, too casually, perhaps trying to impress, he said, "I was on The March, right along with our Glorious Leader." He saw the skeptical look and added, "It's where I hurt my back. Walking through a narrow gorge we took artillery fire that brought a mountain down on us. Killed hundreds. Mao had missed it somehow. I got to say, he experienced more miracles than any of those Loaves and Fishes fables that have gotten around."

Deciding to take this account on faith, he heard this wreck of a man say, "Mao was always constipated, always worried about his bowel movements. It interfered with his sex life." No vulgar euphemisms, apostasy cleanly stated, it was enough for now. "I brought you here to ask a favor. Sinclair looked on as though ready to take notes. "But first, tell me how you got caught up in that dumb drug deal in Cholon."

He saw there'd be no secrets here. "A favor for a friend."

"That small-time clown Boyle is a friend of yours?"

"No, it was about helping the family of a woman I know."

"A woman?" He raised two hands, palms up. "Lord, why must it always involve a woman?" Getting no answer from above or below, he got down to business. 'You may have noticed drugs are everywhere." He had noticed. "Sure, opium and grass is all over the place."

Steele, looking at him with convincing urgency, said, "It's heroin we're worried about. The other stuff was manageable, but the hard stuff is getting into the hands of our troops." There was an oddly moral tone to his voice as he looked for corroboration from sanctimonious Sinclair.

"It shames me to admit it, but we've one big problem on our hands," said Sinclair. "Addiction is taking over fighting units and impacting on the war effort."

Steele waved his general off. "Let me tell you how bad it is. Up in Pleiku, three Noncoms were heavy into distribution and a lieutenant new in country tried to put a stop to it. They shot and killed him. Right in the company street." Before he let that item settle in he said, "Last week an Air Force major had eight million dollars worth of heroin in his plane." Sinclair, in high dudgeon, indignantly said, "Up in Cam Ranh forty MPs were busted for trafficking."

Listening to the two of them, he asked, "So?"

Sinclair continued, "So our guys are returning home desperate for the stuff. They carry it in duffel bags and ship it through the post office. And those still here are running around high as kites."

"So?"

The Money King pronounced, "The Army wants to build a re-hab center right here in Vietnam. The Navy already has two ships in the harbor converted to detox centers. And that's the beginning. Steele looked to Sinclair who went on, "Both projects have to be kept secret. "We need you to get it done through Dupar Construction."

"If its secret how will it be paid for?"

Ronald Steele, pleased with this question, said, "A dummy project will be developed to cover costs, right?" Sinclair jumped to agree.

"What's in this for me?"

The old Maoist, not at all pleased with this, "To redeem yourself."

"Redeem myself?"

"Yes, don't you believe in redemption?"

# SIXTY-ONE

The general rushed them back to MACV Headquarters, locked his private office, and rolled out drawings for plumbing, electrical and other trades. "I don't know anything about this stuff," he told Sinclair. "But I can talk to people who do."

"As long as you keep it on the QT, right?"

"Right."

"Any questions?"

"Yeah. Was Steele really with Mao on The Long March?" Sinclair assayed his questioner long enough to decide how much to reveal.

"Well, he says he was. We have no way to check it out."

"But you have checked him out." Not a question, a simple statement, corroborated by Sinclair. "Sure we've checked him out. He's a real patriot."

"When did he leave China?"

"After Korea," Sinclair said, quietly.

"The Korean War? He was in the war? On whose side?"

Sinclair hesitated only for a moment. "Their side." And hoped to end it there, but his pursuer asked, "What was he doing in the war?"

"An interrogator. The only one in his unit who spoke English."

Sinclair was done. "You've got a car waiting for you." Gathering up the drawings, he felt Sinclair's hand on his shoulder. "We're in this to win. We need your help. We're counting on you." Unimpressed by this fervor, he walked out to the car. "Ronald Steele a patriot? My ass."

Ninh had told him the other morning that heroin use was on the rise. And here he is, being asked to do something about it. He let it go as a coincidence, for now.

Walking into the Dupar compound, he knew the one person who could get this done was John the Greek, who figured something was up with a glance. "A medical facility in Cua Viet? We've already got one there, right near the DMZ. Sure we can do it, but not 'til you tell me what's going on."

Screw secrecy, he decided. "A detox facility. For heroin users."

"A thousand-bed detox facility? Heroin? Lord Jesus."

"That's what it is. And to be kept secret."

"There's nothing secret in Vietnam. Haven't you figured that out? Right now a big secret is that the brig at Danang is jammed with Marines arrested for smoking dope and facing Bad Conduct discharges."

"The Army would rather rehab them."

"Sure they would," said John, who prided himself on being a storehouse of information. "There's a thousand ways to avoid the draft back home, so all kinds of riffraff no matter the criminal record are welcomed into this man's Army. If they are not already drug users before they get here, a good one-third are addicts when they leave." John, flipping through the roll of plans placed before him, asked, "How did you get involved in this?"

The better part of valor was to leave out details. "Lee introduced me to General Sinclair who asked if I could be of help."

"Augustus Sinclair? That loser?" Good old John knew there had to be more. But would have to be satisfied with less.

"Think you can help?"

"It's just another job. By the way, Cua Viet is only reached by sea or air. Construction costs will be billed accordingly." He said this last with a professional, if friendly, grin. What did anybody care about costs? There was money to be made. We had to get our boys back in fighting trim, didn't we?

John rose, plans in hand. "Location, location," he said. "Our boys in detox will be so isolated there'll be no way for them to fill needs or needles. Unless, of course, the medics up there will be their connection." Nothing cynical about that, eh?

A fascination with the Old China Hand led him to bypass General Sinclair, whose driver needed no instruction to bring him to the home of Ronald Steele. The Chinese servant spoke in English. "Mr. Steele resting." About to take his leave, he heard Steele call out and the servant rush to him. A moment later he was taken to a small bedroom, greeted by Steele propped up in a narrow bed. As he took in this ascetic style of life, Steele said, "I prefer not to indulge in creature comforts." He nodded, accepting these mind-reading powers. "It goes back to my years in China. There was never enough of anything and you learned to make do."

"Even for party members?"

Begrudging him the hostility of the remark, Steele replied, "At my level, yes."

"Sinclair tells me you were in Korea during the war."

"Yes, I was," He gave his visitor more than he expected by saying, "When we won the country in 1949 and Mao took over my reward was to become English Language Editor of *The People's Daily*. A nice little job, with an apartment and decent food allowance. A year later the Korean War broke out, Mao went crazy and "Foreign Friends," as we were called, were in trouble. And, since my parents had fled to Taiwan with Chiang Kai Shek, I was especially vulnerable." He paused in this tale from his life while his one servant adjusted the pillows, taking the strain off his back. With a grimace, he said, 'I was purged from the Party, and my job." He knew this was not the end of Steele's story. "To prove my loyalty, I volunteered with the 40th Army and went to Korea." It seemed he was ready to stop there, but went on when he heard his visitor say, "As an interrogator."

"Sinclair told you that."

"Yes, he did."

"Well, before we could interrogate, we had to capture prisoners, so I was a soldier first." He said this so matter-of-fact, it was obvious he'd go on. "I'd fought for years in the Liberation Army against the Nationalists. We were used to meager rations, lousy weapons. And forced marching." He said this last remark with wonderment. "We only traveled at night. Eighteen miles, every night, for eighteen days. Thousand and thousands of us had made it to Korea from Manchuria unseen and unheard. And we attacked at the Cochin Reservoir, with bugles blowing, gongs sounding, causing panic, overrunning enemy positions that never, ever thought we'd be there."

There he sat, in his bed, an old warrior telling a tale of war. Not this war, but another a mere sixteen years before. And here we were, at it again. "And that's when we took prisoners, including a badly wounded full-bird colonel who died of his wounds as I questioned him." Steele paused, then looking at him, said, "I guess Sinclair didn't tell you that colonel was a classmate of his at West Point. Won the Congressional Medal. Posthumous, of course."

Sinclair hadn't, he had to admit, coming to understand the general might have more involved here than Patriotic Gore.

"What brings you here so soon?"

"I picked up plans at MACV, I guess you know that." Steele nodded. "I talked to someone at the office. The project is on its way."

Pleased to hear this, Steele asked, "Whom did you talk to?"

"An electrical engineer."

"John the Greek? Perfect. He's smart enough to figure out what its about, but will keep quiet about it," he said, with an assurance born of experience.

It didn't surprise him John was known to Steele, and asked, "How come you didn't go to him in the first place?"

The Money King, beginning to look weary, said, "I'd heard about you and wanted to meet you. You're a clever guy, and there's not too many of them out here." Looking at him, near to avuncular, Steele added, "You're a risk taker, but you've got to learn how to minimize risk." Accepting this as a compliment, he bade his flatterer goodbye.

"Come by anytime," he said. "There's still a lot to talk about."

That would have been that, but Steele looked at him pleasantly and said, "Enjoy yourself in Bangkok. Arrive home safe."

Ushered out as The Money King closed his eyes in sleep, he had no chance to ask an obvious a question, getting an answer that evening from John pounding the door to his apartment angrily asking, "Why didn't you tell me Ron Steele was involved with this detox joint?"

"And how did he know about my trip to Bangkok?"

"First things first. You don't know what you're dealing with here."

"Enlighten me."

Pushing his way into the apartment, John flopped angrily onto the couch. "The estimate on the electrical was way low, I went downtown to see that idiot Sinclair. He let slip it was a Steele project."

Sitting across from John, whose usual cool manner was long gone, he replied. "But, it's an Army project."

"You're not only a crazy fuck, you're an ignorant crazy fuck. Its his deal."

"Why?'

"I dunno. What I do know is that for fun, I tripled the cost on the job and old Augustus never blinked."

"Is Steele paying for it?"

"John came out of his chair, "No, you jerk, he never pays for anything. I want a beer."

Thrusting a can at John, it was his turn. "And you're the jerk who told him about my trip to Bangkok. And about the girl, too." John cracked open the can, took a swilling pull, denying nothing. "Are you trying to get me killed?"

"No, asshole, I was guaranteeing your safety." John sat back, smug as a hundred-dollar whore. "Your boy Steele hates the Corsicans. It's part of his Chinese heritage." He went back to his beer, waiting to be begged for more.

"What's with him and the Corsicans?"

Taking on a professorial turn of expression, John intoned: "When the Japs took over Southeast Asia in 1941, the Corsicans were collaborators in chasing down the Chinese and all their hidden gold. When the French came back in '45, the Corsicans had taken over Chinese businesses and homes, looted anything that moved. When Ronnie came to town, the Chinese knew he'd been touched by Mao, treated him like an angel, and passed on their happy feelings toward our Corsican friends. End of lesson."

"Well, fuck it, I'm gonna skip on Bangkok anyway."

John, reassuringly, said, "With that kind of protection, I'd go over there and enjoy myself."

"Then be my guest and go in my place."

John spilled his beer, replying, "Uh, uh, lover boy, she's all yours." Trying a pass at sincerity, John added, "Carlos would never touch one of The Money King's boys."

Not bothering to be annoyed he said, "I ain't one of his boys."

"So you say. Too late for that. In like Flynn." Then as an afterthought, he said, "Ronald Steele is one connected guy."

He'd had enough of this bullshit. "How the fuck does he get from Mao Tse Tung and the Chinese People's Army in Korea to all of a sudden being connected?"

John, amused by his question, enjoying the moment, pushed deeply into the cushioned couch.

"So you know he fought with the other side in Korea?" Yes, he did know that. "Well, let me tell you what you may not know." Pausing for effect, John said, "When the war started to turn and a truce was being talked about, our heroic friend slipped out of his uniform and appeared in his underwear at an American outpost. Hard fighting was still going on, Chinese prisoners were being taken and he made himself useful once again as an interrogator, this time for the our side. Cute, don't you think?"

Very cute, indeed, and waited for John to continue what he began to think was a fabulist's account. "Our man from Mao didn't hang around for very long, heading south where opportunity beckoned in the form of liquor franchises, maybe a little call-girl action, having the bright idea to bring over American girls, leaving Korean hookers to the lower ranks."

"And that's where Trafficante comes in?"

"No, not yet," John replied to his suddenly interested listener. "Bigger, much bigger." And asked a question, "Meyer Lansky?" And waited for the nod of recognition which led him to explain how it was that Lansky's grandson had made the bad mistake of being drafted into the infantry and the further mistake of being shipped to Korea where he would join his fellow men under arms as cannon fodder. A story good enough to be true, he decided, watching John unfold the yarn like a Greek storyteller.

"Trafficante had learned about Steele, and on behalf of Lansky asked his assistance in assuring dear old Grandpa about the safety of his only grandson. It took no more than a case of liquor and a winsome threesome, and the boy was assigned as a company clerk so far from the action, the quiet kept him awake at night."

"I got to say, this sounds like fantasy to me. Who's telling you all this stuff?"

"The Money King himself. And he's got more to tell, if you care to listen."

John had calmed down after his angry entrance, helping himself to a second beer. Walking back into the living room, he said, "The Money King all right. And he's got General Sinclair by the balls."

"How come?"

"Ronnie baby was living in Hong Kong, enjoying the fruits of retirement when the buildup began out here. He couldn't resist, an old dog answering a call from the wild, and now supplies every service club in the country with liquor, slots, pinball, refrigerators, generators, you name it." And heard his host add, "And the B Girls. A nice little side line, that."

Finally sitting down, John said without begrudging him a dime, "It's worth millions to him."

"And Sinclair?"

"Ron needed space to store all that equipment and, though not considered an appropriate use of military facilities, got the use of a big Army warehouse at Long Binh. Sinclair got wind of it and asked to meet our man Steele, who wired himself for the occasion, catching the General soliciting a thousand dollars a week for services rendered."

"You get that from him?"

"Uh uh. A Sergeant. Criminal Investigator for the Army. Steele's got him on retainer too. I did him a favor once, and he passed the story on to me."

"Must have been quite a favor."

"That it was."

He looked at John, sitting there, and said to him, "So you know two things, don't you? Sinclair solicited a bribe, and The Money King is paying it."

"John smiled at his willing pupil. "You ain't as dumb as you look. Going to Bangkok tomorrow?"

# SIXTY-TWO

Brutalized by hundred-degree heat and nasty humidity, he fled to the verandah of the Oriental Hotel to catch a breeze. Though it was close to twilight there were few people around as he sat, a tall vodka and tonic for company, in vain hope it might provide comfort against the sapping temperature.

Looking out on the wide, swiftly flowing river, a scene at Bangkok's small airport kept returning to mind. Departure and arrival doors were yards from each other. Lovely Thai women, clutching at young American soldiers, bade tearful, melancholy farewells with an ardor reserved for those most dear. R&R was over for these GIs striding manfully to the flight back to Saigon. Brave soldiers and their girls in last farewells is the stuff of song. And this was no exception, with one small difference. The girls left behind waved bravely for one last moment before dashing off to the arrival's gate, to await another batch of fresh faces. One by one young troopers emerged, some in civilian clothes, others still in field garb, happily taken in hand by those girls so sadly left behind offering, once again, two weeks never, ever to be forgotten.

The overnight bag he'd packed for the trip held a change of clothes and the one hundred thousand U.S. he'd brought along, not to spend, but for purchase of gold. Taking advantage of that tidbit of information Thanh had provided the first day they'd met. Good enough for the generals, good enough for him. If Carlos sent Roxanne here each month he'd draw a double dividend from the trip if she was still game and The Greek's assurances held.

The verandah began to fill with American women and children doting on husbands and fathers who'd also gotten two weeks away from war. Clutching what they held so dear, children clambered over Daddy's lap, Mommy all smiles imagining this forever, not over in a fortnight. The cost of these trips roundtrip from stateside had to be staggering. He signed the bill, being sure to take up his bag and check at reception for any messages.

Nothing yet, or maybe not at all he thought, and went up to his room. Teak was the choice of material throughout the hotel. Its dark browns, set against silk-covered couches and chairs, welcomed him toward a wide four-poster bed. The heat, not abating as night fell, had sapped his energy and he stretched out watching darkened boats glide past the wide window looking out on the river. The luxury was not lost on him, its expense not an issue. He wanted no interruption to a rare moment. One of tranquility against his life an hour's flight away. He closed his eyes, head resting against soft silk.

A ringing phone and a clock beside his bed proved he'd been asleep for two hours. Hating the interruption, he heard Roxanne invite him to her rooms, "The Noel Coward Cottage." She had to be kidding, he thought, checked at the desk, directed to the rear of the hotel where real luxury resided. Cottages posted nameplates. The Somerset Maugham, the Joseph Conrad if anyone can imagine. Roxanne was at Noel Coward's open door. She flung herself at him with youth's exuberance and he lifted her high in the air to share her joy. The cottage was another delight with a bedroom, living room, small study. Furnished as a yacht's interior, a photo of Coward in a blazer and sailor's peaked cap smiled down on those who entered here. He was glad to see Carlos' money so well spent.

"Business, business," Roxanne apologized about her lateness as she nibbled on his ear. "I'm starving, can we go to dinner?" Of course they could. The hotel had Le Normandie and God spare the mark, a fish place called Lord Jim's. Roxanne would have none of it. Off to a waiting taxi, an address given, they were soon seated at a suspiciously grubby Thai restaurant Roxanne told him was the best in town. The great abundance of Thai restaurants in America prepared him for his meal as Roxanne ordered for ten. Plates of broad noodles slathered in a brown sauce and a generous amount of shrimp was served. Roxanne dove in with glee and he joined her by taking a bite of the noodles. On the instant, the chili paste in the sauce assaulted him, allowing barely enough time to pull his napkin to his face to spit out the heat-seeking missile he'd placed in his mouth. The one bite brought tears to his eyes as he felt steam escape from his ears. Roxanne went on with her meal, enjoying every incendiary morsel as he grabbed for water in a vain attempt to cool down the hot oven of his mouth.

"Too hot for you?" she sweetly asked. "Have another bite, you'll soon get used to the taste." Not a chance, he thought, eyeing the shrimp speculatively. "Water wont do any good," she said helpfully. "Put a small amount of sugar on the tip of your tongue." Coquettishly, her tongue moved lasciviously as she demonstrated the way to cool down. "It was the same with Carlos the first time." Such sweet innocence on display before the new man in town, he could hardly be offended.

"He comes with you often."

"No, just one time to introduce me to the people who meet me at the airport each month."

It was a mystification how his women would so glibly mention past or present lovers. Must be some residual affection they assumed would be of interest to him. All he knew was that it was goddamned annoying. The evening had cooled off to maybe ninety-five. He tried sugar on the tip of his tongue. Look at that, it worked for Carlos, and worked for him.

It was well past midnight. Still tired from his nap, he hoped they'd be headed back. Joining Roxanne in a second beer to keep her company, he hoped his lack of conversation would clue her to his wishes. Finishing off her beer she called for the check that he was happy to pay. A gentleman's prerogative, and, not that it mattered, a tenth of what a meal at the Oriental would have cost him.

In a taxi he called out Oriental Hotel, to be corrected when Roxanne said, "No, the Arawan."

It turned out to be a large coffee shop filled with what had to be scruffy, tired whores who perked up when the two of them walked in. Seated at an empty table it didn't take him long to figure out what was next. Roxanne was looking the room over, making up her mind. Settling first on the ugliest, meanest hooker in the room, she stopped long enough at a corner table to invite a woman in kimono to join them. Turned down, Roxanne simply kept on her rounds, choosing a muscular boy who leapt at the opportunity. Ready to go, she gathered up her bemused escort. Pointing to the boy she asked, "Interested?" He shook his head, "No thanks," as he thought, "I bet Carlos would be."

"Well, let's take him along anyway," Roxanne said generously. And off they went, back to the Oriental Hotel that had seen it all. To show annoyance he jumped into the front seat of the taxi, leaving Roxanne to sit between her selections. Feeling her hand on the back of his neck, he looked in the rear-view mirror to see her fondling the sagging breasts of the old whore while reaching for her mouth. Flicking her hand from his shoulder, he looked straight away into traffic knowing he was in for it. What was with her with all this nasty stuff? Was it for him? Is this what she thought men wanted? Over the years, he'd had pleasant moments with pairs of attractive women inviting him into their lives. Conversation, laughs, sharing drinks and meals. And the sex, too, was mighty good. It was a relationship, sort of. This thing in the taxi with that disgusting hooker was degradation, defined.

A security guard at the hotel came over as they entered, prepared to put a stop to this invasion of undesirables. But was persuaded when Roxanne opened her purse, awarding him handsomely to find another dilemma to resolve. Entering the cottage, he took to a soft chair under dear Noel's photo. Roxanne's two guests chatted incomprehensibly, excited as monkeys, taken by the luxury of the place, as she took him by the hand into the bedroom. Once again he took to a chair, Roxanne shrugged and proceeded to set up a tableau vivant for their entertainment. He was growing tired, so very tired, the last thing he remembered before falling asleep in the chair was Roxanne carefully placing a condom on the boy and drawing him to her.

Waking to an empty room, he saw a disordered bed, a still smiling Noel Coward and a clock that read four AM. Leaving the cottage, heading toward his room, the security guard volunteered that the group had gone to Pat Pong Road. An avenue of dives, drugs and anything else a little heart might desire. Allowing a moment for indecision, he opted instead for bed and sleep.

## SIXTY-THREE

Dawn came thundering in, waking him from a bare two hours' rest. Cursing his failure to pull the curtains, he thought for a brief second about Roxanne while heading downstairs to a quiet lobby and coffee on the verandah. At riverside he watched small boats motor up, let hotel workers off at a slip, then continue upstream. Coffee cup in hand he went down to the slip, took a seat on a boat that came along, and was on his way to where he knew not nor cared.

The little water taxi worked past other boats laden with bright flowers headed to market, steered into narrower waters that might have been a canal. Poor houses on stilts stood at waterside, their occupants readying themselves for the day washing faces, pots and pans, a little boy peeing under the watchful eye of a sister, the sun not yet bringing its assaulting heat to the day. The boat moved toward a landing and he joined others on the boat debarking onto a lane with gated houses on each side forming a neighborhood of children preparing for school, parents on the way to work.

Walking away from the canal, he saw some distance from him a blur of orange color. As it drew closer, he saw slim young men, bowls in hands, cone-shaped hats on heads, faces hidden. Monks they must be, he thought, as they stopped at each gate to receive gifts of fruit, vegetables, coins, from men and women in western clothes pausing from their morning rush to offer alms. Bangkok was more than Pat Pong, and hookers, and GIs desperate for surcease from war. Gratefully, he walked down this simple street, forgetting his own mad life, pushing away the goings-on of the night before. Distancing himself, granting himself forgiveness for an accretion of sins that knew no counting. He would change his ways. Take up a beggar's bowl. A beggar all his life, why not take it all the way home?

Luckily his mood was overtaken by song and the sight of taxis coming and going. Seven thirty in the morning it might be, but high-school-age boys and girls were running to and fro from a large house set back from the street in company of Sgt. Pepper. The kids were Americans, all of them. On the way to school, he guessed. Curious, he went up the path to the house and entered a land of Beatles, tie-dyed shirts, and the serious presence of hash in all the rooms. The kids were lined up, cash in hand, for little bags of the brown stuff, before dashing off to school, not to be late for class. No attention was paid to this old guy watching the action unfold as Sgt. Pepper kicked in on a continuous loop when the last cut ended. A handsome American in his twenties, blond and blue-eyed, approached him amiably. He lived in the house, and didn't mind at all explaining he sold stuff from his home to keep the kids from the danger of buying it on the street. Offered a sample, he abstemiously demurred. "Who are these kids?"

"Oh, their parents are in business, or working for our government. There's an American high school nearby." Then by way of further explanation, "Thailand is very indulgent of drug use." Thus it is these young Americans indulge themselves. "She's leaving home, bye, bye," he heard on the stereo, having made his own farewell to this leader of a Children's Crusade.

The narrow street came to a broad boulevard leading toward a large park blanketed with shade trees, and a winding path toward a lake. Morning traffic had begun its inexorable grind, but the park, cool against the morning sun, allowed for joggers, strolling pairs, and children in the company of nannies paddling small boats through flowering lilies decorating the waters of the lake. Lumpini

Park, a sign announced. Something to do with Buddha, he tried to remember, but wasn't sure. Taking a seat under a blue umbrella at lakeside, the disturbances of the night before returned. "Dump your hundred thousand and head on home," he said to small birds flying among the trees. Look at that, calling Saigon home. He'd take care of this easy piece of business first, take on the larger matter of Roxanne soon enough.

At the hotel, the bag kept at the front-desk, he saw a Japanese woman with an older American he recognized. The woman called him Jim. It was James Michener, collecting his room key, and moving away before his admirer had a chance to tell him he'd come to Asia because he'd read when he was twelve, with no business in the adult section of the library, *Tales of the South Pacific.* The first chapter was innocent enough, a dramatic landing of a crippled plane, if he recalled. The librarian allowed him to check out the book, and at home he opened to chapter two and squirmed with wonder before scenes of sex exploding off the page. A first time for everything, and this was a first time that has stayed with him for all these years. He watched Michener's great gray head walk away, knowing he had tales of his own that would forever go untold, collected his bag, spotting Roxanne sitting on the verandah.

He watched her, demure, virginal, in a white dress and sandals, ordering breakfast with a polite smile, glancing out at the river and the temple looming nearby. It was time to walk away, get it over with, bank his money and get the hell out. But lingering, watching, brought indecision. He walked over to her table and sat down. Accepting his presence as acceptance of her in all things, she said, "I went to Pat Pong Road last night."

"I heard."

"Oh, did you ask?"

He let her hostile tone go by. "I was told by the guard."

Reaching for her handbag, she fetched four ten-dollar bills putting them before him.

"Down a side alley, I fucked four of your soldiers for ten dollars each." Pausing, she said, "Here, you can be my pimp."

He let the bills rest before him. "That's a lie. Why are you doing this?"

"Are you judging me?"

"Not in matters of bad behavior. Matters of bad taste."

She placed a hand to her chest and mockingly said, with a sly smile, "That might be the ultimate judgment."

Refusing to play, he rose, "I've got business here."

At this air of dismissal she touched his hand, "A moment in your room, perhaps?"

Not bothering to answer, he began to walk away. Roxanne came after, "I'm going with you."

"As you wish."

"When you are done with business, we'll see the sights. If you wish, that is." And went trailing after him, the forty dollars and her breakfast left behind.

## SIXTY-FOUR

Irritated to feel his pique diminishing, he walked into a nearby bank, pointing Roxanne to a chair. No point allowing her into this part of his life. He'd decided to simply rent a safety deposit box, not bother with gold. The hundred thousand, and any more he chose to add to the pile, would be safe and ready for pickup when he left Vietnam behind. Roxanne watched as he spoke to an attractive officer of the bank, signed some papers, and disappeared with a guard to a vault and a box of his own. He'd never needed such a thing he realized, as he stuffed the bag in, locked the box, pocketed the key, joining the world of clandestine money safely stored.

Sharp-eyed Roxanne asked, "What happened to your little bag?" She knew what she was asking, the clever young thing, but got no satisfaction, no response. With plenty like her to be had at every corner, it was not availability that kept him interested. It was her life and questions to be answered from the night before.

They left the bank and she was pleased to note he followed along, if in silence, as she wandered into expensive stores, feeling textures, examining styles and colors, never checking price tags. Thai women were universally attractive, he concluded. Shoppers or clerks, graced with very sexy figures, eyes large and black, their smooth darkened skin allowing them to wear an array of bright colors. Blue, lime green, red and orange was everywhere, tailored to show off lovely bums, cinched waists. His wandering eye returned to see Roxanne emerge from a dressing room in an electric blue Thai silk jacket and skirt seeking his approval. It was wrong for her. The bright colors against her pale skin, light hair, were shocking, out of place. He told her so. "There are few men that can get me to change my mind about a choice of clothes."

"Or change your mind about anything," he said.

"Oh that," she said. "I suppose we must talk about it." Turning to the dressing room she was gone but a minute, leaving behind the costume offensive to his tender sensibilities.

The heat of the day bothered her not at all. He decided to tough it out, allowing sweat to dampen his shirt, his socks a puddle in his shoes. They halted before a temple she called a Wat, entering the blessing of shade. The darkness within began to reveal an altar decorated at its sides with white and yellow chrysanthemums in clear glass jars. As they approached, Roxanne talked lovingly about the figure of Buddha in gold atop a series of low steps. As he noticed traceries of a wide, gold-leafed frame, she spoke elegantly about the quality of the craftsmanship, the origins of its traditions. The sullied sheets of the night before made no sense. Her soft voice, her passion for beautiful things, tossed him off guard. He went on listening, adding nothing, with nothing to say.

As they left the Wat, sensing a shift of mood, she took his hand. Against his better nature, he allowed the gesture as she led him to an immense four-sided relief of women's heads. Each identical to the faces of women he'd seen in the shops. Women's constancy still applied to appearances, he was glad to see. He asked Roxanne why one of the women — only one — had her eyes wide open and her head in her hands. "It's a look of amazement. For the first time she is experiencing Nirvana."

Nirvana. Nice concept, that. He'd reached for it, with no luck. Too much work, if he recalled correctly. "Can we go somewhere and get out of this heat?" She'd missed out on her breakfast, she pointed out, showing a petulant face that could only have been learned in Paris. Did she think charm could overcome? An air-conditioned dream of a hotel lobby beckoned. They entered its marbled halls and found a café.

"Bad taste. You said, 'I showed bad taste.' " He nodded. "A bourgeois idea, well beneath you," she added, looking over the menu.

"All of us are more bourgeois than we'll admit, don't you think?"

"Speak for yourself. My life, my choices," she said, ordering a large breakfast.

"Well, when you include me in the choices you make, I too can choose."

"And so you did."

"Pornography has always bored me to sleep," he said as she hungrily went at a plate of eggs and rasher of bacon. Raising her fork in his direction while arching her eyebrows, she preened, "So I'm a porn star."

"If that's what you want to call yourself. It was your choice of co-star that disgusted me."

"It was not a movie, it was reality." Then, with the pomposity of an eager adolescent said, "My interest is direct experience with truth." Neither in defiance nor a plea for understanding, added, "I am who I am."

This sounds like an undergraduate seminar, he wanted to say. And wondered if she realized she was quoting Popeye. Toying with a sweet roll he listened as she berated him for thinking anything in this world could be considered disgusting. "While you were sleeping I drew her portrait," she announced proudly. As if this gesture out of Lautrec would have ennobled the hag.

"Not the boy?"

"Of no interest to me."

He left this lie at rest, as she said, "I learned very soon that men, who claimed no interest, would soon enough become engaged." Finishing her breakfast she had to add, "It's so amusing to watch them pretend to be shocked when taken unawares."

"Carlos?"

"Of course, Carlos. Not that I introduced him to anything new, you can be sure." Then grimly she said, "Boys were a break for me from his demands."

This charged conversation had managed to neutralize the subject for him. He had to decide, or choose if you must, his next move. What remained between them lingered at the table along with a mess of dirty dishes. He told her he'd be getting back to the hotel to rest. Let her toy with her big ideas about experience.

In the hotel lobby, outside the restaurant, two epicene men walked toward the elevators. Two tiny Thai girls, no more than eight or nine in company of a motherly woman, caught his attention. They seemed connected to the men. As they waited for the elevator, each man took a child by the hand. Seeing this, he gripped Roxanne by the arm, demanding she watch as the elevator doors opened, the men entered turning with a smirk in their direction. The doors closed and the woman who'd been with them walked into the lobby and sat down.

Dropping Roxanne's arm he said, "Where do you think that belongs on your scale of experience?" She fell silent as he walked away into the heat and a taxi to his hotel.

## SIXTY-FIVE

Things could have ended there. If only. He'd switched his return to Saigon from Sunday to a late flight that evening. Getting back to normal. Saigon, normal? Enough to raise a laugh. He thought about visiting Pat Pong Road. To have a look he promised himself slyly. How could he return to Bangkok without getting laid? An answer came with a knock on the door. Roxanne, a small cardboard cylinder in hand. "A gift for you."

Accepting the gift, as though a baton had been passed in a footrace, he allowed her into his rooms. Fumbling to extricate the contents of the cylinder he passed it back, and she deftly pulled out a drawing as her gift to him. Unrolled, he saw it was the whore of the night before in all her degradation. And, it was remarkable, in fact beautiful. Not the whore, but the drawing, capturing a pathetic dignity in the face and shape of her head, tilted toward the stars. Roxanne watched him, waiting to hear a word.

"Angelic," he said. "It's angelic. Thank you. Thank you very much."

She needed to hear no more. Rolling the drawing back in its tube, she returned it, starting to leave. Of course he would have none of it, forgot about Pat Pong Road, forgot his night flight home. "May I invite you to dinner? At a place of my choosing?" She smiled at the multiple meanings expressed in his invitation. "With pleasure," she said, innocently enough. "I need to change. Would seven be agreeable?"

"Le Normandie at seven, then."

# SIXTY-SIX

The hotel's homage to the great French ocean liner was exquisite in its choice of Art Nouveau. In a curvilinear, voluptuously framed mirror at its entrance he saw Roxanne. In its reflection, an injustice was done to her choice of dress for the evening. Of a color somewhere between turquoise and a deeper green, inches above the knee, high heels of black leather with wispy, sexy straps at the ankles. She moved toward him comfortably; a brilliant smile, an offering of herself he accepted cheek to cheek. It was then he noticed the jade necklace, starting point to their mad time together. The subtle green of the jade, combined with shades of green and blue in the material, the collar spread wide from her neck, so concentrated the mind he lost speech long enough to see that smile once again, before moving toward a river-side banquette.

She ordered a Kir, he joined with a vodka gimlet. A tall, mirrored, mahogany breakfront held flamboyant art nouveau dishware. Drinks in hand, they walked around the restaurant admiring elegant Lalique glass, and small chandeliers hanging from thin metal chains that cast a mellow light through smoked curved glass over each of the tables. A very sexy nude in white porcelain caught their eye. Female, of course. The Normandie had been filled with these beauties. A large poster of the great ship showed off its sleek lines, three angled smokestacks painted red with black trim. Above the keel, more of the black and red with white across the portholes of the top deck. A floating palace, come to a bad end.

They had been walking in silence until Roxanne said, "Pretty, isn't it? Art Nouveau, for the nouveaux riches." It was dismissive enough, and he gave no argument. As they took their places at the banquette, he watched her with the small pleasure of another kind of connoisseurship reserved for men who took careful note of women's movements as she glided into place, unruffled, without a crease across a splendid ass.

Over their disappointing meal, no match for the décor, he asked if she knew the fate of the Normandie. "Of course," she all but bristled. "Every French child knows of the triple stupidity that brought it to its end." He could recount the welder's torch that started the fire, the decision by an American to continue pouring water on the flames despite pleas to open the shuttle cocks to prevent the keeling over that occurred. "I know of two stupidities. What was the third?"

"Your government's insistence on taking it away from France. To become a troop ship, an atrocity in the first place. But to allow it to catch fire and sink was disgusting."

That it was. He'd seen photographs of the great ship keeled over on its side at a berth in New York City. Flames from the fire lit the skies for days, as the ship, stripped of all dignity, rolled over and died. Sold for a pittance to a New Jersey scrap yard at the end of the war.

"My grandfather was at her christening," she said. "We have a photograph of him standing near the largest bottle of champagne ever made. It was on the Loire, the bottle was swung against the hull, the ship was released and hundreds were nearly washed away when she hit the water. It could have been a tragedy, but all grandfather recalls was getting soaked alongside the president and foreign minister."

"Your grandfather was very well-connected."

"Yes, on his way to a brilliant career. In the official party of the maiden voyage of Le Normandie. Until they learned he had a Vietnamese wife and child." Roxanne looked at him, assuming he could never understand such unfairness existed in the world. He was just another American walking the earth with unlimited money and power. "Now he sits in his poor rooms in Paris remembering his son."

"Your father."

"Yes, my father. He would be about your age now."

A quiet came upon them, this odd pair sitting in a French restaurant in Bangkok, Thailand. Recollecting the end of a ship, a career, and a life.

"C'est la guerre," she said with a sneer. "It's always said with a shrug. I hate its passivity. An excuse to accept what should always be rejected." She paused, wondering if he understood. He did, but could find no words to comfort her.

"Your father was a soldier."

"Yes, in order to prove his father was worthy of recognition. And look at how it turned out for them."

"When will you go back to Paris," he asked. A slight change of subject, he knew, but all he could offer.

"Soon enough. For now I'll remain in Saigon."

"With Carlos?"

She looked at him, not at all coyly, "Are you suggesting another arrangement?"

Awkwardly, he shook his head, "No, I'm not."

A tinkle of laughter came over her. "Just as well, Carlos would have made you another casualty of the war."

"I'm willing to take my chances if you are."

Smiling broadly at her victory, she said, "Weekends in Bangkok are not enough for you?"

He smiled back, "Perhaps they're too much for me."

"Well, let's see what the weekend still has for us. Saigon can wait, for now."

## SIXTY-SEVEN

Roxanne knew her stuff about men, offering to join him in his rooms, rather than her desecrated place of the night before. Her sensuality, his sexuality, offered satisfaction guaranteed. Neither would want their money back. But a bigger, better payoff was his. Sitting up, leaning deep into the pillows of the four-poster bed, Roxanne lit a cigarette, filling the room with the aroma of Gauloise. "So, you're planning to see me back in Saigon?" She waited for him to show a bit of hesitation.

"Yes," he said. "I can take care of myself." He knew better than anyone that run-and-hide was his only strategy, but was determined to show brave heart to his French chippie.

"No you can't. Not against Carlos." Ready to show annoyance at this constant calling out of this name, he listened as she said, "But I don't think he'll have time for you. He's working on something very big."

"That's why all the Corsicans are here."

"No, something else. More than the drugs. He was talking with two of his Corsican killers in their vulgar language about an American.

"Killing an American?"

"I suppose so." She said this so casually, adding, "He usually uses his Vietnamese for such things. But can only trust his countrymen for this."

"Who is the American?"

She hesitated, long enough for him to expect a lie. "I don't know the name, a businessman."

Working an obvious hunch, he asked, "What kind of business?"

"I don't know. Carlos thinks taking it over would make him into an honest man." She burst out laughing at this absurdity, dragging on her cigarette to its last measure of pleasure before stubbing it out.

"Do you think you could find out?"

"Perhaps. You seem so interested in Carlos all of a sudden."

It was his turn to dissemble. "No, no, only curious."

It was not the first time Roxanne had been lied to by man in her bed. And let this one go as she had so many of the others, declaring with a winsome glance she'd had enough talk.

"How long has it been since you left Paris?"

A sigh at this intrusion on her mood. "Nearly a year. I suppose you wonder what keeps me here?" That he did, and her answer was one he could have guessed. "Carlos is very generous with his women. It keeps them near and out of the way at the same time."

"And you?"

"I support my family in Paris with what he gives me."

Not a challenge or proposal to him on this variation of hookerdom. She was a working girl making her way in the world. And heaven would protect her. He no longer cared to ask about her antics of the night before. Carlos and his assassin's intentions were far more interesting.

## SIXTY-EIGHT

A complacent Sunday morning found the happy couple together in their bed. A rare treat for the two of them, this sharing of sleep after the night before with God only knows what or whom. He was wide awake, as Roxanne stirred, still half-asleep. She sweetly begged for coffee delivered to the room. Nothing easier, and minutes later a cart came rolling in with anything her little heart desired. A real provider he's turned out to be. Her flight at midmorning, time for her to change out of her lovely dress, offer another bout in bed, and be gone. And so it was. Carlos was unmentioned, but hung between them like a vulture in a tree. Her early departure gave him the break he wanted from all of that. Yet, he felt loneliness at her departure, missing that spirit infused with anger but alive to life's possibilities. This jump from woman to woman led him to remember what devotion to a one and only might bring. A moment's thought, no more.

He dressed without concern for appearances, called down to the concierge and booked a return for late that afternoon. After a night of hookers in a pornographic pile, a golden Buddha, a recounting of bitter family memories, a generous offering of herself to him last night and this morning, he'd had his Bangkok weekend. Without recourse to Pat Pong Road he was quick to remind. In fact, Carlos was on his mind. Not fear of him. He was a clown. Dangerous, but a clown if he thought he could take down The Money King. And, sitting out on the verandah, idling away the hours 'til flight time, he was sure the bedtime gossip Roxanne had passed on had to be about him. Trying to think how to use this information was of little use. He reacted to events. Taking advantage when he could. With no plan either in the day to day, or in this life of his. Easier to muse on Roxanne. Did that complicated morsel have a plan to escape? He'd love to give a boost to that scheme, if only to catch Carlos' reaction.

The American families he'd seen on Friday evening were gathering on the verandah for what had to be a last goodbye. Wives, sad smiles on tear-stained faces, children clinging to their dads, their two weeks gone by so quickly, only time to hug with promises to see each other, soon. He watched as four of the men, with special words for their children, turned away and left. Time for him to go as well. Duty calls for each and every one of us.

## SIXTY-NINE

At the Bangkok terminal, with soldiers and their girls in last embrace, the human comedy of welcome and farewell played out in all pomp and circumstance. The flight, loaded with these boys, carried fragrance of hash, booze, and loud descriptions of their carousing. Photos gleefully exchanged of women plain naked or in seductive poses, laughter, the joy of experiences forever remembered, filled the cabin until the plane began its descent. Then a quiet, near to silence, as Vietnam came back into their lives, and they knew their holiday was over.

Departing the terminal, he paid no attention as MPs with dogs greeted the arriving troopers. Dogs trained to sniff out the nasty stuff bound to be carried back by our boys. Walking toward a line of taxis, he felt hands behind him grasp his arms and escort him to a waiting car. No Welcome Wagon, this. Pushed into a rear seat he found himself alongside Carlos who pointed a pretty little pistol at his eyes.

His only thought at that moment was to come to grips with the fact that Roxanne had indeed turned out to be a very expensive piece of ass. "Enjoy your weekend?" Though Carlos now loomed so large in his life for so many reasons, it was the first time he'd heard his voice. It had a soft, reserved sound that surprised him. A happier surprise was watching Carlos lower, and holster, the pistol. "You can fuck that pervert all you like," he said. Afraid to smile at Carlos calling Roxanne perverted, he noticed he was clear-eyed, sober as Sunday.

He thought he should answer bravely, "Yeah, I had a good weekend, or part of it, anyway."

"Tried to bring in the boys on you, did she? Does it all the time. Weird, don't you think?"

This conversational tone from Carlos was allowing him to relax. He thought this a mistake, but had no way to know where this was taking him. "Do what you like with her. I haven't touched her in months. I can't risk any disease she's carrying. I've got a wife and family to think about."

A family man, he'd announced to his passenger, who found absurd the turn their backseat chat had taken, but wisely held his silence. "The bitch's father was my best friend. I brought her out here knowing it would help her family. I didn't have the heart to seduce her mother." Carlos looked at him man to man, before saying, "Though she was available, I can assure you." That established, he said, "Who knew the daughter would be so out of control. It must be what they learn at art school." He paused again, his way to appear thoughtful. "I say this with regret, but I'm glad her father never lived to see this day." Once again Carlos looked at him, the sincere tone setting him up for something. "Women are the cheapest commodities in this country. Their value more debased than a piastre." A lecture on economics, what gives? "So let's forget our little trollop, shall we?" He was more than grateful to agree, then astonished at what followed when Carlos grandly announced, "You are going to be my business partner."

With that remarkable remark, they came before a grand chateau, the biggest, he would bet, in all Saigon. As Carlos left the car, three children ran to greet him. The family man was home. Along with his passenger, recently away in Bangkok. What the hell, he left the car and joined the fun, noticing that security was everywhere. His wife was no beauty, but Carlos reveled in the warm and happy example of her motherly manner. A ten-year old boy took daddy's guest by the hand, speaking in English, calling him uncle. Young

Vietnamese men stood by, little belly pouches he knew held pistols hidden from view. The price of success in this difficult world.

Turning to his guest, pronouncing, "You must be starving after your strenuous weekend away." Carlos clapped him on the back. "One more for dinner, Dominique." They passed the dining room dominated by a copy of that famous portrait of Napoleon, another Son of Corsica, and entered a darkened room lit by table lamps, and, as he grew used to the lack of illumination, he saw they were alone. It was a library, books in French and English on shelves, and scattered about an imposing desk. Carlos took a seat in a red leather wing chair and had him do the same.

He'd been fucking one of Carlos' women that very morning. And here he was in his company, in his home, no less. It always had been a point of honor with him to stay away from the women of friends and acquaintances. Not quite always, for when circumstances overwhelmed what was a man to do? But a general principle to which he adhered, within reason. Carlos might technically have been a cuckold, but under these conditions, so variable, it no longer was an issue.

He had been given time to conjecture on such things since Carlos jingled coins in his pocket, watching him, saying nothing. At last, he removed his hand, brought the two of them together and said, "You've made a good impression on people in the time you've been here."

Nodding thanks for the compliment, he waited for more. "They say you have a talent for finding things out and getting things done."

"Yes," he replied. "I've met people here and there who have been of help to me." He realized this was too formal a reply, as though sitting for a job interview. And waited for more from Carlos.

"It's what I need. Someone who knows people, gets things done."

"What kind of things?"

"Jewish, aren't you?"

Tired of the question, he responded, "I suppose so." Then repeated, "What kind of things?"

"You know what I do, my business?"

"Of course I do."

"This is something different, legitimate." He said this with a convert's zeal, seeking confirmation for his new faith. "Drugs will always be with us, and bring more trouble along with them." Carlos looked at him. "There's other things to be had here. I need you to be my partner in going after them."

For the third time he asked, "What kind of things?" And finally got his answer. "Thirty million dollars a year in NCO Club business." He'd got his answer all right. "It's my understanding that business is locked up."

"Ronald Steele, The Money King of Vietnam," Carlos said, mocking both the name and title. His voice rising, "Do you know who is The Money King? Me, that's who," and dared anyone in the room to dispute his claim. Hearing no argument, he lowered his voice to its former calm and said, "Your government will only do business with an American, and that's you."

There it was, an offer on the table. No mention of his piece of the action. That could wait, as he answered, "The U.S. Government isn't your only problem." Carlos waited, anticipating an expert's analysis from his new associate. "Steele's got General Sinclair by the balls, and besides, he's dangerous to fuck with, connected all over the world."

"That's my boy," said Carlos, "You present the management problem, I present the solution." There was such an air of delight, not really appropriate to the conversation, he wondered if Carlos had taken a hit. "Sinclair's taken care of. First of all, I tripled what he gets from Steele. Second of all is where you come in." At this, Carlos leaned forward, a general in command of an army at Austerlitz. "We take him out. You set it up for us."

Not considering moral implications, he asked, "Why do you need me, he's completely unprotected."

Carlos stared in dismay. "How did you go from being so smart to so dumb? It's not very Jewish of you. When you met him the first time did you notice anything?"

He let pass, once again, that people seemed to know his movements. "Yes, he was alone, with one servant."

"Alone, sure, but there was no traffic on the street, didn't you see that?" He had to admit he hadn't. "He owns every house on the street, both sides. No one gets near him without being seen. A strange car goes by and an alert mobilizes more firepower than your 82nd Airborne. And this is where you come in, partner." And with that, Carlos bounced from his chair to the door, a boy in the midst of a game. His beckoning finger brought in a Mr. Albertini, and a Mr. Franceschi, executioners, one needed not inquire. It was their eyes that gave away the game. Not staring, too polite to stare, they were assessing, considering what had been brought before them. Carlos spoke to them in Corsican, apologizing, "They speak poor English, but are straight shooters."

Showing appreciation for Carlos' little joke, he shook hands with each, feeling trigger fingers wrap him round. Small in stature, the menace they presented filled the room. He was looking into the faces of killers, with no idea how to get away from all it implied. To clear his mind his gaze lifted from them to the leather bindings of books neatly arranged on the shelves. His eyes settled on Rabelais, but nothing was funny about any of this. He'd never read much of him anyway, in any language. Moving from this poor attempt at distraction to the vicious caper being set out before him, he grew lightheaded for a moment and sat down. Carlos, sensing his disquiet, looked at him with parental affection, "Don't worry about getting used to this, it'll only be the one time." That reassurance was rewarded when Carlos heard his new partner ask, "How is this supposed to work?"

"He trusts you, must be a Jewish thing." Getting no reaction, he continued, "Tell him you've got a business deal that involves our two friends here. That gets them into the house, and the rest is up to them." Simple as that? He didn't think so. Pointing over at the killer twins, hoping their English was meager as described, he wondered, "When the shooting brings out Steele's people, how do they get out alive?" Carlos, with a grin that told everything replied, "Like I said, the rest is up to them." The firm of Albertini and Francheschi was engaged in a suicide mission. Probably told it was an easy setup. And, not incidentally, where the fuck would he be when the shooting started? His ass caught in the crossfire, that's where.

"Sinclair is a better bet to bring this off," he said, hopefully.

Carlos, with immense disdain, replied, "Sinclair is a soldier who is afraid of guns. Lots like him in the army. Anyway, it wouldn't do for an officer and gentlemen to be caught up in such nasty doings. His work for us comes after we put the old Commie fucker away. He'll see to it the fix is to take over the NCO club action." He had an immense confidence in his scheme, smiling at his new partner in the crime, the follow-up into legitimacy. It was the norm for the second generation of gangsters to cover their criminal ways with legit businesses. It was touching to see Carlos trying to accomplish this within his own time.

He looked at Carlos, near to smug in his expectation for the scheme. Time to ask the overwhelming question, "So, what's my end?"

Pleased by his getting down to business, Carlos, expansively, generously said, "When it all goes down, you're in for five percent of the gross." His life at risk, aside from any twinge of a moral bone in his body, was worth ten percent, and told Carlos that had to be the number.

Carlos let what had to be a ferocious temper flicker long enough to look him over, "You penny a can punk, we're talking a million and a half dollars as your end." So, Carlos knows about the beer deal. What else is new? A penny a six-pack, not a can. But why correct him? Better he should think the monthly payoff is in six figures. "Ten percent, three million," was his retort to the putdown of his beer deal. Carlos, standing them both up, grasped his hand in agreement, then a strong embrace. Must be a Corsican thing he thought as Carlos spoke to the watchful assassins, and they all joined together for a family dinner.

# SEVENTY

His teeming brain could barely contain the weekend. Friday night in Bangkok with Roxanne to Sunday night in Saigon with Carlos encompassed too many things of this world. Sex, money and death lined up in orderly row for perusal on a bright Monday morning. Sex an easy deletion from the list; he moved to his part in a killing. For three million dollars. A lot of money. Not for murder, he tried convincing himself, for running a business. A rational way to look at things, he glibly decided. He'd be arranging an introduction. If it developed into a shooting, who would dare call him an accessory? Impeccable reasoning, careful analysis, can move mountains of doubt. Except everything was too neat. The weekend with Roxanne under Carlos' nose, her casual mention of a murder plot against an American, the scary pickup at the airport and what came of that. He knew he was caught between The Dope King and The Money King in a battle of champions.

Who was he to referee, or arbitrate?

Carlos claims he has the General lined up. If so, any American can be his front man on the deal. But not everyone can get to Ron Steele. That's why he's become the new darling of Carlos' eye. Three million dollars, he repeats to himself. But not a dime of it seen yet. Get a down payment, maybe ten percent, before you show your stuff. Peanuts to Carlos. Probably has three hundred thousand stuffed in a sock. First stop of the day would be

The Drug King's mansion. Before the kids are off to school and Daddy's gone to work.

Carlos welcomed an old family friend. Coffee? Breakfast? Anything? Yeah, three hundred thou' earnest money, as proof of our friendship. Carlos threw an arm around his shoulder, "Partners aren't we?" And marching him into the library, reached into a closet, drew out a large suitcase. Not socks dumped on the desk, a mountain of greenbacks. "I hope you don't mind counting it out yourself. Three hundred thousand, is that correct?" With that, Carlos left him to the pile to count and stuff into a handy bag. A Vuitton overnight bag, as it happens. Easy money. Too easy.

Next stop, Dupar Construction to check on progress of the rehab hospital. He would use that update as an excuse to see The Money King. Showing up at the office now and then was always a morale builder for the boys to see Mr. Fixer around and about.

John the Greek, ever himself, welcomed him with, "How'd the weekend go?"

"As expected."

"Quite the party girl, Roxanne."

"Oh, you know about all that?"

"Only heard about it. By the way, heard from Carlos yet?"

John's inquiry seemed guileless enough. But you never know.

He ducked the question. "She hasn't seen Carlos in months, do you believe that?"

"How would I know?" Looking at the overnight bag, John asked, "Where you going with that fancy bag?"

"To the bank," he decided to say. "By the way, where's the Thai chick, the engineer who was here last time."

John, looking serious, said, "Goddamnest thing. She thought she was hired to work at a drafting table. She'd been drafted all right, for a different kind of duty. Then, with a what-can-you do shrug, "She's gone."

"Thai women are really something. Beautiful, at least those I saw in Bangkok.

"And the boys?"

"OK you nosy Greek bastard, Roxanne trots out a threesome, and you know what I do?"

John perked up.

"I fall asleep in a nice soft chair as she goes into her act."

"Want me to believe that?"

"Yep, I do. How's the hospital project going?"

"Right on schedule, a nice piece of change for us. You ought to spend more time around here, if you keep bringing in this kind of business." He supposed that was a way for John to criticize his work habits, but had other things on his mind.

"Speaking of Carlos, Roxanne sort of dropped the news that he was branching out into other kinds of hustles."

John mulled that over for a minute then said, casual as you please, "The Money King," while trying to assay if there was more to come. And broke that silence to remind him, again, that Steele hated the Corsicans. "Carlos' father was a miserable bastard by all accounts. The numero uno collaborator with the Japanese against the French and Chinese. The Chinese thing was about money, but he hated the French, all Corsicans do. A class thing I suppose. Carlos' sweet Poppa took every dime he could find from the Chinese and fingered every Frenchmen who hadn't gotten out in 1940 before the Japs got here."

"Where does he live know?"

"In hell, probably. In '46, on the morning the Japs disappeared, Daddy was stabbed to death while eating his breakfast. Carlos is turning out to be a right honorable heir to his noble father."

## SEVENTY-ONE

Indecision, his regular M.O., allowed an uncontrollable current to carry him along. But there are times in the life of a man when decisions must be made. He was to arrange a business meeting with Ron Steele bringing an offer. Partnership in the narcotics trade with Carlos. With the killers coming along as negotiators. Given this instruction he said, "It'll never work, Steele's too smart to go for it."

"He's a greedy son-of-a-bitch who'll listen to any proposition," said Carlos. "Set it up, and leave the rest to me."

Three hundred thousand in the bag was not a determinant for action. He had a feeling it was all he'd ever see of the promised three million. He thought it a fee for setting Ron Steele up, though he'd be lucky to get out of it alive. Matters of life and death were no more than a next step. Without reality or consequences. Another weigh-station on the highway of life, he told himself with tired amusement.

He knocked on the door of the old lion's nondescript house, greeted by the Chinese retainer. The Money King looked up from a book at this casual drop in with the interest of one familiar with surprises, and waited.

"I've got an update on the hospital deal."

Steele looked at him, with an inquiring voice, "That's Sinclair's business."

Before he could fashion an answer, Ron, closing a book of Chinese watercolors, added, "You seem to have survived your trip to Bangkok."

His only reply, "You know about that."

"I make it my business to know such things."

Wondering, suddenly afraid of what else he might know, it was his turn to wait out a move. Opening the book before him, flipping the pages, Ron Steele said, "You remember Albert Anastasia?"

"The Mafioso who got his in a barber shop?"

"Yes, he sure did. At the Park Sheraton. Two guys with rifles. I've always wondered why."

He looked at Ron, afraid to consider where this might be going. "Wondered why they did it?"

"No, why they used rifles. A barbershop duet they were," he said, not smiling at his little joke. "Anastasia sat there in the chair, facing the mirror, towel on his face, the barber getting ready to lather him up." Examining a detail of a picture in the book, he went on, "The Guinea must have heard something, because he looked into the mirror as the shots that got him came his way. They say he must have been confused, because he lunged at the mirror, trying to get at his killers."

Steele seemed to be done with his account, leaving his visitor to consider the point of the tale. But there was a bit more. "Since then, every made-man insists that his chair face the door, not the mirror, when he gets a shave and a haircut." Finally showing a small macabre smile, he finished with his version of a flourish, "A Jewish comedian owns Albert's chair. Bought it at auction."

"How come you know so much about it?"

"The prick was trying to muscle me with my bar business in Tokyo after the Korean War. I sent a complaint to Lansky, who owed me. Anastasia was trying to get in on his Havana action, so Lansky killed one bird with two shots doing good for both of us. Until Castro. Lansky had a bet big on Fidel against Batista thinking it would guarantee his Havana rackets. He didn't know Fidel was a hard-line Maoist and would run them all out of the country. I could have told him that." His story told, he leaned back in his wheelchair, his hands under a lap quilt at his knees.

"Carlos is planning to kill you."

It was the only thing to say after what he'd just heard. Ronald Steele, showing no reaction, replied, "Someone will come through that door someday and I won't lift a finger to defend myself. But, not now. It's not my time."

Trying to consider that melodramatic reply, he was sure it wasn't a fatalist's response, couched in some vague Chinese philosophy. An agent of his demise sat before him and Ron Steele was wise enough to wait for more.

"He wants to take over your operation. Thinks it will give him a legit cover." Then, to divert attention from himself, added, "He claims to have Sinclair with him. Paying him triple what he gets from you."

"Well, thanks for that, it's something I didn't know. Are you sure?"

"It's what I got from Carlos."

"And what else did you get?"

"An offer." Steele looked up with a businessman's curiosity as he added, "To front the operation after the takeover."

"After I'm dead."

Joining in Ron's ironic review, he said, "That would be part of it."

"And your end?"

"Ten percent."

"Three million, not a bad deal."

"His first offer was five percent."

"And you jumped him to ten? "Now, that's my Yiddisher boy." Then, with no change of expression asked, "Why have you told me this? I haven't offered you a thing."

"I don't know. Solidarity Forever, maybe."

The Money King looked at him with a first smile on his face, amused at his raising up of the old union song and a voice from the sepulcher intoned, "Solidarity forever, solidarity forever..." He stopped short of finishing the line, more important things on his mind. "What exactly is my friend Carlos' plan?"

"He's brought in two Corsican heavies to take you out. I'm supposed to get them to you to talk about doing business." Letting that sit, he watched Steele, mulling things over.

"You know, I've always liked Carlos. Even admired him. Never thought of him as a Corsican. He was born here. It makes a difference, you know."

The Money King was an American born in China, and he wondered what an expat birth meant to him. But this was no teatime conversation. Other matters were at hand. "Go back to Carlos and tell him I'd be happy to meet with his representatives to discuss joining his business with mine."

He stared at Ron, trying to get a feel for what might really be on his mind. "He knows the Chinese want to run him out. And knows I can protect him from that happening."

There he sat, in a half-darkened room, an old China hand talking to him softly about things beyond his experience, out of his element. Asked to broker a deal between warlords involving bribery, easy to obtain killers, commonplace criminality, at a time and in a place calling out to the corrupt.

"I'm growing tired of the game," Ron said. "When things work out, you'll be there to run my side of things."

"Why do you need me?"

"Because you're one smart son-of-a-bitch. But, do me a favor and try to keep your pecker in your pocket. That little thing with Carlos' girlfriend was a close one for you."

It was Ron Steele's way of saying, "You owe me." And maybe he did.

"So tell Carlos what I'm offering and that I'll meet with his Corsican gorillas anytime."

# SEVENTY-TWO

Needing distraction from the past days and hours, his thoughts turned to Roxanne. Carlos had given him a pass, Carte Blanche more or less. As if he'd thrown her in, part of their deal. The fervor of such optimism upon him, he knocked at her door.

"You've survived our weekend together."

Smiling, he said, "Yes, both you and Carlos."

Grateful for that smile, not used to happiness, she welcomed him in past the suspicious eyes of the maid who'd opened the door. "I was sure you'd be met at the airport."

Unless she was playing it dumb, she didn't know what had gone down with Carlos. "I was, by Carlos and his friends."

"You're tougher than you look."

"Not tough at all, we've got a business arrangement."

She had moved to a sofa in the living room, ordered coffee, taking in this news. "I don't know what is more dangerous, playing with me or playing with Carlos."

"He said he doesn't see you much anymore."

"Is that what he says? I suppose it doesn't count last night."

He detected a courtesan's pride in her voice. Competition within an Oriental harem must be a thing to behold. Rivalry for the affections of the one great man distributing favors according to his whim. Pride in the delivery of sons, despair at the birth of daughters. The gossip of eunuchs. The dark side of paradise.

Carlos' attendance on Roxanne the night before, if true, caused him no rustle of covetousness. She treated herself as a property on which he'd already trespassed. And, in the crazy way the world goes led him to a business offer and, by the way, an assassination plot. If he chose to put numbers to it, a ten-thousand-dollar purchase of a necklace had given a three-hundred-thousand-dollar return.

"He canceled my return ticket home."

This interrupted his reverie, "Why?"

"I don't think it was a gesture of affection." She looked him over, gauging if he might be her salvation. "He knows I send most of what he gives me to Paris. The ticket was my escape. He told me last night, as he was leaving to go home to his darlings."

He thought again about the value of the necklace. "You can buy a ticket on your own, can't you?"

"He would know, find out and easily convince the Air France office to find an excuse to keep me from the flight." Examining her fate as though it was a stranger she spoke of, she looked around the room at the drawings of her grandmother. He saw some shift in her mood, a calm the portraits offered. "Carlos was very angry with me last night. Nothing he said. He would never show such feelings to me. It was the sex." She'd caught her guest's attention. "I can always tell when a man is having sex out of anger, the desire is for revenge, nothing more." He hoped she would go on. "He used his penis like a scalpel, probing to cut, cause pain."

"Because of Bangkok?"

She smiled, charmed at this ego on full display. "No, he's used to my using Bangkok to play. It amuses him."

He wasn't so sure that was true. "When will you be going again?"

"In two weeks. A nice change from this boredom."

He hoped her ennui was somewhat diluted by his presence in her life. He wasn't so sure about that either. "What's the delivery you make every two weeks? Cash, I suppose."

"I'm sure you suppose correctly. I've never bothered to check."

Remembering the space his three hundred thousand took up, he said, "It must be at least five hundred thousand dollars."

This was irrelevant to her. It was a package needing delivery, and she was the messenger. A fortnightly opportunity to exact a bit of revenge of her own. He rose, the maid's hovering a reminder that niceties of convention still had to be observed. Plus, he thought she might need a rest from the exertions of the night before. It conformed to his forty-eight hour rule, maintained more in the breach, as they say, to give a woman a forty-eight hour break between partners. One could never be sure of the facts in these matters, but subtle inquiries often provided information allowing him to abide by this ascetic rule. She escorted him to the door, asking his address. On receiving this intelligence she offered, "Noon tomorrow?"

A quick calculation brought him to realize it was something short of his two-day rule, but this was a quibble, it being his rule, not hers. "Why not?" Chaste cheek-to-cheek kisses accomplished, he slipped out into that other world demanding his full attention, shifted from Roxanne to Carlos, an easy transition from one lunatic to another. He looked forward, with a certain lethal joy, to his reaction to The Money King's offer.

# SEVENTY-THREE

Carlos did business from the back room of Milan, a nightclub and restaurant advertising itself as "Saigon's Little Italy, first class with an luxurious atmosphere." That about summed up the place, decorated with overwrought Italianate chandeliers, deep red banquettes, soiled rugs. What the hell, Marco Polo brought spaghetti to Italy from China, didn't he?

A flunky announcing his arrival, Carlos rushed to greet him. With a wave of dismissal, hangers-on and bodyguards quickly dissolved into an outer room and they were alone.

"I know you have good news," Carlos said, leading him to a sofa, where they could plot together.

"He wants to cut a deal with you, become partners in each other's businesses."

Bursting into laughter, Carlos said, "That Mao-loving old Commie bastard, what balls." He stood up, "What else did he have to say?"

"That the Chinese are about to move in on you. He can prevent it."

"You know, it was a fucking Chink that murdered my father. I found him bleeding to death. I was fifteen. He tried to say something to me. But blood came from his mouth instead."

"Is that your answer?""

Carlos looked at him. That twenty-year-ago memory washed away by present concerns. "It's the goddamn Chinese who keep the war going, supplying the North with their arms and ammo. Do you think the Americans will let them take over the drug trade? That's my protection, I don't need no cripple in a wheelchair to rescue me."

His defiance was touching. An attempt to address old family wounds. "Besides, our business is going big time. Poppy production in Turkey is finished, thanks to you guys. The U.S. and European markets need a new source. And guess what? It's coming right out of good old Southeast Asia by way of Saigon." Pointing to his chest, he preened, "And that means me."

"If things go so well with you, why bother with the old bastard?" Carlos did not like the question. It betrayed weakness. "A man's a man, he said with a smile. "It's what men do."

He looked at Carlos, a man engaged in great evil, realizing he himself knew only small-time iniquity, petty stuff. He was out of his class, in with the Big Boys, wondering what got him here. There was no time to muse on such things, when Carlos commanded, "So where does it stand with The Money King?"

"He'll see your boys, thinks it's to negotiate his deal. The rest is up to you."

"When?" He sounded like an executioner, getting the answer he hoped for.

"He's ready anytime. Your call."

"My Corsican cousins will be leaving in a few days. I want them gone before all this happens. Don't want them looking for their piece." Carlos looked at him indulgently. "You've done good. Better than I expected." He acknowledged this compliment, sensing more. "How about a little bonus? You can take Roxanne off my hands." Then as an extra added attraction said, "I'll still be paying all the bills."

Now this was the kind of evil he could handle, as he said to Carlos, "Uh, uh. My mother always told me never to sleep with anyone crazier than I am."

"Sunday morning," said Carlos. "A nice time to blow our Ronnie away. I don't think we'll find him at his prayers." Then, having displayed his humorous side, looked at his accessory to the crime, "Set it up." And was done with him.

Leaving Little Italy behind, he walked out onto Troung Tan Buu and the hum and buzz of the Saigon streets. What he was setting up was a double cross, but why, what for? Carlos had offered the big money, Marty a vague promise, or nothing at all. He knew neither could be trusted, so where the profit for him? "Run, boy, run," he said to himself, not for the first time, as he strolled along, reaching into his wallet for a large note to offer a one-legged beggar. No, he wouldn't be running anywhere. A wheel had been set in motion, not turned by him, but turning him. If that motion were to produce action, it was good enough for him.

## SEVENTY-FOUR

"Sunday morning it is then. Two of them?" He nodded at Ron's casual inquiry.

"And I'll be along, too, I guess," he said.

"So you will. Know how to duck?" Ron Steele was posing a very serious question he simply could not take seriously. Showing that avuncular side once again, he said, "Your Corsicans will be seated right there in front of me." Pointing to a chair off to the side, "You'll take that one."

"Sunday morning," he repeated. "Carlos will be up having breakfast with his family. He reserves Saturday nights for his wife, did you know that?" No he didn't and wondered at such familiarity with his nemesis' schedule and movements. "Quite the pater familias wouldn't you say?" And that was that. No talk of Mao, or the Mafia. All business. For the second time that day he'd been dismissed by one of the two principles in the drama. He had his two-bit part, and would play it well.

# SEVENTY-FIVE

Leaving Ron Steele to his preparations, he saw that noon and his nooner with Roxanne awaited his pleasure. His zeal for promptness went unrequited. She was a no-show and he dozed as a clock ticked off two in the afternoon.

In a sleepy funk, he answered a soft knock at his door. Roxanne, in dark glasses, a disheveled appearance he'd never seen before, begged to enter. It was then he saw the bruise on her face, sat her down on the couch and carefully removed sunglasses. Her right eye was closed, the socket black and blue, the left cheek a raised welt of flesh. "Carlos," he said.

She nodded, bursting into tears. When he went to comfort her, she winced with an involuntary movement. He dropped his hand, waiting for her weeping to subside. "Is this about us?" Her answer brought him to understand Carlos meant him no good. But, this was not about him. He turned to hear more from this battered child.

"He came in with the two men I heard him talking to about killing an American. Do you remember?" He did indeed. "They sat staring at me, while Carlos gave me a suitcase to be delivered to Bangkok this weekend. When I asked why so soon, his voice had meanness I'd never heard telling me I was to do anything he says. Of course, I replied. And that seemed to anger him more. He tore my clothes from me, threw me down, twisted my body to face the floor and brutalized me. When I screamed in pain I heard the other two laughing. I turned over, hoping he was done, to see him gesture those animals over to me. I could only stare as Carlos held my arms down and they raped me one at a time, with a savage grunting I will never forget. When they were done, and I prayed it was all over, Carlos pulled me to my feet, hesitated for a moment, then hit me twice in the face, knocking me down. He stood over me saying, 'Make that delivery and be back here the same day. I'm getting tired of hearing about your weekends in Bangkok.' And then they left me, to gather my clothes from the floor. When I tried to climb the stairs the maid, who must have seen it all, walked away from me with a smile on her face."

She was done, the telling of the horror bringing an end to tears.

He sat there, stunned before the evidence of such violence as Roxanne looked off into some faraway place. "You've got to leave here, go back to Paris." She made no reply. "He'll kill you one of these days." She nodded, indifferent to the obvious.

"Not until he can find someone else for his deliveries to Bangkok."

"So you'll be doing that for him?"

She saw it futile to make this naïve man understand. "He trusts no one else. It's not so much that he trusts me. Carlos controls me because of my family."

"Do they know what you go through for them?"

"My mother has an idea. But we say nothing about it."

He fetched ice in a towel for her bruised face, applying it with a tenderness for which she was grateful. All men were not beasts, he wanted to show her. But knew it would take more than a chunk of ice to comfort her, remove the stains of her morning of terror. His most compassionate response was to act, somehow, against Carlos and his two thugs. His betrayal of the plot against The Money King was not sufficient punishment. His impotence before the desire to avenge Roxanne brought the futility of his life too close for tears. His usefulness to Carlos extended only to the plot to kill his rival. Never mind the bullshit about a partnership. He'd be next on the hit list.

Setting aside a run toward self-preservation, first things first he decided. Roxanne needed care and a rescue. She'd come to him for succor. It was touching and surprising. If it was out of desperation, it hardly mattered. She'd made a judgment about him. That he could be trusted. Might even be able to help. He was touched by this confidence, wanted to be worthy of it.

"Those two bastards who attacked you will get theirs," he told her.

Roxanne lowered the ice from her face, wondering about the confidence in his remark. "I doubt it," she said with full understanding of how little justice there exists in a world without shame.

Letting future action be sufficient reply to her disbelief, he repeated, "Carlos will kill you, eventually." Before he allowed a response, he told her she needed to rest, offered his bedroom, escorting her, pulling back sheets, turning on the overhead fan, puffing up pillows. She followed all this activity, a sleepwalker in search of something lost, left behind. Tucking her into his bed, he saw her eyes close, and whispered to her, "Go to sleep. You're safe here." She opened her eyes for a moment. "Hush," he whispered. "Sleep."

He had a vast capacity for bringing misery into the world. But, once in a great, great while, just when he thinks his life is done, a moment arrives offering deliverance. Seized by that moment, and an idea, he dashed out of the apartment, grabbed a taxi to Tu Do Street. On a mercy mission or so he hoped. He knew that one man's idea of a favor could be another's dilemma. But would play out his plan for Roxanne hoping she'd see the way out, the rescue, he'd prescribe.

In the hour he was gone, Roxanne had revived somewhat, sitting up in bed reading an American magazine. "Feeling OK?" Her reply was a shrug at the inanity of his question. Was it a certain resiliency or fatalism she displayed? Not taking time to consider the question, he said, quietly, I bought something for you. And handed her an Air France ticket to Paris, first class, of course. She stared at it, turning it over in her hand. "I can't use this, I told you why."

Taking the ticket from her hand he showed her it was a flight from Bangkok to Paris for the following Friday afternoon. "Carlos is sending you to Bangkok. Stay at the airport, how would he know?"

"I can't," she repeated.

"Is it about money?" He knew her answer before she nodded, yes. He sat down at her bedside with an even, conspiratorial manner. "You'll have five hundred thousand of Carlos' money, won't you? " She gave no answer, knowing what he meant by the question. "Take it with you to Paris. You could hide in the transit lounge until flight time."

"Carlos would hunt me down, kill us all."

He began to grow exasperated, watching his plot giving over to fear. For one brief moment he considered giving her the key to the safety deposit box holding his hundred thousand. Overcoming this move toward largesse he said, "You don't have to worry about Carlos." Roxanne was beyond dubious. "Look, you can deliver the cash and save your life by leaving. Or, you can skip with the cash, move out of Paris with the money and live happily ever after."

He knew he was expressing more hope than a promise that she'd be safe. But loved the idea of her screwing Carlos out of his bi-weekly deposit. "It's up to you," he said, returning the ticket to her hand. "You'll have to leave everything behind. Carry your jewels in a small bag, nothing more. You can do this, Roxanne." He was near to pleading as she closed her eyes, once again, and fell asleep. It was Wednesday evening. She'd have all day tomorrow to think about it. Too much time, he worried. Then she'd have her Friday trip and a decision. And he'd have his quiet Sunday morning at The Money King's.

## SEVENTY-SIX

A sea of troubles ready to overwhelm him, the arrival of another boatload of beer allowed him to think of simpler times when the money was smaller, threat to life and limb not a looming figure in the landscape. Those golden days, only a month before, now replaced by six-figure payouts with promise of more, and madmen at the top of corrupt empires engaging in a dance of death. He didn't belong in this league, preferred to limp along picking up a few thousand at a time. It was a slower pace, more suited to his tender sensibilities. He was prepared to take the lead in small dramas, happy to visit with Joe Ziegler, chat him up, pick up his loot, take his split and get the rest over to Thanh. The comfort of routine, a regular round, was the way of a normal life. A monthly suitcase of cash for distribution might not qualify for some as normal, but why argue the point? It was good to be back in the small time, dropping in on Thanh and the safety of polite company.

Casually asking Thanh if she knew her neighbor Roxanne, he learned they'd been classmates as children. The best private school in Saigon, you can be sure. Thanh had no curiosity at his question, or her reticence might have revealed an understanding that Roxanne would be known to Americans.

"Did you know her family?" He asked.

"No, we'd only see her parents at school." He had a sense that her simple statement had an exclusionary air. "Roxanne was a mixed-blood and had few friends." Then she added, "Her mother is French, very beautiful. Her father was a soldier, dead now."

Had he been brave he'd have taken Thanh by the neck and say he'd seen pictures of Roxanne's father. That he was magnificently handsome. That he was first in his class at the École Militaire and a hero dying in defense of her petit bourgeoise life. "Mixed blood, my ass," he should have said. But let it slide. Thanh had to know Roxanne's connection to Carlos. Probably was the talk of her circle. A confirmation of the contempt they felt for her from the beginning. He'd had enough; the fetid air seemed fresh against that poisonous miasma. He left without the politesse of goodbye, and what the hell, as long as I'm in the neighborhood, he agreed with himself, why not see how Roxanne was faring?

He was amazed to see her face all but restored to the beauty he knew. "I went to a doctor of Chinese medicine in Cholon," she explained. "Magic herbs, a poultice and leeches did their work." It was a good sign, he thought, to see her vanity restored. An excellent thing in a woman, he knew. "He saw that I was agitated, and gave me a powder that calmed me instantly."

"And now?"

"Powder allows me to get through the hours but can't erase memory." She looked at him, "You said they would get theirs, what did you mean?" Her question was that of an avenging angel seeking satisfaction. Afraid to tell her things that might endanger her more, he said blandly, "Evil comes to doers of evil."

"You don't really believe that." She said this with the hard-earned knowledge of one used to outrages gone unpunished.

"Yes, I do." She waited for more. "Have you thought about my offer?"

Panic came across her face, pointing to her family possessions. "How can I leave all this?"

To convince her he added to her terror. "Would you like to be buried with them? Carlos is a torturer, yesterday was a foretaste of what is to come for you." Desperation, despair was her only reply as she dismissed him with a weak wave of her hand. He left, having done what he could. The rest remained with the tears he left behind.

Musing on these two women who'd been playmates as children, he wandered aimlessly, another morning in the life. That he'd slept with them both was one of those coincidences the flesh is heir to. Daddy's little girls they were. Thanh doing the dirty work of a collector, her body in the service of family as needed. Roxanne, making up for the absent provider by mucking the stables of high-priced whoredom. Dutiful daughters deserving of praise, high-priced victims of war.

He made a side bet with himself that Roxanne would escape. If she takes the satchel of money with her, Carlos would track her down. Friday would bring an end of her story or a continuation of the melodrama. Come Sunday he hoped to see those other vultures hanging by their throats, ready to be plucked and butchered. The band was tuning its instruments. Time to face words and music.

## SEVENTY-SEVEN

A wise man said the prospect of a hanging concentrates the mind. Would that cover caught in a cross-fire between antagonists? With so dire a result looming, he fetched the bag holding three hundred thousand dollars so sweetly provided by Carlos. Solemnly burying the Vuitton in a carton, he addressed it to his son with a short note of affection. He struggled with the words, settling for banality over a pass at profundity. His intention? To leave the box with John the Greek, asking him to send it off unless he fetched it back on Monday morning. That was making provision, was it not, against the possibility that anything could happen?

So ordinary a chore triggered a fright that enveloped him. Tomorrow morning he'd be a not-so-innocent bystander to death, maybe his own. Peripheral, but subject to the whims of errant slugs, with no place to hide. Hands shaking, he sorted the thing through, stomach cramping with anxiety fed by the scenario, fear overwhelming his trembling body. Helpless to act. Passive witness to his annihilation.

Closing his eyes, self-induced darkness brought fiends from the very deep to tear at his guts. Panicked, he opened his eyes to the oblivious emptiness of his rooms. He would die, saturated in the damp of fear, wetting himself, scared shitless, while shitting his pants. This disgusting paradox released him from the dread that swathed him head to toe, allowed him to exit his fate, leave the prison of his festering imagination to spend what he was sure was the last Saturday night of his life.

# SEVENTY-EIGHT

A man living out his last night on earth has options, plenty of them. He might choose to meditate on a life ill spent. Or live his last night much the same as all the nights that went before.

He took to the streets, the more sordid the better; seeking his ease in dear old downtown Saigon, no longer noticing kids selling trinkets, crippled beggars, teenage thugs cruising by on motorbikes. Meandering down the Rue Catinat, its old French name still favored by the locals, he sorted through the choices of bars and clubs available to a man of means, settling on the noisiest, crowded with GI revelers at the bar, and young well-dressed Vietnamese men in slumming mode who sat at tables. Joining his countrymen, he ordered up and turned to watch the comedy of working girls laboring at their trade of enticement. The wiles of seduction were the least of it as young lovelies worked the line of drinkers quickly assaying interest in their wares. An intellectual curiosity caused him to inquire as to price. On hearing, "Fifty dollah for you papa san," he waved off this inflationary effort with a grin, feeling a hand on his arm and a question in perfect English, "Am I worth fifty dollars?" And there stood Sue, in miniskirt and heels. She had to be kidding, he thought, but seeing the ravaged face of a junkie he knew this was very serious indeed.

Sue, all business, refused his offer of a drink, moving her eyes across the room looking for her next mark. Looking at this poor, broken thing he said, "Come sit with me for a bit." She seemed disinclined until he told her she'd have her fifty, no services required. He saw the tracks embroidered down the crook of her left arm. No attempt to hide them, too far gone for that, she did a tale unfold.

Minister Tho had introduced her to the needle well before the whole thing had come apart over her sideline work at The Fuji. Dolores tried to get her home, "She truly did," Sue said, in sisterly adoration. But she was hooked, the stuff was cheap, "And a girl can make a good living out here." For a while, Eddie had kept her going, paying the bills, supplying the Johns, no need for her to be out there hustling. "I didn't even mind him slipping it to me know and then. He has a way with him, you know." Now this was the Sue he knew, always looking for that silver lining.

"So what happened?"

"His sons began showing up after I was done for the night. I'd do my best to fight them off." She looked at him. "You try it with three-hundred-pound gorillas." She let that picture she'd drawn sink in for a while. "When I told Eddy, he just laughed, gave me a 'boys will be boys,' shrug, and handed be a week's supply of hits." Drawing her self up with what dignity she still retained, she said, "I threw it in his face and left."

"And here you are."

"Yes, here I am." Defiance, bred from an old trouper's life, came upon her. He remembered Dolores saying Sue had been giving it away for years, and this is what it had come to. He tried to think how he might rescue her, but junkie see, junkie do, he knew. Anyway, stateside she'd just be another hooker among thousands. Here she had that something extra, the all-American girl, to peddle. Sue looked at her watch, the thirty minutes she allotted him was near to over. Coyly slipping his U.S. fifty-dollar bill into her bra she offered a farewell peck on a cheek. He watched as she worked the line at the bar, a working girl, after all, trolling for her Johnny and going off into the night.

Sitting by his lonesome, his whiskey before him, waves of young beauties offering company were waved off in turn. A desperate air touched their offers of comfort and joy. The Army paid once a month on the first. And here it was, the end of the month, most GIs already broke, and discounts to be had for those with ready cash. Aware of the niceties of economic imperatives, he sought, for the fun of it, the lowest bidder for services rendered. Tiring of the game, he stood up to leave, downing his whiskey, as one of the six or so before him, exasperated, said, "OK papa san, two of us. Fifteen dollah."

Stepping out into the dank air, no longer swallowed by the noise of the bar, feeling woozy after the one whiskey, the chaos of a Saigon Saturday night offered fine distraction from thoughts of the morning to come. Shaking off that scenario one more time, he walked in a blur of color and sound, feeling a part of the place. No longer a heathen, newly converted to the ways of the only world he knew. The beggars in rags no competition for finery adorning lithesome men and women; handsome young officers in uniform offering a reassuring presence in this thing called war; and finally, in the midst of a Dupar mob outside a restaurant, a farewell party for one of his number going home the very next day.

Welcomed as one of theirs, he went along to a large private room set up for the festivities. A full bar, of course. And long tables around a center space for dancing. Except he noticed an odd absence: no women. On making innocent inquiry he was told it was a bachelor party as a token of respect to the guest of honor, Herb Kutchins by name, a pale slight fellow, an engineer so nondescript he'd never noticed him. He did see John the Greek at the head table ready to serve as MC.

It turned out that the little engineer was there as a joke on him. John described him as a Saigon virgin. "The only man in the history of this war to come out here a year ago and leave without once getting laid."

"Bullshit," was the general cry from assorted consuls. John, a Marc Antony before the rabble, raised his hand. Silence fell, a quiet that awaited explanation of such deviant behavior. "Not that you bozos would recognize such a thing, but Herb Kutchins is a man of honor."

"A queer," shouted a Doubting Thomas.

"No," said John, "a promise keeper. A promise to his fiancé to love honor and obey."

"That's after-the-wedding kind of crap," said a shocked older gentleman. Then, a voice of experience added, "And what's she up to while he's been gone?"

At this, Herb raised his head as if to speak in defense, but turned away in silence. John whispered to Herb who produced a photograph of his beloved. Handed around, some simply handed it on; other bolder commentators were heard to say, "Who would ever fuck her?" With that established, the photo came back to Herb who examined it with eyes of love, returned it to his wallet.

John, turning realist, said, "Half you guys got clap, and you know it. That's not the kind of souvenir you want to bring back home with you."

"That's why you'll never go home again," was blurted out. John grinned, more in agreement than amusement. "It's three months of treatment for the cure for anyone interested."

Waiters were bringing in platters of steaks, grilled chicken, western grub for those in western garb. "Enough with this Holy Roller garbage," John was told and he sat down, his peculiar oration over.

He sat there, eating, drinking, and surprised to find that he was enjoying the company. Colonel Lee sat across the room, not bothering to acknowledge him. But, what did he care? Everyone seemed to know Lee was on the take; it was common gossip around the table, an acceptable level of corruption, given his status. The conversation passed on to other foibles. Some had their own farewell dinners coming along. Others here for as long as forever.

As the dinner wound down, the crowd assembled in the center of the room for a last goodbye to Holy Herbie. No one noticed a very attractive young woman who'd slipped into the room. She was for sale, a disturbance to the etiquette that had been established for the evening. Did she represent a Last Temptation for our Guest of Honor?

Surfeited with food and drink, they cynically appraised her as she circled the room trying to interest one or another in the merchandise. With a gesture, each man passed her on to the next, a game she finally understood when she'd completed her rounds without a taker. She stood there staring down laughter and rude remarks she could not understand. But understood enough to know she'd been played, stalking out with a curse on all in who lingered in the room.

Not so drunk that he couldn't see this defilement as a bad omen, he left the boys to their games. Unsteady, out onto the street, lurching toward a taxi, he stumbled, nearly falling into the path of a young couple. The woman, frightened, jumped away. Profuse in his apologies, he let it be known that he honored women above all things, that it had been his mistake, that he begged their forgiveness. The offended party took her escort by the arm in a gesture of dismissal for this thing beneath contempt before her. He watched them walk away, still calling out apologies, until a taxi stopped and took him away.

# SEVENTY-NINE

Beyond the low gate sat The Money King's house. No different than before. Except for two killers, put at ease by his nervousness, amused at his trembling hesitation. One of them, placing a calming hand on his arm, moved him to the front door. He glanced at them, businessmen dressed in Sunday best, suits tailored to accommodate machine pistols in shoulder holsters, and knocked. The servant, bent with age, opened the door, led them inside, and slipped away. Steele, dozing in his wheelchair, awakened, gesturing to chairs placed before him.

The pair, no time to waste, reached inside jackets, a movement met by a shout, causing them to turn and face the charge of the old retainer, firing an Uzi, dropping them to the floor. Ron Steele rose from his chair, weapon in hand, and fired twice. The coup de grace. The old servant, no longer old or subservient, rolled one of his victims over with a foot to watch blood seeping onto the wooden floorboards before triumphantly joining The Money King in the raucous laughter of the victorious.

The warp pace of the past seconds slowed to a speed he could handle. Four men in black entered from a rear room to remove the recently departed. The Money King stopped them with a hand and intoned, in delicious parody, "May God Almighty have mercy upon thee, forgive thee thy sins and bring thee to everlasting life." Then, with a wave of the gun in his hand, "Get them out of here," as a fifth man entered with a mop and pail to wipe spilled blood just like a circus where clowns clean up after the elephants.

"Roxanne's revenge," he said, feeling a cheek go wet. Not tears, but blood oozed to his chin. A bullet fragment must have ricocheted and nicked him. The Chinese warrior examined the wound, touching his cheek with a gentleness that made the Uzi at his side incomprehensible, and left the room. He returned, the weapon put away, with soapy water in a bowl, washed blood from his face, removing a tiny fragment with tweezers, bathed the cut with an antiseptic that made him wince, then handed him the particle of bullet that had wounded him so grievously. As he fingered this fragment, The Money King smiled. "Look at that, bleeding for your country. I'll put you in for a Purple Heart."

He preferred to discuss another level of compensation, but it was suggested he go and tell Carlos what had happened to his best-laid plans. The mild manner of Ron's request alerted him that something else was going on. "I don't consider any of this personal. Find out if he still wants to talk business." Things were turning to normal. Steele, the pistol at rest under a blanket, was once again his inscrutable self. His comrade in arms, sans weapon, returning to the disarming shuffle he affected. Two men dead and gone. His part in it. All routine. The sliver of metal that had cut into him, now no more than a souvenir rolled between thumb and forefinger, he left without a word.

Something was going on at Carlos' house. From the taxi, blocked by police cars at the end of the street, he saw an ambulance, and within a hundred feet of the chateau heard a screaming woman, crying children. Bodyguards and others were running about as he entered the house and saw Carlos, on a child's mattress, bleeding to death. His wife embraced him, kissing his face, ignoring the massive wound that had blown away part of his face, pushing the doctor away, knowing it useless, extracting some last moment of life her husband had left. When he gave it up she quietly, silently, closed his eyes, and went in search of her weeping children.

Bodyguards, true at last to their calling, formed a circle around the man they could not protect. They had stood idly by as his blood was shed, having failed in that one and only task, Carlos the biggest loser of all. A lone gunman had managed to get into the house, slip upstairs to where Carlos was at play with his oldest son who saw his father shot between the eyes. It had to be Steele. He found himself eager to return to the site of those other killings. A macabre curiosity about what might be next had overtaken him. He left the Corsicans to their mournful lamentations. The street had cleared, police and ambulance off to other tragedies of daily life.

Deciding to be a messenger bringing glad tidings, he rapped loudly at Roxanne's door, opened cautiously by the serving woman, who blocked his entrance. Shouldering past her he called out, getting no response. Climbing the stairs to the bedroom, he saw clothes in their closet, shoes stacked in racks. At a vanity table he slipped open a drawer. It had been emptied. Then, a jewel box, bare of contents. His advice had been taken. An envelope covered in French stamps had her family name and return address. Stuffing it in a shirt pocket, he turned to the ugly stare of the servant who said something he did not understand. "Carlos is dead," he said to her in French. The shock on her face showed she understood his simple statement, calculating its meaning, the end of employment. Descending the stairs, he looked over at those precious drawings of her grandmother, still in their frames. For a moment he considered that she could never have left them behind and might return after all. No, his gut told him, she's back in Paris, taking Carlos' dough with her. He took one frame down, then another, until all six were before him on a table. Removing each drawing from its frame, he carefully rolled one at a time in newspaper. The maid stood there, his glare in her direction silencing any idea she might have to complain. He could project imperial power as well as any of them. At a side table he found her gold trimmed stationery and wrote, "Bonjour Mademoiselle, Carlos and your two attackers are no more, shot to death this Sunday morning. À bientôt." Licking his tongue along the edge of a matching envelope, he planned to mail the package out the next day. Filled with pride at this act of kindness costing no more than postage, he walked out into bright sunshine in the direction of Ron Steele, The Money King of Vietnam, prepared for whatever else might be revealed.

Sitting in a chair on a pristine floor, his report was stale news. "This was your deal," he said to Steele. Not a question, a stating of the obvious.

"Sure it was," he said with satisfaction. "Tit for tat. Surprised the cocksucker, didn't I?" He had to agree with Ronnie on that one. "Fancy that, an aficionado of Chinese cooking. How's that for a little touch?" He said this with the laugh of one used to the ironies history plays out before the suckers. "Dim Sum. A passion for Dim Sum. Every Sunday morning he'd order a family feast from the same place in Cholon. All I needed was to switch the delivery boy to one of my guys." Ron smiled. "And that was that. After he did the job, he walked away, past armed guards stuffing themselves, who never heard the shot."

"His ten-year-old saw the whole thing," he said, remembering the feel of the boy's soft hand.

"Oh," The Money King replied, "It must be something that runs in the family. Like father, like son. Unto the seventh generation, isn't it? That's three down and four more to go."

This meager attempt to interrupt Ron's joy of no use, he asked, "What happens now?" This was more like it for the avenger, who drew him closer, "You know Big Eddy over at The Fuji, don't you? Sure you do, he was the one who told me you were a smart little bastard." He let this compliment fly by, waiting for more. "Eddy is taking over from Carlos."

"With the Corsicans?"

Ron looked at him. "Can you be that stupid?" So much for flattery. "Carlos was the only one with brains enough to run the business. Now that his brains are spilled on his kid's bedroom floor, his Corsican snakes will be swarming around with their heads cut off. They'll be looking for work at your construction outfit."

"It sounds too good," he said to Ron. "They won't be handing it over that easy."

"Oh, there'll be pockets of resistance," the old warrior said. "But you've never seen my Chinese comrades in action when the big dollar looms before them." He paused, then added, "It's all for support of the war." This little aside got his interest, and he waited for Steele to offer more. "That rehab hospital you're building in Cua Viet is part of it. That will begin to take care of those GIs hooked on the stuff." He said this as a kindly concerned uncle would, before getting down to real things. "This drug business is making them nuts back in Washington. Senators scared silly that hordes of addicts will be hitting American streets. Drug fiends roaming the cities of the land killing, robbing, raping for a fix." He was enjoying the histrionics, wanted this dire situation to sink in before saying, "The Pentagon knows it has got a problem, wants to cut off the supply to the troops." Another pause, then importantly, "And that's where we come in."

Looking at this Lone Ranger, he wanted to ask, "What's this 'we' shit, white man?" But, not sure Ron would get the old joke let him continue.

"Supply, it's about controlling the supply. The Corsicans will sell to anybody. The Chinese have guaranteed to cut off suppliers to Americans, produce only for export, and local Vietnamese users. A patriotic gesture, don't you think?" The Money King sat back, the grand plan revealed.

"The price of the shit will go through the roof, Ron," he said. "And GIs will get what they need from Vietnamese who can buy the stuff."

"There's bound to be slippage, but you've never known discipline like Chinese following rules. They'll control the dosages so Vietnamese junkies will have just enough, and no more to spare."

This notion of Ron's led him to a vision of GIs stalking Vietnamese who might be holding to mug, even kill, for their little bag of H. But never mind. "To who are Chinese making these guarantees about cutting off supply?"

Ron Steele seemed to take a moment before saying, "At the top of MACV, for openers. And the American embassy is going along. Closing their eyes to flights from the Golden Triangle into and out of Saigon."

Sounding near to sanctimonious he told Steele, "The bulk of it will get to America and our junkies, it's a much bigger problem there than here."

"The High Command out here only cares about its local problems. If this takes care of it they care not at all about the rest. The war would last another ten years. A good thing for everyone. Didn't one of your sages say, 'All politics is local?' Not that I agree. A bit too provincial for my taste."

Ron seemed to be done with his explanations and observations. The whole thing seemed crazy enough to be true. Desperate times called for desperation by all hands. He watched as The Money King played his hand, extra aces secreted away, waiting for the big pot to come along. Probing, strategic, taking advantage of weakness, a Maoist to the end. "How do you want me involved in this?"

"We can talk about that when it all comes together."

"And the NCO club business?"

"Let's wait on that until the smoke clears."

Ron Steele, while reneging on him, casually asked what might be in the rolled up newspaper he'd brought along. Was the old comrade in arms poised behind the arras, Uzi in hand against contingency? The Money King, who trusted no one, was just crazy enough to think the little roll might contain a weapon; that he needed protection from this poor shnook seated before him. "Drawings I'm sending to a friend," he said.

"May I see them?" he politely asked. He removed a drawing of a young woman and displayed it for Ron's delectation. "Roxanne's grandmother," he said without hesitation. "Sending them to Paris?" How could he know that? He was afraid to ask.

His acknowledgement of such clairvoyance received its just reward when Steele said, "Carlos didn't find out until Saturday morning that Roxanne had flown off to Paris from Bangkok and never made his regular delivery. He was berserk, planning to go to Paris on Monday to guillotine that pretty head from her lovely body." As he said this he glanced once again at the portrait of her grandmother. "Tomorrow will never come for Carlos," he said in a mocking tragedian's deep voice. "Roxanne is safe. From him, anyway."

He kept himself from asking Ron about that last remark, or how it was he could identify her grandmother, or why he might know Roxanne had so lovely a body. Instead, he closed the deal by stating, "I happen to know she flew out of Bangkok, First Class, on Air France." Ron accepted this without comment, watching his mark roll up the drawing, carry it out the door, and out of his life.

He had been used. Used up, if a fine point needed to be made. This talk of three million dollar payouts a phony offer from all sides. A pawn he was, who'd switched from one side of the board to the other without gain. He had to give it to Steele, a move ahead at every moment. As he walked away, toward home, the only thing he'd earned was the knowledge he didn't belong in big-time games. He had to be satisfied with the small stuff, take what he could as it came his way. Not a loser, not a big-time winner. A comfort of sorts to one happy enough to settle for less. One of the sheep, bought, resold, and a profit made on his labors. Broken by dragons and covered by the shadow of death. But what difference? When he disappears all that will remain is a shadow.

He'd tried to make a deal with the devil, but old Satan didn't have time for him. Twenty thousand a month delivering beer would have to do. Plus the three hundred thousand from poor Carlos he'd be adding to that little pile in the Bangkok bank instead of shipping it back home. With some happiness, he realized that while Ron Steele had cleverly exploited him, Carlos was his own successful hustle. The Opium King, hot to do in The Money King, had tossed three hundred thousand his way like a tip to a waiter. Along with the added bonus of the goons that'd violated Roxanne cut down within two feet of him. All in all, not a bad week's work. Climbing the stairs to his apartment the welcoming couch drew him in to stretch out and rest for a while.

# EIGHTY

A return to the simple life was called for. Ordinary things, the pleasures of the quotidian. He needed to get beyond ten-thousand-dollar necklaces, three hundred thousand dollars in a Vuitton bag, bullets flying, death dealt with a flick of the wrist.

He would be in harmony with himself, not sweat the small stuff, but revel in it. Return to the regularity of beer bribes and other delights of daily life. Not Prince Hamlet, nor meant to be, he'd been shown his place and stepped forth, a new man, pure and simple.

His woman of choice would be Mara. It had been weeks since he'd seen her. The old familiar began its work on him. Cocksure, it was women he did best. Though it cost him dearly over the years, dashing from pillow to pillow, pouring his life into it. A talent death to hide, he admitted with a sly grin. He fetched the statuette to show off his find as a token of respect, as good a ploy as any. Isn't it respect that woman want, as they slip their knickers down with that little twist to the hips he'd learn to love?

Taking the statue from a soft cloth bag, he placed it before her. "I brought it back from Nha Trang. It's solid gold. Temples up there from a thousand years ago are filled with stone carvings just like this.'"

"So it's stolen, looted?"

"I don't know. I paid for it fair and square."

"But it belongs to the people who live there." She said this with an admonishing voice that was beginning to wear on him.

"I bought it from an old man who does live there." He tried to hide his exasperation, as she persisted.

"It's just another way you take advantage of the people here," she said with sanctimonious reproach.

He had enough hectoring and blurted, "And you don't exploit the situation here at all." Not a question, not an opinion, a fact tossed to the table.

"Exploit?" She looked astonished at the idea. "What am I exploiting?"

He wanted to draw back. Would blow it with her. But he'd gone too far, too deep into defensiveness, and said, "Every time you take a picture and get paid you're exploiting the war as much as I am." This was the end of them, but who did she think she was, a fucking Cassandra?

The teacup seemed to be at rest in her hands and she stared at him, as he prepared to leave, preempting her dismissal. Gently placing the teacup on the table, she softly said, "You might be right. I know you're right. I think about it all the time." She looked at him. "My appetite is for war. Fed by kids in danger. I guess we're all the same. None of us belong here, do we?"

He wanted to say, "My soft life is nothing to what you endure." But stayed silent. He'd been forgiven. Could this child, who exceeded him in wisdom, become his conscience? It was too great a burden to place on one so young. The mood had shifted in his favor once again. He told her about the antique dealer and his treasure trove, suggesting they visit the shop to show off his find. She jumped at the chance, first collecting a small camera, placed in her bag. Not for pictures of war, but you never know.

# EIGHTY-ONE

The old dealer in the antique shop, seeing the Americans, sent two men who'd brought in a trove of wooden objects scurrying away. With a grand gesture, he placed his find before Mr. Dat and watched him use a magnifying glass to study the surfaces of the piece with an intense curiosity. Seemingly satisfied, he reached for a Sotheby's auction catalog. "Look at that son-of-a-bitch," he smiled to himself. "Up-to-date on it all." And near to swallowed his cud when he saw the price a similar piece was estimated to fetch. Twenty to twenty five thousand dollars.

As he sat back with the air of one who'd brought off a coup, the old man placed before him a similar, but seriously deteriorated gold object that barely compared to his little beauty. Thus began a life lesson. By gesture and the occasional word in English, Mr. Dat had him compare both pieces under a magnifying glass leading him to see the almost invisible differences in carving. Those sleight of hand distinctions in the modeling gave him to understand that his piece, though certainly gold, was a fake, a brilliant fake, but a fake all the same. This bit of capitalist cuckoldry did not bother him. He had no thought to race back to Nha Trang demanding justice. He'd been faked out before and been a faker in turn. The dealer offered to take this defeat off his hands for half what he paid. He shook his head in the negative. A cheap lesson and maybe, just maybe, the old guy was working a scam on him.

They left the shop in silence, with Mara more than slightly amused. He would slug her if she made a remark about a Victory for the Proletariat. With a kindly tone to her voice he'd not had bestowed upon him up 'til now she said, "I'm a bit tired, could you take me home? And then offered a blessing. "My roommates are having one of their all-night parties Saturday. I'd love to skip it. If you're free we could have dinner." Then she added in sweet innocence, "And then go to your place, I haven't seen it yet."

And off they went, whistling a happy tune, setting the hour he'd be at her door that evening.

But a little bit of business first. Word had come that another beer-laden freighter had arrived in port that Saturday afternoon.

## EIGHTY-TWO

A knock at the door brought Joe Ziegler who handed over a zipped bag, “My ten percent’s already deducted.”

“Fine,” he said, accepting the bag, you can start picking up the load this afternoon.”

Zeigler told him another boatload was already at sea. Another example of exemplary American efficiency. What a country we live in. But enough talk of patriotism. A contented Zeigler went on his way.

Alone, he separated out Poppa’s share, leaving himself twenty thousand and more to come. This embarrassment of riches needed to be safely stashed or become a bonanza beyond dreaming for a sneak thief or maid. He sank back into a soft chair comfortable in the knowledge he’d found a way to get even, maybe get ahead for a while, looking forward to his evening with Mara.

Another knock on the door, and Thanh’s brother, in what agitated English he could manage, urged him to go to Poppa’s house. More curious than interested, he waved the boy in. Was Daddy anxious about his beer bust dividend? He hadn’t seen or thought about Thanh in the weeks since she’d traded him sex for favors. Lavishing himself with praise at such self-control he showered and dressed leaving with the nervous, waiting boy.

Outside Thanh’s house, a familiar looking pickup held a bag of golf clubs. It was Boyle’s, and Frankie Boyle was sitting comfortable as you please with Thanh's father and a translator conducting a little business. Frankie rose, shook hands, first noting the little bag in his hands, winked at him, left with his flunky. The boy scooted out of sight, his work done. Thanh came into the room. What was going on here? Poppa departed, barely acknowledging him. No explanation offered, he was left to tell Thanh they were dealing with the worst low-life crook, American style, in the country. She seemed not to know what was going on. He was running late for dinner. He'd get it out of Doyle, he decided. And left the house with nary a goodbye or regret.

# EIGHTY-THREE

When they kissed, it was at her behest.

His couch, her decision, he'd wisely decided. Mara had wandered about, fingering books, taking in the flowers, the neatness of the place. A well-kept bachelor pad with a good wine to share, sipped quietly, an eye-to-eye toast, at a point of no return. She'd leaned forward, moved toward him, gently reached her hand to the back of his neck, and eyes wide open, softly kissed him. Lips lingering as long as she would allow, they parted, the distance between them no longer at issue.

"I'm back out there tomorrow." It was a point of fact. A statement of intention, no more than that. But he saw it as a sign, took her hand, silently offering an option she accepted by picking up her wineglass and walking with him toward his darkened bedroom.

A small lamp beside his bed, to steal glances at his lovers in their moments of repose or ecstasy, cast its light on her lovely, inquiring face. She touched the inside of his thigh as they sat embracing at the side of the bed, and seemed pleased when his cock hardened against her hand as she reached inside his neatly unzipped pants.

They kissed as she took his measure while he found his way to the warmth of her as she made the subtlest move to allow him more free play to work his gentle urging magic, fingers inside, hearing her gasp at the intrusion, showing him how to move in out and up to her pleasure dome, which he would love and caress forever.

Her eyes went wide in surprise as she bit into his shoulder and he felt her come in his hand. She kissed him, a thank you sort of kiss, stretching out on the bed, kicking off her shoes.

It brought him another kind of pleasure to see her relaxed and satisfied, and wondered what might be next. After a decent interval he reached for a button on her blouse. Much too quickly she pulled his hand away, then began massaging his cock slowly, sexily, wanting to please him in turn. You got to take what you can get, he realized, but had hoped for something more. It was his turn to draw a hand away. She didn't seem to mind and within a moment slipped down and begin licking the shaft of his cock, then took the head of it within the warmth of her mouth. An expert. All his senses focused on the one thing, his loving dick with her mouth curling, swirling, moving him toward the rumble he began to feel at the back of the balls, that he didn't want, not yet. He raised her head, surprise in her eyes and kissed her.

She asked, didn't he like it, and he said, yes, oh yes, but not yet, and reached once again for the buttons on her blouse, causing her to jump from the bed. Deliberately turning away, she removed her jacket, wriggled out of her slacks, showing a lovely ass. Her back to him, she carefully unbuttoned and removed her blouse. He waited, fully clothed. This was no striptease. She stood and pivoted, a cold challenging look on her face. "Oh my god," he said.

A jagged, horrific scar reached diagonally from pelvis past breastbone to clavicle. Her face had gone from cold to inquiring as he rose and folded her in his arms asking all the questions while touching her face, kissing her hair, loving her, loving her. It had happened two years ago, her first days in country, a supposed milk run of a patrol that got cut to pieces. She was hit by fragments from a mortar barrage and pulled out by Medevac, saved from dying by a young corpsman, then kept alive by doctors who wanted to send her home so she skipped out of the hospital. And here she was. What did he think of her now? "I've always wanted a scar-crossed lover."

"He jests at scars that never felt the wound," she replied, while helping her Romeo from his clothes.

Side to side they faced each other in commingled embrace of legs and arms, kiss for kiss until they fell back on soft pillows, holding hands, ceiling their sky, walls safe boundary, bed the center of the only world they knew.

She turned to look at him. He began to speak, but she silenced him with a quick move that brought her astride him, fitting neatly onto his welcoming cock. The slow up and down riding of him, the feel of her so exquisite, so close to pain, as she took control, so pleased, so very pleased when he reached up and moved fingers across the wetness of her sweet clitoris, causing her to rise up then fall toward him, a happy woman.

She remained atop him, breasts to chest, legs between his, her heartbeat back to normal. She felt weightless, her body returned to that little thing she was, no longer bestriding him, no longer the Colossus she'd seemed a moment before. "Are you OK?" she asked.

"Sure, you're light as a feather."

"No, I mean you didn't come."

"I will." Anticipating her question he told her it was something he'd learned from an East Indian woman, a trick of breathing, more or less. "It has to do with pleasing you first," he told her.

"Can I please you for a while?" she coyly asked. He allowed as how that would be acceptable, and testing a thesis, she reached between his legs and begin an imperceptible massaging of his balls, a flitting across the head of his cock with her tongue, returning to balls again, seemingly hungry to please him with mouth and tongue, fingers and hands, and to show she might just be able to show him a trick or two.

He pulled her up and away from her work, slipping her beneath him, and putting mouth to pussy, using his tongue like a great cat, heard a purr as he reached inside her, lapped at her juices, pressed his tongue back and forth across the little tip at the top of her until she swelled with the pleasure of it, nails digging into him, head tossing side to side and she had come again, and yet again. Then she wanted the feel of his cock inside her for a while, sort of a post-prandial.

She needed a bit of rest, took her ease, snuggled happily, full of compliments he graciously accepted, pointing out she had talents of her own. What tomorrow will bring hung over them, a languid haze, soft accompaniment to their sweet murmuring. She smiled at this old guy, bald of head, sign of paunch, and idly ran her fingers down his stomach past his navel, circled back each time reaching closer to his cock at rest. "That night we met I was in no mood to talk to anyone and here I am." He said, "Was ever woman in such humor wooed?" She looked at him, pleased with the results of her handiwork. "You quote Shakespeare the way the devil quotes scripture." Then pulled him atop her whispering, "Was ever woman in such humor won!"

The here and now beckoned in the guise of soft flesh and it pleased her to feel his hand part her thighs, moving in so-slow motion until she could take the tease no more, pulling his ass toward her with all her strength to feel the fullness of him deep inside her. He allowed her this indulgence, moving in and out, brushing inside her side to side as she moved under him. He felt her improvising around a theme he'd set out awaiting her response. And respond she did, raising her legs to his shoulders, moaning low as he finally gave in to her, then falling toward her for a long remembered kiss. They slept. Each held the other so close they'd never part. Ecstasy had given way to sleep. Sleep to dreams. Nothing to mar their joy.

The dawn's first light reached into the bedroom. Feeling for Mara, he closed his eyes, returning to sleep. Full sunlight flashing in the room awakened him again. A shadow moved across the doorway. His body stiffening against the sight awakened Mara, and she rolled over, seeing Thanh in the bedroom doorway, key in hand as he grabbed for a robe and dashed out. Quickly dressing, she found him talking in a fury to a lovely Vietnamese woman, who cowered before him. When he rushed back to Mara, she slammed at his face. "You bastard. You lousy bastard," she said, so quietly, so evenly. He saw there was no way to explain and let her slip away, a hand to his cheek were she'd struck her overwhelming blow. He turned to Thanh. "What do you want now? You always want something. Give me my key, goddamn you." She said nothing, stood passive, unmoving. Finally, "My father, your friend, it will be trouble for my father."

"Your father never looked at me."

"He is embarrassed."

"About what?"

"Heroin. Your friend told him his money came from heroin. Is that true?" He marched to the door, his open robe floating in his wake. "I want you out of here, do you understand? Out!"

"You won't help me?" It was a question couched in a combination of curiosity and hostility he didn't care to notice. She left without giving up the key.

He stood against the closed door for only a moment before returning to his bedroom, trying to turn away from the past few minutes and restore the hours that had gone before. He would have proclaimed his steadfast love at daybreak, his faithfulness each night. Instead, sadness engulfed him, near to weeping, as he sat on his still-warm bed. He knew there was no repairing this. Mara will go back to her work, and he went to the shower to scrub away at the encrusted filth of his misspent life.

# EIGHTY-FOUR

What drew him to lunch at the most vulgar restaurant in Saigon only the gods in their jollity could conjure. An all-American crowd, raucous and demanding, filled the room with drunken mid-day carrying on. Holding court Frankie Doyle, nothing unusual about that. Save for his companion, the lovely Thanh, sitting across from him fork in hand, smiling now and then. He watched this charade for a few minutes too long, treated to the sight of Doyle rising, offering fat fingers to his grateful lady. They walked past, silence from Thanh, another wink from Doyle. And to put a point to it, Doyle's hand on Thanh's ass, letting it linger as they strolled by.

He kept himself from caring. Tried very hard. How could she do this to him? Is there no loyalty within infidelity? To think of this animal's hands all over her nakedness that he'd once so much desired. Did it have something to do with her begging for help this morning? He'd find out soon enough. Granting them their afternoon together, he knew he'd stop by Doyle's place that very evening.

## EIGHTY-FIVE

Stop by he did, preempted by Doyle as soon as he hit the door. "What a lousy piece of ass. Don't you Jewboys know nothin' about fuckin'? All the time you spent together you didn't teach her a goddamn thing about screwin'? I might as well have been fuckin' a door with a keyhole."

Ah, quiet moment before the Cobra strikes, brief second's pause when the gunship dips, bowing to all, before the hell it holds within breaks loose and fifty, count them, fifty rockets, 75-millimeter jobbies go screaming forth and a pair of mini-guns on max blast and rip not needing a target, only an opportunity. Then 40 missiles more blow life to death, and the Cobra, empty of its load, soars off beating back rough winds at a slow chopper's pace till the ever loving next time comes around and where she stops, nobody.

He was handed a beer. "Don't you know it's our job to turn these bitches into decent pussy?" Boyle sat, amused at his insight into the American Mission.

Giving back the beer he said, "Her father knows about the drug deal."

"Sure he knows, I told him. And why? Because I've got him by the balls." Frankie paused to let this sink in. "You clever little kike, you found us a gold mine. The sonofabitch signs off on every fuckin' container that enters the country. He's the head of export/import for the gook government. I told him he'd have to play ball with me or I'd blow the whistle on his winnings from the heroin deal."

"And Thanh?"

"The chippy? Is that her name? She shows up at my door this morning wanting to talk." She was at my front door first, he wanted to tell Doyle. "After my round of golf," I say and leave. "Sure as shit, she's waiting when I get back. I take her to lunch, she tells me her father is a very important man. Could I find someone else? I tell her she'll have to come back to my place. She knows what the deal is, that's for sure. I fuck her. Forget about it, it was the worst. But listen to this, I send her on her way with papers for her father to sign on a shipment I'm expecting, or else. I told her it was just this once and to bring them to me tomorrow night. Maybe I can teach her to give me a blowjob. What do you got going these days?"

"Nothing much Frankie," he said, rising to leave, lightheaded, staggering slightly.

"You ok?" A kindly Uncle Frankie asked.

"Yeah, sure, I'm fine."

"Listen, if you wanna be part of this I'll cut you in. It was your doin' and I always pay back a favor, got me?" He got him all right, but chose to leave while his pounding heart still resided in his chest.

The adversary had spread his filthy fingers on her. She was no longer beautiful, fallen into the hands of the enemy. She has sinned. Though he honored her, he now despises her. She has been seen naked. Her filthiness pollutes her skirts. She'd not be the cause of his death, but would take it upon himself in the frenzy of digging his own grave.

# EIGHTY-SIX

It was Ninh who said, "We must talk."

"Sure, come in, sit down," reaching for his wallet. Ninh was due his hundred.

Waving off this gesture, Ninh said, "Something more important."

What could more important than his hundred bucks? he wondered.

"Colonel Lee shot himself. This morning. He's dead." Then Ninh added, "Big Eddie and his sons are in jail downtown. They broke their promise not to sell heroin to Americans." The Money King, so sure he had control of the Chinese distributors, had been betrayed. So much for Long March connections.

Imagining those three walruses in one small cell brought him to laughter until Ninh leaned forward and whispered, "Marty Long."

"What, is he in trouble too?"

"No, he makes the trouble."

"What does that mean?"

Ninh crossed over, sat down alongside, putting a hand gently on his arm. Something he'd never come near to doing before. "I will tell you, but it can be big trouble for me, understand?"

He didn't really understand, but waited as Ninh described how our sweet seminarian, Marty Long, was a Special Agent for the U.S. Undercover, of course. But reporting to no one in country, trusting no one, keeping secret files, corruption his special interest. He never made a collar, leaving that to those over here getting orders from Washington based on his information. Long let the small stuff go, until Lee reached a saturation point when he demanded kickbacks from day laborers hired by contractors. Ten percent off a lousy three dollars a day. Have you no shame, sir? No point in asking how Ninh knew all this.

Ninh came to a pause in his telling of the details. It was a pause taken to draw in breath and say, "Maybe you are the next one."

"Maybe?"

Ninh looked regretful saying, "Maybe, for sure."

He let that contradiction fly by and waited for more, and Ninh said, quietly, "It was the heroin."

"But I was doing a favor, I got nothing out of it."

Ninh sorrowfully said, "Everything else, the water, the bribes, the penny a can on the beer, even the radios were OK." But the heroin…he trailed off.

"You son-of-a-gun, you know everything," he said with a smile.

Ninh, nodding his head in agreement, repeated, "It was the heroin."

The shit was all over the country. GIs were into it in so big a way that something had to give. And it might as well be little me, he thought. "When's it going to get me?" he asked.

"Not sure. Not soon. They have Eddie, you they know about. But a really big one is next. Really big." Ninh stated this with assurance, so clearly in the know. There was no need for further talk. The message had been delivered. His hundred a week was paying off nicely. Or was it something else? Had a friendship of sorts developed between them? Time enough to turn sentimental. He was worried, plenty. But worry could wait. Matters of the heart were spinning a web that had a way of taking precedence over clear and present danger.

# EIGHTY-SEVEN

The days slid by. His apartment a prison. Not a drink, barely touching food, emptiness overcame him. Arrest and prosecution seemed a far-off land of make believe. What mattered most was that he'd lost Mara and given up Thanh to Boyle. It sickened him. Wait a minute, he thought, all those hustlers around Boyle being picked up now and then. Is he in cahoots with Long? Or protected by him? Then back to that little bitch. She had hurled a stone and struck. The wound was grievous. He'd not allow her to wound him again. He'd be himself, at last. If only he could break out of time, escape the past, keep its poison from the present, he might leap to freedom. But he'd heard Boyle's every word and its nuance. Every gesture and its intention. He had gotten the message. Played it back and forth inside his head. Fast-forward, reverse or normal speed, it came out the same.

"You were already done with her," he cried aloud. It was over. She'd shown him what she was. But the image of that fat pig ripping the pants from her, crushing her under the stuffed guts of him, pushing his dick at her, in her, was added to the list of other humiliations, all that a man could bear. He didn't deserve this. Hadn't he saved her brother from the army, gotten her father the two hundred thou, brought her to see that kid who probably was hers? What more could he have done? An assuring word was all she needed to hear that morning. But he couldn't think fast enough. It would have done him no good with Mara already out the door.

It had been five days. Mara might be back. He had to see her again. Worth risking her anger. The possibility dragged him from his recurring nightmare. He hadn't thought of Thanh and her doings for at least half an hour. Progress, any mental health practitioner would say.

He felt good, or better anyway, and showered thinking of Mara. How sweet, how smart, how sexy, this waif-like creature who just might be his salvation. As his body welcomed the soap and hot water, thoughts of Mara made him hard. Always a good sign. He stepped from the shower allowing the air to dry him and shaved, oh so carefully, in anticipation of reconciliation. No flowers. No poetry. No bullshit either. Straight talk. He could do it. He could. He knew he could.

But first, breakfast. No longer a condemned man. This would be a first meal. For the forgiven. Was he an optimist, or becoming one? Breakfast on the Continental Terrace filled belly and soul with calories and coffee enough for two. Nothing would get in the way of this era of good feeling. The good ol' boys at their morning beers, the pathetic beggars, the shoeshine boys, were allowed their place in the universe. But he'd dawdled long enough. Mara's house was only a short walk. Fortified against any storm he headed her way.

That abundance of grub brought a wondrous thought: He could learn darkroom stuff, catalog her pics and negs, be her assistant, her helpmeet. It would work wouldn't it? Why shouldn't it work? A happy couple, yeah, hooray! The twenty-year difference in their ages wasn't so bad. For now. But what happens when he turns sixty-three and she's a frisky forty-three and on assignment or assignation, or both? Uh, oh, the snake's in the garden. Get thee behind me, Satan! He would overcome the misery at their parting by offering her his highest compliment. An offering of himself to have and to hold. Irresistible. It had to work.

The gate to her little French Colonial house was open. He climbed three stairs, hesitated for a moment, and entered. Mara's young companions were sprawled on the couch and chairs in the living room. One of them, sipping from a can of beer, looked up at him.

"Is Mara here?"

"Gone."

"Gone where?"

The boy raised his beer. "Gone, goddamn it. Dead and fucking gone.

He stared at him.

"She's at the airport morgue, what's left of her. Go see for yourself."

He turned away, involuntary muscles taking him up the stairs, looking for her bedroom. Looking for something, anything to bring her back to him. The clothes she'd worn their night together were strewn about, her silver necklace on a night stand. He rubbed it between his fingers seeking the feel of her.

"Gone," they had said. "Dead," they had said. Not his comforters, those three. Only the facts. "Dead and gone." Isn't that what they'd said? He gently put the necklace in its place. A paperback on a bookshelf, *Romeo and Juliet*, with Juliet's part underlined and Mara's name inside. She'd played the part in college. "My death will be a grave matter," Mercutio had said, making laughter of his dying. And so said Mara, not for laughs but to brazen with death. She'd lost, she'd won. He put the little book into his pocket and left the room.

His comforters were gone, the house empty. He walked out into the brilliant sun, the street quiet, desolate. Stumbling, he leaned against a wall to rest a while. If only he could tell someone of his sorrow, it might give him ease against the pain that gripped him, coiled about him. Their night together had been so sweet, so filled with tenderness. He would have seen her again, if the world were fair. Tears wet his face, no comfort for his soul, his punishment complete, his lamentation a cry for help, a plea for understanding that would bring down mocking laughter. He felt the rope around his neck, spirit weakened before this calamity. Kept himself from falling, knowing he'd never stand upright again. Trying to remember tenderness torn away by the sweep of a scythe's long blade. "Death, once dead, there's no more dying then," he whispered. No divine dimension to his being, he deserved to be purged from the world.

He would keep this a secret in his heart of hearts. Mara dead, the key he'd given Thanh the cause of it. And Doyle's threats to Poppa bringing her to his place at dawn that morning. Goddamn these accidents of fate. They cried out for vengeance. He'd start with Thanh. He'd show that Mick bastard what this Jewboy could do. If you wrong me shall I not seek revenge?

# EIGHTY-EIGHT

From such despair his only solace was in action. Thanh's brother, frightened by his anger, told him she was in Pleiku, at their father's pepper plantation. The town, not safe for Americans, it was madness to go there. But he had an address, and the next day, bribing his way by paying triple the cost, flew from Tan Son Nhut to Pleiku. On a ticket written for a man who had slept at the terminal for two days to board that plane and stared at him with a hatred he only shook off when the Air Vietnam plane was aloft and flying North to his quarry.

The road out of the Pleiku airport branched at one point, the safe American zone away from the road to town. He pointed the taxi driver in the direction of the town. The driver pulled to the side of the road, looked at the address, and shook his head.

"Goddamn it, yes," he shouted.

The driver formed his hand into the shape of a gun, pointed at him. "Boom, boom," he said, slipped into gear and took off for the town.

He stepped out of the taxi onto a rutted road, houses barely hanging together in the heat and dust, smell of animals kept inside, and hidden eyes watching from windows, behind doorways.

A large walled house stood nearby, and he headed toward it. And there she was, walking down a path, seeing him, showing not a whit of guilt or apprehension. As though it was no surprise for her American to be moving toward her as she carried a basket filled with market purchases. Offering her cheek for a familial welcome, she paid no attention to his non-response and led him into the cool interior of country-house informality quite different from her Saigon home.

After a servant rushed over to take her basket, Thanh sat opposite him saying nothing, trying to assay what he was thinking, what he might know. There was no logic in charging her with Mara's death. What would it mean to her? Another death among so many. And Frankie Boyle? What would that mean to her? Another fuck among so many. Love and Death, those non-identical twins, hovered in the air, dancing before his eyes, wandering through the pathways of his imagining. One lover dead, another his humiliation.

He'd long known the best, the only way to overcome a sexual humbling was sexually. Betrayed? Then pick up on another and watch the last humiliation quickly fade. Thus it was. Thus it would ever be. But this was something different. It came to him, malicious epiphany, that he needed nothing new to relieve him in his agony, His next piece sat before him, changed forever in his eyes. As this mutation did its work, he offered her a smile that she leapt to accept. Her father entered the room. It was high noon, and no matter the distraction, time for Poppa's lunch.

At the table, he had Thanh translate as he told the tale of the two-hundred-thousand-dollar exchange. The trailer in the forest, the shortchanging on the deal, the drug pickup, his smashed face, the bribe to release him. All for you he was saying to Poppa, all for you, nothing in it for me. Father sat there, a Vietnamese Mandarin, holding an audience for this barbarian who'd risked his neck for him, kept his last son from the draft, was fucking his eldest daughter.

In the silence, he reached for his spoon to taste the soup that had grown cold. Finally, the father spoke and Thanh said, "He wants you to tell him about Mr. Boyle." He watched her at the mention of the name, expecting a lowering of eyes in some demure exaggeration. Nothing of the kind. She did wet her lips, her tongue lasciviously reaching from lower to upper lip.

"Tell your father he doesn't have to do anything with Mr. Boyle." He paused and looked at her. "Mr. Boyle is being watched by American crime investigators." He didn't know this, it was probably untrue, a lie, but it seemed to settle the matter, and he was offered a place at the table.

Lunch over, Thanh asked another favor. "Can you help us visit the American base outside Pleiku?" He was sure he could.

A car was called and off they went, the two men in the rear, Thanh in front beside the driver. No words between them, father, silently, ceremoniously, held a red lacquer box covered in gold tracery that caught the afternoon light. At the base, they passed through the first gate without pause, his white face sufficient ID for the passive Vietnamese gatekeeper. The second ring of wire needed more persuasion, manned by two GIs in full battle mode who finally accepted his ID, letting the good-looking woman, the fancy car and prosperous gentleman go to the third ring of wire beyond which they could never pass, though it wasn't their intention.

Out of the car, the father and daughter stood silently, immune to the chaos and grinding noise of an army installation. Father opened the box and dutiful daughter took from it fruit, a red can of Coke, a package of Marlboros, a small altar, and placed them on the ground. It came to him that two years had passed since the attack on Pleiku that Thanh had described their first day together. The anniversary of Number One Son's death. Those simple items from life now before them, he watched clasped hands in prayer, a whispered conversation between father and son, conjured up from the spirit world where he resided. After death the good live on, he whispered to himself. All he could bring to the occasion. They turned toward him. Duty done. Time to go.

# EIGHTY-NINE

Introspection never his strong suit, never the safe haven it was for many, the plane ride back from Pleiku gave him a bit of time to think about things. The night before he'd slipped into a large bed protected by a diaphanous white mosquito net billowing in the evening breeze. A bridal chamber, he thought to himself. The door to the darkened room opened and he watched Thanh come in, into his bed. Silent as always she stretched out beside him. His response a quiet of his own, he found himself embraced by a child seeking forgiveness. Curled within his arms, she rested there. No sound, no tears, nothing more than the heat of her body against his. There was no talk. What was there to say? Not the way it was with Boyle, he was sure. He had taken her down, the ruttish pig of him, roaring as his satisfaction overcame her. Leaving her the mess he'd left behind to wipe away. That was the truth of it. That was for sure.

As he worked his way through the scene, his own hard-on grew, and she moved against it, child no more, knowing she would overcome, knowing he was on his way to forgiveness through the one common language. And fuck her he did, with the fury of a conqueror, sitting her up on the bed, pushing his cock in her mouth for good measure. Love makes the world go round, does it not?

The plane bumped along to its landing. Patiently, he waited his turn to clamber down a short metal ladder at the rear. The terminal beckoned, shelter from the sun, crowded with soldiers waiting to get home or to the golden whores of Bangkok. New arrivals from stateside nervously examined a large hole in the ceiling, a welcome wagon gift delivered via long-range rocket by your friendly neighborhood Viet Cong. A reminder, to some, that there was a war on. Meanwhile, clever civilians changed military scrip into greenbacks, earning 35 percent on the exchange. He'd already seen it all too many times, found a taxi and headed home. Mission accomplished, if only he could remember what it was supposed to have been.

# NINETY

"It's a serious matter to bring someone back from the dead." It was Ninh's reply to a begging request made with all seriousness. Since the little ceremony at Pleiku, where he was sure he'd heard a young man's voice replying to Thanh's father, he'd become obsessed, possessed by the notion he could bring Mara back, if only for a moment.

"Can you help me?" Ninh looked at this crazy American, facing arrest and jail with only a dead woman on his mind and nodded, "Yes, I can. Very complicated. Very expensive. A thousand dollars. The women who do these things are very busy these days."

Ninh's subtlety, his politesse at stating the obvious need this war had created, endeared him to his boss, now a supplicant desperate for help in his mad quest. Each night before sleep, and early in the morning, at the first stirring, Mara would come to him. Never in dreams. Only when awake to the knowledge of her death and his part in it. He lacked the courage to join her in death, needed something or someone else to bring them together once again. He trusted Ninh. Did not mind appearing pathetic before him. Ninh would deliver for him. Mara would come back to him. He had to believe it.

Ninh watched this troubled soul, different from most Americans who came his way. Not that different, really. Trouble with women. On the take, for sure. But a generosity, a gentleness the others lacked or dared not display. Ninh left him with a promise to return when he'd done what he could to bring some solace to his grieving.

And return Ninh did. "Good news," he announced, "Next Sunday. It is arranged. We will go together to Bien Hoa." It was thirty minutes by car from Saigon, near an American airbase. A bit dangerous, but worth the risk. "Where is the girl now?" Ninh asked the question as if she were alive, traveling somewhere.

Barely able to answer, he whispered, "Back in America, I think. Buried there."

Ninh, worried, said, "Without a body here it will be very difficult to bring her spirit back to you. Without a body, very difficult," he repeated. "You need to bring something of hers, something personal."

Remembering the copy of *Romeo and Juliet* he'd taken from her room he said, "I have a book."

"A book? Something she touched, held in her hands? Very good," Ninh spoke with reassuring certainty. "In three days, then. You may not eat the flesh of any animal, bird, or fish. And," at this Ninh hesitated, "no women, no sex." He let this last be taken in, accepted. "To purify you, prepare you."

"Thank you, Mr. Ninh." He said this with gratitude, left alone to think about what would await him in three days.

Three days of celibacy and vegetable plates. No sacrifice too great, he decided, with that usual mix of self-mockery and gravity he'd found so useful. He'd already given up the whoring, been bored with it, didn't miss it at all. A penance being paid? He didn't think so. Penance implied forgiveness, redemption. From other hands, not his own. Convinced of his culpability in Mara's death, he could never forgive himself. No redeeming prayer or act of contrition could repair the damage. A line from a poem popped into his head again, "After the first death there is no other." No solace there. A fact of life, this thing called death.

The ceremony's appointed hour was at sundown. Guide and acolyte took a taxi, picking up the Bien Hoa Highway heading north. Ninh, usually so chatty, had an air of quiet, of contemplation. It suited the mood and they were soon crossing the Dong Nai River toward Long Binh, the site of an immense Army base where every sort of item needed for war was stored. Reaching Route One, the taxi turned west toward Bien Hoa passing another massive American airbase. These bases were everywhere in Vietnam, Pax Americana delivering the peace that passeth all understanding. His reverie was interrupted by the snarling sound of straining engines. He looked out at the sight of giant earth movers, their front blades shaped to a nasty point, joining together in the destruction of a rubber plantation surrounding a one-story building. Those with a leaning toward the classical had dubbed them Rome Ploughs, ripping and scraping the earth to leave no sign of growing things. Precisely what the Romans did at Carthage in days of yore, now matched by our own soldier boys, salt of the earth, working at their task.

They drove quickly along the main drag of the town, past bars and other entertainment palaces. A regular sight, these strips of temptation, wherever our mightiest congregated. Soon enough they were past all this and approaching a small, well-kept house alongside the river. It was nearly dark and the last twilight lit a beautifully carved, painted wooden bird set in an acacia tree. Monkey sculptures cut from large tree stumps encircled the tree. The sound of singing, chanting came from the house as they entered to see lovely young women in white robes swaying slowly to the music. A place had been set for them, and they sat down with Ninh whispering, "The shaman is from my village in the north. She will enter when all is prepared." In the dim light, he saw small ceramic figures in various sex positions alongside figures of pregnant women. He began to notice the intricate carvings on the wall, and plaques with golden characters he thought he'd seen before. Ninh, following his eyes, said, "In honor of the Mother Goddess, she rules everything." His buddy Marty Long had told him the same thing. Odd, he thought, the prospect of arrest, indictment, jail time, was of no matter. Bringing Mara back was what mattered, if only to ask her a question, an overwhelming question, and hope to hear an answer.

The dancing girls left, leaving three older women to continue playing stringed instruments, beat small drums, shake tambourines. Dressed in bright red pants and tunics, their playing reached a crescendo that drifted away to a last lingering sound of the tambourine as a withered crone, lips brightened with a bright red smear of lipstick, dressed in a long, earth-colored caftan glistening in the light, strode in. Her large dark eyes took in the room, saving a special glance for the American who sat before her. Moving slowly, easily, she fetched a long-necked stringed instrument hanging on a wall, sat down and began to play. Her fingers, so claw-like, so tightened in the grip of old age, seemed to lengthen, move across the strings as if possessed by another, playing a different music, more expert, melodious, than what he'd heard before. The three women, true acolytes, studied every move of her hands. When she was done they lit incense, brought highly pitched pipes to their lips as she moved a closed fan back and forth before him. A benediction he was pleased to accept. Trying to clear his mind, he heard her speak for the first time. Sweet sounds directed at him. Ninh, translating, said, "The spirit will return, not the body." He nodded at the shaman, taking in her meaning as she began to chant, a signal to the three women to go to him, remove his shoes, place hemp sandals on his feet and lead him to the nearby river whose waters lapped the shore, a boatman with a long pole standing by, and a man with a long bow of the kind northern tribesmen use for the hunt who faced the setting sun.

Following instructions, he removed his sandals, stepped into the river, feeling cups of water washing across his head. A ritual cleansing to ready him for what was to come. As he stepped from the river, the bowman pulled back his string. A flaming arrow, a call to awaken the spirits, flew toward the sun's last traces disappearing into the darkness. He heard a loud horn and turned to see men carrying torches, long, broad ancient swords, old rifles, circle the house. On the third pass, the riflemen fired up into the dark sky, the procession marched away, and he was led back to the house, a tinge of foreboding beginning to seep into his bones.

The shaman's chants increased in volume, the beat growing more insistent. The three women, quietly chanting in response, lit more incense. While one of them took up cymbals, the other two began spreading rose petals along a path to this supplicant, who watched in wonder as they un-spooled a ball of hemp, circling him and the old shaman in a long, loose loop of thread. She gestured to him and he approached. Taking his hand, she brought it first across her head from brow to throat, pressed both his hands to her breasts, to her stomach, forcing him to feel her deep, inverted navel. The soul resides in those three places, Ninh had told him, needing to be awakened as a spirit to continue its journey. When he returned to his place a tray of food was before him, an offering, should the spirit agree to appear. The shaman moved away in the company of two of her attendants, leaving behind the oldest of the three to chant prayers welcoming the spirit of the dead to the living earth.

The old crone returned, transformed. An ethereal blue, kimono-like robe, trimmed in white, was part of the change. But it was her movements, lithe, at ease, with no sign of age as she stood there, boldly watching him as he stared, transfixed. In a voice drenched in sorrow he called out, "Can you forgive me?" And watched the figure in blue take a small knife, cut the cord between them, turn her back, wail a response, then stalk out of the room. "What did she say? What did she say?" he cried.

And he heard Ninh's funereal reply: "Forgive? For what? Disillusion, or death?" Ninh paused, "She must not be disturbed again." And that would be that. He'd reached Mara and found his answer. He rose and left the house, grateful for the chance, not at all surprised by the result, paying so heavy a price for betrayal, as he had so many times before.

## NINETY-ONE

Cutting through a thick slab of steak slathered in a béarnaise sauce he crisscrossed between berating himself and recollection of the splendor of the night before. "Bloody superstition," he called out to himself, while divining that something important had occurred. Against all instinct he'd given over to a world of darkness. Been allowed admission to mysteries unrevealed to the world he knew. This raising of the dead, a commonplace for any Vietnamese, was a Gypsy fortune-teller's scam back home. It made no sense to anyone used to easy categories of the living, the dead, with nothing in between or beyond to annoy the logical mind.

Masticating slowly through a bite of rare beef, the little house on the river came back to him. The music and dance, the drone of chanting lulling him to a calm he'd never known. He remembered slipping, without cynicism, into the rituals the old woman enacted, his only offering acceptance. He put down his fork, the meal half-finished, no longer hungry.

His upper body, gently rocking in recollection, was brought taut by the sight of Marty Long entering the restaurant alone. He watched as his nemesis crossed away from him to a table near a window and order a drink and a meal without studying the menu. Present reality took little time to replace the calm he felt with an odd curiosity. He moved toward his fate heedlessly, unaware of the speed, no limit to the velocity, hardly aware of actions or their consequences. Long would be moving on him soon enough. A very cool Daniel in the Lion's den, he dared to join Marty at his table to check things out. And Long, equally cool, said, "Frankie's all over town telling people he's porking your girlfriend."

"I was done with her before he got to her and good luck to him." Marty seemed skeptical, but never mind, what difference did it make to him?

"I hear you almost got yourself in deep shit working one of his deals."

"You get that from Frankie" he asked, wondering why Marty was playing him.

"No, Johnny the Greek told me he bailed you out. I guess you don't listen to good advice. Everyone told you to stay away from Frankie's fucking around."

"Some fucking around," he said. "Selling two-way radios still in their cartons to the VC. Then a truckload of heroin. How does he get away with it?" He threw down this challenge about Frankie and his doings sure that Marty Long, Undercover Agent, had to know all about them.

"By finding hungry bastards like you to do the pick up and delivery part. You'll never find his prints on anything. He uses those fat fingers to curl around a golf club, or a tall glass filled with ice and whiskey, or any piece of ass he can buy." He said this last with a touch of admiration. "He's an old pal of mine. We go back a long way. And we Irishmen always stick together." Then Marty said, "Let me tell you again, stay away from him. He's one greedy son-of-a-bitch."

"That he is," he agreed, and left Marty with a wave and a smile. What was going on? Could Ninh have gotten it wrong? Why was he warning him off two-bit Frankie when he was sure to know of his dealings with Carlos and The Money King? None of it figured. Might he be suggesting, say, fifty thousand, to lay off of him?

Never mind, he had a more immediate score to settle with the fat prick. He didn't want to go even-up, he wanted a big win. Wanted him cursing into his whiskey, cursing the day he fucked with the wrong guy.

Should he shoot the fucker? He had a gun, but hadn't handled it in years. Hire a killer? A thousand dollars would do it. There were dozens who'd jump at the chance. Put a bomb in his golf bag and blow the prick to pieces? He laughed aloud, realizing that even in a war zone none of this was going to happen.

He was surrounded by a war all but invisible to him. He fit right in. Living the high life, comfortable among the corruptible. But he needed to focus, god damn it, focus on that greedy son of a bitch. That's what Marty Long had called him. Greedy for money, greedy for sex. Poisonous twins that needed only a clever apothecary to bring the bastard down. This was a return to a level he knew. Not up to the big time of Money Kings and Drug Kings, his thoughts turned to that little golden statue perched upon its stand.

# NINETY-TWO

A sort of serenity came over him, so odd a feeling for one given to agitation. Its source the little golden statue he held in his hand. Fake it might be, but what is more interesting than a beautiful fraud? Deception and betrayal were the common currency, but uncommon beauty washes away all sins. Sitting quietly in his living room drinking tea, of all things, the golden form begat those fallen angels, money and sex to serve as enticement. Marty Long had pointed the way to bait the bear, bring that miserable fucking Mick to heel. A plot was beginning to fester, a scam to drive Boyle, weeping, to his knees.

He'd have to bring the antique dealer in on the dodge. Not trusting his French or the old man's English he would need a translator. Better not use Ninh, it would have to be Thanh, goddamn it. His pride, long since fallen away, had no further to travel. She wouldn't know the details. All she'd need to know was that he had a buyer for some precious objects and he needed the dealer to guarantee their authenticity for a 50-50 split of the profits.

He fetched Thanh and went off to the dealer. No intimacy between the two, this was business, something she understood very well, content with her part in it, no idea it involved Boyle. The clever dealer, wise in the ways of commerce, was quick to understand and needed little to convince him, save when it came to the split. Fifty-Fifty? Uh, uh. Sixty-forty. "My way," the old devil said. And that was that, except that he asked to borrow the Sotheby's catalog for a while. His business over with Thanh, he put her into a taxi and pressed some bills into her hand. She accepted them, the good little whore. He turned as the taxi shifted into gear and was free of her.

Now for the hard part. He had to be careful with Boyle. Hustling a hustler isn't easy. Catalog and little statue in hand, he went to visit his old pal.

"Just lookin' at it gives me a hard on." Thus spoke the connoisseur. The con was halfway home. "Look at the tits on her." Boyle had it in hand, perversely fondling the little thing in his thick fingers. "You can find and fuck an ass like that all over Thailand, but there's nothing to compare here." He seemed ruminative about his musings on comparative anatomy. "I wonder how come?" Rather than speculate, he drew out the catalog and showed it to Doyle, who was mildly impressed by the price it might fetch.

"I paid twelve thousand for mine," he told Boyle, matter-of-factly. "Marty Long's dealer. He's got eleven more."

"Talk to Marty about this?"

"No."

"How come?"

"I thought I'd leave it up to you."

Doyle, subtle as a house of cards, asked, "How's this supposed to work?"

"If you buy 'em, we ship them off to the auction house in London. They've got a sale in six weeks. We double our money." There, said and done. He picked up his statuette possessively.

"How come the old fucker downtown don't do it himself?"

"I dunno. Maybe it's about taxes. They hate to pay 'em. A public sale would cost him plenty."

"Do you think he'd take less for the whole bunch of them?"

"He knows to the dime what these things are worth. It's his business. It's his catalog."

"Is that a no?"

"That's my guess." He watched Doyle go silent. "I'm putting mine up for sale, whatever you decide."

"How come you don't got more than one?"

"It tapped me out. It's all I can afford."

Doyle looked at this poor, broke soul, contaminating by his presence. "Twelve thousand apiece? You're talkin' a hundred thirty thousand dollars right there."

"I'm talking three hundred thousand dollars after the auction," he replied.

Doyle's eyes, shining with greed, betrayed him. "When can I see them? Just askin', don't get no ideas I'm in this thing."

"Look, I don't care what you do. I'm sending mine to London anyway." He waited for this to sink into the thick skull before him. "The old guy will be out of town for a week, buying stuff, I guess. So a week from now is when you can see him. It'll give you time to think about it."

Doyle looked at him. "I don't need you to tell me what to do or what to think." Good, he said to himself. Get the cocksucker riled up. Let him think he's in charge. "I'll see him next Sunday," said Doyle.

Bingo! He thought. Gotcha by the balls. He would have to get up to Nha Trang and buy the rest of them. Not a problem. He'd been a clever apothecary, mixing a potion that Doyle had swallowed whole.

The following Sunday eleven golden girls exuded their charms before Boyle in the antique dealer's shop. Marty Long sat beside him, talking to the old man, then raised one of the eleven and said, "They look good to me." Boyle nodded. The old man sat before them without an outward sign of interest. Boyle lifted an attaché case onto the desk, snapping it open to reveal neat packets of hundred-dollar bills bundled in their U.S. Treasury wrappers. "A hundred thirty-two thousand smackers. You don't gotta count it." With that Boyle gathered up his acquisitions. "Let's ship 'em to London right away. I'm a legit businessman lookin' for a return on his investment."

He watched them leave and turned to collect his forty percent. Over fifty thousand dollars came into his hands. More important, it was Boyle's money. But it would be nothing compared to the look on Boyle's face when he learned what he'd paid for were fakes.

## NINETY-THREE

He joined John for a night of bar hopping and whore chasing with not a word about his hi-jinks with Boyle. The Greek knew about the deal. "Frankie's been all over town talking about it." They found him holding court, surrounded by courtiers. "Drinks all around," Boyle roared, waving them into the circle of his generosity. Orders taken, drinks served, Boyle, in high braggadocio, exaggerated the details of his Big Deal. "Nothin' like being legit," he grinned happily. "I'm lookin' at half a million comin' my way." A wise man raised nose from glass to ask what he'd do with all that money. "I'll buy me a whorehouse," answered our earnest entrepreneur. "If business goes bad I can always say, fuck the business." Unfazed that no laughter followed his tedious joke Boyle carried on. He and The Greek waved their farewells and hit the street.

"I've never seen the fat fucker so happy," John said.

"The transforming power of art," he replied.

"Bullshit. It's the size of the profit. He's never been in on something this big."

This surprised him and he asked about the drug deal. "He's a ten-percenter," said John. "Frankie is the middleman in the deals, making them happen. He's made plenty, and held on to it. But this is a big one for him."

The two of them walked the streets among the crowds, the heat, the noise and smell of traffic, and those lovely young whores.

Resisting temptation, they settled into a booth at a bistro on the main drag. A baguette, sliced and placed before them, was overrun with tiny bugs. Undeterred, John slathered a piece with butter. "It's all protein," he said with a laugh, noting his companion's wide-eyed squeamishness. He'd hardly seen John since his rescue from the cops and they played catch-up, telling of this and that, the stuff of their ordinary lives in this extraordinary place, but leaving out the tale of Mara, her death still an abiding pang in his heart. John had no illusions about Vietnam and where it was heading. His enthusiasms were properly in place and a lesson to us all. Good friends, good meals, plentiful pussy. It would come crashing down one day, he knew, with a certainty that never cramped his good humor. Neither fatalist nor optimist, he played at the game with a plunger's disdain until the last bet on the last card in this game of come-what-may.

Getting around to Colonel Lee's suicide, he learned from John it wasn't the local kickbacks that did Lee in. "Small stuff, of no importance," he sniffed. "That forty-five blowing his head away, and what a mess that made, was his reward for buying defective parts from stateside businesses that fucked up war-essential vehicles." John let that sink in for a while. The gradations of acceptable behavior in this place a wonder to contemplate. "Lee couldn't take the humiliation he'd suffer from his Army pals. So he blew out his brains, a man of honor at last."

Deciding to give John an opening, he said, "So Eddy's busted."

"That he is," said John, showing his amusement at this pretence at naiveté. "You know it was The Money King who did him in?" The look of surprise on his buddy's face led John to realize this he wasn't naïve but ignorant. John sat back, expansively, about to bring enlightenment to the innocent before him. "When Ron Steele took over from Carlos and turned over the business to the Chinese it was to keep shit out of the hands of our GIs."

"That I knew," he told John, a demonstration of his being in one loop or another.

"Sure you knew that. It was all connected to the rehab hospital. Part of Marty's plans to keep the war going." He looked at John, a little boy lost, in need of illumination. "Jesus Christ, open your eyes, and your ears while you're at it. Heroin is all over the place. The smell of grass lingers over every firefight. Dogs sniff for drugs our guys are taking home with them. The Post Office intercepts packages stuffed with hash. Two navy ships of the coast at Nha Be are rehab centers." The Greek, voice rising, was turning from annoyance to anger. "The Lao ambassador to France was caught on his way to the U.S. with sixty KGs of heroin in a diplomatic pouch. The Pentagon is going nuts with congressmen's complaints. If anything pulls the plug on this war it will be the threat of dope-fiend veterans stalking the streets of America." Then, an actor in his own drama, John intoned, "And that brings us back to The Money King."

"To keep the war going?" He hated to sound incredulous, a sure sign he wasn't in the know. John looked at this simple soul, so unknowing in worldly matters. "Our Generals are dumb enough to think they can win this thing. As long as we are here, Ronnie continues to make big money. A happy coalition of interests undermined by our shit-faced warriors." John leaned forward, not out of discretion, his voice not lowering a jot. "He got clearance to take over the business with a promise to keep the dope away from them. It worked for a while, but Big Eddy couldn't resist eighty million in sales and let the heroin slip into the GI market."

"And who'll be involved now?"

"The Chinese will still get their piece, they've got to, but Ronnie's got clearance to bring in big-time Vietnamese."

"Clearance?" He knew the question would bring forth a head-shaking glance but had no choice, this seeker.

"Our embassy. Glad to look the other way, grateful for the favor."

He looked at John in wonder. Is any of this believable? It sounded crazy enough to be true. No general wants to lose a war. And Ron Steele, bless his Maoist heart, was glad to oblige. He didn't want to imagine why The Greek knew all this. Was he in on it in some way? Or working with Long? He was tempted to tell of his part in doing in the assassins. A way to show he too had been in on things. But let it go. Their steak frites arrived, John ordered a bottle of the Beaujolais nouveau, and changed the subject.

He'd been in country six years, "and counting," he said. It was where he lived. Saigon was home. As talk turned away from John he grew uncomfortable, unsure of himself, not knowing why. The transient quality of life here wasn't so different, since he always felt unanchored, unattached. Saigon was perfect for him, if he wanted to think about it. He chose instead to wonder at the French wine they were sharing, the continuing madness of the place, the night-time gaiety untouched by that other world within their borders and the conversation, more a peroration, that John conducted.

Cups of not very good coffee set before them, John let it be known stateside was a place to visit twice a year, tops. He listened, a veteran of nine months in Vietnam with three months to go on his contract, and wondered. Not about the prospect of returning home. Friends and family were a tenuous connection at best. Adventure had always come to him uninvited. Another example of a capacity for remoteness while being in the middle of it. John in his own way was asking him the overwhelming question, what comes next? And he had no interest in engaging the answer.

## NINETY-FOUR

The weeks drifted along undisturbed. A rare quiet, as he awaited the good news out of London. But as more days passed, he wondered if the auction house had been taken in as well. A hammering on his door and bellowing of his name could only be for the best. He opened the door to a red-faced Boyle, near to apoplectic, a shipping box in his hand. He pushed past into the room, dumping its contents on a table. The golden girls came tumbling forth. "Fakes," he squealed, "Fuckin' fakes."

He tried to be astonished at the news. "Who says so?"

"The fuckin' Brits, that's who. Come with me, I'm gonna shove them up that little fucker's ass." He joined Boyle as he raced downtown to the dealer's shop and another disappointment. The place was locked tight. Boyle, berserk, pounding the closed door with his fist, splintered its thin wood panels, attracting attention from the locals who wondered at the fuss. The door gave way, but the place was emptied out, the old man moved to parts unknown. Boyle, kicking at an empty carton, slipped and fell to his knees. Staggering upright, he looked at him. "You dumb Jew bastard, you got me into this."

"What do you mean, I'm out twelve thousand dollars."

"And I'm out ten times that, you poor prick. We got to find this guy."

"Maybe Marty Long…"

"Nah, he'd be useless. I'm gonna be laughed at by every asshole in this fuckin' place.

"Nobody has to know about it." He said this as he drew an extra dividend from the deal. He'd engineered Boyle out of a ton of money, and would tell the world of his folly. Not a bad day's work. A man could get used to this kind of fun. He watched Boyle stalk off without so much as a goodbye.

## NINETY-FIVE

His revenge on Boyle complete, fifty thousand dollars safely stashed, the women gone or forgotten, an old emptiness enveloped him. He walked the Saigon streets, ignoring the whores, avoiding American hangouts, drifting along the lit or darkened way. How could everything he had learned to love, care for, feel inside himself come to this? Would it take a slice of his brain to find the tracings of a schizoid's flaw? Examine the heart, you fools, it is the heart that keeps the record of indecencies. The heart that goes first in a seeming healthy man. It bursts with heaviness. It breaks when it can contain no more.

And the soul? The soul remembers what the heart records. It joins with others, both gone and here on earth, and forms the thing called memory. When he remembers those who've gone it can be said their souls did touch, then part, with promises to meet again.

This reverie possessing him was given pause by a knock at the door. A messenger, envelope in hand, stood before him. On the envelope the engraved name and address of Thanh's father. An invitation to celebrate Tet. Thanh would be there, for sure. He could handle it. Partners in crime, they were showing him respect. He turned the invite over and over in his hand. Had the year already gone by? Who is the keeper of time? Who counts the knockdowns at the bell? May the winner emerge victorious!

# NINETY-SIX

Ninh's warning of impending arrest had not yet come to pass. Not yet. Lee's suicide had been on his mind of late. He might try to fly out of here but they'd be watching, he'd never get on the plane. Not paranoia, this high-wire act the real thing for this trapeze artist, spotlight on him, alone in a darkened tent, drums rolling at a steady beat, leaping into the void without a net.

Walking past the American embassy, a steady barrage of fireworks a merry accompaniment to his mood, he entered Thanh's house. Americans in and out of uniform towered over Vietnamese generals and local big shots. Plus the cast of characters he'd learned to love so well, Poppa, Momma, Little Brother, and Thanh, barely acknowledging him. No Boyle, he was happy to see. It was an A-list crowd, Saigon style. Poppa welcomed him long enough to ferry him to a bar, leaving him to order up the first of too many whiskeys.

He glanced at the main altar, festooned with every sort of food and drink and a photo of the dead son. Momma stood before the altar doting on a little boy in her arms. It was the kid he'd seen in Dalat. Thanh had decided to bring her male heir into the daylight. At Momma's side stood Tu, the boy's nanny awkward in fancy party clothes. He moved toward them as Momma pointed at the photo of her son. "Your father," he heard her say in French. The little boy, squirming, reached for Tu. Grandma reluctantly gave him up, but seemed to smile gratefully at the girl. It hit him, with a blow reserved for the ignorant, that Tu must have been a family servant fucked around with by big brother. The wages of sin revealed and joyously accepted by a family in need of those male heirs. He had been wrong about that one, too. Another confusion to wrap himself around.

Thanh moved about, dutiful as always. A young lieutenant, overly attentive, didn't bother him at all, and he stepped up to the bar for a re-supply of his whiskey. The evening wore on into night. An ever-changing crowd came and went and he stayed, his glass forever filled, dropping into a soft chair as the stupor come over him, having the decency to stay out of the way as his empty glass slipped from his fingers.

# NINETY-SEVEN

Victimized by another hangover, he awoke in a strange, darkened room, still in his clothes, shoes off. Had someone removed them before he'd collapsed on the bed, not bothering to crawl between the sheets? No sign of Thanh, of course. She was at home, after all, a place to perform her very good girl act. He roused himself to his feet in search of aspirin. None was to be found and he staggered back to his room. Curtained windows looked out at the American embassy looming over the silent, tree-lined boulevard.

His watch showed a quarter to three and he hummed the old song. As he turned to what comfort there might be in his solitary bed he noticed a small truck, lights out, followed closely by a beat-up taxi come down Mac Dinh and slowly turn left below him onto the broad boulevard. The Vietnamese cop on duty suddenly dropped out of sight in the shadow of the Embassy's high wall. Before he could reason why, gunfire erupted from the taxi in the direction of two MPs he hadn't noticed guarding a side door to the compound. The MPs returned the fire, jumping behind a steel door to shut it tight. The wonderment of this barely took hold when six or so slight young men wearing neckerchiefs jumped from the truck. Boy Scouts they weren't. A second policeman, roused from sleep by the gunfire, ran off rather than wait to see rocket launchers, other weapons, boxes of ammo unloaded in seconds. One of the MPs was on his radio when a blast tore a small hole in the compound wall through which two men crawled. Firing their weapons, they were met in kind by the two MPs. He watched as this simultaneous equation, this pas de deux, joined them in a dance of death, both pairs moving toward each other's fire as they fell, each and every one, to their graves.

A moment's quiet, a hesitation, seemed to settle in. The dead, as always, followed by the living who lugged weapons through the hole in the wall. A figure rose up from the rooftop, aimed his shotgun at those entering, to let go a lethal blast that never came, since the gun jammed. He tossed it away, drew a pistol, and fired to no effect at those below who'd taken cover behind lovely circular cement planters used to decorate the welcoming green lawn.

The concussion of the first blast had blown out his bedroom's windows and covering him with tiny shards of glass, but his attention was on those who raised rocket launchers to their shoulders and blew through the high and mighty front doors of the embassy building. A jeep raced to the rescue down the wide boulevard unaware that a fusillade of fire awaited them, killing driver and passenger before the little vehicle hurtled into a tall tree. A frail, old Vietnamese man, a watchman no doubt, stood in the middle of the lawn bewildered, confused, too frightened to move when an American soldier ran from the building and dragged the old guy away, gunfire following them to their safe haven. More gunfire from rooftops outside the compound spattered the courtyard and was returned in equal measure. An American soldier climbed to a roof inside the compound and opened up with his M16 until a rocket fired at his position seemed to put him away. After some minutes he rose up clearly hurt but firing his rifle and was felled once more, and did not rise again.

As he began to wonder where the U.S. Army might be, flares began to descend, their eerie candlepower offering what illumination they could as an assault helicopter, a giant alien insect with propellers for antennae and shining lights for eyes, began growling toward a landing atop the building. Met by every rocket and automatic weapon that could be fired from below, the helicopter hovered for a moment then flew away to fight, it seemed, another day. It was 5 a.m. and still pitch dark. Everything below that he could see seemed to be moving at mach speed though he'd been at the window for almost two hours. A handful of men were holding the American embassy, in the middle of goddamn Saigon, for chrissakes. He began to hear the sounds of large explosions and gunfire nearby and far off in the city. Where were Thanh and her family? The house was too quiet. He bet they'd left in the night, knowing more than they were willing to tell their American guest.

A smaller chopper marked by a large red cross managed to land on the roof, pick up a wounded soldier, drop off boxes of ammo, and get out of there quick, real quick. For some reason U.S. soldiers outside never saw the hole blown in the wall and were trying with no effect to shoot the lock off the front gate or ram it open with a jeep. Those on the outside couldn't get in. Those on the inside couldn't get out. A fine mess it could be said had it not involved that little matter of life and death.

He could see the hole directly across the street from his window, would have shouted out to them but they wouldn't have heard. As dawn broke, an armed American in civilian clothes spotted the blasted bricks and began to crawl through. A badly wounded VC soldier, grenade in hand, awaited any enemy. The American, spotting him, raised his weapon as the VC lifted his arm to hurl the grenade. It was as far as his wounds could take him. The grenade exploded in his hand with a brilliantly colored flash that killed him, sending the American reeling backwards.

Unquiet dawn finally turned the day brighter. He was able to see a motley crew of civilians, some armed with TV cameras, others with still cameras, watching, waiting as the effort to break through the gate succeeded with a great crash. Armed soldiers ran through the gates followed close behind by the others. He watched, amazed, as the camera-laden group began taking pictures. My god, he said to himself, reporters, photographers. Acting as though it were the end of a football game.

It's probably all over, he said to himself, and he thought about joining them when gunfire came from a house at the back of the compound. Soldiers blasted away at the unseen enemy firing on them from the house, a teargas grenade was tossed inside, its lachrymose effect wafting quickly on the errant wings of a breeze. It forced an American civilian in the house to come to an upper window. He shouted something, made a gesture with his hand to indicate that he needed a weapon. Our soldiers had taken cover from the gunfire, but into this void a young soldier dashed toward the window, moving as though his body expected the worst, getting close enough to toss a pistol and gas mask to the man upstairs who caught this gift of life and death. Silence descended for a moment, then automatic weapons fire was heard. The unmistakable roar of a .45 came from the house, the American to the window, triumphant. It was all over.

Brushing points of glass from his clothes, he left the empty house, crossed the street and walked slowly into the compound. And saw a ghost. Mara, back turned to him, taking pictures. It had to be. Then the phantasm turned, walked past, paying him no attention. No, it wasn't Mara.

There was no challenge to his presence. He didn't matter at all. The two MPs he'd seen die were sprawled forward, matched by their companions in death. The courage of it, he thought, the crazy courage that brought all four to their demise. Other soldiers, eyes red with weeping, stood before their comrades allowing no intrusion on the privacy of sorrow. Chests heaving in grief they tenderly willed their comrades back to life. Warriors since time began protect their own, cover their dead, keeping them from hot sun, the buzzing flies.

The dead littered the compound, including one Vietnamese man he'd seen frantically waving something in the air before being shot down. An Embassy ID card was still clutched tight in his fingers. Two badly wounded VC were attended by medics. The dead and the blood of the dead spilled everywhere, flaunting the brutal carnage on grass, walls, planters and pillars. A large circular plaque, torn to pieces, carried the remains of the proud American eagle, broken arrows clinging to its talons, now no more than part of the debris.

An assault helicopter finally landed on the roof, soldiers spilling out and disappearing inside the building. A stir at the gate caused reporters to rush over as General Westmoreland, starched Westy himself, a razor-sharp edge to his immaculate fatigues, four stars emblazoned on each lapel, aides-de-camp in tow, strode onto the grounds, barely acknowledging the newsmen around him, and walked over to a sergeant who'd survived the night. A snappy salute between general and sergeant, a man-to-man handshake, a word or two, our leader returned to address the assembly.

Standing on these bloody grounds, at the center of American power where terror of arms had doubted its empire, he pronounced victory, declared the damage superficial, gladly totaled up the enemy dead, body counting his only measure of success, determined in his belief that life in the Orient was cheap. Reporters shook their heads in wonder at this four-star self-deception, and watched as the silvered bird, looking grave, departed.

Next, the dear old Stars and Stripes raised for all to see. Followed, as if on cue, by the entrance of our ambassador dressed in ageless preppy, tasseled loafers an especially nice sartorial touch. Surrounded by his carefully well dressed retinue, and a Major Schwartz, if nametag can be believed, in combat gear. Hillel Schwartz, if that can be believed. One of the Chosen Few providing protection for this self-anointed saintly WASP standing in the midst of his country's humiliation declaring all is well. Why wasn't the Chancery Building still standing? The ambassador excused himself, avoiding dead bodies, hoses washing down the bloody stones. Leaving reporters and photographers to send the truth of the matter around the world through words and pictures.

# NINETY-EIGHT

He walked from the blasted embassy past Thanh's house. Gunfire and the noise of battle covered a city under attack. The war had come to him and he'd seen enough of it. A reporter had said there was nasty fighting around the racetrack. It led him in the direction of Phu To where Marty Long lived. Streets he'd so casually strolled were now littered with the destruction of war. Burnt-out cars, blasted facades of shops, broken twisted trees were the order of the day. He saw no Americans. But Vietnamese, serenity gone, were everywhere. At a wide intersection three dead bodies were ignored by those who hurried past, unseeing or too frightened to care. Black smoke rose in the sky from fires a few blocks away. Trucks carrying American soldiers ready for battle sped down the streets, stopping for nothing in their paths. Helicopters were in the air, the roar of artillery came to his ears, but he kept moving forward indifferent to danger.

He'd been up all night and walked, carefully as a sleepwalker, in the direction of the racetrack and more sounds of war. And found what he'd been looking for, afraid to hope for. Long's house had been leveled. Direct hits had brought down the roof and fire had done the rest. Paintings, scrolls, sculpture, the pretty garden, destroyed. No one inside could have survived. He wandered onto the low pile, picking up the green remains of a Celadon vase. Ninh had told him Marty Long kept everything to himself. This destruction just might be his salvation.

Crossing away from the ruins, he stumbled on a curb and sat down at a table outside a shuttered café. Across the street a truck backed up to a low building and what could only have been bodies were carried inside. It was a makeshift morgue. He went inside to walk among the dead looking for something. Row on row of bodies, most burned beyond recognition, waited for dental records to reveal their names. Others, already stiffened, showed the wounds that had killed them. Then, one burned torso and head, perhaps the worst of all, at which he stopped and said, "That's Marty Long." And learned the melancholy way that he had died: Making a run for it after being taken from his house past neighbors and old whores who must have recognized him but lowered their eyes as Marty Long, Secret Agent, was gunned down and left in the street to die for his trouble.

"I'm a survivor, goddamn it. A survivor," he cried out.

Rolling the little green talisman of good luck between his fingers, he took it upon himself to break the news to Frankie Boyle.

# NINETY-NINE

It had been a while since he'd seen Frankie. "And good riddance," he'd said to himself, wondering whether bringing him the bad news was an act of charity or cruelty. The house was shut down tight. Through a parted curtain he saw Frankie, drink in hand, a grenade launcher across his lap, more pathetic than comic. Boyle rose to his feet at the sound of his name. Cracking open the door and peering outside he dragged his visitor inside, fear showing in every gesture. "The cock suckers hit the golf course. It sure ain't eighteen holes no more." He seemed amused by his wry observation. "Johnny the Greek was holed up with a piece of ass last night, that lucky fuck."

Frankie sat back, the certainty of things as they are, things as they'll always be no longer comfort to him. "Didja hear? Three thousand of our guys killed, right here in the streets. Cooks, and fucking clerks. That's what they sent out to fight those VC motherfuckers. Poor fucking cooks, and clerks. And four of our own guys got it goin' off to work like it was just another day. Jesus, didn't they hear the fuckin' noise? It sure as shit wasn't firecrackers." He took a swallow. "This fucking country. Know what I saw in the market the other day? Body bags being sold for mattress covers, that's what."

He decided not to tell Frankie about the embassy, knowing one thing would lead to another. "I haven't heard from Marty Long," Boyle said, covering his concern with a long pull on the whiskey.

"I saw him."

"Saw him where?"

"In the morgue."

"What the fuck was he doin' in a morgue?"

"Dead, Frankie. He's dead."

Frankie Boyle placed his glass to the side and let the weapon clatter to the floor as he rose, broken, bent, moving toward him. "Whatta mean, dead? His arm rose as if to strike. He's worth ten of you, you pussy-eating Jew bastard." He dropped his arm, turning away. "And ten of me. His girl ok?"

"I dunno."

"You been fuckin' her?"

Appalled, he silently shook his head.

"Don't look at me like that you Jew bastard, you'll fuck anything."

Boyle walked back to his chair and reached for his glass. He sat there, between fury and tears, the whiskey working him, messenger in silence before him. "I promised I'd take care of him. That he'd be safe." He let the promise, the prayer of a promise linger for a moment. "He shoulda become a priest after all." A diabolical chuckle escaped him. "One of those holy rollers who beckons the best of the chippies to his study for private counsel and prayer. Any of them who came to him for confession with tales of this and that would have been fair game for our little padre. Once he had her on her knees, she'd be gone, whoever she was. Single, married, or in her fuckin' widow's weeds, he'd of had 'em up and over. No wasted motion. Quick, see? He had another mass within the hour. Now look at him, blasted away and gone."

"And he was a cop," he said to Boyle.

Boyle, showing no surprise, answered, "Well as long as know that you might as well hear the rest. A couple years ago he got caught in a deal he was running. Some cocksucker gave him up in exchange for a break in his sentence. And the Feds turned Marty. He was a good catch for them. Spoke the language, knew everybody, was trusted by everybody. Made some pretty good collars along the way." Boyle was proud of his boy, never considering the betrayal implicit in his behavior.

"Was Lee one of his?"

"Yep. Blowing his brains out like that, but he deserved it."

Boyle stared into his glass, a quiet coming over him. Raising his head, defiance returning, he announced, "I'm leavin'. Getting the fuck out. This thing is over for us. Indonesia, that's were I'm goin'. We got a contract there. Good golf courses, and pussy the same as anywhere. I'm leavin'. I can't take this shit anymore." He looked at Doyle, this foul-mouthed slug defeated at last by those he'd brutalized. And thought about sticking in the final nail by telling him about the fakes, and his share in the caper. Let it go, he wisely decided. Let the asshole go on thinking he'd been taken by a gook. And left him to his whiskey and whatever else might befall him.

# ONE HUNDRED

Out of his clothes and ready for bed, he showered. An odd thing to do when he slept alone. Soaped, and rinsed, and soaped again, he shampooed his hair, cleansing himself of the evil around him, the evil forever done to him. Slowly toweling himself, he watched his face emerge from the steamed-over mirror, wiping the glass surface to see his eyes give away what he already knew: That at his death there would not be mourners, but mockers. Rubbing his hand across his cheek and chin he decided to shave, lathering his face, running the razor carefully over the surface of jaw and throat. His eyes grew dark as he went about this routine task. The light of the body is the eye, no doubt of that. It was a lesson he'd learned somewhere.

He went to his bed, first turning out the lights, room by room. On his back he listened to the faraway sounds of explosions and gunfire and saw a unity, a symmetry, in the sequence of humiliations that ordered his thinking. He had poured himself into life. And betrayal had been the compassionate response. Why not add one more death to the pile? Join those looking blankly from photograph or padded cell revealing no more than the isolation of their predicament. It would be as meaningless as any of the rest. Thanh's dead brother, maimed children, explosions killing dozens in restaurants. And Mara dead and gone. How he'd struggled toward decency with her. He hadn't forgotten. There'd been no time to think of it. Her death was due to bad luck, wasn't it? Blaming himself was the easy way to explain fate.

While sifting through these artifacts of his life he dug his own grave. Shards of old resentments, other slights, were cleaned, numbered and catalogued against the day when a match would be made, a figure revealed from an accumulation of bits and pieces showing a man and his wound. A wound that will not close, or go away. The smallest of openings yet it festers, it suppurates, leaving heaps of putrescence for all to see and smell. From time to time it will abate, the swelling subside, but never lose its power over him. No skein of decencies to stitch together a coverlet to warm his rendered soul, each day of bright sun, each night of shrouded darkness called forth the old betrayals, called out for death. Knowing that there would not be mourners, but mockers.

In his desolation he saw that the deed, once done, would finally chain fate down, allow for blessed sleep, and force the dung he'd eaten all his life on to another's plate. The Python came into his hand, slippery as a worm. He held the pistol to his chest, ready at last to rip the knot lodged in his heart. He said, still playing the clown, though no one would hear him, "Those that die seldom or never recover."

The pistol never spoke to silence him. He would not become fire and air, leaving earth and water to the vile mud of the world. His punishment was to live, not die. To go on, world without bloody end.

ACKNOWLEDGEMENTS

Anyone writing a novel set in Vietnam during the terrible war years knows the debt owed to those writers, journalists, and photographers who came before. Not comparing myself to those to whom I bend the knee: David Halberstam, R.W. Apple, Jr., Philip Caputo, Michael Hess, Dexter Filkins, Bernard Fall, William Broyles, Jr., Neil Sheehan, Stanley Karnow, Larry Heinemann, Toni Miller, and others who go unmentioned set the stage for future attempts to write a Vietnam tale.

John Balaban kindly gave permission to use his translations of Vietnamese poetry. And, I leaned heavily on Don Oberdorfer's *TET!* for the timeline used in my description of the Viet Cong attack on the U.S. embassy.

My thanks to Peter Plagens, James Walvin, Faya Causey, Joshua Holo, Bob Goldstein, Victor Raphael, Philo Northrup, Yon Frel, Peter Bierstedt, and Scott Chamberlin, publisher extraordinaire, first readers supplying encouragement and sound advice. And Ed Roski who first said, "Write it down!" Janet Cavolini, editor extraordinaire, worked on an early version of the manuscript.

Howard Kaufman, great surgeon and true friend, along with Drs. John Brodhead and Sant Chawla, pulled me through a dire illness some years ago for which I owe them gratitude beyond measure. And the late great Warren Bennis from whom never was heard a discouraging word.

Saving best for less, my dear wife, Selma Holo. No man standing can claim to be as lucky as me. Sweetness, generosity, tough when needed, she heard and read every word I wrote, never failing to cheer or groan as the occasion required. A lucky man indeed.

The novel is littered with references and direct quotations from the Books of Job, Jeremiah, Psalms, and Leviticus; from Euripides, Plato, Cicero, Dante, Shakespeare, Flaubert, John Milton, H.W. Longfellow, Rudyard Kipling, e.e. cummings, Wallace Stevens, Dylan Thomas, Arthur Miller, Bertolt Brecht, Paul Goodman, Rabbi Abraham Isaac Kook, Silvano Arieti, William Maxwell, and, no doubt, others unmentioned. I quote from the old song "If You Were the Only Girl in the World," with lyrics by Clifford Grey; "Too Hot for Words" by Walter G. Samuels, Teddy Powell, and Leonard Whitcup; and the hymn, "Praise God, from Whom All Blessings Flow," by Thomas Ken.

www.ingramcontent.com/pod-product-compliance
Lightning Source LLC
Chambersburg PA
CBHW030524310726
48979CB00010B/1796/J

* 9 7 8 0 9 7 4 5 0 4 2 6 1 *